Ardulum. The planet that va

Neek makes a living piloting the dilapidated tramp transport, Mercy's Pledge, and smuggling questionable goods across systems blessed with peace and prosperity. She gets by—but only just. In her dreams, she is still haunted by thoughts of Ardulum, the traveling planet that, long ago, visited her homeworld. The Ardulans brought with them agriculture, art, interstellar technology...and then disappeared without a trace, leaving Neek's people to worship them as gods.

Neek does not believe—and has paid dearly for it with an exile from her home for her heretical views.

Yet, when the crew stumbles into an armed confrontation between the sheriffs of the Charted Systems and an unknown species, fate deals Neek an unexpected hand in the form of a slave girl—a child whose ability to telepathically manipulate cellulose is reminiscent of that of an Ardulan god. Forced to reconcile her beliefs, Neek chooses to protect her, but is the child the key to her salvation, or will she lead them all to their deaths?

Published by
NineStar Press
PO Box 91792
Albuquerque, New Mexico, 87199
www.ninestarpress.com

Warning: This book contains scenes of graphic violence, which some might find unsettling, including brief acts of child abuse and speciesist behavior towards an enslaved alien race.

Print ISBN # 978-1-945952-65-4
Cover by Natasha Snow
Edited by Sasha Vorun

FIRST DON

Ardulum

J.S. Fields

DEDICATION

To Lauren, without whom this book never would have happened.

ACKNOWLEDGEMENTS

I am eternally indebted to my beta readers, especially those who were with me in the early drafts. Thank you to Seth, who helped make Nicholas a real live boy; to Amber, Glory, and Liz, who slogged through draft zero even though it made their eyes bleed; to Casey and Shannon, who helped me streamline; and to Letty, who helped me work through problematic dialogue.

Perhaps most importantly, thank you to my beta co-op group over in 17th Shard for going through each chapter with a fine-toothed comb. You are an amazing group of people, and I'm grateful to have met you.

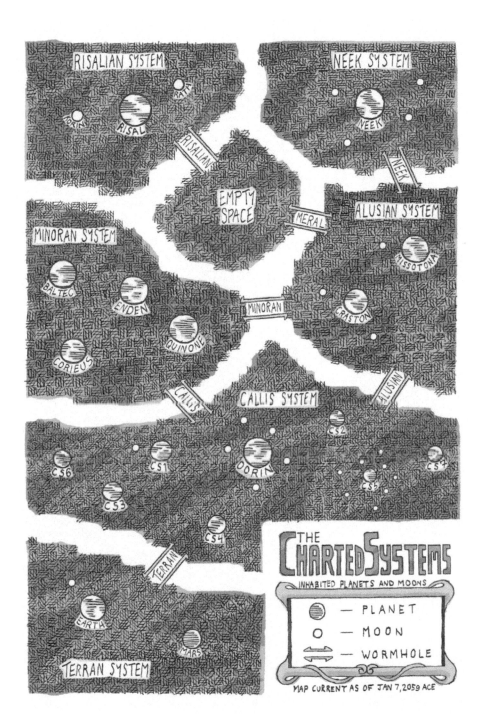

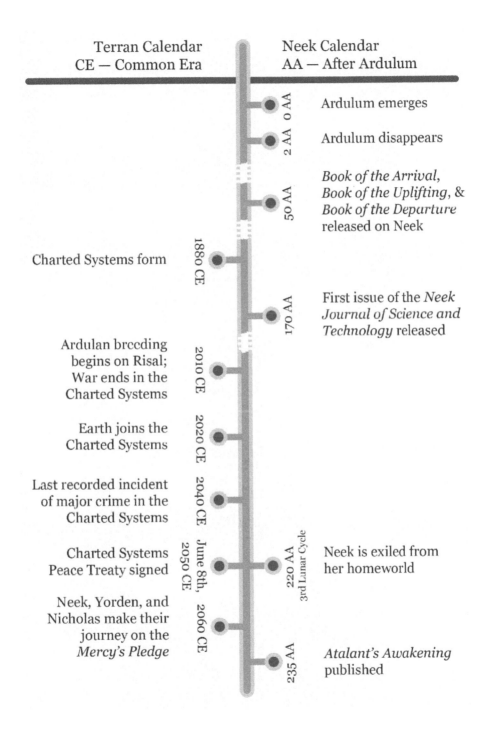

CHAPTER 1: RISALIAN CUTTER 17

Joint Resolution Mandating a Youth Journey

Be it resolved: youths of all Systems should enjoy the benefits of education, cultural understanding, and interplanetary travel that this new age of universal freedom, safety, and peace allows. Therefore, be it enacted that all youths, aged to each species' level of near-adulthood, may embark on a cost-free, two-year Journey off their home planet. None shall interfere with the Journey for any reason, except to provide assistance to facilitate smooth cultural exchange. Youths may travel in groups or alone, may engage in paid or unpaid employment, or may sign on to ships or governmental service as long as such service does not occur within their home system. In this act shall each youth find their own path within the safe, open arms of the Charted Systems.

—Charted Systems General Mandate 27

It was colder than normal in her cage today. The girl shivered as she watched the crystalline strands stride across the metal mesh of her enclosure. Placing her fingertips against the mesh, she giggled when a strand touched her and puffed into a sweet-smelling smoke. With her mind, she reached out to another nearby strand and pushed it, sending the repeating segment bounding alongside the metal into the far corner of the cell.

The strand hovered on the mesh, awaiting her command. It made no sound, and she knew that the beings with the bright-blue skin gathered outside the enclosure could not see it. They clustered around their consoles and trays and screens, and ignored her. That made the game more fun. The girl hopped into the air, and the strand hopped to the next section of mesh. She twirled—creating a cool breeze against her bare, translucent skin—as the strand wove in and out of the solid metal wire.

She flopped to the floor and released her link to the strand, sending the crystalline form back into the matrix of her cage.

She lay on the porous metal, eyes closed, and began to play a new game. In this one she played with sounds, listening to the noises of her world—the noises of the blue creatures. Air wheezed between the slits in their necks, whistled through rows of pointed teeth. Pursed lips forced high-pitched squeaks that, combined with vibrations from their throats, produced a strange form of communication.

Her mother never communicated like that—with noises. The blue creatures never communicated with images, either. Their minds were closed off, unscalable, and no matter how much she tried, the girl couldn't make the same mouth noises. She couldn't communicate with them, but she could listen and pretend, all without drawing attention to herself. Her mother hated it when she did that.

Trying not to attract attention, unfortunately, was a rather hard thing to do. There were only so many times you could push strands around before boredom drove you to other things, and the blues were mysterious. Three times a day, they would bring food and place it inside through a small opening near the ground. They never went past the mesh, and the girl and her mother never left it. There was nothing inside the cage to give to the blues in return for the food, although her mother said giving them something was a silly idea. The blues never made noises at them and never showed much interest in anything. Maybe there was something even more interesting beyond the wall, beyond the door through which the blues came and went at different times. Maybe there were other colors or beings that she could actually communicate with.

The girl longed to investigate those doors—to open every one and learn about what could be inside. How many blues were there? What were the funny things they had wrapped across their bodies? The wrappings looked soft, and she longed to rub the corner of one against her face, or to place it beneath herself as she slept. Where did the food come from, and how was it made? Her imagination spun, images of crazy contraptions pieced together from the blues' artifacts filling her consciousness.

Her mother turned her head and made eye contact, her concern flickering through the girl's mind. A strong sense of disapproval followed the concern. The girl stopped her imaginings and kicked her legs grumpily against the floor. The metal fibers were warm on her bare skin, and she thought, not for the first time, that life was incredibly frustrating. She'd lived her whole life in the cage. Someday, she was going to get beyond the outer door.

Twizzt twizzt.

The sounds of a few strands sparking where her body lay in contact with the mesh disrupted her listening game. The girl watched their brilliance slowly fade on her bare arm, her thin hairs rising ever so slightly and then lying back down. Sounds created by the blues filtered back to her ears, except this time, they seemed louder. Interested, the girl sat up. Mouths were moving more quickly. Flaps of neck skin, purple suddenly instead of blue, slapped against one another. The fine, black hair of each blue was pulled taut instead of let loose down their backs. They stood rigidly, and it looked uncomfortable. It was unusual. The girl edged closer to the mesh boundary and squinted, trying to make out more details between the shimmering strands.

A blue wearing a yellow covering entered the larger room. It grabbed the familiar gray wrappings of another, shorter blue. The mouth noises increased in pitch, and short-blue squeaked the same sound several times in a row. The sound didn't mean anything to her, but she repeated the noise in her head several times, wondering if she should try to remember it. *Captain Ran. Ranranran. RanRANran.* The girl giggled as she changed the emphasis. Blues were silly, and their noises that much more so.

Only young things made mouth noises, her mother had explained once with an image of the girl as a baby making high-pitched sounds in tandem with mental images for food. She'd outgrown it. She wasn't a baby. *She* was almost ready to create the funny wrappings her mother had shown her—the ones that she would rest in for a little bit so she could grow big. After that, she would be as tall as her mother, taller than the blue things maybe, but she still wouldn't make those silly mouth noises.

She looked at yellow-blue, whose neck was beginning to purple. The blues were big, but they still used mouth noises. They weren't very smart. The girl smiled. After she grew, she could teach them, maybe, if her mother would let her. The blues would be a lot more interesting if they communicated properly. She could teach them all the things her mother had taught her, too—about strands and mental pictures and how to eat food slowly so it didn't get stuck in your throat and make you cough.

The girl sent an image to her mother of herself outside the cage, slowly chewing, mouth open, so the blues could see. Concern and fear answered her, sweeping away her proposal. Confused, the girl tried to probe her mother for answers, but her mother buried them as quickly as they'd come. Instead, the feelings were replaced by a reserved calm, followed by a sharp image of the girl inside the cage, far away from the blues.

That her idea had been refused was upsetting, and she stomped her foot—but only a little bit. She recognized her mother's emotional cover-up and, irritated, turned her attention back to yellow-blue. She took a few steps back from the mesh, begrudgingly.

Farther away, yellow-blue's slits were a deeper purple, and the lighting overhead made them shiny. The striking color accentuated the harsh mouth noises. She watched yellow-blue direct three other blues— pointing at her, pointing at her mother, pointing at the mesh. The shortest one came up to the mesh and probed it with the flat of its hand. Yellow-blue let out a string of high-pitched babble, and short-blue fell back, its neck searing into purple.

Fear began to seep past her mother's careful barriers and into her mind. She sent a questioning feeling to her mother, who responded with an image of the girl in the arms of a blue, herself still trapped inside. The girl frowned. She didn't want that to happen. She backed away slowly and stood behind her mother. A protective arm wrapped around her, and the girl peered around her mother's elbow, keeping her eyes on the blues and letting her mother's fear permeate her mind.

Yellow-blue approached the mesh this time, running fingers slowly across the surface and staring directly at her. Blues had never looked at her before—not like that. The girl buried her face in her mother's back and watched through her mother's eyes as the blues touched small, black boxes near their hips. A *clang* filled the air, an acrid smell rose up from the floor, and new layers of mesh surrounded each blue—like individual cages. Only the shortest blue was without one.

Yellow-blue turned a red knob next to the wall panel, a panel the girl had never seen anyone go near before. A soft *hiss* filled the air, and again there was a shot of acrid odor. Then, in between the space of two blinks, the mesh enclosure—the cage in which she had lived her whole life— disappeared.

New scents of metal and an unusual body odor made her tongue feel funny as it hit her nose. The air temperature dramatically warmed. Her mother's emotions became chaotic—the only concrete desire the girl could make out was one of protection.

Despite it all, she was curious. No walls meant she could touch a blue, if she wanted to—could feel the little bumps on their skin, touch their shimmery, dark hair. That thought was appealing, so the girl peeked her head back around. Maybe she could touch one without stepping from behind her mother if they kept coming forward.

They were close now, surrounding the girl and her mother in a tight semicircle. They held strange bent tubes, ends pointed at her mother. Strands hopped along the tubes' surfaces in a merry game. The girl reached out with her mind to touch a strand, but a wave of rage from her mother cut her off. Frustrated, the girl slowly stretched her hand towards the shortest blue, keeping her mind blank so her mother wouldn't know what she was doing. The short one looked at her—right at her—and the corners of its mouth turned up, revealing rows of pointed teeth, and took a knife from its covering.

She drew her hand back quickly, unnerved by the image, but short-blue caught her by the wrist. Her mother spun and swung a fist at the blue's jaw. It dodged, shifting its body to one side, and pulled the girl along with it. The grip on her wrist was strong, and she was slammed to the floor, the metal digging into her knees.

Before she could process what had happened, short-blue hauled her to her feet and pushed her into the blue with the yellow coverings. This blue grabbed her by her hair, which was much more painful. She tried to pull back, to return to her mother, but the tension on her scalp made her eyes water with pain.

The strands stopped moving.

Stillness filled the room even though the blues persisted in making their noises, the short one ripping at her mother's arms with long claws. The girl knew what would come next, so she went slack, the weight pulling down the blue that held her as well.

Her mother pushed the strands around them with her mind. Crystalline units shot from the walls, the protective mesh, and the bent tubes, and bound together into a thick cord in the middle of the room. The blast that followed rammed into the short blue's back. The blue dropped the knife and fell into her mother, who quickly moved to the side and allowed the blue to slam face-first into a wall and then onto its back, leaving it crumpled at an odd angle on the floor, smoking.

Yellow-blue produced several low noises from its mouth and gestured as a strange, foul-smelling tendril of smoke wafted up from short-blue's now empty eye sockets. The girl gagged. She had seen her mother push the strands before, but it had never smelled this bad. She hadn't realized *anything* could smell this bad.

Her mother stumbled forward as two other blues took hold of her. Moving the strands was hard work—the girl knew from practicing. Her mother would be tired now. Instead of calling again to the strands, her mother reached for her, and the girl pulled against the blue that held her. Their hands locked, and the girl's skin burned as her mother dug in with fingernails, trying desperately to keep them together as the blues pulled them apart. But her mother was tired from strand pushing, and the blues that held her were very strong. Finally, they were connected only by the fingertips, and then, not at all.

Her mother sent another image. This one showed the girl kicking and biting yellow-blue. Nodding in understanding, the girl began to thrash. She jerked her body left and right, swinging her arms wildly and pulling her head at odd angles.

Stomping and biting, her mother gained a few centimeters towards her. Excitement rose in the girl but was dashed just as quickly. Holding the girl tightly by her hair in one hand, yellow-blue lunged forward. The creature picked up the fallen knife, grabbed her mother's arm, and slashed it right at the elbow joint. Pain seared through her mother's mind and ripped into hers. The shock of agony made the girl's body go limp, and she slumped to the floor.

Yellow-blue turned back to the girl and made more noises, gesturing for her to resume standing and move towards a strange cylindrical structure behind it. When she didn't respond, yellow-blue sighed and gave a quick yank to her hair. She continued to slump, the biting pain in her arm and growing dread eclipsing the sharp pulls at her scalp and neck.

Three pushes came in rapid succession from her mother, targeting the blues that held her. Unlike the short one, however, these blues were protected by individual mesh barriers—the strands hopped wildly off the surfaces and shot around the room. A long strand hit a stationary console, which burst into flame. Another bored into a wheeled tray. At impact, the tray exploded and metal shards ricocheted off the walls. None of the blues were hurt.

Suddenly, yellow-blue grabbed the girl's leg with a free hand and hoisted her up off the ground, swung her a couple of times to gain momentum, and then roughly tossed her into the cramped space of the cylinder, forcing her limbs inside with its foot.

The impact of her head against the metal wall sent white spots blooming behind her eyelids. The girl tried to pull her legs in tightly, but yellow-blue's sharp toenails raked her translucent skin and drew blood from the prominent veins underneath. Wetness streamed down her face. She wanted to close her eyes, but she couldn't look away from her mother.

Wild with fear, her mother sent a message of warning. Pictures began to form in the girl's mind—pictures of her breaking out of the cylinder, of running into the main room and smashing the black boxes, of running out the door...

The image stream broke when a loud *CRACK* reverberated through the room. Energy had discharged from one of the bent tubes the blues carried. In the first heartbeat, strands shot forth and hung in the air. In the second heartbeat, they moved into her mother's head. There was a pause. In the fourth heartbeat, her mother's head shattered. Bits of skull and gray matter splattered the legs of several of the blues as the body slumped in its captors' arms. An eye, intact, rolled across the floor and stopped a meter from the cylinder, the pupil looking right at the girl.

Yellow-blue holstered the bent tube and turned, its expression blank, as the cover was placed over the cylinder. The girl's world turned dark, her mind turned dark, and there were no strands left to give her the illusion of safety.

CHAPTER 2: MERCY'S PLEDGE

The planet that vanishes,
the planet that sleeps.
Bring knowledge to our world
that we might keep.
Until such time as you are needed again,
we bid you good journey,
our celestial friends.

—Neek nursery rhyme

Neek lightly tapped her head against the crumbling wall of her quarters. Dust and bits of metal rained onto the floor with each impact, creating pyramids of debris on the tops of her boots. Frowning at the mess, she shook one foot and then the other, sending the lighter bits into the air. The particulate cloud hung near her knees for a few moments before settling back to the floor, this time more evenly distributed.

That she was interested in the falling patterns of broken wall told Neek a lot about her current mental state. How long had this delivery run taken? One month? Two? If they couldn't manage to get a decent payout soon, the tramp ship she piloted, *Mercy's Pledge*, was going to disintegrate around them from lack of basic maintenance. At this point, the only things holding the crumbling infrastructure together were the integrated cellulose microfibrils and the captain's pigheaded stubbornness.

Neek checked the interface near her desk. Five minutes to exit. They had run out of fuel halfway through the Callis Wormhole and had been coasting to the exit for ages. How or why they had run out of fuel she hadn't asked—the *Pledge* was falling apart in so many places that a leaky fuel valve would be the most mundane explanation. The endless wait had driven her to her quarters. Her other option was listening to the

Pledge's Journey youth, Nicholas, extol the virtues of metallic cellulose integration. Again. He'd only joined them on the *Pledge* a few months ago, and Neek already wanted to strangle the gangly hopefulness from him.

Their last Journey youth had lasted six months. Nicholas would be lucky if he lasted four, especially if he kept harping on the ridiculousness of her people all sharing the same name as their home planet. It was awkward. She knew that. She'd had to grow up with it. You got used to using modifiers after a while, and considering she was the only Neek currently off-planet, it shouldn't have been that big of a deal, regardless. Terrans were just a little too individualistic, and it didn't help anything that her people's name resembled Nicholas's so closely.

Exhaling, Neek wiggled her toes inside her boots and sat back against the desk chair. This haul was, mercifully, about to reach its conclusion, but she couldn't put off her monthly obligations any longer. If she ever wanted to be repatriated, she had to follow the guidelines her uncle had negotiated. One call per month. One lesson from a Neek holy book. One discussion afterwards. A recording of each call, sent to the president of her homeworld to review her progress. Once a year, the president met with her uncle, where the possibility of her return was discussed. Thus far, her status had moved from "never" to "making progress," which probably meant she was getting better at faking interest in the old texts. Clearly, she needed to be even better, however, if she wanted to return before her hair fell out.

Neek let the gentle, steady movement of the ship work on her muscles, slowly releasing the knots of tension that had built during the past hour. When she was sufficiently calm, she leaned forward against the desk and placed her hand on a pocked, round panel on the upper right corner. A thin light scanned her palm, and another row of lights turned on slowly from beneath the surface of her desk—shining clearly despite the opaque biometal.

The panel emitted a soft chime, and Neek pulled her hand away. The lights from beneath the desk merged together to form a wide, white beam that went from desk to ceiling. "Eldest paternal uncle, capital city of N'lln, Planet Neek," she said clearly. A soft *click* of recognition sounded from the panel, and the white beam turned gray, indicating the call was processing.

The speed of the response, at least, was uplifting. She'd spent a month's pay on upgrading the communications panel in her quarters. The cellulose reinforcements made for a crisper transmission. She suspected the company responsible, Cell-Tal, was already working on new technology to replace it. Still, this unit was light years faster than her old one, and given how often she actually placed calls, having the newest in cellulosic technology was a bonus.

The beam turned white again and then began to separate into distinct colors. In the center of the beam, a full body image of Neek's uncle appeared. She took in his tall, wide frame—similar to hers. Their hair was also the same reddish blonde, their skin the same bronze, but their eyes differed: his were a pale olive and hers a brilliant green. Much unlike her, he wore a welcoming smile.

There was a fluttering in Neek's stomach. Today, with his gold robes and long hair pulled back into triple braids, he looked identical to her father. Melancholy rose in Neek, but she squashed it quickly.

"Niece!" the older man greeted in their native language. "I've been expecting your call! We haven't spoken in over a month. How are you? Is everything all right?" He grinned and tapped a thick bark-bound book against his other hand. "Ready to tackle the next chapter in *The Book of the Uplifting*?"

Neek paused to reorient her brain. The wet, popping sounds of her native language seemed foreign after such long disuse. When she did respond, her words were slow and awkward, her tongue thick in her mouth.

"It's always good to hear your voice, Uncle. Nothing new, per usual. Trying to finish a delivery, and we're stuck in a wormhole without fuel. Unrelenting peace is good for business, at least, and since I have nothing else going on, we might as well get to it." She paused and then leaned in. Her voice softened. "Before that, though, how is father?"

Her uncle's face fell. "He's well, Niece. As well as can be expected, certainly. You know he misses you. We all do. He'd call himself, but, as you know, he'll not challenge the president's ruling on your exile."

Neek closed her eyes and rubbed them. Her fingers came back wet, but not from *stuk*. It'd been ten years since she'd last seen her family. Her mother had been sick when she'd left, but Neek knew better than to ask about her or her gatoi talther—her third parent. Neither worked for the president, and questions regarding them could be misconstrued as personal. If her mother were dead, her uncle would tell her. Otherwise, that type of question could get even this small communication access rescinded. It was best to stick to safe topics. Have the discussions. Keep her dissenting mouth shut long enough to gain entrance to her homeworld so she could see her family again.

A knocking sound came from her uncle's side, and when she opened her eyes again, it was to the serene smile her uncle used when running a service. They were usually left alone for their discussions, but now she could see another set of feet—and the hemline of a gold and green Heaven Guard robe—in the upper corner of the transmission. Neek felt instantly sick. She sorted through mental images of her cohort from her time at the academy. Her roommate probably wouldn't have made the robes this early—she was terrible at piloting in space. Her cousin had scored the same top marks as Neek, but the skin tone of the feet was too pale to be from her genetic line. It was an older student then, someone she had maybe known but not socialized with. Someone who flew an agile Neek settee ship around her homeworld instead of a dilapidated tramp in the middle of the Charted Systems.

"It is, of course, always good to hear your voice, regardless of the reason. Every time you call, I thank Ardulum you're safe. Your distance from home distresses your family, as always. To be our planet's only exile, it is a hard road to walk. Our prayers are with you." Her uncle's left hand closed around a glossy, wooden pendant at his neck. Carved, Neek knew, by master crafters to resemble the planet Ardulum of Neek myth. The planet was fabled to move on its own from system to system, and in reverence to that freedom, devout Neek often wore a planet somewhere on their person. Neek had ground hers into a fine dust with the heel of her boot the day she'd been forced from her homeworld.

"Remember to light your prayer candle tonight and thank the Ardulans for their help, Exile. Their benevolence keeps you safe. Now then, let's begin on page two hundred and seventy-three. 'For two years, the orange planet glistened...'"

Neek let her uncle's voice drone on while she half listened. She ran long fingers through her hair, snagging on a tangle near the end. The *stuk* moistness on her fingertips, thin now from irritation, helped her work the mat loose as he continued to speak.

"'On the blue arcs rode the Ardulans.'" Her uncle looked up from the book. "In this particular passage, we view through our ancestors' eyes what the Ardulan technology must have looked like. Impressive. Mind-shattering. Imagine, Exile, that you were one of those Neek to first see Ardulum. How would you feel?"

Neek snapped an honest answer before she could catch herself. "You know how I feel about those stupid myths. I've seen the whole of the Charted Systems. Unsurprisingly, there are no mystical, traveling planets out here."

"Consider your words," her uncle responded sharply. "You should know better than most the consequences they can have."

Neek snarled and was just about to let loose a string of curses that would better explain how she felt about the president and Ardulum as a whole, when the *Mercy's Pledge* jostled violently. Neek spilled halfway out of her chair and had to right herself.

"Fuck. I think we just hit something." She forced a smile. "We can pick this up later. It was nice chatting with you, Uncle. My love to Mom, Tal, Dad, and Brother. I'll call again soon, I promise."

Before he had a chance to respond, Neek closed the connection and bolted towards the cockpit.

* * *

"Get those skiffs off our tail!" Captain Yorden Kuebrich yelled as Neek rounded the corner.

She looked out the viewscreen just in time to see the *Pledge*—her engines dead—exit the Callis Wormhole into the middle of a much-unexpected dogfight. A wedge-shaped Risalian skiff zipped past the *Pledge*, catching the edge of the ship on its wing, and started her into a slow spin. A pod, deep purple and about half the size of the skiff, chased the skiff and grazed their starboard flank. Neek braced herself against the console and heard Yorden tumble into the wall behind her, his substantial girth denting the aluminum.

Mentally cursing the ship's poor artificial gravity, Neek launched herself into the pilot's chair, grabbed the yoke, and scoured the latest damage report. "Aft stabilizer is shot," she called out after checking the computer. Other skiffs near them suddenly swooped back into a larger group, and the *Pledge* was, for the moment, left alone. Neek released the yoke and let her fingers move deftly over the interface. "Those new spray-on cellulose binders for the hull are holding, but only just. What's left of the Minoran armor plating is now officially cracked beyond repair."

She swiveled to see the captain buckling himself into a much larger version of her own chair. His brown hair puffed about his head, per usual, but his body language spoke of surprise and tension. That concerned Neek because Yorden was old enough to have lived through actual conflicts. If anyone knew how to react in a situation like this, it was him.

"Were we just *attacked*?" she asked incredulously. Neek took a closer look out the viewscreen. The rectangular cutter that sparkled with pinpricks of light and the wedge-shaped, agile skiffs were Risalian. The pods—both the smaller purple ones and the frigate-sized, maroon ones—were unfamiliar. Their formations were just as strange, stacked in columns like stones on a riverbank instead of in pyramidal and spherical formations like Systems ships would. "Are those all Charted Systems ships?"

Yorden threw up his hands in disgust. "They're not just Charted Systems ships—they're *Risalian* ships. The cutter and skiffs are, anyway. No clue on the pods. What those blue-skinned bastards are doing out here with fully weaponized ships, I can only guess. However, they're firing lasers. If we lose our armor and take a hit from any of those, we are space dust."

"Comforting," Neek mumbled. She hadn't noticed the laser ports on any of the ships, but now that she looked closer, all of the vessels were covered with armor plating and had at least two laser turrets each.

Neek continued to watch as the pods begin to cluster around a Risalian cutter. A pod ship zipped beneath the cutter, firing wildly at its underside, before making a quick right turn and heading back to a larger pod. Five others followed suit. The cutter's shielding began to splinter, but the ship remained where it was.

Neek leaned towards the viewscreen, still unsure what she was seeing. "The Risalian ships aren't chasing, they're just defending. What is going on? If they're going to appoint themselves sheriffs of the Charted Systems, they could at least fight back."

Yorden smacked his hand against the wall, loosing a shower of dust. "Something on that Risalian ship is holding their attention. Get us out of here, before either of them gets any closer." He pointed to a cluster of ships to Neek's right, and her eyes followed. Little flashes of bright light sparked and then died intermittently as ships were destroyed, their flotsam creating an ever-expanding ring. A large piece of metal plating floated past the *Pledge*'s port window. The edge caught and left a thin scratch in the fiberglass as it slid off.

"What are they protecting that is so damn important?" Neek wondered out loud and then snorted. "Something worth more than our hold full of diamond rounds and cellulose-laced textiles?" she added cheekily.

Scowling, Yorden pushed Neek's hand away from the computer and began his own scan of the *Pledge*'s systems. "Communications are still up, but I don't think either party is listening right now." Frustrated, he kicked the underside of the console. "Try one of them. Better than being crushed."

"Captain, come on. We are dead in space. If another one comes at us, why don't we just fire at it? It's better than being rammed." She pointed upwards at a circular hole in the ceiling. "What's the benefit of flying a ship so ancient it falls apart if you're not taking advantage of the grandfathered weapons system?"

Yorden's terse response was cut off when a short burst impacted the ship. Another group of skiffs flew past, depositing laser fire as they did so. The *Pledge* banked to port, carrying momentum from the impact. From the direction they had come lay a trail of shattered ship plating.

A panicked voice called down from the laser turret. Neek bristled, steeling herself against the inevitable irritation that came whenever their Journey youth spoke. "That skiff just *fired* at us. How does it even have weapons? I thought we were the only ones in the Systems with a ship older than dirt."

Neek wrapped her right hand back around the steering yoke. Each of her eight fingers fit perfectly into the well-worn grooves, and the brown leather darkened a shade as her naturally secreted *stuk* smeared from her fingertips. She smiled to herself. Flying a geriatric tramp was still better than flying nothing at all.

"Look, Captain," she said, keeping her eyes on the battle. "I can steer this thing if we get pushed, but that is it. We don't have any other options. They have guns. We have guns. Well, we have *a* gun. Why don't we use it?"

Yorden stared at the approaching ships and then took a step back. "I am willing to ignore the illegality of what you are suggesting because I don't want to spend my retirement as incinerated flotsam. Attracting more attention to ourselves is a terrible idea, but we won't have a choice if a ship comes at us again." Neek raised an eyebrow, and Yorden snorted. "Better incarcerated than dead, I suppose."

A large plume of yellow smoke burst from the far wall panel as Yorden spoke, almost as if the *Pledge* were agreeing. Two more shots impacted the tramp and sent the small transport into a tight spin. Neek gripped the yoke with both hands and pulled hard, trying to steady the ship. Yorden's hip smacked the main console, and the thin metal scaffold dented.

"Do it!" he bellowed, rubbing his hip. "We can worry about Risalian consequences for owning weapons if we live past the next ten minutes." The captain got onto his knees to inspect the new cloud of smoke that was billowing from underneath the console. Neek fanned the computer interface and coughed, attempting to assess the damage. The smell of burning wood wafted towards her, and she suspected some of the new Cell-Tal bindings were on fire.

"I don't hear any firing, Nicholas," the captain called, his voice hoarse.

"I don't know how to work any of this stuff," Nicholas yelled back as the sound of frantic button pushing could be heard over the panic in his voice. "I'm just supposed to be observing!"

"Just press buttons until something happens," Neek called up to him. Her head rolled back slightly as she relaxed the *Pledge* from a tailspin to a gentle rotation by opening the gas vents. As the internal gravity system began its whirring to adjust to their decreased movement, laser bursts—sporadic and utterly uncoordinated—began to ring from the *Pledge's* turret. The bright streaks of yellow light shot in the general direction of the fray.

"Try to *aim*, Nicholas!" Yorden bellowed over his shoulder. "Did they teach you nothing useful in school? We're not trying to piss off both fleets, just keep them away from us." He bent down and opened an access panel beneath the yoke, searching again for the source of the smoke that was now seeping through the upper console.

"Half of these switches don't *do* anything!" Nicholas yelled back, his voice muffled by laser fire.

"Why not try hitting the ones that *do* do something?" Yorden retorted.

"Ha!" Neek exclaimed. She entered the final series of commands with her left hand, and the star field outside the viewscreen stabilized. "Did a little back-alley reroute, so I think this waste of space might just stay upright for a little bit. We're far enough below the battle that maybe we'll be left alone for a while."

As Neek finished her sentence, she watched a Risalian skiff break formation and align perfectly with the *Pledge*. Neek's breath caught in her throat.

"Uh, Captain?" she said, not wanting to turn around.

"Figure it out, Neek," came Yorden's terse response. "If I don't fix the air quality breaker, we're going to suffocate to death."

The skiff edged closer, staying in their direct line of sight. Neek assumed they were being scanned, but with the archaic technology on the *Pledge*, she had no way to confirm it. She wondered briefly if the pilot on the skiff was staring as intently out the viewscreen as she was. She tried to imagine the mindset it took to fire on an unarmed ship that was dead in space and, as she contemplated, rubbed the back of her head. Of course, the *Pledge* was *not* unarmed, but the likelihood of the Risalians having pulled the ship's registration since their emergence from the wormhole was low. Neek ground her fingertips into her temples. A funny tickle was starting there—one she couldn't quite place but hoped wasn't the start of a headache. Likely, it was just residual tension from speaking to her uncle.

A pod disengaged with the Risalian cutter and swooped on top of the skiff, showering it with laser fire. The skiff banked to starboard, avoiding each blast, and then righted. The pod moved to the other side of the *Pledge* and bobbed around her edges.

"We're being used as a shield," Neek muttered. Louder, she yelled, "Nicholas, pick one and just fire already!" The pressure in Neek's head grew. Irritated, she pressed a *stuk*-covered finger to the affected area and visualized pushing the pain away.

A ringing sound came from the laser turret. A bright-yellow shot appeared from the top of the viewscreen and opened a hole in the skiff's hull. The ship began to list and, a moment later, exploded when two additional shots were added by the pod.

"I got one!" Nicholas yelled. The sound of his whooping could be heard distinctly through the ceiling. "Take *that* you tiny skiffs!"

"Get the other one! Don't stop until—" Neek cut herself off as she took in the battlefront. Nicholas's destruction of the skiff caused a ripple effect among the others. The rest of the small Risalian skiffs had broken formation and begun flying erratically. Some were running into each other, others simply heading off course. One was listing at an odd angle, expelling occasional bursts of red fuel. The Risalian cutter was left unattended, and the strange pod frigate was closing in.

"Were the skiffs on autopilot?" Neek asked incredulously.

"Autopilot doesn't work for those kinds of maneuvers," Yorden responded. "It is only useful for fixed points and straight lines." Both watched in confusion as the smaller ships continued to drift apart and the largest pod docked with the cutter. "The round ships aren't firing anymore," Yorden murmured. "That's something."

"Do you want me to keep shooting, Captain?" Nicholas had come down the ladder from the turret and into the main cockpit. He was noticeably shaken, and the sweat stains on his shirt spoke of the stress he had been under moments before. His expression darkened as he asked, "I didn't kill anyone, did I?"

"Maybe," Neek responded casually, trying not to think about the implications. She'd forgotten how sensitive Journey youths could be. She tried to mitigate the snark in her tone but couldn't quite figure out how to do it. "It saved our lives though. Something worth writing home about, anyway."

Nicholas shifted uncomfortably on his feet but remained uncharacteristically quiet.

A tiny, purple light began to flash at the base of the console. Neek tapped the area. "Incoming hail from the pod that's docked with the Risalian cutter. You want to answer?"

"The troublemakers are contacting us?" Yorden considered and then shrugged his shoulders as he accepted the hail. "This is Captain Yorden Kuebrich of the *Mercy's Pledge*. We're a tramp ship on our way to Oorin. To whom might we be speaking?"

A grainy image finally materialized on the comm, revealing a hovering, purple-black, spherical being with no apparent appendages, eyes, or mouth. It did, however, have distinctly human-looking ears that protruded from the sides of the sphere.

"That's a giant, sentient beach ball," Nicholas stated flatly.

"At least it's not a traveling planet," Neek muttered.

Yorden glared at both of them and then turned his attention back to the comm.

The ball creature bobbed up and down twice. A lateral slit formed right in the center of its body and slowly opened.

"We're off course," the creature said in perfect Common. "We've sustained heavy damage and must dock for repair. As you are also disabled, we can offer you a tow to a planet with repair capabilities."

Yorden looked quickly to Neek, who shrugged. They had to get a tow from someone. Why not a beach ball? There was no way the Risalians would give them a tow after what they'd just done to their fleet, and they definitely couldn't just spin near the exit of a wormhole forever.

"That'd be Oorin. We've got a pull loop just under the port plating. I'll have my pilot extend it, and you can latch on however you want." Yorden gestured at Neek, who, in an exaggerated movement, brought two of her fingers up into an arc and then back down onto a blue button on the far upper section of the console.

"Pull loop extended, Captain. Can we have Nicholas get out and push?"

The young man scowled, but his retort was cut off when the *Pledge* gave a large jerk as one of the alien pods latched onto the pull loop with a coiled metal rope.

"Prepare for towing," the sphere said before cutting off the communication.

There was silence in the cockpit for a long moment before Yorden exhaled and slumped into his chair. He leaned back, and the chair reclined, groaning under his weight. "I think that took twenty years off my life. We need to get answers from Chen when we hit the spaceport. If the Charted Systems are being invaded—or whatever just happened to provoke the Risalians—the Systems are not prepared for it."

"This is just another notch on your belt, I'd imagine, Captain."

When Yorden didn't respond, Neek playfully punched him on the shoulder before she settled back and closed her eyes. Notch on his belt, and another irritation on hers. She'd have to put off calling her uncle back for at least a few days now, which wasn't going to look good on the yearly report. Maybe she should just write this year off altogether and send the president a few recordings of her actual thoughts. Neek grinned. That would be incredibly satisfying but, unfortunately, detrimental to her goal.

At least the funniness in the back of her head was gone. Whatever the last ten minutes had been about, Neek was glad things hadn't gotten more serious. Hopefully, they would soon be far, far away from the Risalians, their ridiculously overpowered ships, and whatever it was they wanted so desperately to protect.

Chapter 3: Callis Spaceport

For two years
The orange planet glistened
Propulsion tail dripping flame
Our atmosphere burned in blue arcs of laughter
Blue arcs through which our future came.

On the blue arcs rode the Ardulans
Pale and dark and etched like stone
On the blue arcs came our saviors
Our future carried in open palms.

With their guidance did we build our cities,
Towers glittering in majestic height.
With their guidance did we leave our heavens
Our ships strong with orange tails of light.

All things do we owe to Ardulum
All things do we divine from them
And when they left on blue arcs turned orange
Did we weep and mourn for them.

—Poem from *The Book of The Uplifting*, published on Neek in 50 AA

The *Pledge* was a mess. Neek slapped an access panel shut near an exterior wing, but the metal refused to latch and swung back out at her. She cursed and added a broken door to the list of repairs. There was no way the payout from this job would cover everything, which meant, once again, they'd be forced to triage.

Too frustrated to continue, Neek walked out of the ship and to the docking bay exit. Directly across from the *Pledge* was a Minoran galactic liner, its fresh scarlet paint glossy in the overhead light. Neek took a moment to admire the long, oval-shaped ship's soft curves and streamlined front. It was three times the size of the *Pledge* and easily five times the size of a Neek settee. She'd never even set foot in something so large.

"Bet it flies as smooth as it looks," she muttered to herself as she trailed a fingertip over the shiny surface. "Probably not a tight turn radius, but it'd be great to get my hands on the yoke and see what she is capable of."

"Neek!" Yorden's voice snapped her out of her daydream. The captain stood near the exit, tapping his foot impatiently, a fat satchel of what she hoped were diamond rounds hanging from his belt. She'd forgotten they were to convene before lunch to price parts. Neek reluctantly peeled herself from the liner and jogged to meet him. He didn't say anything when she came close, instead turning and walking briskly out of the bay and into the main section of Callis Spaceport.

The commerce area was nearly deserted. The usually bustling port—the main commerce attraction on the otherwise uninhabited Oorin—currently showcased only a few dozen shoppers, most of whom were Terran. Neek could see Yorden physically relax, the tension from the dogfight easing away as he was surrounded by his people. She felt the opposite, however, as every pair of eyes that fell onto her hands changed from curious to apprehensive. Neek. *The* Neek—the only one of her species out and about in the Systems. Her planet was backwater enough to stay out of the news feeds, but important enough, due to the andal exports, that other beings knew enough to name it. To name *her*. The *only* Neek off the planet, barring the occasional diplomat. The Exile.

Neek ignored it. She'd grown used to the gawkers over the last decade, and the dogged stares no longer cut so deeply. Besides, she had other things to think about. The incident with the Risalians still weighed on her. Neek had never been in a fight before—not a real one. She wasn't sure what it meant, or even what to think about it. Were there going to be consequences for firing on the Risalians? Were the beach balls a new potential member of the Systems, or were they, too, on the wrong side of the strict Risalian laws? If things got too heated in the Systems, maybe she could use that to her advantage. She wouldn't be a useful lesson in disobedience to her planet's president if she were dead. Maybe she could manage to negotiate some on-world religious indoctrination, with a side of family visits.

Yorden answered one of her questions before she managed to vocalize it. "It's been, oh, thirty years, maybe forty, since I was involved in something like that. I was about Nicholas's age, all elbows and knees but not nearly so naïve."

They paused in front of a fast-print food shop, the neon lighting advertising perf catching Neek's eye. A group of quadruped Minorans sat on their haunches near the front window, flicking their ears with pleasure as they lapped up perf suspended in a container of water. The owner of the restaurant, another Minoran, began to wave Yorden and Neek in with a front hoof, but then stopped when she noticed Neek's hands. The owner's face fell to a frown and she turned, flicked her spindly tail across her rear, and walked back into the shop.

With a sigh, Neek rammed her hands into the pockets of her flight suit, ripping one of the internal seams in the process. "What do you think the Risalian attack means?" she asked. "Not so much for us, but for the Charted Systems."

Yorden flipped a diamond round into a wishing well near the shop and then grumbled. "That the peace isn't holding, more than likely. That the Systems are about to get a wake-up call." He fished his round from the water along with a handful of others. Once the dripping stopped, he opened his palm and let the shimmering diamonds plink back to the bottom of the shallow well. "You have to remember, Neek, that things were really different when I was young. Earth had all those wars going on, and space travel was still in its infancy. Risalians weren't in the picture at all, much less their highly effective sheriff forces. This peace—this unrelenting, omnipresent peace—hasn't been in existence for that long. Besides—" He slapped his hand against the water, splashing the nearby wall. "—peace is unstable at best. Usually more of a time to gather forces than anything else. Risalians are great at posturing."

"I don't know the first thing about war," Neek muttered as they resumed walking, her hands encased to the wrists in cotton fabric.

"No, but you're halfway decent at subterfuge. That's something." Yorden snorted. "Cheer up. You've got a job on the *Pledge* as long as you need it. I'll never find another being with a hand wide enough to use the ship's yoke and computer panel at the same time."

Neek stopped walking and glared at Yorden. She debated a number of Common curses, but Yorden spoke before she did.

"I'm only kidding, Neek. Your piloting skills can't be beat. You know that."

Neek bit back the curses and resumed walking, debating whether or not to take a verbal shot at Yorden's deteriorating ship as payback. As they turned another corner to where most of the small parts dealers were located, Neek forgot their conversation and her discomforting celebrity status. There—between an Oorin condominium and a Terran sausage shop—was Nicholas deeply engaged in conversation with a large member of the beach ball species who had given them the tow.

Yorden's tension was back. He stomped over, and Neek could see the tips of his ears starting to turn red. She thought back to six months ago, when Nicholas had lost them an Enden hauling job by refusing the native's offer of a small pebble from the shores of her home continent. Nicholas had argued later that it looked stolen, and he had no intention of accepting stolen goods. No amount of lecturing from Yorden about how you accepted gifts even if they *were* stolen had made Nicholas change his mind.

Steeling herself for another diplomatic incident, Neek kept off to the side. When the captain reached the youth, he stepped just in front of him, cutting Nicholas off from the beach ball.

Silence followed Yorden's entrance. The captain cleared his throat.

"Captain!" Nicholas hissed. "We're in the middle of a conversation."

Yorden looked over his shoulder and narrowed his eyes. "I know. What's going on?"

Nicholas stepped cautiously from behind the larger man and then took one more step closer to the sphere. Yorden eyed him suspiciously.

"Captain Llgg," Nicholas began, and Neek cringed at the obvious butchering of the name. "Meet Captain Yorden Kuebrich." Nicholas turned back to the beach ball captain, whose ears were now rippling. "Captain...Captain Lug commands the ship that towed us into the Callis System. Her species is called, uh...Muh-nu-gul, and they're from one of the uncharted systems—the sector out behind Risal. She told her government that we saved their lives, and now they want to hold a ceremony for us. She seems pretty serious about it."

Yorden looked surprised. Neek toyed with the inner seam of her flight-suit pockets, now slightly sticky, and considered. A new species meant new contacts. New contacts meant new jobs. New jobs meant more money for the ship, and maybe some extra for one of those new printer pens that extruded wood-metal composites. She'd seen some models on display a few shops back, the store window loaded with accessories like nozzle tips, support scaffoldings, refill cartridges... With something like that, they could draw out their own parts instead of buying them. Biometal was always cheaper raw than formed, and Neek always loved a new toy.

On the other hand, these Mmnnuggls were having some sort of conflict with the Risalians, and getting involved any more in *that* mess was probably not going to sit well with the captain. He'd already lost any Neek planetary hauling jobs because of having her for a pilot. He didn't need his potential clientele whittled any further.

Yorden turned to Neek and raised an eyebrow. She shook her head. She appreciated getting a vote in the matter, but likely Yorden had already made his decision.

"Look, Captain...Lug." Yorden coughed as he, too, caught on the name. "We just want to get our repairs done and leave. No need for any ceremonies or anything. If you hadn't been there, we'd have never made it to Oorin in the first place. We're very grateful."

Llgg bobbed up and down twice, purple ears rippling. "Our laws demand you be compensated for your trouble," she said in her strangely perfect Common. "You and your crew will meet us tonight in docking bay forty-seven, where our ship is berthed. There will be a meal and ceremony, followed by a presentation of your reward. This is required."

"Reward?" Yorden sputtered, looking bewildered. Neek leaned against the wall and tried to remember if they had ever received a reward. Hauling freight wasn't exactly glamorous work, nor was it likely to get you noticed by award-giving institutions. Still, the idea made her reconsider her position. Nicholas's lucky shot didn't seem particularly award-worthy, but then again, what did she know about the Mmnnuggls, or whatever they called themselves? Maybe they had one of those "no debt" cultures. Maybe they liked to give gifts. Maybe the gift would be a long-range riot rifle that she could fire from here and hit the Neek president in his heavily jowled face. Maybe they'd follow the *Pledge* around the Charted Systems until Yorden accepted something. Did Yorden want to risk pissing off a brand-new species just to avoid more drama with the Risalians? The Mmnnuggls did seem to have better technology, and none of their ships had fired on the *Pledge* in the dogfight.

Yorden's response came slowly, each word deliberate. "Maybe...we do have time for a...ceremony."

Before Yorden could talk himself out of it, Neek walked over with a wide smile.

"Wait, reward? Of course we'll be there!" She clapped an arm around Nicholas's shoulder and grinned as the *stuk* on her fingertips wicked into his flight suit, leaving long, dark stains. Nicholas wriggled under her arm, trying to evade the wetness. "You know, I was just telling our captain here how we don't spend enough time getting rewards these days." She gave a practiced sigh. "The price of honest business, no doubt. Self-sacrifice for the greater good always has to play second fiddle to affording food."

"Please be in attendance at the end of the Third Cycle." Llgg bobbed again, flattened her ears against her body, and then, without turning around, accelerated away from the group so quickly that a small breeze ruffled Yorden's puffy hair.

When she was out of sight, Yorden turned to Neek, who dropped her arm off Nicholas and glanced out the nearby window.

"Gross, Neek," Nicholas said as he rubbed at the wet spots on his shoulder. "Personal space, remember? We talked about it."

Neek ignored him. "What do you think of this ceremony, Captain?" she asked. "Possibility of a trap? It doesn't really sound like it, but these things *did* try to take out a Risalian cutter and then docked with it. Think they're after something? Think they *stole* something?"

Yorden nodded. "I agree. We need answers. Why don't you take the kid down to Section D and talk to Chen. You and I haven't been to Oorin in a while, but you should be able to find your way back there." He gestured back towards the *Pledge*'s berth. "I'm going to find parts. Be sure to pick up some weapons if you can. Legal ones, old enough to be grandfathered in."

This time, Neek's smile was genuine. She took a few steps to the right, gave a mock salute, and smacked her hand onto Nicholas's back, leaving a small, wet spot from each of her fingertips. Nicholas hunched his shoulders and sighed.

"Onward," Neek said, mind already dancing with thoughts of the guns she might find in Chen's haphazard piles of goods. "To the shopping!"

* * *

It wasn't as hard to find Chen's shop as Neek had feared. He still had the bright-orange *SPACE STUFF!!* sign above the doorway, which she could see from halfway across the plaza.

The shop itself had not changed. Goods were stacked in piles on the floor, loosely separated by type. Several shoppers milled about inside, and the area still had the same musty smell Neek remembered from years before. As she entered the shop, Nicholas trailing behind, a tiny human male emerged from behind a pile of clothes. His white hair was long, thin, and dyed purple at the tips, and he had just as many wrinkles as she remembered. Unlike the typical drab clothes of the spaceport, Chen was brightly dressed in blaring rainbow print. He looked shorter than the last time Neek had seen him, or possibly he had only ever come up to her hip. It was hard to remember. She left her hands out from her pockets just in case.

Chen recognized her immediately, a wide smile crossing his face when they made eye contact. "Ah, the exiled Neek. With a Journey youth this time, I see. Trade Yorden in for a younger model?"

Neek smiled sweetly. "Come now, Chen. You know I'd only upgrade to someone older." She nodded her head towards a pile of weapons in the center of the store. "Mind if we look around? We ran into some trouble outside the Callis Wormhole. Beach balls and all that. Can never be too careful, even in peacetime."

Chen's expression darkened at the mention of beach balls, but instead of speaking, he disappeared back behind the clothing pile. His disembodied voice called, "By all means, take your time. I'll be around if you need me."

Without looking to see if Nicholas was following, Neek brushed past a pile of thick canvases and headed to the weapons. Her boot caught on a loose thread and caused the entire pile to collapse as she walked by.

"You know, they make shelving for this sort of thing," Nicholas commented as the canvases spread out in front of him. "Besides, wasn't that guy supposed to give us information? He has got to be, like, ninety years old. Maybe he forgot."

Neek stepped around another messy pile and worked her way to the weapons stack. "Judging people on how they appear can get you killed, Nicholas," Neek said as she wedged her hand between two sticky handles to grab what looked like an antique dueling knife. She grasped its hilt and carefully extracted the delicate object. Upon closer inspection, however, she realized she had been mistaken. The blade of this knife bent upwards and back towards itself. It had a decorative hilt made from finely carved wood, which made it all the more confusing.

"Huh," she said as she held the knife out to Nicholas. "Take a look at this. Why do you think someone would put such a nice handle on a vegetable peeler?"

Nicholas blinked several times in confusion and then batted the knife away. "Could we focus on our task?" he asked loudly, startling a nearby shopper. The Minoran quadruped perked her ears towards them and then, upon seeing Neek's fingers, cantered to the back of the store. "We didn't come here to shop—we came to get information."

Neek put the knife on a nearby countertop. It was worth purchasing just for the hilt, which looked suspiciously like andal wood—a species native to her homeworld and the organic basis of most of Cell-Tal's biometals. "Chen is clearly not yet ready to give us that information. Have some patience." Neek smirked, slapped Nicholas on the back again, casually strolled over to the case where the owner had reappeared, and began browsing the pistols under the crystal-paneled surface.

After several minutes of deliberation, Neek pointed at the most expensive-looking pistol, a piece with an exceptionally long barrel. "Let me see that one," she said to Chen.

"It looks like a pistol," Nicholas said in an irritated tone. "A ridiculous pistol."

"Hush," Neek breathed as she ran her slick fingers over the weapon. There was elegance to its design that offset its inherent loss of functionality. Ancient, long-barreled guns simply did not shoot true, in her experience, but this one didn't look old at all. Chen wasn't legally allowed to carry new weapons, however, which made this particular one a mystery.

The owner frowned as Neek continued to inspect the weapon. "That one is a little tricky. I bought it from a Risalian who needed some fast cash. Xe said the gun was a specialty weapon—one of Cell-Tal's noncommercial models. Xe showed me how to work it, but it doesn't appear to be lethal. I gave the Risalian fifty diamond rounds simply because I'd never seen anything like it before."

"It looks just like every other pistol here," Nicholas commented. "What if it is just some prototype that never made it into mass production?"

"I'm inclined to agree with the boy," Neek said. She handed the pistol back to Chen. "What is so great about it?" Neek leaned her elbow on the counter and rested her head in her hand. She raised an eyebrow. "Feel free to wow me."

Chen flipped a switch Neek hadn't noticed before on the side of the pistol. A soft hum began to build in frequency until she couldn't hear it anymore. He then leveled the pistol directly at Nicholas's head.

"Whoa!" Nicholas cried, jumping back and to the side. "What'd I do?"

"Relax, kid," the proprietor said. "It doesn't kill or stun. It's a containment gun. Here, watch." Chen pointed the pistol back at Nicholas's head and fired. Neek watched in fascination as Nicholas froze in place. All around him pulsed some sort of sparkly mesh. Strange little strands of light shot across the mesh, launched towards his skin, and then immediately shot in the opposite direction. It was oddly beautiful, but she couldn't figure a practical use for it.

"Now go try to move him," Chen instructed. Confused, Neek went over to Nicholas and slowly put her palm up against the mesh net. To her surprise, her hand moved right through and contacted with his arm.

"Very interesting," she commented, noting the buzzing feeling where the field touched her skin. She grabbed a bit of Nicholas's sleeve and gave him a tug. Nicholas took a step forward to counterbalance.

"Hey!" he cried out. "I didn't tell my legs to do that! I can't even feel you grabbing me!"

"Yet you still appear to be able to talk," Neek remarked. "Seems like a very specific targeting system. Highly advanced." She reconsidered the usefulness of the weapon. Being able to freeze someone in place *and* move them could solve a lot of problems during some of their off-the-book runs. Since they did those off-book runs mostly for the Risalians themselves, having a piece of Risalian tech to help seemed fitting.

"Does it work on all species?" Neek asked.

Chen shrugged. "If it was made by Cell-Tal, then it's likely cellulose-based—andal cellulose, specifically. You know they import that tree like crazy from your home planet, Neek, or at least as much as your government will sell it. You can see the microfibrils running across it in the right light. A lot of Risalian weapons I come across have this type of modified laser field. The cellulose changes the properties somehow, makes the fields more malleable." He paused, flipped another switch on the pistol, and fired it again at Nicholas. The mesh net immediately vanished. "All the Risalian said was that it was developed for a specific species but would work on most of the Charted Systems inhabitants to varying degrees. That gives you a few trillion beings to shoot at."

Neek took the pistol back from the proprietor and ran her fingers over the surface, leaving clear trails of *stuk*. It was a unique weapon—an elegant weapon—and a weapon Nicholas might actually use. Their last Journey youth had refused to carry any form of weapon, even a knife. A containment gun, however, would likely have broader appeal.

"Want to purchase it?"

Neek glanced at Nicholas and then back at the pistol. "Definitely." She grabbed the strange knife and a two-handed riot rifle from the pile as well, and placed them in front of Chen. "These too."

Chen bent below the counter and pulled up several pieces of cotton cloth. He wrapped the items deliberately, taking his time with the folding and tying of the material. As he began to pack the parcels in a canvas bag, he spoke slowly, in a barely audible whisper.

"Those Mmnnuggls you tangled with are from outside the Charted Systems. They're not entirely organic, according to speculation, although those stupid ears are quite real. I've heard talk of their homeworld somewhere behind Risal, but I don't have any real confirmation of that." He added some extra padding around the stun gun before tossing in several brightly colored flyers, which advertised his next day's sales. "They have excellent linguistic skills, but seldom use our wormholes as transport. Their weaponry looks more advanced too, from the pieces I've been able to acquire, and they've been at the Risalians for years."

When the last item was in the bag, Chen held it out to Neek, who took it reverently. Her fingers closed on the handle, but Chen did not let go and instead yanked it forward so that the pilot spilled over the countertop, her ear right up against his mouth. "Encrypted Risalian communications refer to them as pirates, Neek. Minor irritants, but irritants nonetheless. Today, I heard a report of more-than-minor theft. They took something off that cutter—something the Risalians care enough about that they are launching a full squadron to hunt down this group. Best stay away."

He released her and then, with a final nod, picked up a cloth and a glass object and began to polish it, whistling as he did so. Neek grabbed the bag and Nicholas by the cuff of his flight suit, and headed back to the *Pledge* to prepare for dinner with the pirates of the Charted Systems.

* * *

The crew of *Mercy's Pledge* sat together in a soft, round depression in the floor of the Mmnnuggl pod. The room was bathed in bright green lighting that felt considerably disquieting. Neek tried to move to her knees to block the reflection coming off of the round walls, but the ceiling was so low that she cracked her head against it. Grumbling, she sat back on her bottom and tried to distract herself with Nugels instead.

She counted roughly thirty in attendance, their spherical bodies ornately painted in vivid shades of yellow and gold. Captain Llgg sat to the left of Yorden, issuing orders to the serving spheres in the strange monotone beeping of their native tongue.

"We would like to thank you for attending the ceremony," Llgg said in Common, turning her wide vocal opening towards Yorden and his crew. Her earlobes rippled. "My crew is now going to perform an interpretation of 'The Battle of Ggunllrnn' for your entertainment. Eat the provided refreshments."

Several trays of food, all round and firm to the touch, were placed in front of the three guests. Neek blinked and looked up at Llgg. "Sorry...battle of what now?"

Another set of ripples cascaded through Llgg's ears. "Cgunllrnn. The battle in which the tramp, *Mercy's Pledge*, provided a brilliant attack on a Risalian skiff, coming to the aid of the Mmnnuggl people. You honor our Gods and those that serve them. None of us would have known which ship contained the Ardulan interface. We would have surely perished without your help."

Neek choked on the sphere she had been trying to swallow. Yorden delivered two quick whacks to her back, and the round food came up and out, rolling across the metal floor. Ardulan? As in, beings from Ardulum that her people worshiped as gods? Surely she had misheard. In fact, she was certain she had misheard. Neek pushed the entire conversation to the back of her mind, determined to not let it spoil her evening.

"Right. Well, you're welcome," Neek said, forcing a smile. "Let's get this play or whatever it is under way."

Llgg bobbed three times, and several spheres started darting around just above the middle of the sitting area. The beeping noises imitated the sounds of laser fire as they recreated the battle in front of their audience. First came a large sphere, painted silver like a Risalian cutter. Then, a group of smaller Mmnnuggls—children maybe?—also painted silver, clustered around the "cutter." A group of unpainted Mmnnuggls entered then, a large one in the lead. Finally, a small, haphazardly painted Mmnnuggl spun into the scene and began a slow list to one side.

More imitation laser fire. Finally, the *Pledge* sphere emitted its own beeping, and a Risalian sphere dropped quickly to the floor.

"Hey, here's the part where I hit the Risalian ship!" Nicholas whispered somewhat loudly to his companions when a number of spheres began to spin drunkenly away from the center of the stage.

Neek felt a sharp elbow in the ribs. "This is your fault," Yorden hissed. "You picked his application. He's the one who managed to hit the lead ship."

Neek wiggled her fingertips at Yorden. "Don't doubt the *stuk*. He saved our lives in the process."

"I still don't buy in to your finger voodoo."

Neek shrugged. "It's not like either of us have any skill with large laser guns. The crossfire would have destroyed us anyway in another few minutes. Just ignore that it was a Risalian ship. They'll never ID the *Pledge*. We scraped off the perma-ID with Baltec acid, remember? Besides, we do enough hauls for the Markin Council that I doubt they'd consent to our destruction."

"Risalians are more resourceful than you think." Yorden folded his arms across his chest. Nicholas continued to watch as the reenactment of the battle drew to a close, with one Mmnnuggl "docking" with a larger one.

The two paused their whispered arguing as the mock battle ended, and Nicholas began to clap loudly. Belatedly, Yorden and Neek joined him.

"Honored guests," Llgg said, rising up from the rim of the seating area and floating towards its center. "While Mmnnuggls are mostly unfamiliar with the cultures of your 'Charted Systems,' we do understand the importance of gratitude. Today you saved many lives. Our government has sent instructions that you are to be granted our cargo as a token of goodwill and gratitude between your ship and our homeworld." Llgg quickly turned her spherical body counterclockwise several times and gave a loud chirp. A few other Mmnnuggls exited the main chamber and returned with a heavy-looking cylinder the height of from the floor to Yorden's waist.

"A bomb?" Neek asked hopefully. "We don't have any of those onboard. They always take up too much cargo room."

The cylinder was brought to a halt just in front of Yorden. The Mmnnuggls paused and were silent.

"It's...lovely," Yorden managed. "We know just what to do with it."

"You have the facilities, I assume, to care for this?" Llgg asked.

"Yes, of course," he responded. "My ship is fully equipped for..." He peered more closely at the cylinder. "Fully equipped for stasis capsules."

"Then our debt is paid, and our gratitude fully expressed." Llgg whirred loudly, and several Mmnnuggls began to move the cylinder forward again, towards the boarding ramp of the ship. "My people will accompany you back to your ship with the capsule. You may instruct them on where it is to be placed."

"We thank you for the gift," Yorden responded, recovering from his confusion. "Should you ever require any sort of goods transportation, we hope you'll consider the *Mercy's Pledge* in the future."

"Indeed." Llgg responded. "Safe journeys to you, Captain, and to your crew." With that, Captain Llgg and the rest of the crew retreated.

"Stasis chamber," Neck mused as they headed back towards their ship. "Great. They could at least have given us *some* form of explosive. What are we going to do with the whatever-it-is inside?"

CHAPTER 4: CALLIS SPACEPORT

I refuse to follow a man who places tradition over progress. I refuse to bow down to a man who preaches morality yet practices infidelity. There is nothing in those books that you cannot teach yourself! Impeach the president and elect a new head of Neek who will not cauterize this planet's growth with two hundred years of myths and fables!

—Excerpt from a political rally in N'lln, Neek; Third Lunar Cycle, 220 AA

"Are we going to open it?" Nicholas asked. He nudged the cylinder with a toe, and a string of white and green circles lit up on the side panel. "It's pretty small. I guess it could hold a monkey...or maybe one of those giant space slugs that are native to this system."

"If it's space slugs, we're tossing it out the bay doors. I don't do slimy." Neek shuddered.

Nicholas wrinkled his nose. "But *you're* slimy."

Neek tipped the cylinder onto its side and tapped experimentally on the metal. "Mucus and slime are completely different things." She looked up at the Journey youth. "I thought they made Terrans take advanced biology classes before they shipped them off-world."

"Enough, please." Yorden ran his hands over the outside casing. "It's smooth the whole way around. No levers or buttons of any kind. Not even sure where a seam would be on one of these."

Neek studied the cylinder and then produced a fine-tipped laser scalpel from her flight-suit pocket. "Fuck it. Sucker is ours now, and I never could wait to open a surprise present." She squatted down and began making an incision near the top. The laser cut through the first layer of metal with ease, but sparks started to fly as the beam encountered the second layer.

"Probably some sort of security system," Yorden commented as he shielded his eyes. Neek increased the settings on the scalpel and continued to go over and over the same line. The sparks grew in intensity, although they curiously did not burn when they hit her arm.

"Almost through the second layer, I think," Neek called over the increasing pitch of the tool. "Whatever is in here can't be that big."

A loud *POP* filled the cargo hold, and a blast of putrid air and smoke blew out from the cylinder. Neek fell back, knocked off her haunches. Yorden and Nicholas took several steps backwards as well. When the air cleared, Neek could see a large, burst seam running across the cylinder. The indicator lights had ceased functioning. The entire unit appeared to be dead.

Placing a hand on either side of the seam, Neek slowly pulled the two edges apart. The metal seemed to give way easily, and a rush of sparks accompanied a preadolescent female as she tumbled unceremoniously out of the tube and onto the floor.

"What the—" Neek fell backwards, scrambling away from the child, certain her eyes were deceiving her.

Before the pilot was a little girl. Her translucent, white skin showed a patchwork of purple veins running just underneath the surface, the mass so thick that her organs couldn't be seen. Her body was also, Neek noted in horror, covered in a substantial amount of blood and nothing else. Her hair was long, chestnut colored, and pulled back behind her neck in a rough tail. A small, black triangle, roughly the size of Yorden's pinkie nail, showed through the skin just under her left eye. She was completely unconscious.

"I *thought* I heard Lug mention Ardulans," Yorden commented. "You okay, Neek?"

Nicholas moved forward to touch the girl, and Neek grabbed him by the shirt, hauling him away. "Don't touch her! Don't go near her!" Neek was certain she was hallucinating. "Ardulum is a *fairy tale*," she whispered. "This is someone's idea of a sick joke. This is not real. This is a *joke*."

"A very intricate joke, apparently." Yorden nudged the girl's arm with his toe. "The vein work is exquisite. Tattoos maybe?"

Neek shook her head, her eyes wide. She released Nicholas and ran to the communications panel—slapping the door open with her palm. "Who cares? Let's get Captain Lug on the comm and tell her we're not amused by this." Neek's hand shook as she tried to tap in the docking berth number of the pod, *stuk* rivulets cascading down the panel. On her third try, she felt Nicholas tap her on the shoulder. She spun around and glared at him.

"If she's alive, then she sure looks like she's in rough shape. Don't you want to, I don't know, check her pulse or something? Maybe she needs help."

Yorden moved closer to the girl and rested a hand on her forehead. "She's warm, and she's obviously breathing, so she's alive. Nicholas, give me a hand to get her scrubbed off. It might wake her up in the process. Once she's awake, we can get some answers...and figure out where to drop her off."

"Drop her off?" Nicholas asked, incredulous. He walked to a water port near the door and filled the bucket there. "You don't drop children off. You *raise* them."

"*Mercy's Pledge* is *not* a crèche," Yorden responded sourly as Nicholas handed him the bucket. He pulled a piece of cloth from the top of a nearby container and began to wash off the blood. "Although that does bring up an excellent point. Where is the best place to drop off a maybe-Ardulan child?" The captain looked pointedly at Neek. "This is an unprecedented opportunity for you. 'Religious heretic returns with god' would be a headline that might give your president a heart attack and would certainly get you past the upper atmosphere of Neek."

Yorden's words blurred together. Nicholas said something in response, but Neek didn't hear it at all. Her mind rang with words and images from her childhood, all tumbling over one another and piling into a dark, seething mess. An old nursery rhyme came to the forefront, and Neek found herself repeating it silently. *The planet that vanishes, the planet that sleeps...*

It was all too ridiculous to even consider, but that didn't stop the thoughts from racing across Neek's mind. Every Neek child knew the stories of Ardulum. They were forced to read all the sacred texts in school, to memorize all the ballads, to recite the genealogies. Every statue in every town square had an Ardulan carving. Every art gallery was covered with Ardulan murals, and that girl—that unconscious, blood-soaked little girl—looked like she had fallen out of a painting, out of time itself, and right at Neek's feet.

"Neek." Yorden's voice filtered into her mind. She tried to focus on the captain, on Nicholas, on anything other than the girl.

"I remember some of those myths you told me about your planet. This doesn't make them true." A large hand fell on her shoulder. She shrugged it off. "Besides, how often does exoneration fall at your feet, even if it might not be real?"

"Doesn't it make them true?" she snapped. "How many times did I lead those rallies against Ardulum? Against our president and his archaic worldview? What would *you* call that girl? Dark hair with red highlights, translucent skin, black markings, bipedal—do you know of another species that has those characteristics?"

"Neek, no one in the Charted Systems has heard of Ardulans other than your people," Nicholas said. "A moving planet can't be real. The physics don't make sense. Besides, she just looks like a sickly, tattooed Terran."

Yorden wiped his hands on the sides of his flight suit while Nicholas wrapped the girl in a soft, yellow blanket. The bath had cleared the blood and grime, but her skin was still just as pale, the mark under her eye just as striking. Neek moved forward then, propelled out of her stupor by a sudden desire to touch that translucent skin, to trace the black outline under the eye and see for herself. She took two steps and stopped again, something nagging at the back of her mind. Something was amiss.

Neek closed her eyes and sorted through all the Ardulan stories she'd been going over with her uncle. Was it in the first holy book, *The Book of the Arrival,* where there was mention of the markings? Maybe. It was something about Talents, something about those funny tattoo things that were really just busted veins and how they linked to specific skills...

Neek's eyes flew open in realization, and she leaned in more closely. The mark under the girl's eye—Ardulan *children* didn't carry markings. Those developed later, during the second *don,* when the new adult would manifest her abilities and the corresponding bruising would appear and remain. The bruising was a permanent indication of the adult's Talent. Ardulan children couldn't manifest. They were also wholly dependent on their mothers—Neek vaguely remembered something about telepathic bridgeways and mental development.

She released a breath and relaxed her shoulders. The girl couldn't be Ardulan. She was a fabrication, had the markings of a fraud. It was all an elaborate hoax. Ardulum was still a myth. But maybe, maybe, she could use it. There were enough similarities, certainly. Was it enough to convince her home planet? Her uncle? Kid could get a home with some nice Neek parents who'd spoil her rotten, maybe get to lead a planet one day, and Neek could...what? Suppress her disgust at the entire system of governance long enough to see her family again? Help her mother get better while fielding persistent questions from reporters? Be trotted all over the planet by her uncle as validation for the Ardulan religion?

"What do we do with her now?" Nicholas asked the captain, bringing Neek back to the immediate problem. "That bath didn't seem to wake her up. Think she's still in stasis?"

"We'll put her in the other cargo hold for now, on top of some blankets. She either wakes up or she doesn't. I'm no doctor, and with the price I'm paying to have the armor and fuel tank on this ship repaired, I certainly can't afford one either." Yorden glanced at the small girl, and his tone softened. "Ardulan or not, that's all we can do for her."

* * *

Neek wandered around the *Pledge,* running her fingers over the decaying walls and listening to the sounds of the repair crew as they peeled old armor plating from the transport and replaced it with modern sheets pressure-treated with bioreflecting spray. It was a noisy task, and one that was scheduled to take most of the day. She'd spent a fitful night tossing in bed, finally waking up in the very early morning covered in *stuk* and clutching the strange vegetable peeler she'd purchased from Chen.

She thought back to last night, when Yorden had contacted the Mmnnuggl pod only to be informed that it had departed Callis Spaceport immediately after the ceremony. That meant the girl was theirs now, whether or not they wanted her. Yorden had let Neek decide where they'd take the girl. Now the pilot just had to make a choice.

As she turned the corner towards the cargo hold, she ran into an equally sleepy Nicholas. "Hey, Neek." Nicholas rubbed his shoulder. "She's still out cold—hasn't even moved."

Neek wrinkled her nose at the pungent, sweet aroma in the air. She peered down the hall from which Nicholas had just come and saw the broken cylinder and rust-colored puddle surrounding it. "Disgusting, Nicholas. Really. Is it that hard to use a mop?"

The young man rolled his eyes as they walked into the cargo hold. The walls here were higher than anywhere else on the ship, but most of the available space was packed with bins and tubs filled with cargo and various cargo "leftovers."

"Bigger issues at hand, don't you think?" he asked. "How long can Ardulans go without food or water?"

"She is *not* Ardulan," Neek spat, her tone more acerbic than she intended. "Ardulan children are never separated from their mothers before the second *don*. They can't survive without the telepathic connection. If she were Ardulan, we would have no way of saving her. That stasis chamber...it would have been designed to incubate her into her second *don*, a stage past puberty—somewhere between adulthood and advanced maturity."

Nicholas pursed his lips and leaned against a corrugated cardboard box overflowing with biped dresses. "What if she's Terran? There are only three bipedal species in the Systems, and no way is she Risalian. Mom gave me a genome analyzer before I left for Journey. I could do a scan and see if it matches any on record."

Neek turned to Nicholas. "Why...never mind. I have a better idea. Let's try a more direct approach to answering our questions. Something a little less scientific. We need more information before we go around pretending we have an Ardulan onboard." She pulled back a section of blanket, exposing the girl's bare shoulder. Slowly, she placed the fingertips of her right hand onto the flesh.

The *stuk* from her fingers hardened upon contact, effectively sealing Neek in place. "That's...different," she commented as Nicholas looked at her quizzically. "I wonder what..." She didn't finish her thought.

The girl's eyes abruptly opened and stared directly at Neek. She felt a tugging at the back of her head that made it feel like someone was trying to compress her brain. A blinding pressure dropped into her skull. Then Neek started to scream.

CHAPTER 5: MERCY'S PLEDGE

The planet arrived on a crisp evening during the month of Yvet. It appeared a pale orange in our sky, a comet tail streaking behind it that outshone our sun. It stopped between Neek's third and fourth moon and took orbit—the sheer size of it filling the night sky and making it appear as if the heavens were on fire.

—Excerpt from the Neek text, *The Book of the Arrival*

Risalians in gray tunics held a struggling woman. The girl was dragged away towards a stasis cylinder. Wordless terror filled the room. A laser pistol discharged into the woman's head, and then came an anguished mental scream. The scene replayed yet again.

I'm dreaming, Neek thought, not for the first time. *It's a horrible, never-ending dream.* Shoving the child into the cylinder, the Risalian shut the latch, sealing her inside. The world blanked white for a moment, before starting again. Risalians entered a room of metal mesh.

Neek screamed. If she had to watch the scene again, she would lose what remained of her sanity.

Neek shoved at the cage of metal mesh, but there was no door, no control panel, no exit... No escape. The woman's emotions were building again, the mental images ripping through Neek's mind. The thoughts were chaotic, disordered, and simplistic. Reactions drenched in fear.

Neek banged her head against the mesh wall. There was no pain, which didn't help to alleviate her frustration, but it did keep her from having to watch. She kept her eyes closed and her head bowed as the laser shot reverberated through the memory. She waited for another reset, but this time the floor underneath her feet shook. Neek opened her eyes and looked around. The little girl stood next to her and, while Neek paused, clasped Neek's hand.

Neek tried to make eye contact. The girl's eyes were unseeing and glassy, as if there wasn't anything behind them. Neek snapped her fingers in front of the girl, but there was no response.

The scene began yet again.

"Is this how you got into the cylinder?" Neek asked. The girl continued to stare at her mother, as though she hadn't heard. The mother's translucent skin caught Neek's attention momentarily, the tattoo prominent on her face. "Hey, yoo-hoo!" Neek gave the girl's arm a gentle swing. "What's this all about? Is there any chance we might return to the world of the living at some point?"

At the swing, the child turned her dead eyes up to stare at Neek. Neek felt a slight pressure on her mind, like someone was timidly stroking the inside of her skull. She chased the feeling and crashed into a wave of loneliness and despair so thick she forgot how to breathe.

Neek gasped, clutching and clawing her throat. Eyes widening with alarm, the girl released Neek's hand and backed away quickly. The feelings abruptly ceased, and Neek fell to her knees, trying to breathe normally.

"Are you trying to kill me?!" she demanded. The girl wasn't paying attention to Neek anymore. A *BANG* went off, and the mother's body again slumped to the floor. Blood seeped over pale skin as the prominent veins faded with each passing moment. Bits of brain matter stuck to dull red hair.

"Think maybe we could talk about this? Who are you? Why are you impersonating an Ardulan?" Neek surveyed the scene, which was just about to refresh. "Why am I watching this again?"

The girl kept her eyes fixed on the body. Neek got up, stomped over to her, and put her hand on the child's shoulder. "I'm talking to you," she said.

The pressure played at the edges of her mind again. This time, Neek drew away quickly. "Uh-uh, kid. Not doing that again. Let's try to talk, like normal sentients." The girl looked up at her with a perplexed expression. The pressure came again, firmer this time. Neek tried to push the girl back, but she skirted through Neek's mind, evading. Searching. Prodding.

A memory came.

Neek was standing with her cohort at the graduation ceremony. She stood at the front, silver robe billowing behind her in the wind. She was first in her class. She would move on to master training and, once she passed the skill tests, would be invited to the Heaven Guard. Crimson settees flew overhead, and Neek's stuk began to thicken in anticipation. One of those was now hers to train in for the next five years until she became a full member of the Guard and was gifted a brand-new ship. She would become a protector. A searcher. A sentry. She would be free of her family's legacy.

The crowd cheered. Her three parents, seated just meters away from her, clicked their tongues wildly. Neek felt awash in their praise and the adoration of her friends. She was the first in her family to make it this far in training. Nothing could rival this moment.

There was movement then, from the corner of her vision. A sleek, gold hovercraft pulled to the edge of the crowd. Neek's smile fell. Who would interrupt the ceremony of the elite Heaven Guard? Her roommate shifted, and Neek put out a hand to steady her.

Silence fell in the crowd. The door to the hovercraft opened, and the president of Neek stepped out, flanked by three guards. Murmurs began behind her. Her classmates scooted away. Neek's heart rate increased. He couldn't. Not here. Not now. This moment was too important.

The president came towards her, the crowd parting. The guards stripped her of her robe, the silver fabric tearing as rough hands pulled at it. The fabric caught in the wind and blew back into her cohort, catching on her roommate's foot.

She tried to fight them off, but they were bigger. She was pulled away from the cohort, towards the hovercraft. She heard her parents' screams but could only see the face of the president before her, grinning.

"I warned you to keep your mouth shut," he whispered into her ear. The hovercraft door slammed closed, cutting off the sounds of the crowd, the whine of the settees, and the pleas of her immediate family. It was the last time she saw any of them.

"Get out!" Neek screamed. "If you want to communicate, then talk. You know, move your lips. Make sound come out." Neek placed several fingers on her lips and moved them up and down, pantomiming the concept as best she could.

The child cocked her head to one side. Her eyes narrowed in concentration as she opened her mouth. She took a deep breath and expelled it in a loud burst, managing to emit a sort of huffing sound.

"That's it? Neek asked. "That's all you've got?"

The child looked pleased with herself and stared back at Neek. The pressure returned again, this time shockingly gentle.

"Your way or the spaceway, got it," Neek muttered to herself. She buried her own memory and chased the pressure again, connecting with the sensation in the far back of her mind. The grief was still there—hanging in the space between the two of them like a curtain. This time it wasn't threatening to overwhelm her senses. Neek probed a bit deeper and found the girl, her consciousness a dull, throbbing light. The girl felt hopelessness but also curiosity. Curiosity about her.

You'd think the ancient scribes could have mentioned that the Ardulans can't speak, Neek mused. *Except she's not Ardulan.* Neek knelt down and looked the girl directly in the eyes. The girl looked back, and Neek got the distinct impression that she was hungry.

"So break us out of this world of yours, and let's go eat!" Neek said. Preferring telepathy, she'd not projected mental imagery since she was a child, but, slowly, Neek managed to pull together an image of a table of food in the galley of the *Pledge*. Then she sent an image of herself and the child as they had appeared in the cargo hold, with Neek touching the unconscious girl's shoulder.

The girl sent back a wave of loneliness, tempered this time. She took the images from Neek's mind and rearranged them, showing Neek at the table with the food and herself huddled in a corner. Metal mesh walls formed around her small body, cutting her off from view.

With a groan, Neek withdrew the image. "You won't be isolated, not like you are now, anyway." When the girl's frown only deepened, Neek crouched to one knee to look the girl in the eyes. She reformed the image again, with the girl sitting next to her at the table. This time she added Yorden and Nicholas, laughing and eating food off one another's plates. She raised one of her hands up in the image, constructing a copy of the *stuk* on her fingertips. She brought her fingertips to rest on the girl's arm and then pushed as best she could at the girl's mind.

The child stared at her, sending out confusion. Neek sighed. "The *stuk* will allow a faint connection. I'm not a telepath, but Neek—my people—have a sort of mental reading ability. If you'd just break this damn dreamscape, I could show you!" Neek watched the child's eyes for some form of comprehension. "You don't even hear the words I'm speaking, do you? That's just great."

She stood and turned away from the replaying scene just as the main cage collapsed and the Risalians entered. There, in the corner, was a door. She hadn't noticed it before. Neek marched over. "There's a reason I don't have offspring," she said, knowing full well the girl didn't understand. "I don't have patience for this." Neek opened the door with her free hand and stepped into the next room. The door swished shut behind her, and the background melted from a dark corridor back into the room she had just been in. The scene continued to play.

"We are leaving!" Neek proclaimed emphatically. She walked over to one of the Risalians. "Is this the issue?" she asked, making sure to maintain the mental link she had with the child to ensure her attention. Neek grabbed the Risalian by the tunic, took a gun from hir holster, and shot the Risalian in the head. Xe crumpled to the floor as hir skull blew apart in the exact manner of the girl's mother.

"This is over, see? Done. It's not real. It has no hold over you." Neek continued through the Risalians, firing at each one in succession. When she reached the adult Ardulan woman, the scene was drawing to a close, with the Risalians holding the headless torso. Neek punched one of the Risalians in the face, and xe fell to the ground, releasing the body. She fired her laser gun execution style into the back of hir head. The second struggled to maintain control of the torso. The girl looked on with huge eyes.

Neek stalked back over to the girl and grabbed her arm. "End this," she insisted, placing the gun into the child's hand. Neek built an image of the girl firing the gun at the one remaining Risalian and the Risalian crumpling to the floor. Then Neek changed the image back to the *Pledge*'s galley, overflowing with food.

Comprehension dawned in the girl's mind. She approached the Risalian with halting steps. The Risalian continued to struggle with the mother's body. Xe made no move to counter or avoid her—Neek assumed the girl's mind could only utilize memories it had previously experienced.

She moved as close as she could to the Risalian and then glanced back at Neek. She sent a questioning feeling through their link. Neek sent back assurance.

"One way or another, end this nightmare."

The girl fired the pistol. The Risalian's head shattered, and as the fragments fell to the floor, the dreamscape began to melt. Neek felt stabbing sensations in her head, as if the child were trying to burrow into it. Neek sent a memory of pain from her own childhood—a spill onto a gravel road from a hover sphere, and the child backed off, maintaining only peripheral contact.

The dreamscape turned white around them, and the white faded into gray. Sounds—real sounds—began to penetrate the haze. She could feel someone's touch...

"Neek!" Nicholas shouted, shaking her shoulder. "Captain! I think she's coming out of it!"

Neek found herself on a pile of blankets, with Yorden standing over her. Her fingers were still stuck to the girl's shoulder.

"Neek!" Yorden crouched down, cupping the sides of her face.

Neek groaned and tried to sit up, but her attached fingers kept her from completing the action. "Ughhh," she moaned. "I feel like I just woke up from a night of bad drinking with a Nugel."

Nicholas laughed and wrapped Neek's free arm around his shoulders, supporting her weight. "Between dogfights and ceremonies, when have you ever had a drink with a Mmnn...Muh...oh, man. With a Nugel?" he asked.

"I haven't," she responded, trying to get her eyes to focus. "But I imagine this would be the result." Neek glanced down at the child, who was stirring. "Not the child, obviously. The headache. Definitely the headache."

"We're glad to have you back, Neek," Yorden said. She could see the stress lines on his forehead and drew a few conclusions.

"How long was I out?"

"Couple days," Nicholas responded. "We're en route to Craston. It has the closest physician who can operate on Neek patients."

"I don't think that will be necessary," Neek said, returning her attention to the child. Through her *stuk* link, she sent a feeling of friendliness. "Our little friend here is about to wake up as well. We both want food."

The girl's eyes blinked open. She squinted at Yorden and Nicholas, only to rear back, burrowing into Neek.

"Oh, they're harmless," Neek said, but at the girl's mental questioning, Neek sent soothing thoughts. "You two want to put together some lunch? There are a number of things I think we should discuss."

* * *

"Best I can guess, she's some kind of telepath," Neek said mid-chew. They had all congregated in the galley, and Yorden had thrown together most of the available food on the ship. Neek took her time sorting through the bits of cold meat and fruit, leaving the fibrous plant material for the girl, who tore through it all at an alarming rate.

"So, uh, Neek," Nicholas said warily. "Why is she jittery? She was pretty mellow right after you two woke up."

"Fuck off, junior," Neek growled. "Kid's got *problems*. Risalians are protocol-strict, sure, but what I just saw..." Neek trailed off, and her voice softened. "I know it speaks of my upbringing, but execution? I—we can talk about it later. Maybe after I get separated from my new accessory."

Yorden huffed. "The Charted Systems' goal of absolute nonviolence has made all of you incredibly naïve. Peace always comes at a cost." He looked pointedly at Nicholas. The youth's expression turned defensive.

"Don't start," the captain warned. "I was alive when Earth joined the Systems, back when morality was negotiable."

"Morality is not—" Nicholas tried to argue, but Yorden cut him off again.

"No. Listen. I'm not saying peace isn't a great goal, but it takes time for beings to settle into it. This peace—" He gestured widely. "—came on the backs of the Risalians, and it came *overnight*." He nodded his head at the girl, who looked up from her vegetable with a wary expression. "Secret Ardulan-creatures in stasis cylinders? Could be pretty powerful if used correctly, if Neek myths are true."

"Which they're not," Neek said quickly as she wiped her mouth. "And if they were, a kid telepath can't possibly be of that much use. Right?" Neek reconsidered her words after she finished speaking. She'd been forced from her homeworld just as violence left the Systems. It hadn't seemed unnatural at the time, but now...

"I do not like where this puts us," Yorden continued. "We've got Risalian skiffs we're responsible for destroying and a kid who was probably stolen from one of their ships." He paused and looked right at Neek. "Did you forget that this is a *transport* vessel? We move cargo. We don't always move *legal* cargo, but cargo nonetheless. Minor illegalities are one thing but this—" He pointed to the girl. "This is going to get us killed."

"Captain," Nicholas sputtered as he buried his hands in thick, black curls. "Killed? They're Risalians, not villains. We don't kill sentients in the Charted Systems. Our laws won't allow it."

Neek caught the flutter in his voice and managed a smile. "Calm down, Nick. I don't think the Risalians are suddenly going to pull all their transport ships off the borders to come after us. Doubt they meant to shoot at us. They're certainly not going to take the warships out of dry dock for a kid." She looked down at the girl on her lap and sent her a questioning tug.

The girl looked up at Neek and smiled, patting her stomach.

"As for her," Neek continued, "she's no Ardulan. A telepath, yes. Traumatized, yes. Responsible for forcing peace on trillions?" Neek raised an eyebrow at Yorden. "I think that's a little unrealistic. Look at her, for andal's sake. She's a fucking kid."

"She's not human, either, if that helps," Nicholas added. "She doesn't match any species in the Systems. I scanned her while you two were out."

"I want her off my ship, Neek. The Nugels knew exactly what they were doing when they gave her to us. Time to pass the problem on. Are we or are we not taking her to your homeworld?"

Neek leaned her head back against the wall and stared at the crumbling ceiling. The wispy presence in the back of her mind flitted forward, and a tickle that felt surprisingly like a question surfaced. Of course, the girl could be asking for something as simple as more food, or a blanket, or for Yorden to shave his beard, so Neek ignored the possibility that the girl was inquiring about the pilot's current mental state. Hell, Neek wasn't even certain what she felt right now. Taking the girl to her planet had seemed like a great idea before, when Neek wasn't thinking clearly. The last thing the girl needed was to be used as a political tool, even if her uncle was well-meaning. Still, the Neek people were isolationists at best, and the Risalians would have trouble recovering the girl if they got her on-world. Neek would just have to make sure to remain with the girl, filter out some of the crazier zealots and such. She'd talk with her uncle first. Maybe her own parents would be up to raising the girl, which would of course involve many visits.

"I would need to make some calls first, Captain. Get things sorted."

The captain stood from his chair and made his way towards the cockpit. "Get yourself separated from her. We'll be at Craston in two days. After that, I need coordinates, one way or another." His voice dropped. "I have contacts on Craston, Neek. They could find the girl parents there, too. Help her disappear, if you think your planet isn't the right place for her."

Neek brought her head back down and turned to the girl, who was looking at her quizzically. "I'll keep it in mind. Until then—" Neek made an exaggerated movement with her bound arm. "Would one of you be kind enough to bring one of the galley knives? I'd like to see if I can separate us."

"Nicholas, help her out," Yorden said, swishing his hips between two ceramic pots thick with bamboo as he headed out of the galley. Still upset, Nicholas grabbed a pointed meat knife from a drawer and brought it over to Neek.

"Oh, cheer up," Neek said as she awkwardly tried to pry at the dry *stuk*. "She's alive, isn't she? We got her out of that stupid cylinder. I'm not going to just dump her on Neek, if that's what you're worried about. Probably not on Craston, either." Neek handed the knife back to Nicholas. "See what you can do. It's a bad angle for me, and I'd rather not slice either of us if I can help it."

"This isn't okay, Neek. Why are the Risalians—who are supposed to keep the peace   trafficking a kid?" He sighed and plunged the tip of the knife in the center of the *stuk* on her first finger. It slid in with a little push, and he began a gentle sawing motion around the perimeter. "I've read things in some of the old law books of Earth. Really bad things that Terrans did to kids even sixty years ago. Do you think...I mean, that stuff isn't supposed to happen anymore." Nicholas finished one finger and then moved on to the next.

"I think we have a lot of unanswered questions. Why anyone would want to mimic an Ardulan, especially when I'm the only Neek off-world... I just don't see the point." Another finger popped free, and Neek wiggled it gratefully. "Although I will say that Yorden doesn't see demons where there aren't any. Something's up."

Nicholas frowned as he cut through the final millimeters of hardened *stuk* on Neek's littlest finger.

"Finally," Neek said. "I want to take a nice, long soak in a tube and try to forget the past few days." She pulled her fingers off slowly, allowing the still-wet tips to glide briefly over the girl's arm. Finally, she broke the link.

The child's eyes went wide, and she dove for Neek's hand. Neek evaded her, shaking her head, but that only made the girl more hysterical. It didn't help that Neek's mind had a distinct emptiness in it. Neek found herself disconcerted by her sudden dependence on the girl's mental link.

"What's going on?" Nicholas asked, trying to get his arms around the girl's torso and pull her off of Neek.

"Broke the link," Neek answered, dazed.

"She's going nuts!" Nicholas exclaimed, bracing the girl in a modified bear hug. "Do something!"

Neek blinked a few times and stood. "Okay, here's what we're going to try." She reached down and grabbed the girl's hand.

The link snapped back into place, clearing the strange fuzziness in Neek's mind. Panic and fear slammed into her, past the places she had shown the girl she wasn't to go. The girl dug into more memories.

Her father was going on a long trip, and she wouldn't see him for months. She was leaving for flight school. Large hands were pulling at her as the sounds of the settees streaked through the sky. She was placed on a light transport with only the clothes she wore. The sound of the door closing and locking. The pressurization of the cabin. The starfield that filled the window as she left Neek's orbit.

"Fuck!" Neek said as she choked back a sob. "I don't have time for this." She sent a strong wave of frustration towards the girl.

Surprised, the child pulled back.

Neek gathered her emotions and forced her voice to steady. "Try to grasp this. I'm *not* your mother, okay? I have a life, and it doesn't involve little girls." She shot an image into the child's mind of herself sleeping in her quarters, and the girl sleeping on the pile of blankets in the cargo room.

The child stared at her blankly.

Neek let out a small scream of frustration. "Let's try a different tactic. Nicholas, keep holding her." Nicholas nodded, tightening his hold.

Neek sat back down in her chair and dropped all her inner barriers. She gave a gentle pull, inviting the girl in. At once, the girl's mind wove through hers, looking at memories, emotions—anything that caught her attention—but not bringing them to the surface. Neek drove her towards the pool of her current emotions and towards the memories of their recent encounters.

The girl paused in this area for a bit, probing into some sections more deeply than others. *Get it?* Neek thought in words instead of images. *You can't stay here. It's not safe. I can't take care of you.*

The girl's head shot up, and Neek felt her consciousness zip off into another area of her mind. Confused, Neek tried to follow, but the idea of poking around in areas of her own brain made her nauseated. Suddenly, Neek felt a jolt of pure glee come from the child.

You...are...mad. At me, the girl spoke into her mind. *At me! Please...no.*

You suddenly have language? Neek responded, incredulous.

In your mind, the girl said. *You communicate like...like this? With words? They're like...symbols to represent images, instead of using images directly.*

Me and the rest of the galaxy. Neek gave a gentle push with her mind. *You want to back off a bit? We need to talk about boundaries.*

The girl retreated to the far reaches of Neek's mind. *I do not...don't like being alone,* she said, fear creeping into her tone. *You don't like it, either.*

Learn to deal with it, Neek responded. *I've got a ship to fly. Besides, you're not alone. Yorden, Nicholas, and I are here. We're just not, you know,* here.

She tapped the girl on the temple gently.

I guess, the girl responded hesitantly. *Why are you so sticky?*

Huh? Neek puzzled over the question until the girl sent a mental picture of Neek's fingertips.

Oh, that. It's *stuk. My species produces it from our sweat glands, but predominantly from the fingertips. It's supposed to boost empathy, but mostly it just gives away your emotions.* She wiggled her free hand, and small droplets of *stuk* fell on the girl's leg. *Once it dries, it crumbles off.*

The girl remained quiet, but Neek could feel other questions forming. Several times, Neek tried to ask the child's name, but forming the question without...without sounding utterly rude was impossible. *Let's make a deal,* Neek offered. *You go sleep in the cargo room for a few hours. When you wake up, you can come find me, and we'll talk a little bit.* She paused, and tried to add emphasis to her words. *Just for a little bit. Then you go back to the cargo hold, and you stay there, unless I say otherwise, until we get to Craston.*

The girl's eyes started to tear up. *Okay,* came the weak reply. *You'll be lonely then, too.*

Yes, but I'm going to work my way through it. See? She sent what she hoped were feelings of confidence.

The girl didn't seem convinced but didn't object when Neek carefully peeled her fingers off.

Neek gingerly handed the child to Nicholas, trying to ignore the sudden emptiness in her mind. *Not an Ardulan,* Neek told herself firmly. *Just a kid. There is no reason to get attached. She will be fine.*

The girl reached out for Neek again, but the pilot retreated towards the cockpit. She had to get out of that room. Getting off the ship, too, would be a relief.

"Would you take her to the cargo hold, Nicholas? I'm going to take a look at the ship's laser and see if I can tune it or something. It'd be nice to have a reliable means of defense if anything happens between here and Craston."

Nicholas nodded and carried the girl out of the room. Neek watched them go, the wide eyes of the child full of questions Neek wasn't ready to answer.

CHAPTER 6: OUTSIDE THE MINORAN WORMHOLE

You are not going to believe what these beasts can do. We need to start retrofitting our electronics immediately. Cellulose isn't just the polymer of the future—it's the tool that is going to help us finally bring about peace.

—Transmission from Cell-Tal to the Risalian Markin Council, date unknown

Captain Ran stood, motionless, as Cutter 223 raced through the Minoran Wormhole to intercept the *Mercy's Pledge*. Dark, starless space filled the viewscreen and made it appear as if the ship were not moving at all. A tremor ran through Ran's right hand. In a well-practiced motion, the captain moved hir left hand over the right, smothering the shake, and then straightened hir pale yellow tunic. Xe had lost the stasis chamber. Xe had lost the stasis chamber *to the Mmnnuggls*. Sitting on the board of directors for Cell-Tal had not been enough to protect Captain Ran from this failure, nor was hir invention of Dulan Field technology. The time of preferential treatment was over—the Markin Council had made that very clear. But hir time in the Reeducation Center was over as well. Xe had paid in full for hir mistakes, and now it was time to rectify the situation that xe had caused.

Hir hand shook again, and this time, Ran steadied it by placing it on the containment gun at hir hip. Dulan Fields were so simple to incorporate into a standard laser pistol. Print the pistol with biometal manufactured with over fifty percent cellulosic content, and you had a pistol capable of handling an enhanced beam. Integrate andal cellulose into the ruby from which the laser emanated, and you created an amorphous barrier so utterly confusing to Ardulans that they could not break free. The field functioned not only as portable containment, but when reversed, as protection for Risalians in the unlikely event an Ardulan became out of control. A containment rifle was a sturdy weapon, a comforting weapon—especially considering all the Ardulans Ran currently had onboard.

The young male sitting in the chair next to Ran, however, was far from warranting concern. He was early into his second *don*—just over twenty years old—had red-tinted, translucent skin, and bore the marks of the Mind Talent. The male was currently not in use, as the automated skiffs docked within the cutter currently required no direction. His hair was short and deep black, and he wore no clothing. His slight build, especially juxtaposed against the musculature of a grown Risalian, spoke of emaciation, although the way he sat in his chair—with his back hard and straight and eyes fixed directly ahead—made him appear larger than he was.

Ran stifled a gag and pulled hir long, black hair behind hir back. Research projects aside, the beings were hideous to look at, especially juxtaposed to a cutter as lovely as this. Xe had personally worked on the genetics of the Ardulans currently housed on hir ship, which made them slightly easier to stomach, but still—translucent skin and persistently breaking veins was a terrible adaptive strategy. How the creatures had managed to evolve to this level of functionality, Ran couldn't even begin to imagine. They were a genetically mutated, albeit highly useful, sexually trimorphic race of mute idiots. Hir offspring's pet *titha* had more personality.

Ran's disgust was threatening to make hir vomit. Xe rubbed at hir neck slits, which felt troublingly warm, and then turned away from the Ardulan male and instead addressed the crew, currently a mixture of first, second, and third ranked pilots, who sat dotted along the convex platform of the bridge. "Do we have an ETA on *Mercy's Pledge*?"

"Yes, Captain," a third pilot responded. Xe adjusted the height of hir chair and swiveled to look at Ran. "We estimate they will be at the entrance to the Minoran Wormhole in approximately three minutes, based upon their departure time from Craston. They weren't there long—only an hour. It is unlikely they transferred the cargo in such a short period of time."

Unlikely, but still possible. Ran felt the warmth on hir neck and rubbed hir slits again, hoping to ease the purpling away. Four days ago, xe had found the pod frigate that had attacked hir cutter. Upon questioning, the Mmnnuggl captain had spoken of a meet-up with the *Pledge* and a transfer of the chamber, which was an absolutely ridiculous course of action considering how much work the Mmnnuggls had gone to acquire it in the first place. Logic was clearly not their best species feature. Regardless, Craston was a large planet, and it would be best to deal with the *Pledge* now and worry about other possibilities later.

The regular starfield slowly grew in the main viewscreen as the cutter stretched through the end of the wormhole and returned to normal space. Watching attentively, Ran frowned and fidgeted with the computer controls to nonessential systems. Patience would be the key with the *Pledge*. Terrans and Neek were such skittish species, and, according to Markin Kelm, Captain Kuebrich already had a distrust of Risalians that stretched to the previous Markin Council and some poorly handled andal deliveries. Ran had only dealt with the other captain indirectly, but knew enough to avoid angering the Terran. A misstep could end with their interaction splattered across the Galactic News Network. That needed to be avoided at all costs.

Ran ordered the cutter to maintain position just outside the wormhole and wait. Xe considered their cargo hold full of diamond rounds, enough to buy a brand-new skiff, including one of Cell-Tal's latest model ships—a model xe hirself had designed. The sleek edges and revolutionary cellulose content—almost eighty percent—made the new line unsurpassed in speed. It'd be ideal for the barely tolerated smuggling Kuebrich performed, potentially making Ran's life more complex in the future, but a strong bribe for the present.

"Captain," the third pilot called out. "A ship is approaching. It's a Terran shuttle of unknown class with a laser turret that qualifies under the antique protections laws. Her beacon isn't transmitting any code."

"That's them," Ran said, hir voice a little higher than intended. "Third, please hail the ship."

"Yes, Captain," came the quick reply. A moment later, Captain Yorden's scruffy, unkempt face filled the large viewscreen in front of the bridge.

"Yeah?" Yorden asked, his eyes narrowing. "What do you...?" He paused before he registered what he was seeing. His eyes opened wide, and his mouth gaped slightly. He took a step back from the console. "What can we do for you, Captain?" he asked hoarsely. "We don't want any trouble and certainly aren't causing any."

Captain Ran tilted hir head to the side and regarded the other captain. When Ran spoke, hir Common words came out slowly and heavily accented, but the tone was even and unwavering. "Honestly, Captain. I find other species' hostility towards Risalians utterly confusing. If I wanted to take something from *Mercy's Pledge*, I would have done so the moment she appeared on our sensors. The very fact that I am *waiting* for you and bothered with a hail should tell you that my crew and I mean you no harm. We are only here to conduct a business transaction."

Yorden's eyes narrowed. "Business with Risalians never ends well. The Markin still owe me three hundred rounds from the Missotona run. I delivered all those trees *alive*. I don't care what the Alusians say."

Ran attempted a reassuring smile. "I have your back payment here for Missotona, as well as any others you think we may have missed." Xe clasped hir hands behind hir back. "In addition, I'd like to discuss your assistance of a Mmnnuggl pod some time ago. They gave you cargo. That cargo, however, did not belong to them. It is Risalian property, and we would like it back."

"Why would I give you my reward? If you want to pay me hush money for the dogfight the *Pledge* stumbled into, just do it. Drop the façade."

Ran sighed. This was why Cell-Tal didn't like to employ Terrans. "Captain, whatever your past dealings with the Markin, let me assure you that this is an unrelated matter. A *delicate* matter. The cargo you received was stolen from us and is an integral part of our ability to keep the peace. You are risking the safety of the Charted Systems by harboring it."

Yorden scoffed. "An integral part of peace is an empty stasis chamber? I thought Risalian tech was supposed to be the best in the Systems."

Ran's smile grew stiff. "Empty?" That tingle in hir neck—the same Ran had felt when the Mmnnuggls took the cutter during the battle—was back. It was the same tingle that turned Ran to shaking when the Mmnnuggls burned the three hundred andal saplings hir cutter was carrying, the tingle that singed hir neck when all the Ardulans onboard were systematically executed by the spheres and the cutter left to drift, dead in space.

"Yeah," Yorden responded, seemingly now disinterested with the conversation. "We'll sell it to you, but not cheap. If it's worth enough to send a cutter for, you're going to pay dearly for it."

"You wouldn't..." Ran began, trying to keep the waver from hir voice. Hir hand began to shake once again, and xe hastily shoved it into hir pocket. "You wouldn't happen to know what became of the *contents*, would you?"

Ran sincerely hoped Yorden was lying, that he was perhaps too scared to mention that the thing inside was dead because they'd tried to open it. Dead or alive, it didn't matter much to Ran. Cell-Tal could clone new offspring easily enough. But if that wasn't the case—if the Mmnnuggls had emptied the cylinder before giving it to the *Pledge*... How many hours had hir team put into making that thing? How many generations of breeding were involved? Xe had dedicated hir life, as did many others, to working out its genetics—only for petty pirates to snap Risal's greatest triumph away. Now the beings of the Charted Systems might never know how close they had come to securing the peace for good. They only knew kindness. They only knew trust. Who was going tell them what had happened? Who would explain the implications?

Yorden shrugged and sprawled back into his padded, brown chair. "Nope. Came to us empty. Looks like someone cut it open with a laser scalpel."

Ran tried to think quickly. Xe had to be smooth. Xe had to be nonconfrontational. Ran *could not* make confronting the *Pledge* Systems-wide news. "Hypothetically," Ran said slowly, trying to give hirself more time to think. "If you had found something in the cylinder, and it was now dead...we would certainly not hold you responsible. It is the genetic material we are hoping to recover. Vitality is not required."

"Sorry. Nothing in it. Maybe there are a few cells you can scrape from the bottom or something." Yorden leaned into the screen. "How many rounds do you have on that ship? Enough for me to establish faith in Risalian leadership?"

Ran refused to take the bait and remained calm. "Would fifty thousand be sufficient?"

"No," Yorden responded smugly. "But it's a start. I'll have my pilot align our ports and extend the bridgeway." He pointed to Ran's left. "Have one of your thirds bring your captain's chair. It looks big, and I could use an upgrade."

* * *

Yorden nodded and terminated the communication. "Neek, get the ship lined up properly." He turned and yelled up into the gun turret.

"Nicholas! Go grab the girl's capsule and bring it to the docking pad. I'll meet you there."

"Captain..." Nicholas trailed off.

"We can debate your morality later," Yorden said. "Get the chamber and get it to the docking pad. I don't have time to argue with you right now."

"Dangerous game you're playing, Captain." Neek took a moment from aligning the ships to raise an eyebrow at Yorden. "Hoping to buy our exoneration with a broken stasis chamber?" The ship lurched as the two docking pads aligned, and the bridgeway extended from the Risalian cutter.

"Exoneration, and maybe a blind eye to transgressions of the future." Yorden looked smug. "We could do a lot more work if we didn't have to constantly worry about getting our wrists slapped. Besides—" He pointed to the turret room. "—we don't have a shot in hell of beating a cutter with that rusted BB gun. And since you've decided to try begging your planet's forgiveness with the aid of our youngest crewmember, we need the Risalians off our tail."

"That doesn't mean—"

"I'm not just going to hand them the kid. Anything I can do to dismantle the network of passivity the Risalians built, the better." Yorden clasped Neek's shoulder, the weight heavy but not unbearable. His voice softened. "I see your *stuk* trails, Neek. I'd not hand a kid over to executioners. Calm down. I know you want to get home. I always said I'd help if I could. You just have to have a little faith."

"You demanded the captain's chair," Neek countered, rolling her eyes at the captain's word choice. "That's sure to put Ran in a good mood."

Yorden chuckled. "I've done enough 'delicate' runs for the Markin over the decades to know when things are serious. If a captain is still involved, there's wiggle room. Besides, they have nicer furniture." He pointed to the indentations in his chair.

Neek nodded and looked away. "I just fly the ship." She took her hands off the yoke and sat back in her chair, arms crossed over her chest. "Docking complete. Do what you have to do, Captain."

"The girl will be fine, Neek. Everything will be fine." Yorden stepped away from the cockpit before turning back to address her. "Of course, there is also a possibility we will all die. It's hard to tell at this point. Keep the engines on, just in case."

CHAPTER 7: MERCY'S PLEDGE

We had a rudimentary understanding of science before the intervention of the Ardulans. Our medicine was crude, our understanding of chemistry, physics, biology...all centuries behind other sentient worlds. The Ardulans sent their best scientists to work with us. They were patient teachers, going over each elementary concept until we understood it and could emulate it ourselves. They never grew angry at our ignorance, and each uncovered inability lead to an ever-greater pool of knowledge.

My great-grandmother worked on a farm just outside the capital, growing andal. She told me stories about the plantings before the Ardulans came—about how each would take fifty to sixty years before the plants could be harvested, and even then, so much of the plant was wasted in processing.

One day, an Ardulan woman came to the farm. My great-grandmother described her as a pale, short woman with red hair and black tattoos across her wrists. Her clothes were soft, gold—the color of the soil. She brought a small machine with her, so small it fit in the palm of her tiny hand. The Ardulan showed my great-grandmother how to use the machine, how to scan each plant for its lignin content and void space. She explained how the voids caused weaker wood, the lignin stronger wood, and how scanning the plants as saplings and eradicating defective individuals would benefit the entire crop.

It's funny—it all seems so simple now. To Neek in my great-grandmother's time, this was life-altering information. The Ardulans only stayed for two years, but even now we reap the benefits of their knowledge. Some of the plants growing now in that field were planted during the time of the Ardulans. Can you imagine? What would it have been like to work alongside a god?

—Transcribed conversation from an aged Neek male just before death, seventy-five years after the departure of Ardulum

Fuck the cockpit. It might be where the captain wanted her, but Neek had other ideas. Instead, she stood in the corner of the cargo hold, suppressing a smile, as the girl meandered and investigated the hold's contents. Their link was thin without direct contact, but impressions still trickled into Neek's mind. When the girl managed to wedge small fingers between gaps and pop lids, Neek delighted with her at the brightly colored textiles and smooth textures that spilled forth. The clothes were scrap, just something Chen had provided to camouflage the smart textiles they were hauling for Cell-Tal. When the girl trampled them in her eagerness to open another box, Neek decided to let it be. What harm could a little kid do, anyway?

Neek did appreciate that the girl had found a dress to wear amongst the piles—a bright-yellow dress that ended just above her knees and twirled when she spun around. The visual was calming and made the child, well, a child. Not a god. Just a little girl in a twirly dress, secure in her surroundings.

The girl turned and waved at Neek, a blue ribbon clutched in her hand. Neek smiled and began to step forward, when pressure edged her mind. Her smile dropped, and she pushed back into the wall. The pressure eased, and the girl's face fell with the ribbon, which fluttered to the floor.

Neek banged her head back against the bulkhead and groaned. What the fuck was she doing here, getting the kid's hopes up? All the girl wanted was to communicate, to have a friend in the world who wasn't trying to keep her locked up or blow her brains out. Hell, she'd even seen Yorden in here a time or two, playing some stupid Terran hiding game. Why couldn't she just treat the kid like a kid? What was wrong with her?

There was a tug on the sleeve of her flight suit. Neek looked down into wide green eyes dripping concern, which only deepened her personal disgust. She could do this. She could interact. She could be fucking maternal if she needed to be, surely.

The pilot scooted back several centimeters and knelt down, trying to maintain eye contact. The girl watched, cocking her head to the side, grinning. Unexpectedly, she took a deep breath, jutted her chin out, and forced a chest full of air up from her lungs, producing several tortured bleats.

Neek laughed. She couldn't help it. The sounds were so similar to a type of water fowl found on the Neek planet that the image rose within her mind without prompting. The girl scrunched her nose up in a proud grin. A light pressure returned to Neek's mind and, curious, Neek allowed it to proceed.

Honk honk, the girl sent, practicing with Neek's words. The bird from Neek's mind morphed, and the letters for "duck" appeared, surrounding it. Which wasn't right—there was nothing on Neek that even remotely resembled a Terran duck, but Neek had no desire to correct her.

I'm a Neek duck, the girl sent, twirling away from Neek. She took several large, wide steps and let out another, louder honk. *I'm calling to my mother to come walk with me.* She took a few more wide steps and then hopped high into the air. *Duck jump!* She giggled in her mind.

An image of Neek's own mother as she had last seen her, flushed with pride despite gaunt, sickly skin, threatened to spill over the mental link. Neek squashed it.

I'm not your mother, she sent as the girl landed from another jump. *Just a pilot. A friend.*

The girl shrugged her shoulders. *My mother is dead. I know that.*

Neek didn't know how to respond. The girl was doing her best to suppress her sadness, but their link had tightened too much since Neek entered the hold. Hopefully the intensity wouldn't be permanent. Neek didn't need someone else's parent problems on top of her own.

The *Pledge* lurched, and Neek fell onto her backside. The girl ran over, words tossing in her mind in an unintelligible jumble. Neek grabbed the girl by the shoulder and pushed her away, the skin contact filling her head with a rush of images and emotions she didn't have time to sort through.

Stay here. I've got something to do. The pilot pulled her hand free, *stuk* trails arcing across the distance between them. Pressure chased her mind, but Neek ignored it, instead bolting out the door and down the corridor. Her boots slammed onto the metal flooring, but it was the sound of another, heavier footfall that warned her to pause. As she rounded the next corner, she saw the backs of Nicholas and Yorden, the cylinder already held by a cluster of gray-clad officers on the Risalian side of the causeway.

BLUES!

The color shot through her mind first, followed by the word. Feet shuffled behind her, and then a small body slammed into the bulkhead. Neek spun around to grab the girl, prepared to haul her back to the hold, when the girl lost her balance and fell belly-first onto the floor. Air forcefully expelled through her mouth, resulting in a loud *HONK*.

Yorden, Nicholas, and the Risalian captain turned towards them. Yorden's eyes stormed. Neek sheepishly shrugged in response.

"It would seem, Captain, that you have not been completely honest with me." The Risalian captain moved towards the girl, a small pistol in hir hand. Neek began to move towards her as well, when an image of a broken skull flashed across her vision.

"Just my niece, Captain Ran," Yorden said as he slid around Neek and blocked the girl with his bulk.

"Really, Captain? Do we have to do this dance?" Hir expression turned cool. "You've done a remarkable job of keeping her alive for someone with no knowledge of stasis technology or animal husbandry. I don't care how you did it, but know that this is no longer a negotiation." Xe pointed the barrel of the gun at Yorden's stomach. "That *thing*, uncontained, is dangerous. Deadly. I need her on my ship immediately."

"Why? So you can take her to Cell-Tal and dismantle her? Fuck off, Captain," Neek spat. The girl took a step towards Yorden, but a wide hand motioned her back to Neek. The pilot grabbed the girl—careful to touch fabric instead of bare skin—and tried to pull her back down the corridor. The girl resisted, not taking her eyes from Ran. Neek had recognized the captain in the same moment that the girl did, the dreamscape image playing across her vision.

The tip of Ran's pistol wavered as xe tracked the girl. In a moment of distraction, Yorden pulled out his own gun and leveled it at Ran, the tip almost brushing the other captain's hair. The Risalian dropped to the ground, dodging, and shots rang from the connected cutter, sending cellulose-infused mesh at Yorden's chest.

Neek had seen the officers pull up their weapons but reacted a second too late. Her launch into Yorden's side resulted in her rolling off as a containment field surrounded the captain. It was better than a straight laser shot, but now she was on opposite ends of the causeway from the girl—something that Ran had already noticed.

By the time Neek stood up, Ran already had the girl over hir shoulder, the child kicking and honking in protest. Neek cursed and sprang for Ran's midsection. Before she could connect, masses of letters and images grew thick in Neek's vision. She couldn't see the causeway at all—only cluttered visualizations. She hit the floor on elbows and knees, missing Ran and knocking the wind from her chest. Her riot rifle shifted uncomfortably in her left pant leg. She'd missed her chance to draw it. Until the girl calmed down enough to stop transmitting gibberish, Neek couldn't chance firing with spotty vision. Instead, she stood cautiously and tried to push through the images to the girl. *Calm down,* she sent, more tersely than she intended. *I can't help you if I can't see.*

The girl honked again, loudly, and Neek's mind showed her the girl's mother—or rather, the mother's brain matter—spread out over the floor. That was just the vote of confidence Neek didn't need right now.

"Shut up!" Ran yelled at the child. There was a loud smack, a childish cry of pain, and the glittering brightness of what had to be a shot from a containment gun. Neek's vision cleared. Not completely, but enough that she could sweep the imagery to one side and process her surroundings. She didn't appear to be sparkling with reinforced laser bits, but if the shot wasn't for her, then who...

"Stop!" Nicholas's voice squeaked from somewhere off to her right. Andal help him, if he didn't have his new gun, she'd strangle him—sight or no. Through her partial vision she could make out a weapon in the youth's hand, which, mercifully, was pointed at Ran, the tip jostling wildly.

"Reverse the goddamn fields," Yorden hissed. "You've got the same weapon they have. Fucking teenager."

"Teen—" Ran's mouth hung agape, and hir gun fell to hir side. The girl dangled limply on hir shoulder, surrounded by shimmering cellulose. Neek slid the riot rifle from her pant leg and eased it up, slowly. If Ran turned another five degrees, she could almost certainly get a clean shot off—if the other Risalians didn't contain-shoot her first.

"You have a *Journey youth* onboard?" the Risalian yelled at Yorden. "Are you insane? You would expose a child to your...your—" xe trailed off, little flecks of purple dotting hir neck. Neek had never seen a Risalian so upset, but likely Yorden was enjoying it far more than she was.

The tip of Nicholas's gun continued to go around in wide circles, as if he were using it to divine water instead of threatening a being's autonomy.

Neek considered. As satisfying as it would be to shoot Ran, the officers would certainly put them all in stasis and take them to the Council. If Ran wasn't in a mood to shoot anymore—which, judging by the continued purpling of hir neck and the now holstered pistol, xe wasn't—then maybe they were back to negotiations.

Clearly, Yorden had come to the same conclusion. "Shoot at me, Nicholas, not Captain Ran," Yorden spat. "Then why don't you tell the captain about all the amazing things you're learning on Journey, like how to fire a ship laser, how to bribe for information, and how to break up child trafficking rings."

The youth's expression darkened. He fired at Yorden and then at the girl in quick succession. "This isn't supposed to be what the Systems are about," he said, turning back to Ran. "You're supposed to *protect* us, not take advantage of our most vulnerable."

"You..." Ran stumbled over the Common words, neck now a searing violet. The girl landed a kick to a soft spot on hir chest and tumbled to the floor when Ran dropped to hir knees. "That isn't a *child*, Terran. She was made in a lab—*my* lab. I arranged her genetic code myself, base pair by base pair—hers and her siblings. She isn't sentient. She's barely alive."

Yorden scooped the girl from the floor and snorted. "I'm not interested in debating this particular morality. What'll it be, Ran? Dead traders, easy to explain. Dead Journey youth? The Systems won't forgive that. Get off my ship before you become the first gunshot victim in two decades."

There was silence then—one long enough for the girl's fear to settle into unease and Neek's vision to clear completely. At least she was right. The girl wasn't Ardulan. She was a Risalian construct, a product of some strange convergent laboratory evolution. Oddly, that didn't make any of the tension in her shoulders dissipate, nor did it lessen the strain in her chest.

"You win, Captain," Ran said slowly. Xe clasped hir hands and began to walk backwards towards hir ship. The officers behind hir reluctantly followed. "She was designed to save lives, not cause deaths. We'll take the chamber, which should have enough genetic material in it to clone. I'll have ten thousand rounds transferred to the account the Markin have on file for you." Ran pointed at the girl but didn't look at her. "Kill her," xe whispered as Yorden lowered his gun. "You don't know what she is. I didn't make her to be a pet."

"You forgot my chair," Yorden countered evenly. "Now fuck off."

Ran picked up the cylinder and backed down the bridgeway, eyes never leaving the other captain. Yorden waited until the Risalians closed the hatch door before grabbing Nicholas by the arm. "To the cockpit. Now. This did *not* go well."

* * *

Neek grabbed the yoke and slammed fingers onto the computer screen, conscious of the thin layer of *stuk* she left behind. She hadn't realized how much of the girl's fear was still bleeding into her. That or it was her own apprehension. It didn't matter.

The pilot took several deep breaths as the *Pledge* rotated starboard, away from the cutter. A smooth calm overcame her. Her hands stopped shaking, and her movements became fluid. Confident. The *Pledge* was complicated to fly, with its archaic yoke and patched computer interface, but she was anatomically suited for the job and...it was *flying*. The "what" didn't matter.

It was only as the ship began to accelerate that Neek chanced talking. "We can't outrun a cutter, Captain. Maybe Nicholas can help out. Maybe we can distract them long enough to get to a decent speed." Neek's fingers flew over the interface as her other hand maneuvered the yoke. The engines on *Mercy's Pledge* sputtered and then refired. The ship bobbed. The starfield on the main screen began to blur. It was never a good sign when that happened.

Except the starfield wasn't blurring. Neek blinked several times before she realized that another image was superimposing her vision. The girl stood and was staring at the console, transfixed by the bare patch of metal. Whatever had her so fascinated was transmitting far too clearly for Neek's liking, but she had no idea how to tune the link.

See the strands, Neek? The girl smiled.

The ship let out a series of beeps, indicating it had reached maximum speed. She'd already set a course, so Neek took a moment to really look at what the girl was showing her. *I see cellulose microfibrils,* Neek returned. *Which is creepy. No one should be able to see glucose polymers without some type of scope. What the fuck are you doing?*

The girl didn't get a chance to respond. A shot from the Risalian cutter hit the *Pledge* in its main engine and sent it careening to port as the backup engine whined in an attempt to take over. Even more alarming were the packets of information flowing into Neek's head from her connection to the girl. The kid was...she was *reading* the information transmitted on the cellulose-infused biometals. That shouldn't have been possible, but there was no other way to explain how Neek suddenly knew that the armor plates had melted, that the engine was vulnerable. Through the girl's eyes, she saw the plates peel off, pinwheeling into space.

"How did I know that was coming? Looks like Ran can't kill a Journey youth directly, but blowing up a ship with one on it is just fine. Hypocrite." Yorden slammed into his oversized chair and yelled, "Cover the damaged area, Neek!"

"I know!" Neek yelled back. She couldn't see, not really, but she *could* still steer the ship. She just had to do it through the girl's vision instead of her own.

The ship rotated as it continued to speed through space, undamaged side now facing the cutter. Another shot came, this one a steady, orange beam. The distinctive smell of burning wood wafted from the biometal.

"They're opening a seam," Yorden said, slamming his hand onto the console. "Attacking a ship with a Journey youth onboard could get the entire Markin Council overthrown. That's a huge risk to take, especially for a lab experiment."

Alarms screeched as Neek put the ship into a tight tailspin. Wherever Neek moved the ship, the laser followed, concentrating on the same spot. The computer warned of oxygen loss. Neek's eyelids felt heavy.

"God or not, it won't matter if we can't get away." The ship spun to starboard and then back to port, the laser never wavering. Neek's panic backed the girl from her mind. Grainy patches of console bled into computer stats and mingled with sudden images of Neek's parents. She felt the girl linger on the images—the face of an older woman who looked much like Neek, her skin an unhealthy yellow. A tall, broad-shouldered man with a stern expression. Another adult with wide hips and long, braided red hair.

Nicholas's voice broke through. "None of my shots will connect!" he yelled from the turret. Shots streaked from the top of the ship, each somehow managing to launch on the correct path but ending up just wide of the cutter.

"The ship is ten times the size of ours!" Yorden yelled. "It can't be that hard to hit!"

"I don't understand what's going on," Nicholas responded, his voice starting to wheeze as well. "The system says I'm locked on the target. The shots go straight. Then they just...well, they just veer off." The sound of Nicholas's fist ramming into the control panel vibrated through the cockpit. "I don't want to die!"

"If these are our final moments, Captain," Neek said, halfheartedly continuing her attempts at evasion, "then I want you to know that your pickup lines are terrible."

Yorden chortled and then burst into a coughing fit. "They're better than yours," he managed as he recovered. "I learned mine from the Markin themselves. And I can still drink more Oorin wine than you."

"That was shady counting on your part," Neek responded. Her tone sounded flippant, when she hadn't meant it to. The girl picked up on it and prodded Neek for an explanation.

Sorry we couldn't help more. Neek sent images of the seam on the ship opening, the crew gasping for breath and eventually falling over.

The girl stamped her foot, climbed onto Neek's lap, and pushed the pilot's hands off the controls. Neek stared blankly.

You can fly ships? she asked incredulously and then pointed to the triangular mark under the girl's eye. *That isn't the marking for a Mind Talent, but hey, why not try? I only spent ten years in flight school. Clearly, I don't know what I'm doing.*

The girl didn't respond. Instead, she focused on the computer screen. Looking inside the child's mind, Neek watched her identify cellulose in the navigational computer and the ship's main computer core. Outside of the primary bundles, loose crystalline cellulose strands spun, buffered by laser light. The light cut through the crystallites, targeting the amorphous regions in the cellulose and snapping hydrogen bonds. The biometal buckled. The seam in the hull widened.

The laser shouldn't be there, the girl said. *It has to go out.* She focused on the laser—scoured crystalline chains until she found the same amorphous regions. Then, somehow, she broke them apart.

A crackling sound started coming from the burning seam in the panels. The smell of burnt metal and wood filled the remaining air. Yorden pointed wildly at the viewscreen, which showed the laser beam— previously a tight, straight line—beginning to wobble and arc.

"What is she doing?" Yorden asked, rubbing his eyes at the encroaching darkness.

"Creepy telekinesis. I think. Or microkinesis. Whatever. I don't really know."

Still too hot, the girl thought and pushed again. This push was stronger, and she strained as she leaned into it. A slow trickle of blood started to drip from her left nostril and onto the computer console. Neek thinned their connection, surprised by the physical reaction. This had definitely not been mentioned in any of the holy books.

The girl couldn't generate enough energy from herself. She was too tired, and the air was too thin. She needed a secondary source of power, which meant she had to form bonds, not break them. There was plenty of cellulose, however, hovering in every piece of metal, every plastic. Neek watched the girl trace relay lines, identify systems, and reach out with her mind. Instead of following the laser, however, the girl commanded the cellulose, pulling it across the *Pledge*'s systems, building thicker and thicker chains.

The crystalline chains bonded together instantaneously, and energy surged into her. Each new bond sent a pulse directly into her body. The girl gathered the energy, pooled it into a single ball of blazing current, and pushed. It threaded across the laser line, destabilizing the weaker amorphous regions as it went. The more areas destabilized, the faster the process became. The beam sparked wildly, shots of white light spilling across the viewscreen, causing blinding flashes across Neek's double vision.

That's enough, Neek sent. The console was getting softer under her hands, the metal around the ship groaning as the girl continued to collect cellulose.

The girl didn't seem to hear her. Instead, she let the energy follow the beam as it disintegrated, all the way back to the cutter. When the energy hit the already weakened infrastructure, the impact shattered a reinforced window near the laser port and continued throughout the ship, blowing out the power lines. The ship stilled, the lights on her hull blinking intermittently.

Enough! Neek yelled inside her mind, trying to push the words to the girl, but the child was too caught up in the interior of the ship. Crystallite forms began to visibly emerge on the console. There was so much fodder at hand, so many integrated systems to pull from. Cellulose was bound in the fabricated metal that made up the shell of the ship. It roamed in electrical systems and coiled tightly in weaponry. More and more came to the girl, bonding in a horrifying chain reaction Neek had no control over.

The pooled energy grew bigger. Unwieldy. The girl struggled to maintain her control. With the laser beam disintegrated, the girl had nowhere to channel the raw energy, so she drew it into herself.

That knocked their link back to the thinnest of threads. Unsure whether she should be relieved or terrified, Neek watched an electric corona build around the child until the energy began to seep out of her and consume the console with thin, cracking tendrils. Panic overtook the child's face as her body slumped, her control over the energy waning. There was a brief complete stillness in which Neek hoped everything had managed to dissipate back inside the *Pledge,* before the console exploded, sending bits of metal, glass, and plastic all over the cockpit.

The blast slammed everyone to the floor.

"What happened?" Nicholas slid down the turret ladder, teetering and choking on the acrid taste of the air.

Neek coughed several times and moved away from the child, hoping she hadn't crushed her. "You okay, Yorden? Nicholas?" she asked. The pilot raised a hand to her face and slowly slid her fingers over its surface, noting the small shards of diamond sticking out in various places. Rivulets of *stuk* trickled from each cut.

Yorden groaned and coughed heavily as he sat up. "I think I'm fine," he responded. "Most of the shrapnel missed me. Thanks for getting in the way."

"The kid," Neek croaked, pulling her seeping fingertips off her face and gently rolling the girl onto her back. Their eyes met, and the girl tried to smile reassuringly.

Are the Risalians still attacking? she asked.

No. And you're bleeding. Blood seeped from the girl's nostrils and down her cheeks, running onto the floor. Neek wrapped her arm around the girl's back and gently set her upright. The blood flow from her sinuses increased, and Neek ripped off a portion of her sleeve and held it to the child's face.

Nicholas squatted down next to the girl, his eyes watering. "Hey," he said. "Look." On her right cheek, a bruise was spreading from the side of her nose almost to her ear, with the tip reaching just under her lower lip.

"Fuck." Neek whispered. All three watched together as a second, larger triangular bruise began forming under her other eye. The small triangle that had been there before was soon engulfed by the purple stain.

Just some blood, the girl told Neek. *Sometimes if you push too hard, capillaries break. They heal quickly.*

Capillaries...cellulose. Neek shook her head. *I can't process this right now. Just...are you okay? Pain anywhere?*

The girl shook her head. *The only pain I have is coming from you.*

Yorden's voice interrupted. "Ship's dead in space. Again. I just rerouted our remaining power to gravity, air systems, and containment foam over the breaches." He looked pointedly at Neek. "Want to tell me what just happened? Looked like some wicked god magic from here."

Neek turned to look at the open seam near the exploded console, which was slowly filling with blue mesh foam. "No. Just...science, I think. Telekinesis is common enough in the Systems, but this—this was a whole new level of weird."

"Who cares why it happened?" Nicholas asked slowly, his words slightly jumbled. "We're completely vulnerable. If the Risalians shoot us again, we're toast. What are we going to do?"

"We wait," Yorden responded. "Have a chat about what exactly Ran was trying to create in our little stowaway here and hope someone comes along for us before another Risalian ship comes for them."

CHAPTER 8: RISALIAN CUTTER 223

Results from the repeated measures one-way ANOVA found a significant decrease (45% ± 0.05%; P<0.0001) in andal tree occurrence from the forestry survey of 25 BA to the most recent survey performed in 220 AA (Fig 1). This study changed the error structure to account for time. These results indicate that andal coverage in Neek forests has decreased, rather than increased, over time. The authors hypothesize that technology developed during the 'Ardulan' time period may have played a role in this decreased production, as the recorded systematic genetic and physiological manipulation of the plant was proven to be detrimental to long-term growth in laboratory trees (Forest Reports 219 AA). The trend in the data suggests that wild andal tree growth will continue to diminish over the next forty years and that, potentially, in fifty years the only andal trees left on Neek will be those commercially grown.

—Excerpt from "Trends in wild andal growth in Neek forests," published via peer-review in the *Neek Journal of Science and Technology*, 222 AA

"Report!" Ran demanded as xe entered the bridge.

"The laser disintegrated, Captain," a second responded. Xe tapped the interface in front of hir to display a diagram of the ship as Ran ground hir heel into the metal flooring below. "Something started a chain reaction in the cellulose bindings, targeting the amorphous regions in the microfibrils and...the hemicellulose coating was stripped. The cellulose broke apart into glucose monomers."

Ran focused the diagram on the laser unit. Blinking purple lights highlighted damaged areas, and chemical formulas for cellulose appeared. Cellulose tech wasn't that complex, but the cellulose harvested from andal trees could behave...erratically. The extra boost it gave to electronics made up for the unpredictability, but this was ridiculous. Hydrogen bonds didn't just snap, and microfibrils didn't just unwind.

"Let's pretend for a moment, shall we, that what you are talking about is even possible to do outside of a laboratory. We have other weapons, including at least fifteen laser turrets, three of which contain refracting lasers and all of which are computer automated. We also have an Ardulan gunner to interface with the computers. They can't all be broken."

"When the first laser disintegrated, it appears that the whole weapons system went offline, and parts of it may have unbound as well. The tech Ardulan is on repairs, but fixing an entire ship system...even an Ardulan can't fix an entire ship. Apologies, Captain. We estimate at least three hours before main weapons are operational *if* we don't have to replace every single part. There is no way we will get the entire ship fixed without returning to Risal."

Ran winced as memories from the Reeducation Center xe had been sent to after losing the girl the first time dredged to the surface.

Harsh green lighting. No view of water. Endless vegetables. Endless lectures. Endless assessments. Toiling in the intense heat of an andal plantation on one of Risal's moons, the leaves wilting in the poor atmosphere. Memorization of so many genetic sequences and cellulosic chemistry formulas that Ran could still see them all, every time xe closed hir eyes. They layered on top of one another, intermingling, sometimes bound so intrinsically with one another that xe couldn't sort out which was a base pair and which a microfibril. No chance to communicate with hir offspring. No chance to communicate with the Cell-Tal board. No access to hir experiments.

Ran's hand shook. Xe looked over hir shoulder at the large, wide panel that was nestled in the corner of the bridge. Images of waves of deep-blue water crashed over the surface. Ran calmed. Hir head cleared. Xe had things under control. Xe would not go back to Risal empty-handed. Ran swiped the schematic from the screen and queried the computer. Text began to scroll in tight packets, just slowly enough to be read once before being replaced with new information.

...power. Systems currently at 75% functionality. Suspected abnormalities within main housing as well as secondary systems.

Housing experiencing loss of structure conducive to structural integrity damage. Primary analysis shows removal of hemicellulosic binding and fractures along amorphous cellulose. Repair time unknown. Crew assigned to repair duty: fifteen Risalian thirds and one tech Ardulan...

Ran tapped the screen and queried the weapon status. The text changed quickly.

Minor damage: two hundred forty-seven fuses, four empty charges, twelve Risalian injuries.

Major damage: Unable to quantify. Larger components required for weapons operation no longer exist in useable form. Electrical harness for weapons system offline.

"Fantastic," Ran muttered to hirself. "So, even if we could repair the weapons, we'd have no way to power them." The captain smashed hir fist into the console and then queried the computer for information on *Mercy's Pledge*.

Estimated time to repair propulsion: one hour
Estimated time to repair main laser: three hours
Estimated time to repair secondary lasers: no secondary lasers
Estimated time to full electrical repairs: thirty hours
Estimated time to complete all repairs: two hundred thirty-three hours

At least the *Pledge* was damaged more than the cutter. That was good news. Feeling more confident, Ran called out to the bridge crew. "Get as many crewmates as we have with technical training to the damaged weapons immediately. We'll build them from scratch if we have to. The rest of you, head to Electrical and see if you can't get the harness working."

Ran watched the crew hurriedly flow out the two main doors to the bridge. As the second began to follow, Ran grabbed hir by the arm and drew hir aside. The second's neck slits tinged purple immediately. "Second," Ran breathed, trying to temper hir voice. "Whatever our tech Ardulan is doing, she is not doing it fast enough. Why don't you see if you can't motivate her a little? I'll deal with the ones here."

The flustered second saluted by placing two fingers on hir right temple, spun around, and sprinted off the bridge.

That left Ran alone, save for the two Ardulans assigned to the area. *Just sitting there,* Ran fumed, *like nothing at all has happened.* Except things had gone horribly wrong. Again. Ran had only wanted to damage the *Pledge* enough for towing, not blow it and hir own cutter apart. Still, at least the *Pledge*'s crew still lived. There was no way Ran could justify killing a Journey youth, no matter how badly the Markin Council wanted the Ardulan progeny. Captain Kuebrich had insured his safety with innocence, and that in itself was more infuriating than hir failure to retrieve the girl.

Ran's hand shook, but this time xe did not hide it. There was no one left on the bridge to see, no one except the mindless pieces of living equipment. There had to be a malfunction in one of them. This failure did not lie with the Risalians. Only equipment could perform so poorly.

Ran walked slowly over to one of the Ardulans and stared at the side of his head. "Where did Cell-Tal go wrong with you?" xe breathed. The captain nudged the Ardulan's leg with hir toe. "Too stupid to talk. Too mindless to react. Another broken piece of machinery on this poor cutter."

Ran paused, considering. A faulty Ardulan was dangerous under the best of circumstances. They could misfire, even shut down an entire ship as their mind entered the mental tangle of age. A malfunctioning Ardulan could easily account for a stray shot hitting the *Pledge*. A malfunctioning Ardulan would have no qualms about killing a Journey youth. A malfunctioning computer system, which is how it would have to be spun to the media, could easily be forgiven.

Ran smiled then—a wide, toothy smile that stopped hir hand from shaking and caused hir to straighten. There would have to be a consequence, of course. Faulty Ardulans couldn't be allowed to live— they were too dangerous. It was only logical to destroy a dangerous piece of equipment after it malfunctioned. After all, the safety of the Systems was at stake.

The screen in front of Ran flashed an update. A laser—a secondary refracting laser that barely had enough capacity to burn through metal— was online. Whatever the second was doing to motivate the tech Ardulan was certainly effective.

"Gunner!" Ran barked as xe walked over. The Ardulan turned and fixed her dark, empty eyes on Ran. She was third *don*—Ran could tell from the small creases around her eyes and mouth. She was also battle-trained, having served the past fifteen years on a border patrol ship that frequently encountered Mmnnuggl pirates. She was certainly old enough to misstep. Her mistake in firing on the *Pledge* would be so easy to explain, her death unquestionable. If Ran was going to spin this tale, however, it would need to be believable. When Ardulans went bad, they went in spectacular fashion, often causing several misfires in a row. That meant the *Pledge* needed a few more shots in her.

"Fire at *Mercy's Pledge*. Aim for the cargo hold farthest from the cockpit and hold the beam so the *Pledge* can't repair. I don't particularly want bodies, but if they occur, I want them intact, if at all possible."

The Ardulan turned back to the console and placed her hands on top. Ran looked to the viewscreen, eagerly waiting for the laser to materialize. Images of a suffocated Yorden, eyes wide in surprise and fingertips bloody from trying to repair what would be a persistent hole in the hull, danced across Ran's vision. If that happened, at least xe wouldn't have to put up with any more of Captain Kuebrich's smugness. Seeing the Terran at spaceports was bad enough. Having to entrust him with Cell-Tal's delicate transport jobs because the Markin trusted *him* over a Risalian courier was entirely different. He was *Terran*, for andal's sake.

Blood pounded in hir neck. The thought of Yorden as space-flotsam was really appealing.

One heartbeat...then a dozen...then two dozen. The laser didn't fire.

Ran growled. Was the gunner *actually* malfunctioning? Her fingers remained on the console but lacked movement. Her eyes were unblinking, staring straight ahead.

Ran slapped the back of her head. "Fire!"

The Ardulan made no indication she heard the captain, remaining still.

Why did all the equipment have to be broken? What sort of feedback loop had that idiot girl caused? A third *don* Ardulan was fully capable of bypassing any minor damage that might exist within the targeting system. This particular Ardulan had an exemplary record of service on border ships. For her to fail *now*... Ran seethed.

"Try again." The command was smooth. Controlled. Getting mad at a tool accomplished nothing. Xe had had only a small hand in the genetics of this particular Ardulan. Maybe the genetic code had been muddled somewhere along the way.

This time, the fingers moved. Commands scrolled across the screen in front of her. The captain dug hir nails into the shoulder of the Ardulan. Pain was a motivator even in the dullest of animals. Even the lumbering *titha* grazed quicker when faced with its own demise. The thin skin broke easily, and blood pooled around hir nails—bright-red drops that contrasted with the dried, maroon splotches that lay splattered on the console and the female's thighs.

"Faster," Ran whispered into her ear. "I know what you are capable of."

More commands scrolled past, but the laser remained dormant.

Slowly, Ran placed hir free hand into a pocket, pulling out a long knife with a curve at the tip. Xe caressed the intricately carved andal wood handle. "My Dulan knife," xe whispered to the female. "Awarded to every new captain at their graduation ceremony." Xe traced the flat of the blade against the Ardulan's cheek. "I have had extensive training. I never did think I would have to use it."

The captain continued to trace the blade from the female's cheek to her neck and then slowly down her spine. Xe stopped just above the hip bones and brought the knife to tip. "Fire," xe commanded steadily, voice still in a whisper.

A whimper came then from the Ardulan. She did not turn her head, but her fingers continued to move with increasing speed, dancing over the console. Ran double-checked the laser status on another monitor. The laser was still working. The Ardulan was not. Xe didn't have time for faulty equipment.

"Fine." Ran braced one hand on the female's shoulder and used hir other to make a plunge-and-swipe motion, severing the spinal column. Blood soaked the captain's hand and sleeve as the Ardulan slumped to the floor. Ran looked over at the male Ardulan, who, as xe suspected, was still just sitting at the communication console, staring at the viewscreen with no signs of recognition. He didn't even sniff, Ran noticed, as the bridge filled with the sweet smell of wet blood.

"Remove it," xe commanded. "Then bring up the secondary gunner from storage." Eyes vacant, the male got up, picked up the body, and left the bridge. A trail of bright-red blood—both his and the female's—trailed in his wake.

CHAPTER 9: MERCY'S PLEDGE

"Ardulum? Be serious, Governor. I think we're well beyond such childish thought in this day and age. Although I would appreciate it if you would not share that sentiment with my wife."

—Overheard conversation between the president of Neek and the governor of N'lln, 225 AA

"You're insane, Yorden, and this is going nowhere. Ardulans can talk. We have transcriptions. They had one of four Talents. They were marginally telekinetic, insofar as they could integrate within their Talent structure, but that's it. They sure as hell couldn't manipulate cellulose." Neek angrily kicked the leg of an empty chair next to her, sending it onto its side. The resulting clatter was loud, too loud in the echo of the galley as the crew continued to toss around theories.

Yorden bent down and righted the chair, groaning as he did so. "Would you suspend your persistent disbelief long enough to have a conversation? We're stranded until someone picks up our distress beacon, so we might as well be civil."

"Captain." Nicholas held out a pocket communicator. "I uploaded the *Pledge*'s contacts into my personal comm, but it says we don't have any contacts currently in the Alusian or Minoran Systems. There's no chance of us being found before life support gives out." When Yorden crossed his arms instead of taking the device, Nicholas frowned. "I'm not a magician or Ardulan or whatever. I can't just make a ship appear." He rapped the comm against his knee and then brightened. "My family has legal contacts throughout the Systems. Want me to inquire?"

"No. Legal would route through the Risalians. That is the opposite of what we need right now." The captain cursed and slammed into his chair. The wood creaked in protest. "If we do get a tow and ever get the ship repaired, I need to have a *long* conversation with the Markin. I'm especially curious as to where they think they will find another tramp to haul Cell-Tal's off-market products at the rates they're willing to pay. Speaking of Cell-Tal—" The captain pointed at the girl by Neek's side, who was staring back at him critically. "I think it's time we took a less literal look at those old myths of yours, Exile."

Neek winced at Yorden's use of her clarifier.

"So, then," Yorden continued, "let's blend theories. A planet moves into orbit around Neek through some weird physics—a planet inhabited by Ardulans. They teach the primitive Neek people some agriculture for whatever reason, then leave. Maybe they traded or were explorers. Not gods, as you so loudly remind us."

The girl shifted, and the pilot handed her another long twig of Yorden's lucky bamboo; any guilt Neek had initially felt at letting the girl eat Yorden's prized monocot was fading with his persistent hypothesizing.

"That plant is older than you are, Neek," Yorden said reproachfully. He grabbed the potted remains and moved them to the corner of the galley. "So where would a moving planet go next? Why not Risal? This is hundreds of years ago. Maybe some Ardulans decided to stay. Maybe Risal had a hot tourist trade. Who knows? If we get over the logical leap of a moving planet, the rest isn't too hard to imagine. Risalians get their hands on a species with unique abilities. They enslave them, breed them. In order to maximize Ardulan use, they engineer cellulose into everything. It's *brilliant*. Horrible, but brilliant."

The girl finished the bamboo stalk. *More?* she asked Neek while sending the pilot an image of the four stalks that remained in the pot.

"No, you can't eat the rest of it," Yorden growled. "Don't need telepathy to figure that question out."

"It's a huge leap," Neek retorted. She handed the girl a *bilaris* fruit from the table, which the child pushed away. "But if Ardulum is going to be real, I'd rather it be a race of explorer-traders than gods."

Yorden and Nicholas stared at her expectantly, but Neek ignored them. Instead, she let her mind drift for a few moments, letting the sporadic beeping of Nicholas's personal comm steady her breathing. She knew what she needed to do—the Neek people might be xenophobes, but they were connected xenophobes. There was a strong chance her uncle had contacts nearby; she just needed to contact him and convince him to send them out. What she would have to use as motivation, however, kept her from springing to action. This was not how she had intended to introduce the child to Neek society, but her options were now limited.

Neek pushed that issue aside for the moment. Journal reports dredged from her memory—the expanding monoculture plantations, Cell-Tal's demand for increased production... Yorden was right. It made a lot of sense. Too much sense, in fact, to be dismissed. They had no way of proving it, however, without Risalian cooperation. They'd die before they got that, which meant she had to act. Except she couldn't call her uncle directly without his ID code, which was locked in her fried personal comm system. She'd have to call Customs directly.

Neek held her hand out to Nicholas. "Hand me the comm."

Nicholas raised an eyebrow, but handed it to Neek without protest.

"I'm getting us rescued," she muttered as she keyed in coordinates, leaving smudged fingerprints in her wake. A heavy hand fell on her shoulder but then, just as suddenly, left. Yorden would never ask her to make this call, and she appreciated his willingness to suffocate to death in order to spare her humiliation, but her desire to avoid further scorn wasn't worth their lives. Probably.

The call began to process. The communicator slid between her fingertips as her *stuk* secretions thinned and her heart rate sped up.

"Careful! It's the only working communicator on the ship, and Mom will kill me if it breaks!"

Neek snugged the device in her palm just as the comm chirped. The insides of her boots felt damp, and Neek licked her lips, trying to moisten them. *Stuk* rivulets ran from her fingertips inside the sleeves of her flight suit, tickling her fine arm hair. She wiped her eyes clear with the sleeve as the screen filled with a humanoid male with dark red hair and copper skin.

"Neek Customs Operations," he answered in Common, his tone bored. "Which agency are you trying to reach?"

Common. She couldn't do Common right now. With a kid in her brain and Risalians waiting to blow the *Pledge* apart, the last thing Neek needed was to talk to her own people in a foreign tongue. Instead, Neek sucked her cheeks into her mouth and produced several wet popping noises.

The operator grinned, recognition in his eyes, as he spoke in the Neek language. "Exile! You're allowed to call in now for your theology lessons? Fantastic! You must be doing well. I can see the light of Ardulum in your eyes, *stuk* or not. The high priest works such miracles."

"Speaking of," Neek cut him off.

"Oh, right, yes." The operator fumbled with a panel offscreen. "I'll try to get through to your uncle, but his office is closing in five minutes. Just hold on a moment." He turned from the screen, and the communicator darkened.

"Why would your government rescue us?" Nicholas asked. "I thought you said Neek bureaucrats had no souls."

"Shut up," Neek shot back, trying to keep her voice low. "I can't deal with your Journey youthness right now. This is a delicate situation." Nicholas looked taken aback, but she didn't have time to explain. Instead, Neek looked back to the screen to see the broad smile of her uncle and, mercifully, no one else. His braids were unraveling near his neck, the weave bunching at the end clasp. Her *stuk* production slowed. Her uncle always looked like that at the end of a long service, riding the praise of the masses. He was always happiest then, too, which boded well for what she was about to ask him.

"Niece!" her uncle exclaimed. He followed the greeting with several sounds similar to the ones Neek had made.

It occurred to Neek that she would have to use Common. Fucking Nicholas wouldn't be able to understand a word she said otherwise, and she didn't want to rehash the entire conversation later. "Good to see you too, Uncle."

Her uncle's eyes narrowed, and his smile dropped. "Two communications in such a short period of time. Common language formality. Are you all right? I didn't expect you to resume our conversation, even though it was abruptly ended. It's not like you to willingly request more time with the books."

"Uh, no." *Stuk* dripped into her eye, and Neek wiped it with the back of her hand. The movement shifted the comm enough that it slid over slick skin and onto the floor. It skittered and spun until coming to a rest on its edge against the leg of a chair, the camera facing the girl.

Neek heard the gasp through the audio feed. She hoped her uncle wasn't having a heart attack. That wasn't the way she'd planned on breaking the news, but it was likely more effective than anything she could have come up with.

Neek let the comm sit near the chair for several heartbeats—long enough for her uncle to take in the swinging legs, the translucent skin, and the triangular marks on the girl's face. As great as it was having a

Journey youth onboard as insurance, a potential Ardulan was even better. Assuming, of course, that her uncle bought it.

When she finally retrieved the comm, the face staring back was a different person. It was still her uncle, of course, but there was no mirth to his eyes, no upturn of his mouth. *Stuk* began to bead on his forehead, and Neek was almost certain he was shaking.

"Praise," her uncle managed to choke out. "Praise Ardulum. They've come back. I always knew they would. We always knew they would." The older man scooted closer to his own screen, causing only his eyes and the bridge of his nose to show on Neek's end. "She chose you, Exile?" he breathed. "The planet...did you see the planet?"

Neek's face flushed, and she fumbled again with the comm. "Uh, no. No planet. Sorry. Just the kid. And, uh, I want to bring her personally to Neek. You know, do things right. Do you think you could arrange that? Right now," she added, closing her eyes firmly as she tried to shake the image of the girl's facial bruises from her mind. This was a ruse, she reminded herself. The girl was not an Ardulan. Lying to her uncle was far better than the crew suffocating to death.

"Right now none of us are going to get out of this system, much less to Neek, without a lot of help." She ran three fingers over a small keypad on the back of the communicator. Numbers scrolled across the screen. "These are our coordinates. We're dead in space with a Risalian cutter trying to figure out how to destroy us. They want to destroy *her*. We have no weapons, we're missing part of our shielding panels, and main communicators are down."

Her uncle's hands came up and covered his face for a long moment. He brought them down quickly, exhaled, and turned abruptly towards a large, white panel off to his left.

"Risalians... She can't be destroyed," he mumbled to himself. Whistling and plopping noises began to filter through the audio. "I'm sending out a planet-wide alert. If we have trading partners near you, we'll know soon." He turned his attention back to Neek and gave her a pained look. "Regardless of your views, Niece, the child needs you. She needs your faith."

Neek brought the comm closer to her face. "I don't need a conversion—I need a tow."

Several chirps went off on a nearby screen, and Neek's uncle diverted his attention. "Responses are starting to come in. There are two Minoran galactic liners scheduled to exit the Minoran Wormhole in one hour. They've confirmed their assistance."

"I hope it's enough," Yorden said, getting up from his chair. "I'll see if I can repair any of the damaged computer systems while we wait. Thank you, High Priest. It will be...interesting to see you again." He gestured to Nicholas. "Come on, kid, lend a hand."

Nicholas smiled weakly at Neek and the girl before hopping out of his chair and following the captain out of the room. Neek terminated the connection to her uncle, unwilling to prolong the conversation. She caught the tail end of a "Niece, we should—" before the screen went dark.

As the clomping of Yorden's feet drifted into silence, Neek collapsed back into her chair, *stuk* still falling in thin layers from her fingertips. The girl stared at her—eyes unblinking—her presence in Neek's mind patient as the high priest's words danced through her skull. Minorans were coming. They would be rescued. She was going back to Neek. She would see her parents again. She was going home.

The wispy presence shifted, and Neek finally looked to her left. No words or images came into her head. The girl had been quiet since the incident with the cutter, and Neek couldn't figure out if she was frightened by the event or merely being respectful of Neek's personal space. Curious, she gently prodded the presence.

You okay? You can stay here in the galley, if you'd like, Neek offered. *Chairs are more comfortable than the floor. Sorry we didn't put you here to begin with. We were all a little shaken up.*

I didn't mean to frighten you, the girl returned. She took a cushion from Yorden's chair and dropped it onto the floor, sitting down in a twirl. *I'm not a god, Neek.*

Neek sat down cross-legged on the floor opposite the girl, trying to process that comment. Already the bruised areas on the girl's face were starting to fade, leaving purple-green blotches surrounded by the strong, black outlines of the triangular marks under her eyes. It gave the child an ethereal look, and Neek considered how beings so pale with such dark markings could have made an impact on a primitive culture like the ancient Neek—had they existed at all.

The pilot took her pointer finger and traced the outline of first one marking and then the other. The girl was so little, so obviously a juvenile, but there was no denying what she had seen her do.

She'd grown up with her parents telling the old tales as bedtime stories. Her primary school staged pivotal moments of history as little plays. Like all Neek children, she'd pretended with other young Neek countless times—games where the children were Ardulans of different Talents, coming to teach the Neek.

I'm not a god.

The words came again, but Neek mused on old memories. Each child would pick a Talent and emulated the skills. Neek had always been partial to the Aggression Talent—she'd never had any qualms about shooting imaginary beings. Her friend, Ikorin—at least that had been the girl's name before she'd grown and taken the common name of their people—had always been of Science, and her other friend, Belkuy, of Hearth. They were a perfect trio of Ardulan power when they played together, and Neek thought fondly on all the imaginary antagonists she'd slaughtered to protect her friends while they befriended their wooden toys and "taught" them a better way of life.

That was all before she grew and gave up her child-name. It was before her brother had gotten her a subscription to *The Neek Journal of Science and Technology*, and before she'd really started to *think* about things. It was before Neek realized that she had a lot of opinions that other Neek didn't share.

Now, there was a child before her that could be Ardulan. A *real* Ardulan, not some exaggerated deity with questionable motives. A girl who, despite the matted, blood-soaked hair framing her small face, could be older than Nicholas. The first *don* lasted twenty years, which meant the girl might only be a handful of years younger than Neek herself, especially if she was surviving without her mother's presence.

What are you, then, Neek asked the girl, *if not a god? Are you a genetically enhanced slave? A member of some long-lost species that shaped Neek civilization?*

The girl looked thoughtful. Their connection tightened, but this time, Neek didn't fight it. Why should she? The girl had already dredged up her most painful memories. What was there to hide? They were already way beyond personal boundaries.

I'm just me, the girl said finally. *I want a name.*

That took Neek by surprise. Of course the girl would want a name once she understood the concept, but it was embarrassing that she'd had to ask.

Well... Neek frantically ran through child-names from her homeworld. If she named the kid something foreign, her people would never forgive her. Again. If she named her something the Terrans couldn't pronounce, that'd be one more headache she'd have to deal with. If she named her after an Ardulan from one of the holy books...she didn't want to think about all the ways that could backfire. She needed a simple name. Something easy to pronounce across the Systems.

Neek picked the first single-syllable name that came to her mind.

Emn, she sent. She said it out loud then, too, so the girl could get used to the sound. "In the old language, it means something like 'motherless child,' which seems appropriate, and it's still a common enough name on Neek that no one will ask questions."

Emn, the girl said slowly, picturing each letter. The smile was slow to come, but when it did, Emn's face lit up in a grin Neek couldn't help but return. It made the question that came next more disconcerting than it should have been.

Why don't you use your other name?

Neek's mouth opened and shut several times before she managed to speak. Child-names were never spoken aloud on Neek after the child's ascension ceremony. They were beneath adults, beneath society, and irrelevant to daily life. Of course Neek still remembered hers, but speaking it seemed almost blasphemous, especially in front of Emn.

"I..."

Neek was cut off midsentence when the ship juked to port. Both Neek and Emn tumbled from their sitting positions and rolled, slamming into a nearby metal pillar.

Stay here! Neek instructed as she pulled herself to her feet, pushing away from their connection and lunging for the door. Racing down the corridor, she skidded to a halt in the cockpit and found both Yorden and Nicholas staring at the viewscreen, unmoving.

"They're early," Yorden said. The crew watched as two galactic liners continued to decelerate near the *Mercy's Pledge*. The first maneuvered between the *Pledge* and the cutter, physically shielding the smaller ship. The other transport, which had already sent out several clamping rods, killed its first set of engines and fired a second set on the opposite end of the ship, effectively reversing its direction and towing the *Pledge* after it.

Neek pushed the men out of her way and stared out the viewscreen. She absentmindedly flicked a small crystal shard across the broken console with her finger, ignoring the skittering sound it made as it bounced along the jagged surface. The Minoran galactic liners were *huge*. How did one even fly something with so many curves?

"Think the Risalians have raised their shields?" Neek wondered out loud. "With that liner in the way, we have no ability to see what the cutter is up to."

"I hope the liners have better armor than we do," Nicholas commented, his eyes glued to the screen.

"The Minoran liners are reinforced for extra security during financial transactions. They'll be fine." Yorden pointed a thick finger at one end of the screen. "They're a long way from Baltec. See those pocked markings on the underside ship ports? They all look full. Must be some important people they're carrying. Your uncle has quite the connections, Neek."

Neek refused to take the bait. "The Risalian cutter just opened fire with one of their smaller lasers. See the yellow discharge bouncing off the starboard end of the liner? I'd say the Minoran armor is getting scorched but appears to be holding."

"Minoran galactic liners can take a beating, but they're no match for a Risalian ship. Nothing is, because the Charted Systems won't let any of the rest of us have real weapons." Yorden finally broke his scrutiny of the screen. "Let me see Nicholas's comm."

Neek fished the little disc from her pocket and handed it to Yorden. The captain activated the connection, his thick fingers finding it hard to gain purchase on the slick surface. Finally, the Minoran captain materialized on the tiny screen.

"Captain Yorden Kuebrich of the tramp, *Mercy's Pledge*," the female Minoran said, her long face dispassionate. Neek glanced over to the comm disc's screen. She could just make out a quadruped form, but little detail. "This is Captain Elger Tang of the *Galactic Baltec Wind*. We have your ship clamped to ours and are about to fire our lightspeed engines. We should enter the Neek Wormhole momentarily. Please ensure all passengers are secured for the flight."

"The other liner—what about it?" Yorden asked, glancing back at the big screen. "It's taking damage."

"The Risalian gunner appears to be having some issues working hir controls," Captain Tang noted. She pivoted slightly on her four feet and then sat back on her haunches, gesturing with a front foot, the long, yellow claws separating widely in an imitation of pointing. "My sensor operator has been tracking the Risalian cutter since before we left the wormhole. All that tech and they can't seem to hit the same spot twice. You must have damaged their auto-targeting system. If they can't maintain a steady laser stream, we don't have much to worry about."

"If you say so," Neek muttered.

Tang's ear perked, and she tilted her head to one side, letting her brown hair fall over her eyes. "Ah, Exile," the captain said, blowing the strand from her face. "The high priest mentioned you. Used to be a pretty fancy pilot back on your homeworld." Tang's eyes roamed the screen. "I can't imagine a tramp transport is as engaging to drive as a settee."

Heat flushed Neek's cheeks, but she refrained from speaking. Once, just once, she'd love to run across a species in the Charted Systems that *didn't* know who she was.

"Captain, we're entering the wormhole," a Minoran called somewhere offscreen. Captain Tang nodded. "Strap in, friends. We have access to some of the less traveled lines. Should be able to get you to Neek in a few days at top speed."

"You have our thanks," Yorden responded heavily. "*Mercy's Pledge* out."

When the screen blanked, Yorden faced the crew. Neek watched several emotions play across his face. Around the captain, loose panels and frayed wires swayed and clapped in the poor internal gravity. He'd had the *Pledge* when they'd met in the Terran System, nine years ago. It was one of Earth's first private spacecrafts, nearly as old as Yorden was. To see it like this now—a softened mass of biometal and fried circuitry—had to hurt.

"Neek," Yorden finally managed, rubbing his temples with his fingertips. "Any chance your people won't be as cool to us as they were the last time we tried to enter your system? We're barely holding together. At this point, a rock thrown by a religious zealot would break the *Pledge* apart, and I remember how many of those we had to dodge the last time we tried to get planetside."

Neek sighed and then stood as straight as she could manage. "We're bringing back a god. They should throw andal bark, not rocks. Besides, I have it on good authority that I am much more charming now than I used to be." She took a step towards Nicholas then and put her arm around his shoulder, giving him a tight hug. "Right? I'm downright charming."

Nicholas pushed her off. "Neek, you are overbearing, loud, and devoid of emotional depth." He started up the ladder to the turret and then turned his head back. "Why don't you deal with this Ardulan thing, instead of acting like an ass all the time?" He finished the climb, slammed the hatch door closed, and yelled in English, "Why do we keep calling them wormholes? They're *tesseracts*. Common language is stupid!"

Neek forced a smile, debating the wisdom of either punching someone or screaming. When she gathered herself enough to speak, she did so through gritted teeth. "Just wait until we get to my homeworld. You think I lost my shit over the girl? Wait until you see an entire planet lose their minds over the return of a child god."

Chapter 10: Markin Council Room, Risal

The Neek people alone are responsible for their past and their future. How long can we expect to coast through time on the advances of our ancestors? Fill the empty place in your hearts with progress instead of legends! Stop being afraid of becoming more than you are now!

—Excerpt from a dissident rally speech in N'lln, Neek, 220 AA

Another emergency meeting of the Markin Council to deal with the growing Mmnnuggl problem. How many had already occurred this cycle? Six? Seven? Markin Kelm shifted in hir chair and tapped a cluster of gems on the inlaid conference table. Xe had promised to take hir child, Belm, on a tour of the Cell-Tal nursery today—a new batch of Ardulan offspring were being born, and Belm had begged for weeks to see a live Ardulan birth. They'd actually made it as far as the crèche building before Kelm's communicator pinged, calling hir in for another meeting.

The current ostentatiousness of the room's decorations only added to hir frustration. The room had been recently renovated, and Kelm briefly wondered which of hir cohort approved that unnecessary expenditure. For the past two years, the motif had been Risal-specific—mostly andal wood furniture and paintings done by artists on Cell-Tal grants. The current designer had gone with a more intergalactic look, with tapestries and gemware from across the Systems littering the walls and writing surfaces. The conference table was the same, however—made of andal wood and polished to a high gloss. The chairs, too, were andal, all made from Neek trees so old they'd been planted before Kelm's last two progenitors had lived.

Kelm looked at the table again. The five markin, each of whom represented a sector of Risalian life, sat equidistant around the circumference. They were all identically dressed in blue tunics, with their scaled, black hair tied back from their necks in the style of their respective provinces. The overhead lighting brought out the different melanin contents within their skin, making a striking monochromatic blue ring around the wooden table. Hovering just above the table lay a glittering patchwork of finely woven cellulosic cables and colored diamonds—one of Cell-Tal's finer creations. Thin, translucent cables ran to the seats of all five markin, allowing each one to control the holographic interface. Recessed in a wall just behind Kelm were two printers—one for food and one for tech. They were both the newest models and superior to anything currently available on the consumer market. The food printer had code for over fifty thousand fast-print perf entrees, able to produce three a minute. The tech printer, when loaded with andal cellulose, produced the highest quality biometal in the Systems.

Kelm hoped one of the markin had something useful to present this time. Xe had no update from Captain Ran yet as to the recovery of the girl, and Markin Sald, of the Capitol sector, and Markin Raek, of the Genomics sector, had been so completely consumed with the new genomics project that Kelm doubted either of them even knew what day it was. Markin Xouy, of the Science sector, had been out on border patrol, and if xe had called the meeting, Kelm didn't want to hear the report. There had been too many Mmnnuggl attacks recently and too many Risalian casualties. They couldn't take any more losses, and the Systems couldn't afford any new weaknesses. There were too many gaps in the Charted Systems borders now—too many opportunities for invasion. If they didn't recover the girl soon, the entirety of the Systems would dissolve into chaos.

The sun had yet to rise, and the glow of artificial lighting within the meeting room reflected off the embedded gemstones in the tabletop mesh, creating harsh glares when looked at with too sharp an angle. All five markin were in attendance, and all five, Kelm thought, looked haggard.

"There was a Mmnnuggl incident at the fifth intersect yesterday," Xouy began, hir tone weary. Xe bent over the biofilm in front of hir, and a cascade of hair fell onto the table. Scales fell from the strands and clinked onto the wood. "The third since the attack on our cutters near Oorin. The Mmnnuggls grow bolder." Xouy pulled several additional pieces of thin biofilm from the inside of hir tunic and pushed them towards the others. "These documents show the locations of the Mmnnuggl attacks, plus the other, smaller skirmishes over the past cycle."

Kelm studied the sheet, absentmindedly rubbing hir right neck slit. This was going to be a long meeting, judging by the reports. It was unlikely xe would make any of the births today, not even the evening ones. Belm would be disappointed, but hopefully they could make the next cycle. It was a shame Belm was too young to have witnessed the birth of the missing girl. Her genetic line had been in development for fifty years, and she was the last offspring her progenitor was capable of producing. To have been present at the birth of Risal's greatest achievement would have been something Belm could have impressed hir friends with for decades.

"Intersects thirty-seven and one hundred and five were also attacked," Kelm said, returning hir attention to the sheet. "But those two intersect attacks were not attributed to the Mmnnuggls." Xe pulled one of the sheets closer and studied the ship schematics presented near the bottom. Being the head of the Ship Operations sector had its advantages, one of which was being a little too familiar with ship architecture. "They're not Mmnnuggl and don't follow the design patterns from any Charted Systems manufacturers." Kelm flipped the sheet around and tapped one of the images, expanding it to fill the screen. "Despite all the noise we made at our last meeting about Ran's unfortunate decision to separate the girl from her mother before her metamorphosis and speculation about her mother's unusual Talent usage, we now have a bigger issue to deal with."

Markin Sandid, of the Sheriff sector, raised a thick, gray eyebrow and responded with a less than impressed tone. "A few new ships aren't that alarming, all things considered. Especially since the only ships being attacked appear to be randomly selected and are of no strategic or monetary value."

"I agree," Raek said, taking the sheet from Kelm and studying the image. "The girl should be our top concern, not more inconsequential pirates. Without her, the Talent breeding program is completely over. We have no genetic base from which to start again, unless we want to clone. This means thorough testing will have to be done on all our remaining stock to determine suitability for a secondary breeding program. The data could take years to gather, even with Cell-Tal's resources. Going on a hunt for that stupid traveling planet is completely out of the question, and even if we did find it, there is no guarantee they would trade with us again."

Kelm felt warmth creep up the sides of hir neck and took a deep breath. "I'm not arguing that retrieving the girl is inconsequential. But look—*look* at that ship. Look at the mark it bears on the wing tip."

Raek squinted hir eyes, brought the sheet up to hir face, and then looked back at Kelm questioningly.

"We've had reports of three different ship architectures thus far—other than Mmnnuggl—and all have this same marking. They're allied."

Sandid dropped hir head back and closed hir eyes. Xe tugged at the neckline of hir tunic, which was too snug and pressed into the sensitive flesh. Kelm watched with detached fascination as the gemstones reflected glittering specs of light across the markin's throat and deep-blue tunic. "Unified, but as to what? If they're looking to start a war—why? There hasn't been a war in the Charted Systems since we implemented the entire Ardulan program. The Systems are completely incapable of defending themselves. No one here has any concept of true conflict. There hasn't even been any serious crime within our borders for the past twenty years. We have a completely demilitarized populace—by choice, I might add. What could this outside alliance hope to gain by taking out random Risalian cutters?"

"It's a good question," Kelm responded. "For years, the Mmnnuggls have only been interested in petty thievery, taking small items that are easily resold. Whether they have always been working within an alliance or whether this is a new development doesn't matter. Their tactics are changing. Something has moved them from hit-and-run to outright frontal assault. I'd like to know what, or who, is responsible."

Xouy nodded. "Beginning with the theft of the Ardulan girl, the Mmnnuggls are now more focused. They're coordinated. The last two ships they attacked were reduced to rubble, and recovery teams found evidence of currency and other valuables. The ships were not sacked prior to attack. Monitoring of the communication relays shows that before each attack there was no communication, no attempt at bargaining." Xouy dropped hir voice an octave. "We've lost over five hundred Risalians this cycle alone to a group of aliens that won't even tell us *why* they attack, or how to appease them."

"That's unacceptable," Kelm said. Xe rubbed hir neck slits harder, willing the purple tinting to fade with the encroaching sunlight. "The loss of Risalian life is discomforting under standard peace conditions. To lose so many for no apparent reason—we cannot allow this to continue. What should we do?" Xe turned to Sandid. "Diplomatic envoys maybe? Negotiations? If they're using faster-than-light travel, how will we even get to them?"

Sald interrupted Sandid's response. "I'd be more interested in understanding why our ships aren't defending themselves." Xe turned the document around so it faced the other markin and pointed to the second line on the sheet. "Cellulose runs throughout every component on those ships, from the hull to the lasers. Every Systems member in a Cell-Tal ship is, in theory, protected when an Ardulan is nearby. Every ship is also a potential weapon, depending on need. But look—take this attack at the twelfth intersect. Our ship is identified as patrol skiff 1154, carrying a second *don* Hearth Ardulan; 1154 was attacked by *one* unknown ship, which fired four short burst shots from a refracting diamond laser and managed to obliterate 1154."

Sald dug hir claws into the andal table. "How is that possible? Our shield-trained Ardulans are tested extensively, can withstand over one hundred *repeated* laser shots before collapsing! This one lost control *after just four*. The other reports show similar issues—cutters with gunners never firing a penetrating shot; patrol skiffs with second and third *don* shields unable to even attempt escape." Sald pointed at the bottom line on the document. "Perhaps most disturbing, a medical ship carrying three second *don* Ardulan healers recovered with no one left alive. There is a pattern right in front of us—we just don't want to see it."

"Genetic failures, Sald?" Raek asked, frowning. "Or something more insidious? We are working with a limited gene pool, true, but our scientists can find no compatible species with which to broaden the resource."

Xouy frowned. "Correct me if I'm wrong, Raek, but from what I understand, genetic failures occur at first sporadically, then with increasing frequency in a given controlled population. To see a slow increase in defects would be one thing, but to have so many at once...to me that seems more of the type of failure that could only occur through some type of link. Our Ardulans do not have telepathic ability outside of the mother-child bond, unless they have the Science Talent, so I don't know how something like that would spread."

"Mutation?" Raek asked. "Perhaps simple degradation of the genome? We do a fair bit of cloning along with selective breeding. Our process has never been perfect." Raek folded hir hands. "As you all know, we've replaced so much of the original DNA that at this point I don't think any of us would know how to reset the species back to their original parameters, and the Ardulans themselves tinkered with the livestock they gave us for years before we even saw them. Who knows what they were originally capable of."

Xouy looked thoughtful. "Could a mass failure like what we are witnessing be due to simple genetic degradation or sudden mutation?" The markin frowned. "It just doesn't seem like it would happen all at once. We should have seen other problems arising, slowly, over the past ten years or so."

Raek shrugged. "Some sort of external stimulus may have started a chain reaction. As to what that stimulus could be, I don't know."

"Stop using your brains so much and just *look*." Sald grunted, and pushed the sheets towards Raek. "Forget genetics, genomics, whatever. We can debate mutations and lack of defense later. What's more important is *what* is being attacked. All these attacks have one thing in common."

Kelm scooted over to Raek and examined the documents as well. Exhaustion hung in the air, and the smell of body odor and clean linen assaulted Kelm's nose. Bright sunlight was just beginning to filter into the meeting room, and Kelm wished to go home, wrap Belm up in a warm blanket, and forget about the brewing war. Except if Sald was right, if they were missing something big, then they all needed to see it.

Kelm read and reread the text. Ships of unknown classes. Destruction after one or two hits. No looting and, if Sald was right, no genetic failures. What did that leave? The only thing the ships had in common was that they were Risalian and contained Ardulans.

Kelm's communicator pinged again. The text on the biofilm in front of Kelm changed from the meeting minutes to what appeared to be a hastily typed note from Captain Ran. Kelm pushed any hope xe had of seeing Belm today from hir mind. Sald was right.

"I think I may have our answer," Kelm said in a low voice. "And I think we need to have a long conversation with Cell-Tal. The girl is alive, and she is manifesting. And somehow—somehow, the Mmnnuggls know it."

CHAPTER 11: NEEK

Intersects 201 through 250 are compromised. I repeat—attack by heavily armed Mmnnuggl pod-frigate and six unknown alien ships occurred approximately three hours ago. Attack appears to have been coordinated. All Risalian scout and defense vessels along intersects 201 through 250 have been destroyed. Estimated total life loss at over six thousand. Send reinforcements immediately.

—Distress call from Risalian Cutter 7 to the Markin Council, September 30th, 2060 CE

The utter ridiculousness of her current situation struck Neek as she sat before the yellow sand beach that ran along the border of her home province. Positioning herself right at the edge of the surf, she shuddered every time the cool, blue water lapped at her shins. The sun was just finishing its set, and she could barely make out Nicholas and Emn splashing around in some of the tide pools.

The arrival of *Mercy's Pledge* on her home planet had been kept quiet due to Emn—and the potential for planetwide riots. With the exception of several medics and government officials, no one had come to see the crew since their landing. They'd been placed in a small house just on the edge of Neek's home province of T'billk, near a small fishing village where she'd spent her youth.

Neek wasn't sure what she'd expected upon returning. She was home, and that should have been enough. It was still a pleasure to watch the moons rise each evening, to revel in their pale green and purple hues. Each time a settee flew overhead, however, it felt like another piece of herself was torn away. They were only a few hundred kilometers from the Heaven Guard training facility, which meant every day Neek awoke to the engine whine of novice pilots on their training runs, and every night she went to bed watching the advanced pilots practice formations.

The constant reminder stung more than she cared to admit. She wasn't Guard. She would never be Guard. She was sitting on a beach *with an Ardulan*—real or constructed—and yet what she truly wanted was still just out of reach. Neek had given up on the concept of "fair" long ago, but the cruel irony was not lost on her.

It didn't help that the only thing to have changed in her absence was, well, her. It was now two hundred and twenty years after the departure of Ardulum by the Neek calendar—and ten years after Neek herself had been exiled. Yet, when she watched capital broadcasts, the same bills were debated in the government, the same prayers said at temple. The *Neek Journal of Science and Technology* still published the same types of articles on andal production and potential reasons for the increasing crop failures.

It was as insufferable as the day she left. Neek had since piloted alien ships, been in firefights, gotten drunk in bars, and now—*now* was in possession of an Ardulan. Maybe. Didn't that warrant news? Religious fervor? Movement of some kind? At the very least, it should have bought repatriation and a chance to see her family.

Her frustration was compounded by their isolation. Even with all of that news, all the stories Neek could share with her family, the government forbade her from contacting anyone. They were functionally prisoners in the small seaside house. Nicholas's little handheld communicator hadn't even been able to reach her uncle. The only outside contact they received was the steady stream of medics that came by to take samples from Emn, who always smiled at Neek even when the needles hurt.

Neek stood slowly, brushing the sand from her pants and watching the small grains crystallize with her *stuk* and fall in a lazy loop from her fingertips. Wisps of light hair, pulled from her braid by the wind, waved in front of her vision as she called for Nicholas and Emn. The temperature was dropping quickly, and the last thing she needed was to have one of them get sick.

"Come on, you two, time to come in." She motioned towards the house. Nicholas looked up, nodded, and scooped Emn into his arms, carrying her out of the water. She looked quizzically at him, and he pointed to Neek and then the house. Emn's face broke into a large grin as she waved back at Neek.

Neek smiled at the girl as she traversed the rocky path to the small bungalow where the crew was currently housed. It was newly constructed, and the wall planks still smelled of sweet andal sap. Although Neek guessed it had been erected solely for their containment, the builders had not skimped on design despite the time crunch. The edge joinery was hand-carved, alternating between hidden hook-pin and locking trapezoid cuts. The roof was thatched andal bark, the black, curly periderm unmistakable. The windows were even decorated with reliefs of andal trees, their long, extensive root systems entwining across wooden frames. There might be doubts within the government about Emn's godhood, but clearly the president was not willing to completely toss the idea aside. Architecture like this was not taken up lightly.

"Those two should sleep well tonight," Neek commented as Yorden looked up from the ship schematics he had spread across an antique andal table. Neek pulled out one of the small stools, the covering of which she suspected was made from andal rayon, and rested one knee on top. She pushed some of Yorden's scribbled notes aside to clear a small space and then leaned down onto her elbows. "How's the ship? I hope you're taking my suggestion about paint color seriously."

"No magenta, Neek. However, if your government is serious about all these upgrades—" Yorden motioned to the pile of papers. "—then we've hit the jackpot. We should have picked up an Ardulan god sooner. The *Pledge* is getting Flex-Plate, the new bioplastic from Cell-Tal that uses only andal cellulose. It's supposed to be super pure—the best stuff on the market. Much more resistant to laser fire, and they've got some new coating derived from fungi that absorbs UV and helps power the ship. We'll save tons of fuel."

Neek looked pointedly at Yorden. "This is just a distraction to keep us from getting restless, and you know it."

"Yes, but I'm not willing to pass it up, either. We're not going anywhere, so we might as well get something out of it." Yorden sifted through the pile. Schematics, drawings, and a few sheets of what looked curiously like doodles were scattered across the work surface. Finally, the captain pulled a bland piece of paper from the edge of the table and handed it to Neek. "Take a look. New comm line, rebuilt engines, a few new sensors, cellulosic food printer. We're losing part of the cargo hold for a battery to store the solar cell energy we collect from the fungus stuff. Shouldn't be too big of a deal. The only time we ever use the full capacity is when we haul andal for the Markin, and after the last few weeks, I don't see that happening again."

"Those hauls make ends meet," Neek pointed out, tossing the paper back onto the table. "That food printer better come with extra cartridges, or we'll starve to death. Especially if we—"

The tickle in the back of Neek's mind ballooned, and her eyes unfocused. The mental link with Emn—a persistent, dancing presence—drenched her mind as the girl entered the bungalow, Nicholas trailing behind. Neek caught images of sand and surf, small aquatic life forms, light and airy emotions, and, clamoring to the forefront, hunger. The pilot pushed it all to the side, tucking it into the far corner of her mind until her vision cleared. She'd have to figure out how to regulate their connection before she tripped or drove the *Pledge* into a star or something equally uncomfortable.

The cooling unit—older, likely, than the table Yorden was composing the rebirth of his ship upon—shuddered as Nicholas pried the door open. He took a large, leafy vegetable from inside, broke it in half on the countertop, and offered half to Emn. Emn shook her head and made a set of hand motions to Nicholas, who shrugged his shoulders. Curious, Neek prodded their link, and an image of andal sapling twigs sprang into her mind.

"I think she wants more of the little trees," Nicholas said. "They look like epicormic sprouts of some kind. The food basket yesterday had some in it, and she took them out before I could get a good look. We didn't get any new ones today."

"Andal twigs," Neek muttered. "Because of course she would eat andal." Louder, she added, "The holy books don't mention anything about Ardulans eating andal, just planting it. Just another mystery, I suppose. Although why the Risalians would engineer her to eat an endangered tree that is in high enough demand to be nearly unaffordable is beyond me. Also, it only grows on Neek, as far as I know. Those Risalian attempts at plantation farming never seemed to yield anything."

The mental question came again, this time with a touch more force.

Sorry, Emn, Neek sent. *We don't have any more here. Could you eat a vegetable instead? I think there is some more lettuce in the cooler.*

Distaste strong enough to border on disgust was the only response Neek got.

"Look, I don't understand how you're even digesting the wood," the pilot said out loud. "Unless you are harboring some intense gut microflora, your body shouldn't be able to digest woody tissue. Young shoots, sure, but stems? Those are some highly specific enzymatic requirements."

"She's been eating like that since she came out of stasis," Nicholas said. "How is this the first time you've noticed? You spend all that time talking to her—or creepily staring, I can't tell which. You really hadn't noticed?"

Neek put her head in her hands. The words that came next were more guttural than Common, but she didn't care. "I've got a lot going on right now, junior. Fuck off."

You're cranky, Emn sent, her tone indicating more of a question than a statement. Neek forced herself to calm down. The last thing she needed was tears. She'd be remembered as the heretic that made the Ardulan child weep, which would go over about as well with the general populace as when the president broadcast the anti-Ardulan manifesto she'd written her first term in flight school.

Instead of responding, Neek forced herself to yawn. Complex emotions and religious reevaluations could wait for another day. "I need to get some rest," she said, getting up from the stool and walking towards the sleeping quarters. "If anyone comes..."

"We'll let you know," Yorden responded. "See you in the morning, but don't forget: the science minister will be here right at daybreak for testing."

Damn it, that was right. She'd completely forgotten. Either the government had gotten over its initial wariness, or whatever tests they wanted to run could no longer be entrusted to low-grade medics. The science minister was second in line to the president. A visit from her was risky, considering how things were left between Neek and the president. What was to keep Neek from just shooting the woman in the face, other than morality?

Neek fantasized on that course of action for a few moments as she stood and walked to her room, a grin of smug satisfaction creeping over her face. Tantalizing as it was, she wanted answers, too. She could always shoot the science minister later, after she'd gotten clearance to see her family.

Another few steps brought her to her room. A gust of wind from the open window in the hall slammed the door shut behind her, bringing with it the smell of salt water and andal sap. It smelled so much like home. If she closed her eyes, she was certain she would wake up in her childhood bed. Her father would be cooking breakfast, and the smell of crisp meat and fruit would be hovering just on the other side of her door. Her mother would be working on some crop rotation project—she was always working on something related to their farmland. Her talther— her third parent—would have already gone out to swim with her brother, their morning exercise never skipped no matter what the weather. All Neek had to do was get up, open the heavy andal door, and join them.

A wind current crept in from underneath the door, funneling several young leaves as it entered. Neek opened her eyes. There was no thick, woolen pad here for her to sleep on, no paintings of settees adorning the walls, no trillium flowers in a vase near the window. She couldn't look at the bare walls, sap still leaking from joinery incisions, and pretend to be anywhere else. She was never going home. It was time she accepted that.

Neek fell onto the bed face-first, her mind awash in stupid, irrelevant memories. As she drifted to sleep, the faint whine of the settees seeped through the wood walls and brought with it swirling images of a torn robe falling at her feet, gold and green colors intermingling with crimson and the pale, auburn glint of her own blood.

* * *

A gentle shake roused Emn from a dream about crimson ships and Neek people who wore far too much yellow clothing. Rubbing the sleep from her eyes, she padded after Nicholas towards the largest room in the house. Her stomach growled. Emn hoped more andal would arrive today. The Neek vegetables tasted terrible and made her feel sleepy, and the thought of eating meat turned her stomach.

A delicious smell wafted as she entered the room. A woman stood in the center of the area with a large basket of andal near her foot, the twigs fresh-cut with thick, white sap beading at the ends. Emn licked her lips and stepped past Nicholas. The twigs would make a delightful breakfast. Another quick step brought her within grabbing distance of the basket. She reached out, hands centimeters from a thick twig, when Neek's hand fell onto her shoulder. Caution bounced across their link, bound up in some complex memories Neek was trying to suppress. Emn's hand dropped, and so did her smile. Breakfast had to wait, apparently.

Since no words were chasing the emotions, Emn filed the warning and turned her attention to the other Neek woman. She was tall—almost as tall as Neek, but nowhere near Yorden's height. Her skin was the same copper color as Neek's, but her hair was a deeper red and her build much thinner. She looked frail to Emn—too wispy to carry out important tasks like ship repair or piloting.

Emn looked at the other Neek in the room. Everyone kept staring at the woman, the other Neek bowing their heads when she addressed them and constantly handing her biofilms to read. She seemed important, but Emn couldn't figure out why. The woman had a deep purple dress that swished around her legs when she walked, which was pretty and a color Emn had not seen before on this planet, but other than that, she didn't seem that special. She certainly didn't seem important enough to be causing all the leaky emotions Emn was getting from her Neek.

The woman sneezed, and her nose contorted upwards, giving her more of a Risalian look. Something about the action made Neek's emotions flare and then quickly extinguish. The hand on Emn's shoulder tightened, and the girl took a step closer to the pilot. She decided she didn't like the science minister. The woman made her Neek uneasy, the pilot shifting on her feet, her *stuk* thin and dripping. That was unacceptable. Emn decided she wouldn't be nice to the woman. Her Neek was more important.

Neek lead Emn backwards from the basket, each step a disappointment as the andal basket became farther and farther away. They finally stopped near the wall of the pentagonal room, opposite the door leading outside. Emn had been in here a few times before, primarily in the evenings with the crew. After the sun went behind the horizon, Neek and Yorden, and sometimes Nicholas, would talk out loud about the Neek planet, the Risalians, and sometimes even Ardulans. Emn's comprehension of spoken Common was getting better, and she could follow the dialogue, but every once in a while, Yorden spoke in languages called Polish and Yiddish, and Neek wouldn't translate the words.

Today the room was hot, the air stagnant with the windows closed. Bright sunlight streaked across the panes and highlighted the andal basket, making it even harder to ignore. The Neek spoke to one another in their native tongue, which Neek was not translating for her. Emn didn't want to push Neek to share, since all her previous attempts to strengthen their connection had been met with Neek pulling back even farther. Since the science minister wasn't interesting, Emn focused on the andal, imagining what the fresh twigs would taste like, how sweet the sap would be when she took that first crunch into the cambium. The Neek needed to hurry up so she could eat.

Finally, the sticky hand on her shoulder shifted, and Neek pressed on her mind. "This is Emn," Neek said in Common to the woman in the purple dress. "Get whatever-it-is done, Minister. We have a busy social calendar to keep."

"Exile, enough. We have to be sure. You know that. How do you think it looks, having *you* bring an Ardulan back to our planet? If the president is to go down this road, there can be no doubts, especially not about your intentions." The minister smoothed wrinkles from the side of her dress and picked a twig from the basket, offering it to Emn. "I heard you favored these, little one. Please, help yourself."

Two fat, glistening drops of sap landed soundlessly on the polished wood floor. Emn pleaded with Neek with raw emotion. She was so hungry. One twig would get her through the testing. She just needed one.

Neek relented, and Emn shot forward. The twig end was in her mouth before the minister knew what was happening, a small gasp Emn's only indication that she might have startled the woman. She didn't care. The wood was springy, fresh, and, while difficult to masticate, absolutely delicious.

"We'd like to start with a simple mechanical test," the minister said, her eyes fixed on Emn in fascination.

The girl flipped the end of the twig into her mouth and crunched loudly, relishing the final release of sap. She licked the lingering sugar from her fingers and then wiped them dry on the hem of her dress. The fullness in her stomach made her feel better about the minister. She had thought to bring andal, after all. Maybe her Neek was overreacting.

The minister took a small, black pistol from a holster on her hip. She offered it, hilt-first, to Emn and then knelt before her.

"Do I want to know why you have a gun?" Neek asked with a frown.

The minister gave Neek a withering glare before addressing Emn. "I'm the minister of science on Neek," she said as Emn took the gun. "You've been patient with us, been through many tests. Thank you. What we need now is a physical demonstration of your Talent. It's outside the defined structure we have on record for Ardulans, and we would like to better understand the mechanics."

They want to watch me break cellulose? Emn asked Neek, wrinkling her nose as she did so. *Why? It's boring, and the last time, I blew up a ship and hurt you. I don't think this is a good idea.* She ran her fingertips over the scarring on Neek's arm, where glass shards from the console had shredded her skin. Neek jerked under her touch, and the pilot pulled her arm behind her back.

"Emn has a point," Neek said caustically. "If the goal is for her to blow up the house, this seems a solid method for achieving that."

"We've taken precautions, and we just want a small demonstration." The minister's eyes narrowed, and she stood, turning to Neek. "Your opinions are not needed here, Exile. Keep them to yourself until I ask for them."

Neek jerked at the "exile," and although retorts seethed through her mind, she made no attempt to block them from Emn. Confusing suggestions about mating positions with various native animals and discussions of the minister's parentage wove into the girl's mind, the corresponding visual images shocking. Emn narrowed their link and took the pilot's hand, and the vitriol slowed to a trickle.

"This is a standard laser gun," the minister continued, turning back to Emn. "Please take your time looking it over."

This gun is really ugly, Emn sent to Neek.

Agreed, Neek returned, her anger morphing into sarcasm. *No decorative work on the sight at all. You'd think they'd pull better machinery out for a god.*

You want me to do this then? Break the gun?

There was a mix of emotions from Neek. All entangled so thickly that Emn pushed it aside, the idea of unraveling it all overwhelming.

Yeah, Neek sent reluctantly. *Just...it's fine. Maybe if you do whatever it is they're expecting, they'll let us leave the hut.* Neek smiled down at her then, the warmth reaching her eyes. *Don't worry. I'm sure you'll keep it under control.*

Not entirely convinced, Emn took the gun and turned it over in her hands. Slowly, she let her mind wander into the physical structure, following the cellulose as it wove through the plastic casing. It was a simple design, and she intuitively understood its function. After using the lasers on the *Pledge,* this would take no effort at all.

"This pistol has been modified to emit a continuous stream once fired. We've set up some ship plating just over there." The minister pointed to the far wall where a jagged piece of biometal was propped. "Aim for the metal. I want you to fire the pistol and then disrupt the beam by breaking the integrated cellulose, just like you did on the *Pledge*. We only need you to break one linkage. Polymer to monomer, that is all. The computer chip on the side of the pistol will transmit data directly to my computer here as you do." The minister backed away a few steps and nodded. "Whenever you're ready."

Emn looked up at Neek for reassurance. One break didn't seem likely to go out of control, but it still seemed stupid to risk when Neek was standing right there.

Go ahead, Neek sent. *Firing a weapon inside a house is definitely not the dumbest thing that has ever happened on this planet. Just try not to hit Nicholas or Yorden, okay? Break the bond, then stop. No explosions.*

It sounded easy enough, and the basket of andal was tempting her again, so Emn studied the gun one more time before raising it up and aiming at the plating. Taking a deep breath, she flicked the small, red switch on the side, initiating the beam.

Her aim was true, and a consistent white beam began to singe the biometal plate.

"One linkage, Emn. That's all we need."

I didn't forget, Emn thought. *Why does she talk to me like that?* She felt Neek's hand give hers a small squeeze.

She's an ass. Just do what she wants. Then we can be done with this so you can steal the rest of her andal and I can punch her in the face.

Emn giggled at the silly imagery Neek sent as she focused inside the beam. The cellulose looked almost alive here as it coursed with the light. She picked a strand at random, choosing the easier amorphous region over the more tightly packed crystalline areas, and told it to stop moving.

The strands froze, quivering in place as its compatriots dashed around it.

Emn heard a sharp uptake of breath. "Is...is the laser *frozen*?" she heard someone ask.

"Only part of it, it would seem," the minister responded. "How very unusual."

Ignoring the comments, Emn brought her focus closer until she could see the repeating glucose units. She wove through the tightly packed crystallites to the amorphous zone, focusing on a single glucosidic bond. When the bond was completely in focus, she forced it apart, pushing with her mind and snapping the bonds. She did the same on the other end of the glucose, separating it from the longer chain.

There was a soft snap, so soft Emn wasn't certain anyone heard, and a tiny glucose unit fell from the laser beam and onto the floor. Emn was certain no one could see it other than her. She released her hold on the broken cellulose, and the strand flopped back into the stream, its broken length causing the laser to sputter.

Neek tightened their connection. *Thanks for giving me the view.* Emn smiled, pleased nothing had gone wrong, and handed the gun back to the minister.

"So, you got what you came for?" Yorden asked. "Questions answered, mystery solved? I don't care one way or the other whether or not she falls into a god category, but how about you let us venture farther than this delightful beachside resort."

The minister didn't answer. Instead, she continued to read and reread her screen. Emn frowned. She'd done what she was asked. A tiny piece of sugar was on the floor, and she hadn't blown up the house. What more did the minister want? She honked indignantly, and several of the Neek attendants took a step back. Ducks could be mean, especially Neek ducks. There was plenty of cellulose nearby. If the minister kept bothering her Neek, maybe she would use it.

Neek nudged the minister with the toe of her boot. "Emn's impatient, and so am I. I don't know what the computer chip told you, but it looked like straightforward microscopic manipulation. Just microkinesis. It's clearly a Talent, just not one we have on record, or she's just an Aggression Talent with a lot of focus. Who cares?" When the minister still didn't respond, Neek kicked her again—this time, with an audible sound. "Hey, come on. You can't keep us here forever. Let's take her to my uncle at the very least. He can pray over her or something. Just *let us out.*"

"It's not that simple, Exile." The minister stood, her eyes darting from Emn to the screen in her hand and back again. "This is unprecedented. The holy books are the words of the Gods. We *know* what Ardulans look like, how their Talents work. If there were a Talent like this, we would know. We would have records. She—" The minister began to point at Emn and then hastily shoved her hand into the back pocket on her dress. Emn hopped forward, head low, lips pursed out in her best impression of a menacing duck. "Emn isn't like any other Ardulan we have on record."

"We don't have records," Neek retorted. "We have conjecture, hearsay, and some very sketchy, thirdhand eyewitness accounts. That's all those books are."

The minister handed the small computer to another Neek and began to back out of the room, nodding at her attendants as she did so. "I'm grateful for your sudden interest in the Ardulan religion, Exile. It is a miracle within itself. But this... If she is an Ardulan, we have to arrange a proper welcome. We have to consult with the high priest. However, if she isn't Ardulan, if she is instead some other species...if what you have told us about her origins are true, then we have a weapon on our hands."

"She's a *child*," Neek hissed.

The minister blinked several times, looked at Emn, and then lowered her voice. "Exile, we have to determine range. Capacity. If *Mercy's Pledge* is an indicator, she can utilize any cellulosic structure that she is directly connected to, and that connection does not appear to need physical touch. If she can boost her range by using energy from formed bonds, somehow harvesting any cellulose within an unknown range... Well, in a galaxy of high cellulose saturation, where does that leave us? On a planet full of forests, where does that leave us?" The minister took a step closer to Neek—lips tight and hands clenched. "She's not of Science, she *defies* science."

A heaviness settled over Emn, and she straightened, forgetting her game. She struggled to clarify the feelings and imagery from Neek. She saw a small house silhouetted in moonlight, much like the one they were in, on the shores of a beach. Three adults stood in the doorway, their faces blurred. Her chest hurt. It was hard to breathe.

"You're not going to let us leave here, are you."

It wasn't a question.

From the doorway, the minister shook her head. "Not any time soon. Be patient, Exile. The president needs time to consider the implications. He needs time to take precautions."

Neek's grip tightened as her words crashed over one another. The whine of a ship overhead made it harder to hear. "This is your *chance*," she hissed. "It shouldn't matter to you, or the president, whether or not she is a real Ardulan. The population refuses to progress without Ardulan influence. Emn could inspire them, encourage them. People wouldn't have to worship some fairy tale anymore. They could have something tangible, something real that they could form a new, educated belief structure around. The Neek people don't have to be held captive by dogma anymore. No one on this planet will do anything unless it has to do with Ardulum. Why grow traditional forests—the Ardulans promoted monoculture. Why travel the Systems—the Ardulans came to us. Why develop new technology—the Ardulans gave us all we need. Fuck that. This is about stopping the stagnation of our planet, our culture. While the rest of the Systems move forward, we stay here. Never learning. Never exploring. Why? Because we are waiting for some stupid planet to reappear and tell us what to do!"

"Where's her planet, Exile?" The minister's tone made Emn shiver. The warmth in her eyes was gone, and the woman's posture had turned rigid. Cold. "Why would some creatures from outside the Systems give you a little girl and no information? Her Talent, her markings, her manifestation in what appears to be a first *don* life stage—it isn't consistent. You can't fault the president for caution. She's as if someone was constructing a caricature of an Ardulan without doing in-depth research."

The whine of the ship increased, and a settee landed in front of the house, sand pluming into the doorway. Neek stepped back, her sudden apprehension apparent to more than just Emn.

"You're not going anywhere. Your Terran friends may leave when they choose, but you and the girl will be with us for a while. Be happy," she said, the corners of her mouth lifting slightly upwards. "At least you're on your home planet again." In a twirl of purple, the minister ascended the ramp to the ship, leaving only a trail of Neek's raging emotions in her wake.

CHAPTER 12: IN ORBIT AROUND NEEK

I saw the aliens first in an andal field. They walked smoothly with heads held high, eyes boring straight ahead. The stalks of the andal, threshed on the ground after harvest, made no crunching sound under the soft, brown boots of the aliens. As the small group drew closer, I dropped my son's hand and pushed him behind my back. The skin of the aliens was pale and reflected the orange light of their hovering planet. Deep, black lines covered areas on their bodies. I was afraid for myself. I was afraid for my son.

—Excerpt from *The Book of The Arrival*, second revised edition

"Two minutes to Neek," a second called out from the front of the bridge.

Captain Ran stood from hir chair as the speck of a planet grew in the viewscreen. As the cutter drew closer, Neek's four moons came into focus as well, their nondescript, stagnant surfaces a reminder of the technological hole that was the Neek system.

The Markin Council's instructions had been clear, and Ran hoped to follow them without incident. With the crew of the *Pledge* trapped planetside, Ran felt more confident, although how the Neek would react to the request xe was about to make was unknown.

The cutter pulled past the first moon, and Ran allowed hir mind to drift to the few interactions the Neek people had had with the other members of the Charted Systems. Cell-Tal had quarterly andal shipments from Neek, of course, but Ran had never accompanied the Risalian couriers. Captain Kuebrich made additional runs for the Markin, of which Ran knew even less about. Ran had personally spoken with the Neek president once, over comm, to renegotiate andal prices after the invention of cellulosic food printers, and had very recently given serious consideration to strangling the Neek that traveled with Yorden. That was it. Xe could recall no other recorded instances of Neek interaction. Xe had never given it much thought, but considering the andal situation now, how much more could have been harvested, Ran wondered, if xe had ever taken the time to visit the planet as a Cell-Tal representative? Did they have untouched forests? Were their exports maximized? Why types of rotations were their plantations on, and could something as simple as nitrogen fertilization speed up harvest?

"Second, can we get a detailed topographic map of the planet up on holo?"

The gray-clad Risalian queried the computer and then shook hir head. "Apologies, Captain, but no topographic data exist for Neek."

That explained a lot. If the planet had never been seriously mapped, then no one knew anything about the forest cover. Ran tapped hir personal interface and repeated the query. An error message returned. The question of *why* the Neek planet was left out of the Systems' planetwide database was intriguing. The Markin sent surveys to all planets in the Charted Systems yearly. Updated census information, economic reports, land mass...it should all have been available.

"There's an endnote in the database, Captain Ran," the second called out. "Neek has declined surveyors yearly. A secondary footnote from a previous council notes that technologically delayed systems don't represent a serious need for mapping, and as such, the issue will not be pressed with Neek and Earth if they continue to decline."

"So they've declined official surveys, but I can't imagine a scientist or archeologist has never entered some data into the common repository. Check there. Even a little information is better than none at all."

The second tapped a series of commands, and text began to scroll across hir display. "There is one report in the commons," xe said. "Neek is a basic humanoid planet. Carbon-based, liquid water, yellow sun. It has four continents, three major provinces, and four moons, all of which are undeveloped. Andal is native to this planet, growing in both wild forests and plantations, and estimates provided by the Neek government put the forested portion of the planet at ten million hectares. There is one major intelligent species with two distinct phenotypes, three genders, and a low occurrence of genetic drift." Xe tapped several other panels, and a scrolling list overlaid the planet view. "This is the commerce information provided by the Interstellar Trade Route Commission. No major imports or exports except the occasional andal shipment to Cell-Tal. Emigration estimated at one in the last decade; immigration tightly controlled to the point of prohibition."

"What does that say in the corner there?" Ran asked, pointing to a small, unreadable section of text.

The second enhanced the image. "Tested and confirmed telepathic rating of two on the ten point Carew Scale affects roughly seventy-five percent of the populace."

Of course they were telepaths. Ran sighed. That complicated matters but did explain why the Markin had never set foot on the planet. "Once we're in range, get the Neek president on the comm and transfer it to my office. I'd like to avoid the planet as well, if at all possible."

* * *

An aged Neek filled Ran's screen, his short hair a mass of orange curls, his green eyes piercing. The andal bench upon which he sat blended with his dark skin, making his form difficult to discern. He eyed Ran, frowning, as he sipped from a delicate wooden mug with andal reliefs carved into the base.

"Captain Ran. I received your communication that you would be visiting, and the *Pledge* crew has been held, per your request. While the Neek people are, of course, always happy to comply with sheriff investigations, I am still unclear as to why you have chosen to visit us personally. Would you care to elaborate?" The president set the mug down and dabbed at the corners of his mouth with his shirtsleeve. "Perhaps the last wood shipment to Cell-Tal was not satisfactory? I can assure you that what the andal now lacks in heartwood, it makes up for in fiber length and decreased lignin content. Plantation growth does have its drawbacks, but you cannot argue with the increase in cellulose."

Ran leaned over and entered a code into the computer, transmitting the specifications of hir ship and hir very delicate cargo. "President, I am here today representing the Markin, not Cell-Tal. The girl that travels with the *Mercy's Pledge* crew is a nonsentient piece of property belonging to the Risalian government. I have been charged with recovering her but not, of course, without due compensation for your planet's cooperation."

The president's eyebrows rose as his attention was drawn to a nearby computer interface where, hopefully, Ran's transmission was scrolling.

"I see," the president said slowly, eyes dancing between the computer and Ran. "One hundred thousand diamond rounds makes this a very serious negotiation indeed. I assume you have substantiation of the claim required under Systems law?"

Having expected this, Ran tapped another line of code and sent a second transmission. "For your consideration, President, I've sent the genealogical history of the progeny, along with her genetic sequence. If you also require, I can send video of every moment of her life up until she was removed from one of our ships. Amusingly, I can also recite approximately twenty-five percent of her genetic code from memory. She took a long time to make."

"Make..." the president trailed off as he read through the text. When he'd finished reading, the president ran both hands through his mop of curls. "Your claim appears irrefutable, and under normal circumstances, I would not hesitate to return stolen property, sentient or otherwise. I understand the potential delicacy of your operation, Captain. However, I have some questions that need answers, specifically about her genetic lineage."

Ran frowned at the unexpected turn of events. The conversation was taking too long, and xe wasn't entirely certain what a Carew Rating of two got you in terms of telepathy. Could the president see into hir mind from their communication? The last thing Ran needed was extensive knowledge of the Ardulan breeding program in the hands of a backwater planet.

"Her parentage only concerns my geneticists," Ran replied sharply. "I'm more concerned about why *you* seem to be so interested in her."

"Fair enough, Captain." A light flashed to Ran's left, indicating the president had sent a file. A large file. Ran opened it on a secondary screen, and a delicate script began to scroll. The captain's confusion lasted only a moment, before a word in bold text caught hir attention.

Ardulum.

These were encounter stories, descriptions that, while protruding and flowery, mirrored a history Ran knew very well. Except the Ardulans here had been met as gods, not equals. They were worshipped, revered, and, if the president's cautious attitude was any indication, still held a surprising sway over the modern population.

Ran grinned, the edges of hir lips pulling high, allowing hir tongue to flick across pointed teeth. If only the Markin had visited. Xe made a note to send a Cell-Tal team out immediately, accompanied by a Hearth Talent. Cell-Tal could make significant strides in the export market here if Ardulans were so cemented into the native belief structure. Bring a few Ardulans with them, and Cell-Tal could likely access even the andal trees in old-growth reserves. In the interim, however, there was a clear way around the current hurdle, which would satisfy both of their needs.

"President Neek," Ran began in an even tone, spreading hir hands in an open gesture. "The girl is not a god, but I can see her usefulness to you in such a capacity. She comes from a small group of defective stock that was traded to us by the ruling class of a visiting planet. Ardulum. In much the same way you might keep beasts of burden, we have cultivated these Ardulans...trained them in the basics of language so they can be useful to the sentient species. I see no reason why you should be left without one. Certainly a being such as yourself could manage to keep the existence of such creatures quiet—we wouldn't want every planet in the Charted Systems clamoring for their own." On an adjacent monitor, Ran brought up photos of the four Ardulans currently on Cutter 77. "I'm sending you a manifest with Ardulans we'd be able to provide immediately in exchange for the preadolescent. Their Talents are listed below the profile. Select any one you feel would be most important for your task."

When Ran looked back at the viewer, expecting to see the president delighting over the Ardulan manifest, xe saw only a pale face and searing eyes boring directly into hir own.

"Ardulum" the president whispered, his tone soft and dangerous. "The planet that vanishes."

"Technically, it propels, but that isn't important. About that list."

The president shook his head, blinked several times, and began to scroll through the options. "Aggression, Science, Hearth, and a menagerie of specialties from each. Just as in *The Book of the Uplifting*." His expression turned from guarded to impressed. Ran snorted at the quick transition. "Still concerning. I have a planet that believes in Ardulum, Captain, and in the majesty of its highly intelligent species. The girl you're after is sentient, there can be no doubt about that, and powerful. If the Ardulans you carry are merely chattel—some defective off-breed—they can be of no use to me. I will not put my people's belief structure in jeopardy, even for the Risalians."

"The girl has shown promise in weapons in the past," Ran noted, trying to drive the conversation. "And the adult Ardulans on my ship are quite powerful as well. Other than that—the girl can't speak, and neither can any of the others. As religion is mostly interpretation, that should only work in your favor." Ran sent the document again, to press the issue. "We have two options if you'd like to stick with that skill set, both very well trained and highly obedient."

The president was silent as he considered. He ran a sticky fingertip over the rim of his mug, circling the dark contents as he did so. Ran waited patiently, the whine of the cutter's engines and the swaying of green branches outside the window in the president's office helping hir to soothe the anticipation.

After another few heartbeats, the president looked back at the screen. He placed the mug down and splayed his fingers widely across the tabletop in front of him. "For my purposes, and in the interest of interstellar peace, I would prefer the second *don* female. She looks enough like the one we have here that we could pass off a younger adult as the girl just into second *don*. And I want the exchange done here, on Neek. We can't risk our ships being dissolved by the girl when attempting to transport her."

Ran put the requisition into the computer as the fluttering in hir chest settled. "Done. I will have the second *don* Aggression female prepared for transport. I appreciate your cooperation in this matter. Should you encounter any issues with your Ardulan, please do not hesitate to contact me on this channel. Cutter 77 out."

The screen blanked, and Ran leaned back in hir plush chair. Xe would have to oversee the transfer, unfortunately, but if it meant retrieving the girl quickly and without fanfare, it was worth the risk. If the process took much longer, xe would be risking the girl's metamorphosis. If she began her incubation into second *don*—or worse, emerged—outside of Risalian control, there would be no way to contain her. There would be no way to protect anyone; not the Risalians, not the Neek, and not the other innocent beings of the Charted Systems from the unfocused telekinetic power of an untrained adult Ardulan. Cell-Tal had experimented with that scenario before, at their former laboratory on the Korin moon. Mercifully, only a handful of Risalians had lost their lives, but the lab had been reduced to glucosic sludge, and an entire genetic line had to be sterilized.

That couldn't happen again. Not with this line. There was time. Ran just needed to be patient. In less than an hour, xe would be on a skiff, bringing their second *don* gunner onto Neek. The swap would be made, and Ran could return the girl to Cell-Tal's holding facility, hopefully before she began her transition.

Patience. Ran inhaled deeply and then closed hir eyes. Xe pictured the waterfalls of Risal, the sparkling, green water, fish arcing through river foam. Hir progenitor swam in the clear water, diving for silver fish and long, black eels while Ran stood in the waterfall's path, letting the cascading pressure wash away hir tension. Edging on the idyllic scene, however—just in the corners of Ran's mind where xe couldn't chase it away—was the image of an unfettered second *don* Ardulan female, free in the cellulose-drenched Charted Systems.

CHAPTER 13: NEEK

Destroy the blasphemers! Burn their temples, demolish their ships! They have transgressed against Ardulum, and only through Ardulum can one walk in the light.

—Excerpt from a network broadcast outside the Charted Systems, October 22nd, 2060 CE

Neek awoke with a start, the whine of settees fading into the distance. She tried to throw off the sheets, but they stuck to her torso as she sat up, copious *stuk* streaming from her fingers. She'd had that stupid andal dream again—the one with the weeping trees in the too-still forest. The erratically recurring nightmare had haunted her since she was a child, but now it occurred with frustrating frequency.

Neek knew better than to expect a return to sleep. Instead, she ran a sticky hand through her hair—managing to mat the fine strands even further—before standing and throwing open the shutters to her window. Two moons were up in the early morning light, and the tide was just cresting the horizon. The stillness in the air calmed the pilot's breathing but not her mind. To the east, a squadron of settees practiced formations, the reflected crimson apparent even at a distance. Neek's hands jerked in tandem with the movements of the teardrop-shaped ships. Circle down and in for sudden thrust. A full counterclockwise rotation followed by an upwards jab for a descending loop that just brushed the treetops. The gentlest of strokes to send the settee into a smooth lateral glide.

A settee dropped, plummeting directly downward. Neek watched the nose of the ship struggle to right itself, the pilot likely slipping over *stuk*-covered controls. The settee leveled off, but only after shearing tops off of several andal trees in the nearby plantation.

"Idiot pilot." Neek slammed a shutter over the window and turned away. She didn't need to be watching training exercises. She needed to get off-world before Emn became the president's new religious figurehead. Any escape attempt, however, would require Emn's assistance, which Neek wasn't certain how to request. Besides, the knowledge that she was only kilometers from her family—and that she would have to leave without seeing them—weighed her down.

"Hey, Emn, want to help me blow up part of my planet? Maybe you could just impale the president on an andal twig and then we could steal his ship to get off-world." It felt ridiculous to say out loud, even as she tiptoed down the empty hall. Just to her left was a small end table with a piece of chewed andal lying on the top, the curly bark still attached in some places. Curious, Neek popped the unchewed end in her mouth and tried to rip off a section with her molars. Bits of bark and sapwood came off, sticking to the roof of her mouth. She gagged. Once the material dislodged, she chewed slowly, noting the surprising spiciness of the wood, and finally managed to swallow.

It felt grainy going down her throat. She coughed, trying to move bits that seemed stuck. *Not one of my brighter ideas*, she thought to herself. She put the twig back down and decided against mentioning her experiment to anyone. She wouldn't put it past Yorden for having given the andal a go, too, but likely he'd had the foresight to wash it down with something alcoholic.

Her wanderings ended at the door to the room that Emn and Nicholas shared, the two beds divided by a wood partition. She pushed it open, careful to minimize the creaking. Emn had chosen the left side of the room. In a towering bed carved from a single andal tree, the girl was still fast asleep, curled into a ball with the sheets splaying out around her in a pinwheel pattern.

Neek's feet carried her inside to Emn's bed, where she knelt. It'd been two days since the science minister's visit. Neek had avoided the girl since, making excuses to leave the house or lock herself in her room. The avoidance made Neek feel childish. That some part of her clung to a fairy tale religion was embarrassing. Emn came from a Risalian lab. She didn't use magic. She used cut-and-dried science with some skilled telekinesis. If fungi could break down cellulose with enzymes, why couldn't a sentient do it in a more mechanical fashion? Perhaps the Ardulans of legend were the same—just travelers with an extensive scientific potential, capable of impressing a primitive planet in their attempts to make contact. Except that line of reasoning led to the possibility that there was in fact a planet moving around in the cosmos, which brought a whole separate set of issues and far too many possibilities.

Asleep, the girl seemed too small to be the cause of the constant tickle at the back of Neek's mind. With the morning light reflecting off the girl's translucent skin, she could imagine Emn older—a young woman Nicholas's size, with determined eyes, and carrying the ceremonial two-headed spear described in Neek's childhood history texts. She imagined them sitting together at a fast-print shop, eating perf food so standardized you could taste the outlines, or together in a divey spaceport, discussing Neek politics and history. She imagined Emn with children of her own, happy and carefree, on a planet where no one feared her.

A smile crept across Neek's face as she gently wove her fingers into one of Emn's loose fists. The girl's sleeping mind slipped into Neek's, and she felt the familiar pressure build near the base of her skull before tapering off into a lighter touch.

"I wonder if you'll ever get to see Ardulum," Neek whispered to Emn. "If it does exist. Our artists paint it with reverence—this place they've never seen. We all dream about it. Even the president, I bet. Even me." She paused as Emn shifted in her sleep, clasping Neek's hand tightly as she turned onto her other side. "I wonder how things will change, now that you're here. Or if they will at all."

Neek felt Emn's mental connection alter as she slowly came into consciousness. *I didn't mean to wake you up*, Neek told her. *Go back to sleep. I'll go away.*

An emphatic negative pushed its way into Neek's mind, and she laughed softly. *Or not.*

Emn sat up, still clutching Neek's hand, and rubbed the sleep from her eyes with the other. *What am I supposed to change?* Emn asked sleepily. *I don't have any other clothes.*

No, little one. Not clothes. Lives. I think you will change lives, if the president lets you. If you want to.

What I want is— Emn's thoughts halted at the loud rapping on the front door.

The noise jarred Nicholas, who leaped out of bed. "I'm ready!" he shouted sleepily. "Let's get 'em going out fight ship!"

"Somehow I don't think that will help, but I appreciate the thought." Yorden yawned as he walked past the bedroom door. "How about we start with seeing who it is." Yorden pulled at the coppery handle, paused, and then took a step back. "Can we help you two with something?" Yorden asked. "Seems a bit early for more testing."

Neek's heart stopped, or at least, that's what it felt like. In the doorway stood two heaven guards. Their gold robes just brushed the floor, the edges of the fabric trimmed with a deep green. Crimson piping followed the collar and swooped over the shoulders. Their feet were bare, indicating command posts. Behind them, Neek could see a settee idling on the beach, the crimson paint reflecting a glowing halo in the light of the sunrise.

No one spoke. Neek stood rigid, unable to move. She didn't recognize the man or the gatoi—they were easily a decade older than her, but she knew their caste well enough. With bone-white skin and red-tinted eyes, both belonged to the oldest family line on Neek, a line that prided itself on being able to trace back every ancestor for thirty generations.

"Did you need something?" Yorden asked gruffly. "We haven't had breakfast yet."

The gatoi stepped forward, zir jawline tense. "Orders from the president came this morning. The Ardulan girl is going to be field-tested at the president's northern facility and then given a new physical this afternoon. She should be back in the early evening."

"Wait, you're taking her away?" Nicholas asked, joining everyone else in the main entryway. "The medics have always come here before. Why do you have to take her to this facility?"

The gatoi's eyes wandered from Nicholas and casually took in the room. "These tests cannot be done on-site without danger to bystanders." Zie offered Yorden a clipboard with a legal-looking document attached.

Yorden glanced at Neek before handing her the clipboard. "An official seal and everything. Emn must have really shaken someone up yesterday."

Neek's mind raced. The Heaven Guard had no medical training, nor were they used for routine transport. Their sole purpose was to patrol the sky, searching for signs of Ardulum. To be called in for this—it was too official. Too formal. Adding to the mystery was the presence of the gatoi guard. Neek's third sex was in decline, the unique chromosome set destabilizing with each successive generation. A gatoi wouldn't be risked in any type of conflict situation, unless zie was sent to diffuse Neek's own suspicion. Zir presence was a clear warning, except Neek couldn't determine for what.

"I assume you require an interpreter," Neek said, wrapping an arm around Emn's shoulders. "No doubt you're well aware of the communication difficulties between her and, well, pretty much anyone else except me."

The guards looked at each other, unsure. The male then turned to Neek and crossed his arms across his chest. The wide sleeves of his robe fell to his wrists, exposing more brilliantly white skin. "Exile, would you just shut up and let the president do his job? This is a matter of science, nothing more, and the paperwork doesn't specify for a translator."

Yorden moved forward and addressed the guards. "Obviously someone screwed up the paperwork. Imagine how much time it's going to save when you show up with Emn *and* her translator." He clasped the gatoi on the shoulder. "As a captain, I can tell you that crew initiative and ability to think on one's feet is essential for promotion. No one likes a guy, er, sentient, who can only follow orders."

The guards looked at each other again, the gatoi shrugging zir shoulders. The male dropped his arms and looked from Neek to Yorden, and then back again. "I—"

Neek moved forward and pushed herself between the two guards. "Well? What are we waiting for? I'm sure the president doesn't want to be kept waiting. Let's go."

The gatoi shrugged and placed zir hand on Neek's elbow, guiding her towards the ship. "Let's just take her. We can always send her back," zie muttered to the male.

"Okay, but if anyone asks, it was your idea," zir colleague responded as he trailed behind. "I refuse to be the one responsible for her if she goes after the president again. You didn't see what happened the last time they were in the same room together."

* * *

The settee landed just outside a large government building on the outskirts of the capital. The guards ushered Neek and Emn off the landing pad and into a small, empty, sterile-smelling room just inside the entry doors. There was nothing within—no furniture, no decorations, and no beings. Neek's *stuk* crystallized on her fingertips. They'd been in the settee for just over two hours, the guards alternately staring at her with open disgust or bantering about other guard members. Some of the clarifiers Neek recognized—most she did not. Some of the events they discussed—the most recent graduation ceremony, the training exams, the flight drills—brought back sharp memories. Memories that needed to stay buried.

The guards ushered Emn and Neek to the center of the room and then stood at attention. They were facing another door some ten meters away; the door from which they'd come was still open and letting in a warm breeze and the smell of summer.

The emptiness of the room bothered Neek. For a private meeting with the president, it made sense. He had most of his meetings in private rooms, including the ones that involved her. For heaven guards to escort an Ardulan to such a room, however, seemed contrary to the Heaven Guard's mission. If they knew of Emn's existence, yet brought her here…

"What now?" Neek asked the male guard. She began in an even tone, not wanting to escalate the situation, but was unable to keep the sarcasm from riding into her voice. "No parade?" She picked at the gold sleeve of the male's robe, fingers stroking the green edge. "Shouldn't you be bowing to Emn? That is your job, after all—searching for, protecting Ardulum." Neek dropped the sleeve and wrapped her arm back around Emn's shoulders. "You've got one right here, genius. Consider the implications."

"Exile." He nodded back towards the settee through the open door. "I fly your ship. Did you recognize her? They never bothered to remove your designation from the hull. When my old one needed too many repairs, this one was the only available."

Neek's eyes flicked to the hull where, just under the seam for the hatch door, three letters in gold paint—her unique Heaven Guard identifiers—reflected in the sunlight. She suppressed the impulse to run over and glide her fingers over the imprint. She'd never gotten to see it. The ship would have been given to her after the ceremony, had she actually made it through.

"It's been ten years. I'd think you'd be more embarrassed to have a command position and still be flying a ship marked with a heretic's lettering," Neek said.

The guard's lip twitched. "Better than not flying one at all, wouldn't you say?" He looked to the gatoi guard, who looked away. "Why don't you tell us about your tramp? I've heard that Terran shuttles can maneuver about as well as *titha*. Would you agree?"

She'd clearly hit a little too close to the mark. "I thought there would be testing," she said, changing the subject. "Shouldn't we be in a hospital, or maybe somewhere with more cellulose?"

"What we're doing," the gatoi said, placing a hand on Neek's shoulder, zir fingers firmly pressing, "is waiting. I would prefer you did so quietly."

Neek snorted but remained where she was. Instead of answering, she reached out to Emn, both with a hand and mentally. *How are you doing?* she asked.

The ship made me feel sick, Emn responded, and a pinch of nausea laced her next thought. *Those ships fly a lot faster than the* Pledge.

Yes, I know, Neek returned sullenly. *We have much more stable access to andal here, so our ships—*

There was a tap on the door in front of them. The large wooden handle turned, and with a slow creak the door swung inward. The cross-breeze formed instantaneously and pulled small strands from Neek's braid, impairing her vision. She could, however, tell by the gait and the brilliant orange hair who was coming towards her. Neek rubbed at the crystalized *stuk* on her fingertips, peeling off the thin film, and sent a warning to Emn. There was no reason for the president of Neck to be doing the testing himself. Then again, there was no reason to do testing at sunbreak, either, even if the minister had come in the early morning once before. Something was wrong.

The president's dress was formal today, his long, black tunic and pants trimmed on the edges with gold ribbon. On his left sleeve, five andal leaves were stitched in green thread—the mark of his office. He'd let his hair grow longer since Neek had last seen him, the bright curls now brushing his chin. He was within an arm span of her, his face radiating a sticky hubris, when the last puzzle piece fell into place.

Captain Ran came through the door, yellow tunic straight and bright, hands clasped behind hir back. After hir trailed someone Neek had not expected to see, and she hastily wiped the strands of hair from her face to make sure her vision was true. A woman followed Ran. She was tall, almost the height of the captain, with a thin frame. That alone wouldn't have been enough to make her stand out, but her hair was just the right shade of dark red, her skin translucent, but brown instead of pale. There was no mistaking what she was, not after seeing Emn. The pilot pulled the girl closer to her and tensed as the guard's hand on her shoulder began to dig in.

Neek tried to rationalize the presence of the Ardulan woman and Ran on her planet. Cell-Tal worked with the Neek government for andal exports. Ran was on the Cell-Tal board. That made sense, even if the Neek government seldom granted visas. To have Ran and the president together, however, *with an Ardulan*, was beyond plausibility. Her mind couldn't wrap around another Ardulan. Intellectually, she knew there had to be others—she'd seen the images of Emn's mother herself. But standing in front of one, seeing those same blank eyes look through her, was surreal.

Ran and the Ardulan woman stopped just behind the president. There was a cough—a pretentious, throaty cough that brought Neek's attention back to the man in front of her. Deep-set green eyes stared, skin slack and marked near the edges of the lids. Jowls hung loose near a small mouth that was turned ever so slightly upwards. The air smelled stale and old, a tired circulation of clichéd governmental power grabs and Risalian meddling. Her breathing quickened. Small crystalline patches began to form on Neek's skin. The long, slender fingers of the gatoi moved from her shoulder to her arm, encircling.

"Exile," the president greeted her warmly, a ripe smile close to rotting on his face. His voice hadn't changed, nor had her desire to grab a handful of those ridiculous tangerine curls and bash his head repeatedly into a wall. The male guard moved to stand next to Ran, the yellow tunic of the Risalian garish against the gold hues of the Guard robe.

"I'm delighted to see you again, of course. A decade is far too long for a politician to go without death threats." The corners of his mouth twitched. Neek looked to his fingers, curious to read his underlying emotion, but the tips were dry.

The president noticed the direction of her gaze. "Only peasants and heretics can't control their emotions. You should try breathing exercises. I'm sure the guard behind you would be happy to give you lessons. Zie is used to dealing with the uneducated."

Neek took a step forward, but wet fingertips dug into her skin. "Don't," the gatoi whispered into her ear.

Neek stopped, but only because Emn tugged at her flight suit. Alone, she'd have taken her chances. With Emn, the risk was too high.

"So we are left, then, with what to do with you." The president came forward until he was almost nose-to-nose with Neek. His breath coated her mouth in the smell of fermented *bilaris*. He reached a hand out and ran it from her shoulder to hip. *Stuk,* thick and beading, curled off the president's fingertips and melded her flight suit to her waist. "You weren't supposed to be here, but I'm not surprised."

She'd been nineteen the last time the president had been this close, and last time, she'd still been too much in shock to know how to react. Her time with Yorden on the *Pledge,* however, had removed that particular hurdle.

Neek's knee came up, ramming between the president's legs. The gatoi guard had her on the ground, arms pinned behind her back, before she could follow through with a punch, but she was still able to watch the president fall to the floor, groaning. Pain in her tailbone aside, it was exactly as satisfying as she'd thought it would be.

Neek? Words lilted through her head. The male guard had the child by the hand, and while Emn clearly did not like the situation, the guard wasn't doing anything more than holding on. She was probably safe. No Heaven Guard would actively harm an Ardulan, even a construct. She, on the other hand, was likely going to pay for that kick.

As the president recovered, Ran moved towards Emn and the guard. Neek pulled against the hands that held her, but the gatoi was stronger. Without access to weapons, she wasn't getting free without help. "Stay away," Neek warned, her voice low. "She's not yours to take."

Emn honked defiantly at Ran, twisting in hir arms as xe took her from the guard and secured her over hir shoulder. Her bare feet kicked, toenails raking across Ran's tunic, but the Risalian held her in place.

Neek! This time it was a scream. Neek shifted her weight, moving her right leg under her left, and tried to slip beneath the guard's arms. Her shoulders cleared one arm, and she flipped back onto her other hip, desperate to dislodge the rest of her torso, when a sharp blow landed on her head.

White swam in front of her eyes. Memories from Emn slammed into Neek's mind and intertwined with her own. Neek batted them away, desperate to keep her vision clear. *Ran at her graduation. Neek's mother held back while guards dragged Emn away. Emn screaming...*

Neek pushed the jumbled memories down and focused on her vision. She was on her feet again, although when that had happened she was unsure. A guard was on either side of her, each pinning one of her arms painfully against her back. It was hard to see. Emn was still calling to her, and she could hear Ran's grunts as Emn's kicks hit sensitive areas, but without the support of the guards, she didn't think she could stand on her own. Emn's panic fed Neek's disorientation, keeping the pilot off-balance, unsure how to break free.

"President, *please.*" Neek's pleading grated against her ears, but she had no alternative. "Think of what she means for our people!"

The president's face loomed over her then, bright curls of orange turning her stomach. There was a sharp, thin prick of pain in Neek's right shoulder, and an image of a needle shot across her vision. Emn's consciousness grew sluggish, and it took Neek a moment to realize it wasn't she who had been drugged.

"We find ourselves here again, Exile," the president said softly, his lips centimeters from her ear. Emn's presence thinned, her panicked memories groggy.

Sleepy, Neek, Emn managed to send.

You have to stay awake. We can't get out of here without you.

"What would your parents say, do you think?" the president continued. The male dug thick fingers into Neek's braid and pulled, forcing her head up. "Your mother in particular," the president breathed. He moved to face her. Two slippery fingers ran down the side of her face before tugging on her chin. The tension on her braid relaxed. "Mentioning an incident like this might put too much strain on her system. Her status has been critical for weeks. Did you know that?"

Words spun through her head but none reached Neek's lips. She pulled against the guards, her teeth clenched in a rage to help her ignore the popping of her right shoulder and the nails that tore at her skin. She could no longer see Ran, but she could feel Emn bobbing in the back of her head, fighting unconsciousness. The president had no right to talk about her mother, had no right to bring her family into this again. She could end this ridiculous game *right now* if she could just pull free and get her hands around the bastard's throat.

A blast hit Neek from behind, directly between her shoulder blades. Her muscles spasmed as the guards released her, and the president took three steps backwards. A mosaic of light and cellulose surrounded her, and Neek mentally cursed each tiny, shimmering microfibril as the pain in her shoulder caught up with her.

"That should give you some time to think." The president nodded to the guards. "I appreciate your assistance. Please remember that I require a contingent of fifteen heaven guards tomorrow, at two hours past sunrise. Have them meet me in the lower medical bay in this facility."

"She's an Ardulan!" Neek yelled at the guards as they nodded and headed towards the door. "You're supposed to *protect* her, not give her to the Risalians. *Help her!*" Emn's presence had reduced to a whisper, but Neek couldn't keep fighting the containment field, fighting to keep their connection, and fighting the damn president all at once. She needed help.

Emn, can you do anything? Manipulate something? Crush some bonds or bones or science us out of this? Emn struggled to respond, but the returned imagery barely formed.

Emn, please. *You blew up the* Pledge. *Can a little sedative really be that effective?*

A sharp image of andal clouded Neek's vision, before deconstructing into a rolling hunger. Neek finally understood.

Do you have to eat the andal? I took a bite of that disgustingness early this morning. I'm sure it's still around. Could you use it?

An incomprehensible jumble of images came from Emn, packed so tightly together that Neek couldn't decipher any of it except the sharp warning that followed.

Just do it! We can worry about repercussions later.

That seemed to fix whatever held Emn back. Pressure built in Neek's lower torso—a bloating, uncomfortable pressure that made her feel nauseous. She felt the skin over her stomach peel apart, internal organs shifting. Something warm that wasn't *stuk* ran down Neek's legs. The front of her flight suit shredded. The remains turned a copper color, and she could smell the metallic sweetness of blood. Of course Emn had to get at the cellulose somehow, but for some reason, Neek hadn't envisioned such a direct approach.

The field around Neek grew brighter, bulged inward, and then burst apart. Neek sank to the floor, a sleepy, drugged stillness encroaching on her mind as her flight suit saturated and *stuk* seeped across her abdomen, attempting to close the wound. Emn's presence dropped away.

Crazy science magic, Neek thought wanderingly. Emn was gone. Her mind was empty. Everything happening around her felt jagged. The edges of her world were blurring, her vision taking on a dreamlike quality. For a moment, she was certain it was she who was still struggling ineffectually against Captain Ran, not bleeding onto a dense wood floor. Her mind continued to wander. *I wonder what Risalian soup tastes like? Do Risalians eat soup? Why don't more people wear shoes in space?*

Reality seeped back in. It was patchy at first—checkers of gold and green giving way to the president, his hands roaming across the front of the Ardulan woman and leaving *stuk* trails in their wake.

"Interesting display, but not very useful." He turned the Ardulan around by the shoulders and inspected her back. "What do you think, Exile? We should be able to pass her off as Emn without too much of a problem. A little makeup and creative lighting should do wonders. We'll get her a dress, too, just like your Emn. Adorable and yellow. The people will love it."

That comment focused her mind a little. Neek would castrate the president. Castrate and remove his tongue. Maybe swap the two organs if she could figure out how.

"You'll respond to 'Emn' now," the president said to the Ardulan. The woman turned around slowly, each movement thick and deliberate, until she faced the president. "Nod your head if you understand."

The woman brought her head down and up once, her auburn hair bobbing over her shoulders. Grinning, the president slapped the woman on the rear.

"Excellent! Go with the guards down to the infirmary. They'll find you some clothes." Neek followed the president's gaze to the long geometric pattern on the woman's side. "Lovely. Very lovely."

I should have killed you when I had the chance, Neek thought vehemently right before she passed out.

* * *

"Come on," the male guard said to the Ardulan woman, taking her arm and guiding her out the door. The woman followed, mind processing only the direction change, as the guards navigated several flights of stairs and entered the infirmary. On the nearest bed lay a yellow dress with strapped sleeves and a trim cut at the chest and skirt.

"Here," he said, shoving the dress into the woman's arms. "Put it on."

Slowly, every moment deliberately debated before execution, the woman stepped into the dress and pulled the straps over her shoulders. The right side of the dress was open with a sheer mesh sewn in, allowing the markings to show.

"Fits," the other guard said. "Now we just wait for the president."

"What do you think we should do with her?" the male asked. "Doesn't look like she'll be causing much trouble."

"You," the other called, snapping zir fingers to get the woman's attention. Zie waited until the Ardulan faced both of them. "Sit on that bed and stay quiet."

The woman turned, this time taking in the length and height of the hospital bed. In a smooth and graceful movement, she hopped upon it, resuming her empty staring at the door. The thin, yellow dress clung strangely to her form and made the woman conscious of the material. The sensation of the fabric over her skin was unusual and tickled, but she did not itch. She didn't wonder about the not-itching. She didn't wonder either about the sudden change in her surroundings, or the unfamiliar species giving her orders. Instead, she watched in her mind's eye the child break the Dulan field. She remembered the feel of the snapped linkages and released energy. She remembered the clarity of thought and determination the girl didn't realize she was broadcasting and felt again the waves of unfettered emotion hit her and seep through the dense fog of her mind.

Before she realized that she had instigated the motion, the woman brought her fingertips to the material hanging from her shoulders and pinched part of the dress together, running her fingers down the length to her hips. The fabric was smooth to her touch, and the tactile sensations traveled up her arm and into her mind. She liked the feeling. Touch was something new, something she hadn't thought of before. It was hard to focus on the feeling of the dress, however. The deep fog in her mind made it impossible to focus on anything other than mechanical weapons, but there weren't any weapons here. There were just new things to touch.

The woman ran shaky fingers through her hair, noting the texture and sensation from the strands. She felt the fabric covering of the hospital bed, running her hand along its length. Concepts of "coarse" and "soft" tugged at her, just beyond reach. She tried to focus, tried to chase the ideas down. When she pressed into the back of her mind, trying to penetrate, the fog rose up and covered the thoughts. It seeped from her skull through her body, where it chased the thoughts of texture and eradicated them. The feeling of the dress, the texture of the hospital bed, and the smoothness of her hair all disappeared.

When the fog finally subsided, the woman's mind was once again empty, except for the persistent image of the girl and the *snap hiss* of energy, the tiny capillaries breaking just under the girl's skin. She knew the signs, had seen them enough times in her own stolen offspring to never forget.

The time had come for the girl's metamorphosis.

CHAPTER 14: RISALIAN CUTTER 77

We've had no communication with intersects 20 through 25 in over three days. Scout ships sent to investigate have not returned. We are forced to conclude that Risal has lost control of the aforementioned borders.

—Intercepted communication from an unidentified Risalian cutter to the Markin Council, October 17th, 2060 CE

Emn awoke with weighted eyelids, blinking back the harsh, yellow light that streamed overhead. Next to her lay a basket filled with thick sticks of andal. Steam rose lazily from the branches, the smell of something in between cinnamon and syrup thick in the air. Emn was entranced. She sat up and buried her face in the steam, letting the thick tendrils obfuscate her vision and overwhelm her olfactory senses.

The smell brought back memories of her mother, of the dinners they shared together in their small room. Emn hadn't had andal since—not properly prepared like this, at least. Would it taste as before? When she bit into a stem would the springwood crunch and the summerwood dribble fresh, white sap down her throat? Would the bark crumble on her tongue, adding a caramelized flavor that would linger long after she swallowed? Emn's mouth watered. Raw andal was much tougher to chew, and while the sap still flowed, it left her more irritable than satiated. To be able to have the properly prepared variety was surreal, and she lingered for long moments in the aromatic draft of flavors and memories.

As the steam began to dissipate and the andal began to cool, Emn looked up, suddenly conscious of her surroundings. She was certainly in Risalian custody—there was no mistaking the architectural similarities and the aftertaste of extruded bioplastics. However, this room was different from the one she'd occupied with her mother. Instead of porous metal, the floor here was a solid sheet of silver. The walls and ceiling were identical—all cool, metallic surfaces joined with petrochemical plastics. Without the steam from the andal, the room stank of chemicals and volatile organic compounds. The smells lingered too long in Emn's nose, irritating her mucosal membranes and causing her to sneeze repeatedly.

In an attempt to clear her sinuses, Emn put her face to the pot of andal, her nose touching a stem. The spicy aroma returned, however diluted, and helped her relax. She took a deep breath, held it, and then sat up, taking a look around the room. The most curious thing about her surroundings was the lack of cellulose. She couldn't find the strands— the microfibrils—anywhere she looked. Releasing her inhalation and grumpily returning to normal breathing, Emn let her mind slip into the floor beneath her knees. Inside, she found nothing organic, unless she counted the extended history of the petrochemical sealant. It was the same in the walls and the ceiling, and in the mesh that sectioned the room in half, sealing her from the door.

Her concentration slipped as nausea rose up.

Hematoma, a dispassionate male voice said in her head. *Minor blood collection due to cranial impact. No permanent damage. Eat the andal.*

Emn ignored her intense need to vomit and chased the presence in her mind. *Who's there? Where are you?* There was no one in the room with her, unless invisibility was something beings could do. It *felt* like telepathy, like when she communicated with her mother or Neek, but she couldn't talk to just anyone, could she? Neek had *stuk*. Her mother was, well, her mother. The male voice in her head was completely foreign.

Hello? she called out again. *Who are you?*

No answer came—neither in her mind nor her ears. Isolation settled back in. Emn listened, but everything was silent. She was alone again, and this time, not even the cellulose was around to keep her company. Her head spun, and the urge to vomit rose again, stronger this time.

Suddenly, the smell of the andal, which had tapered to a mere whisper, assaulted her nose. Her stomach rumbled in response, and without bothering to wonder why, Emn shoved the nearest branch into her mouth. She fought the desire to grab another even as her molars made quick work of the thin twig.

The andal was everything she remembered. This piece had been cut during early spring, when sugars ran high. Cloudy white rivulets of juice ran down her chin and onto the front of her dress, staining the bright material in sticky streaks. A familiar buzzing began in her head, and Emn closed her eyes, enjoying the waning of her hunger pains.

The cooked andal in her stomach began to break apart, microfibrils of the cell walls peeling from the masticated pieces. The microfibrils churned slowly, rolling around in digestive enzymes that cleaved the long chains. Freed glucose absorbed instantly into her stomach lining and moved farther into her body, where it converted to energy. She felt strong, almost buzzing from the saturation of sugar and power.

Properly cooked andal behaved very differently than greenwood. She'd tried to explain it to Neek once, but her jumpy conglomeration of words and images—especially the pictures of chemical bonds—only confused the pilot. She'd given up after that. Emn understood that her thought process was different from everyone else's, but it frustrated her that only she could see where the differences lay. She wasn't a child, not like the Common word connoted, but she wasn't an adult either—not yet, anyway. She was sort of like Nicholas, stuck somewhere in between, except Nicholas didn't have to struggle through nonverbal, mutually exclusive forms of communication to get his point across.

Having her energy stores replenished meant she had more options. Emn sat back up and again considered her surroundings. How much energy would she need to escape, assuming she could find some cellulose to break apart in the first place? Even if she was on a cutter, breaking apart a floor or wall wasn't a big deal. Disabling an entire ship was. She couldn't afford to get tired halfway through just to be thrown back into a cell, or even put back into stasis. She needed as much energy as she could get, but there were several other matters she needed to attend to before attempting escape. The first was the nausea that was again rising up, and the other the pressure she felt in her head. She could take care of both—she just needed a bit more to eat first.

Emn returned to the andal, devouring her piece and several others of similar size before releasing a large belch and lying back down on the floor. While she waited for her body to process the wood, Emn let her mind drift back to the *Pledge* crew—to Neek in particular. She'd taken the cellulose from Neek's stomach, had ripped it from her body and left her bleeding out amongst enemies just to free her from the containment field. In the end, Emn's actions hadn't even mattered, as the wound had incapacitated Neek. Would the other Neek care for her, help heal her wounds, or would Neek be left to die because of Emn and her foolhardy attempts at rescue?

Emn looked down at her dress and poked a sticky finger at a juice stain, the fabric lifting slightly as her finger pulled away. She had to find a way off the cutter, away from the Risalians. Neek was in trouble because of her. Neek might be dead because of her. The entire crew of the *Pledge* might be dead, all because they had helped her. Emn looked to the ground, fighting the tightness that constricted her throat. She had to get back to the planet, had to help the *Pledge* and her crew. She needed off this stupid ship!

Emn got to her feet and turned in a circle. As she tried to assess her options, the nausea returned, and she retched, sending the remains of andal onto the metal floor.

An image entered her mind of the lump on her head. *Heal it,* the male voice said again. This time, the male caught her consciousness and led her into the damaged areas. Emn watched, fascinated, as layers of capillaries and skin came into focus. A diagram overlaid the area, showing indicators of what was in the right place and what wasn't.

It's not cellulose, Emn sent to the strange man. *I can't move it.*

You are not constrained in this way, the voice returned. *Heal the area.*

Emn let out an exasperated sigh but drew on her energy anyway. She moved her consciousness inside herself, focusing on the capillaries of interest. Her mind moved around them, studying them, and mapping their topography; then, when she thought she had enough information, she pulled at them as if they were cellulose.

The capillaries moved apart. Surprised, Emn switched tactics, pushing the platelets seeping from the open capillaries into clots, sealing the flow. She then pulled at a small section of skin just over the bump, separating the skin in half. The trapped blood flowed out of the opening and down the left side of her head, the red drops bright on her dress and the dull gray floor.

When the flow stopped, Emn slowly eased the skin back together, moving layers of dermis slightly so that a seal formed. She did the same for the capillaries, pushing off the scabs, moving the lines back together, and then growing clots around the junctions.

Smugly satisfied with her work, Emn tapped her head with her fingers. *Thank you*, she sent to the male that slid from her mind before the last word formed. As his presence slimmed into nothing, Emn grinned. The ability to manipulate her own body—and possibly those of others—was fascinating, and she knew exactly where she wanted to start. Emn finished the last of the andal and, still grinning, turned to the mass of tissue in her throat. She understood the importance of this mass—the Neek scientists had studied it thoroughly over the past month, and she had prodded it herself several times while practicing her vocalizations. The speech impediment was bothersome, and while the Neek scientists hadn't done anything to make it better, Emn had a sudden idea.

I bet I can make it like Nicholas's, Emn thought, drawing on a small amount of energy and probing the throat-mass with tiny mental pushes. *Neek's is complicated and has lots of funny little holes, but Nicholas's just has muscles and ligaments. I have those too—they're just not in the right places.*

Emn brought up a mental image of Nicholas's larynx, an image she had put together from days of watching him laugh and talk to her while playing games in the water, and from the diagram he'd shown her when she'd tapped his throat. Emn studied the picture carefully. It would take too long to move each piece individually—rerouting the blood vessels alone would take hours, and Emn doubted she had enough andal to sustain that level of concentration.

Instead, she gathered the energy and pulled it together. Emn took her mental picture from Nicholas and overlaid it onto her larynx. She then coiled the energy around both the image and the physical area, binding them together. When she had surrounded both with as much energy as she could, she pulled, forcing the image of Nicholas's larynx onto her own.

Ligaments unwound and snapped straight off her hyoid bone, muscles and cartilage correcting their alignment accordingly. Emn felt pressure ease off her trachea as the inner membrane settled into place. The girl took a deep breath and watched blood pump out of her heart and through her veins, all of which now connected properly.

Cautiously, Emn pulled back out of herself. She drew a breath, jutted her chin out past her front teeth and brought her lips together, pushing air out of her lungs and through her voice box at the same time.

"Emn," she sounded, her new voice wavering. "I'm Emn."

Emn grinned and clapped her hands in delight. She was talking! She didn't have to be a duck anymore. She could *tell* people what she wanted, join conversations. Even the Risalians would be easier to deal with now. After all, only *sentient* beings could talk.

Emn was startled out of her thoughts as a rectangular panel dissolved at a corner of the little room. She felt a distinctive pressure change and jumped back in surprise as the metal floor shifted under her feet. Captain Ran tentatively stepped into the room, the familiar gun held at attention. Xe lingered in the doorway, watching Emn, shoulders tense.

A Risalian in gray poked hir head around Ran, taking in the room. The edges of a conversation came with hir.

"...over here. I know you think most of Cell-Tal's business is moving to the external market, but forcing the entire Risalian fleet to speak Common when off-world seems extreme."

"Enough, First." Ran inclined hir head towards Emn. "I brought you here to do a physical, nothing more. I've already reset the pressure plating so it won't electrocute you when the weight distribution changes. Get in there."

The first stepped gingerly around Ran and into the room. Xe knelt before Emn, who took a step back. "I'm glad the board suggested installing the floor before the cutter left dry dock. It doesn't have its cellulose reinforcements installed yet, but in this case, that seems fortuitous."

Ran nodded and remained silent, running hir big toe slowly over a small section of the floor. The first let hir eyes linger on Emn's stained, yellow dress before extending a finger past the mesh to trace the hemline. "Clothes. On a juvenile. *Yellow* clothes, as if she had tested and passed the Captain's Exam." Xe tugged at the material near Emn's shoulder, knuckles grazing Emn's bare skin.

Gross, Emn thought to herself.

"Captain, I think you should come over here. Her eyes are following my movements. She's fidgeting, like she's upset I'm touching her." The Risalian turned to face the captain. "How much did you change in this model? The behavior is atypical."

Ran did not move, but hir eyes flicked to Emn uncertainly. "I didn't ask you for your opinion, First, just a physical assessment. Has the healer Ardulan spoken to her? Has she healed herself sufficiently? Is she well enough to be placed back in stasis?"

"The bump is gone, and I don't see any traces of blood." Xe stood. "We could try to put her back in stasis, but that technology has never been tested on an Ardulan postmanifest. If she can break a Dulan field, as you mentioned, chances are she could break the cylinder as well."

Ran's lips pursed as xe knelt to one knee, looking quizzically at Emn. "She's eaten the last of the andal, and it wasn't enough to do anything more than the healing. I'll deal with her from here. You're dismissed." Ran holstered the gun and nodded to the doorway. The first's eyes went wide, but xe left swiftly, the door swishing shut behind hir.

Emn stared up at Ran, a rage-filled curiosity melting her insides. She would not remove her dress. Neek had said she could wear it. It was hers. Besides, she could talk now. Removing her dress was just stupid. Maybe she should take off the captain's tunic and see how xe liked being naked in a cold, metal room.

"You're watching me, aren't you?" Ran looked Emn in the eyes, the Risalian seemingly uncertain. When xe spoke, the tone was different too—softer, the words more of a question than a command. "You can't wear yellow, you see. Or clothes. Juveniles don't wear anything on Risal, and only captains can wear yellow. Just hand the garment to me, and I'll go. No fuss."

"Why? It won't look good on you."

She couldn't have asked for a better response. The Risalian's neck seared violet, and xe fell backwards, head slamming against the wall.

"Well, it wouldn't," Emn added. "So I might as well keep it. If you want it, you'll have to shoot me, like you did my mother." Those words hurt to say—the vocalization somehow making the past event more real than just reliving it in her mind. Captain Ran could not be trusted. Captain Ran was dangerous. Captain Ran was, for some reason she couldn't discern, perpetually *in her way*.

Several words whispered from Ran's mouth, the hissing clicks unfamiliar but the tone very similar to Neek's when she was surprised.

"Where's Neek?" Emn asked, leaving the clothing issue behind. "I want to find her."

"You're not supposed to be able to talk," the captain managed finally as xe pushed hirself upright. "I didn't code you for that. We prepared for multiple Talents but this...this near-sentience..." Ran struggled to collect hirself, eyes wide and breath heavy. "Ardulans don't talk. They don't ask questions. You're...you're not a child. You're a weapon, a piece of living machinery." Xe grabbed at hir tunic, hands riffling through fabric folds before finally reaching the hip holster for hir gun. Ran launched to hir feet and grabbed Emn by the throat, lifting her off the ground. Hir eyes turned dark, and Emn could hear labored breathing and a faint whistling as air drove through the Risalian's neck slits.

Emn gasped for air while she tried to pry the blue fingers from her throat. Her legs swung and kicked, but Ran held her at a distance. "This is rudimentary intelligence," Ran sputtered. "Like in a beast of burden. No different than the basic instinctual responses of your mother. Talking is...it's a simple mistake. An error. Perhaps a mutation—that's all." Black spots began to swim in front of Emn's vision as the Risalian shook her from side to side. "We can fix mistakes. I can fix you. Just have to tweak your code a little. Once we get to the Cell-Tal lab, it will be fine. You'll see." Ran ended the last words in a higher pitch, the sound hurting Emn's ears.

The fingers released her, and Emn fell to the floor. Ran put the gun back in the holster. Emn sucked in mouthfuls of air, coughing loudly. A hand hit her across the face before she completely recovered, sending the girl backwards and bouncing her head off the floor.

"Remove the cloth. Failure to do so will result in additional beatings. Further disobedience could lead to more drastic measures."

Emn managed a sitting position. It was still hard to breathe, hard to see. Everything hurt.

Then Ran was down at her level, tracing two fingers against Emn's swollen cheek. Soft words came again, the jagged gentleness drawing tears from Emn's eyes. Blue filled her blurred vision as the confusing tone lulled her, made her long to be back in her mother's arms.

"If you do have some flicker of life, think about this. Helping the Risalians means you'd help save everyone in the Systems. Isn't that something you'd like? Helping your friends? Your Neek? You just have to listen to what you're told. Take off the clothing."

"No!" Emn screamed, although the sound came out more like a honk than she intended. She was tired of being told what to do, tired of having no control over her life, tired of the Risalians, tired of Ran. Neek had fought back. Neek *showed* her how to fight back, and she didn't need cellulose to do it. Drawing on her memory of Neek's actions in the dreamscape, Emn got to her knees. Ran's hand rose and swung, aiming for the same side of her face. In the moment just before impact, Emn lunged forward and grabbed the gun with both hands, pulling it from the holster.

The captain grabbed for the gun, but Emn rolled right, jabbing a kick at hir knee. Ran yelped as hir knee buckled, and xe crashed back against the wall, denting it.

Her mother's execution filled Emn's mind, and the image of Ran—of yellow-blue—fueled her rage. Behind it came a memory of Neek, her interference in the dreamscape, and a kneeling Risalian. Emn moved squarely behind Ran and leveled the gun right behind hir head. Before xe could react, Emn pulled the trigger. Laser light shot from the gun in a tight beam and entered Ran's skull. Silently, Emn counted in her head—*one, two, three*—and on the last count watched the skull suddenly bulge and then shatter. Brain matter splattered onto every available surface, including Emn. Jagged skull fragments dropped at her feet, irregularly sized and deep violet. Emn kicked at one with her toe, and watched it skitter over the floor before careening off the wall.

"Risalians don't control me anymore," she said to the bits of skull as she stuck the crook of the gun into the front bib of her dress and walked out the open door. "I can save everyone on my own."

Chapter 15: Neek

Today's top news story—debris from a Minoran ship of unknown class was found adrift just outside the Callis Wormhole. Investigators at the scene told our reporters that the ship was likely battered by a comet's tail. Hull fragments showed characteristic large impact abrasions, and portions appear to be melted, possibly due to an internal fire on the ship. No survivors have been found. Our hearts go out to all the families affected by this tragic accident.

—Broadcast from *The Galactic News*, October 22nd, 2060 CE

She was still alive. Still alive and wearing all her original clothing. Pleased that at least she had those things going for her, Neek opened her eyes. The first thing she saw was a smooth, white ceiling crisscrossed with andal saplings. She spread her fingers out in wide arcs at her sides and then pulled them into her palm, gathering the fabric underneath. It was soft, drawing the *stuk* from her fingertips and absorbing it so her body didn't become sticky when she rolled.

"I hate hospitals," Neek muttered to herself. After sitting up, she swung her legs to the side and stood. Several loud beeps rang out from a monitor next to her bed, and then the room returned to silence.

Neek peered at the monitor's readings, tapping at the screen jutting from the top. The image on the screen contained her bio stats—heart rate, blood pressure, brain activity, and *stuk* production rate. She was healthy, judging by the numbers, and her stomach didn't hurt anymore, which left the question of why she was in a hospital room to begin with.

"Hello?" she called loudly. "Is anyone around?" Neek noted the three additional beds and the small lavatory off to the side, all untouched and clean. That didn't bode well.

"Hey! What do you do for food around here?" she called out again, raising her voice.

"You wait until it is served." Neek whirled around quickly as the president entered through a hidden opening in the far wall. Behind him trailed the Ardulan woman in a yellow dress, her hair braided down her back.

Neek blinked several times, trying to make sense of the apparition. "You..." she stammered, attempting to make eye contact with the woman. "You look so much like Emn." The dress, the hair, the way she stood just a little off balance, the way her hands didn't fidget at her sides...Neek shivered.

"She's a cousin of some form, from what I understand, but that's beside the point," the president responded. "She *is* Emn, for all practical purposes. Freshly emerged into her second *don* and ready to return to her humble home." The president tapped the woman on the shoulder, and she took several steps towards Neek. When she was an arm's length away, she stopped and nodded her head once in apparent deference. Again, Neek tried to catch the woman's gaze, but the Ardulan's stare seemed to go through her instead of registering Neek's presence. She'd seen those eyes before, on Emn in the dreamscape. Not dead eyes, but eyes that didn't process sensory information in the same way as most. At least, that's what she had assumed about Emn. Whether this Ardulan had similar mental capacities to the girl, Neek didn't know.

"You expect me to, what?" Neek asked, pulling her eyes from the woman. "Just forget the real Emn and go around introducing our planet to a substitute?" Neek took a step towards the president, her hands balling into dripping fists. "You can't possibly expect that to happen. At no point in our delightful history together have I ever gone along with one of your ideas. I wouldn't be quiet ten years ago, and I won't now. The entire planet needs to hear about you—about the Risalians and the Ardulans. You have no right to keep it from them."

The president's eyes grew cold as he clasped his hands behind his back. He took a step towards the Ardulan while considering Neek with detached scorn. "What I would prefer would be to dispose of you in a convenient accident, ship your Terran friends off-world with their shiny new ship, and personally guide our young Ardulan around Neek. However, as my cabinet pointed out, there is a certain poetry to including you in the equation." The president cupped the backside of the Ardulan and gave it a hard squeeze. The woman did not respond.

"You're disgusting," Neek spat, slapping his hand away. The president caught her by the wrist and held tightly, pressing until pain shot up Neek's arm, and then released her. She pulled back, rubbing her wrist and letting colorful images of the president in uncomfortable positions dance in her mind.

"You *know* Ardulum is a fairy tale, yet you insist on perpetuating a lie to keep our planet isolated." Neek spat at the president's feet and suppressed the desire to punch him.

The president brushed a hand down the side of the Ardulan's dress, straightening a wrinkle. "Exile, what I do or do not know about Ardulum does not concern you. I'll not have this planet further under Risalian control, and if the only way to keep our people on-world and to keep our technology unaltered is by working within the Neek belief structure, then that is what I will do."

He looked back at Neek, a small smile creeping up his cheeks, and ran a *stuk*-covered fingertip down the Ardulan's spine, pausing at the base. Neek shivered. She could feel that finger, its slippery unwelcome touch a memory she had tried hard to forget.

"Now you, Exile, have a choice to make. Option one: take Emn here back to the home we've assigned you. I've seen to it that the travel restriction is lifted from your area. You'll be provided with a small planetwide transport ship that can take you anywhere on Neek. Take Emn around. Show her off. Talk to people about how she came to be with you." The president paused, his tone dropping. "Rather, tell them about how you found the young Emn, and how suddenly she entered into metamorphosis upon reaching Neek. How you waited patiently these six days until she emerged as this lovely creature we have standing before us now. How you don't know why her metamorphosis was so short, but how you always knew those old texts couldn't be *all* right. Vindicate yourself a little. Show the world that charming smugness. Most importantly, tell everyone how you're doing everything you can to teach her about Neek so she can begin teaching us again, just like her ancestors did."

Neek had been eighteen the last time she and the president had had a conversation like this. She'd hacked into government records and been caught. There had been an official investigation. A formal envoy had come to her house. Her uncle had been called, her parents talked to. The president had given her a choice. That time she'd been able to buy herself another year on Neek with lies and caution. At nineteen, the president had exiled her indefinitely. This time...

She shuddered at the memories. "You can't be serious."

"Deadly serious," the president responded. "I won't play around with banishment anymore. You will cooperate, or I will end your life here, now, in this medical bay." He leaned in. "Now's your chance to make up for past offenses and do something good for your planet. That *is* what you always worked towards, isn't it? The best for our planet Neek? The best for your family? Here is your chance. Be the guide to our new savior and remove the stain you placed on your family in the process." The president's smile broadened, dimples pocking his fleshy face. "I'll even throw in a settee. Not crimson, of course, but close enough for you to feel comfortable."

The hook. She'd been waiting for it, knew it would be something she'd find nearly impossible to turn down, but this time the president had misjudged her. As much as Neek longed to step inside a settee—to place her fingers around a yoke built for Neek biology and skim through clouds as if she were born amongst them—that wasn't why she had come back. She allowed herself a moment, however, to imagine herself finally inside a crimson ship...before the image of Emn superimposed on it. Behind that image stood her three parents, her brother, and her childhood home.

"I will not lie to my people," Neek breathed. Her eyes darted up and around, searching the room for exit points. "If you kill me, who guides this Ardulan around? Your presence wouldn't have the same impact as mine."

"No," the president conceded as he produced a small gun from his belt and pointed it at Neek's midsection. "But your uncle's might. The high priest carries a lot of weight, even in these modern times. The death of his niece is sure to cause him sadness. He can find solace in our young god."

Alarmed that the president would even have a gun, Neek raised her palms in front of her torso and took a step back. "No. You cannot have the highest religious leader on our planet give credence to this...this *deception*." Neek pointed at the woman. "She is *not* an Ardulan! The Risalians made her *in a lab*. The planet will stagnate completely if my uncle gets ahold of her. He will shut down science on this world. We will revert to *nothing*."

"Then be her guide. Help moderate her influence on your people." There was a pause. Then, in a lower tone, the president added, "Get your ship."

Neek exhaled through gritted teeth and considered. She looked at the Ardulan woman, noting the slight ruffling on the bottom hem of the dress, the gentle reliefs of andal leaves embroidered in yellow stitching. The forced air in the hospital room moved her own hair, tossed wisps of tangerine about the president's head, but left the Ardulan woman untouched, her hair firmly in place. Her eyes remained unfocused, unmoving.

Her uncle, as well-intentioned as he was, would destroy the Neek people with an Ardulan at his side. But the alternative—her leading around this new Emn, lying, pushing her people away from the progress they were trying so hard to make despite this ethereal shadow of a sentient... She couldn't do it. She couldn't let the real Emn remain with the Risalians, either. The Neek would still be alive, even if not moving forward, if the Ardulan went with her uncle. Neek herself—she would die if she did what the president asked. She wouldn't be able to live. She wouldn't want to live. If she died now, by the president's hand, she knew Yorden and Nicholas would pursue Emn and rescue her. There was only one choice to make.

"I won't participate in your games." Neek tried to muster as much confidence as she could. "I choose death."

The president's eyes widened, and he took a step forward. The gun moved higher, until the tip pointed right at Neek's nose. "You're sure about this? The thought of me parading around our Ardulan here with absolute control—that doesn't bother you?"

"Not as much as misleading my entire race." She held the president's gaze and tensed her muscles. Could she juke fast enough to avoid the laser? Did she have anything to lose by trying?

Making a snap decision, Neek dropped into a crouch and rammed her head into the president's midsection. As he fell backwards, the small gun fired with a soft *pop* and released a flurry of white powder. The shot, barely concentrated, sped towards Neek's head and smelled like...sugar?

Startled, Neek stopped in her tracks. Was the Ardulan woman protecting her, or was she protecting herself?

The president recovered quickly. Jumping to his feet, he leveled the gun back at Neek's head and fired again. This time, a small wisp of smoke curled out from the tip before the plume of powder shot out. "Stupid collectibles," he muttered as he brought the gun back in and flipped open the protective outer case, inspecting the mechanisms inside.

Taking advantage of the distraction, Neek planted a hit on the president's ankle with a booted heel. This time, the blow was enough to collapse the man, who shrieked in pain as he crumbled. Neek kicked the dropped gun under the far bed and grabbed the Ardulan woman by the arm. She paused momentarily, startled by the lack of connection at their touch.

"Time to move!" she ordered, pulling the woman behind her as she exited the room. She could spend time figuring out mental connections later.

Neek quickly scanned both left and right. The corridor was white and neither side bore any descriptive markings. Discounting the whimpers behind her, it was quiet, and although the passage stretched indefinitely in either direction, Neek couldn't see any other living beings. *What sort of moron doesn't bring guards?* she wondered as she picked left and pulled the woman down the deserted hallway. Several meters behind, she could hear the loud footsteps of the president running after them.

"Stupid Neek architecture," she cursed her voice irritated. "I never liked the whole hidden door concept. We have to find an exit or at least another corridor." Without breaking stride, Neek looked at the Ardulan. Unseeing green eyes bored straight ahead. Her bare feet thumped rhythmically on the floor as she kept pace with Neek, and her breathing stayed calm even as Neek's became ragged from the exertion.

"I don't suppose you have any idea how to get out of here?" Neek asked between breaths.

The Ardulan gave no response.

"Never hurts to ask," Neek said, sighing.

Ahead, the hallway began to curve gradually to the right. Before following the bend, Neek took the opportunity to glance back over her shoulder. She had just enough time to register the president and his gun before another bullet ripped from the shaft. Neek caught a quick jerk of the Ardulan's head out of the corner of her eye. The man screamed, the sound echoing through Neek's ears as the bullet entered her left eye socket and tore through her brain.

Everything went black.

CHAPTER 16: RISALIAN CUTTER 77

And in our final news story of the evening—parents will want to make sure their young ones are tucked in bed before listening—a new correctional institute has been approved for construction by the Oorin government, in the outskirts of the Callis System. Oorin President Gtwyn stated that the institute was completely unrelated to the sudden spike in petty crime within the Callis System. President Gtwyn could not be reached for comment.

—Excerpt from a network broadcast within the Charted Systems, October 22nd, 2060 CE

Emn's bare feet smacked against the familiar porous metal as she ran down the deserted hallway. The bruise on her cheek stung, one of her eyes was swollen shut, and she kept stumbling, the gun threatening to spill from the front of her dress each time. Finally, she placed a protective hand across the weapon, enjoying the sudden sense of security.

With her depth perception impaired, Emn failed to see the protruding column as she turned a tight corner. She hit it face-first and fell onto her back. As tears welled up in her eyes, she braced herself on the cold floor and put her free hand to her nose. Gingerly patting it, she noted that it hadn't broken.

Have to get off this ship, she muttered angrily in her mind. She took a deep breath and tried to go inside her mind to fix the damage, but she simply didn't have the energy.

Shakily, Emn pulled herself back onto her feet. *I need a ship,* she reasoned. *If I can get a ship, I can leave and find* Mercy's Pledge. *I can rescue Neek.* She cocked her head to the side as she considered how she might accomplish that task.

Cutters carried numerous smaller ships. Neek had taught her about big ships and small ships. The little ones would be easier to fly; hopefully, they were similar enough to the *Pledge* that the transition would be intuitive. She just needed to find one, preferably without any Risalians around.

Emn began to tiptoe down the hallway, concern growing that she had not yet encountered any Risalians. A fresh scent of cooking andal mixed with the sickly sweet smell of gray matter and blood on her dress, making the journey that much more unpleasant. Small parts of the Risalian's shattered head had also adhered to her skin and hair, and when Emn reached out to steady herself against a bulkhead, the residue stuck lightly to the surface.

Gross.

Emn pulled her hand away and bent down, wiping the sticky remains on her dress. Once her hand was somewhat clean, she stood back up and stepped just to the left, placing her hand on a fresh area of the bulkhead.

The gentle vibration of the ship ran along her arm, and Emn's thoughts briefly jumped to her mother—to a memory of sleeping next to her with one side of her body pressed tight against the mesh, feeling the pulse of the ship lull her to sleep. Her body relaxed, but the smell of cooking andal persisted.

If she could find food, she'd have a better chance of fending off Risalians. Did Risalians eat andal, too? It was possible, she supposed, since Yorden said they transported andal trees a lot. She could start by finding a mess hall, but that would require a map. A map was likely to be inside a room, which meant she had to open a door.

She removed her hand from the bulkhead and scanned the hallway. It was still empty and quiet. The lighting was bright and harsh and focused over a doorway three meters ahead on her right. *Rooms have Risalians,* she reminded herself. *But I have a gun.*

Emn stepped towards the door and paused just before it, considering her options. She knew it was unlikely that her isolation in the hallway would continue—eventually, she would need to find cover. Without extensive energy reserves, she couldn't readily defend herself and certainly couldn't sync with the ship. That meant she had no way of knowing where she was going, and she couldn't read any of the Risalian scripts near the doors, which might indicate what lay behind them. She would have to go inside somewhere, find a quiet corner, and begin manipulating cellulose. Now seemed like as good a time as any.

Emn reached for the handle. The door opened easily as it was pulled open from the other side. Not expecting the lack of resistance, Emn stumbled forward into a gray-tunic Risalian, who reached out to steady her.

"Hey, everyone," xe called out in Common towards several tables. The Risalians all looked up immediately, their dinners forgotten. "Did someone let the Ardulan out for a walk?"

"Probably wandered off," one answered from the back of the room. "Go take her back to the holding area."

"Aren't there supposed to be Dulan fields around those cells?" another asked.

The Risalian holding Emn looked down at her. She stared back defiantly through her good eye, only for the Risalian's gaze to fall from her face to the gun handle hanging from her dress front. Emn realized suddenly that it would be very unusual for an Ardulan to have a gun.

"I got lost," she said, trying to sound scared. "Can you help me get back?"

Off to Emn's right, an eating utensil clattered to the floor. There were several coughs, a chair tipping over, and then silence. Every Risalian was staring directly at her, food forgotten. Ardulans didn't talk. She probably should have remembered that.

"That thing just spoke," one said.

Hir table companion, a slightly taller Risalian with pale blue skin, smacked the other on the shoulder. "She has a gun. Clearly something has gone wrong."

The Risalian Emn had bumped into took a few steps back, hands raised in front of hir face. "Look, girl, why don't you give me that gun, and we'll walk you back to your room, okay?"

They're afraid of me, she thought with satisfaction. *But there are a lot of them. Too many to shoot. I have to be smart.*

Emn chanced a quick look around. There were four energy ports, all located near the food service area, and all bordered by metal mesh. She could see the cellulose coursing over the surface, sparkling dimly in the light. It had a heavy enough concentration to give her a substantial boost without having to spend excessive amounts of time harvesting strands. The closest port was only a few steps away, but a Risalian stood between her and her goal.

Emn opened her good eye wide and slowly pulled the gun from her dress. She offered it to the Risalian on small, open palms. Xe took it gingerly, with only two fingers, as if Emn had poisoned it somehow. Emn suppressed a giggle. The only things on the gun were the remains of another Risalian.

"There now," the gray-tunic Risalian said as xe holstered the gun on hir side, locking it in place. "How did you get this?"

"Don't know. The shimmery thing went away. No one came. I walked outside to find someone, but no one was there. The black thing was in a locker near the room. I didn't know what it was, so I took it."

The Risalian eyed Emn skeptically, hir eyes drawn to the dried blood. Emn watched as hir neck slits bloomed to lilac.

"Hey, Aarn," another Risalian called from the back of the galley. "Why don't you just take her to Captain Ran? I'm sure the captain can sort it all out. Above our rank, you know."

Aarn turned around to face the seated Risalians. Emn watched the back of Aarn's neck phase from lilac to lavender and then slowly creep to violet. "Don't any of you think it's kind of strange though…? She's *talking*. She's wearing *clothes*. It's like she's…like she's an adult, you know. Not like an Ardulan at all." Aarn's voice lowered. "It's like she's sentient."

Emn took the opportunity to pretend to lose her balance, inching a step closer to the port.

Some of the Risalians shifted uncomfortably in their seats, and a low murmuring began. "Your examination score doesn't qualify you to ask those questions," another Risalian called out. "Just shut up and take her back. Markin'll send you to a reeducation center so fast your slits won't have time to color if they find out otherwise, I'll bet."

Aarn's neck was almost black as xe turned back to Emn. The girl kept her eyes wide, her face confused.

"Yeah. I heard what happened to Captain Ran." Aarn gestured to the door. "C'mon, girl," xe said in a kind voice. "Why don't we take you back before anyone finds out you're missing." Xe offered hir hand to Emn.

Emn had to make a decision. She was a solid lunge away from the port and thought perhaps she could avoid the Risalian with an unexpected bolt. However, the kindness in the Risalian's words tugged at her. A part of her wanted to take Aarn's hand—have Aarn tell her that things would be fine.

She blinked a few times and realized Aarn was looking at her quizzically. "Everything all right there, little Ardulan?" xe asked.

Emn reached her hand out, fingers just touching Aarn's, when another utensil clattered to the floor. She startled as an image of her mother's skull—and then the dead Risalian's—flashed across her vision.

Risalians couldn't be trusted. Risalians would kill her, and they would kill Neek. Resolute, she batted Aarn's hand away and lunged for the port. Emn thumped against the ground as her lunge came up several meters short and then scrambled onto her hands and knees, closing the distance. She launched her fists at the port, crashing against the wall in a bruising impact. Crystalline cellulose chains stopped their movements, and Emn targeted the closest ones, pulling them into thick cords. Bonds formed. Energy began to flow into her, and the lights in the mess dimmed as Emn rerouted the cellulose from the systems nearest her. Emn dove deeper into the systems, pulling and coiling every piece of cellulose she could find.

Chaos immediately erupted. She opened her eyes as the energy flowed into her to see Aarn's face melt into concentrated anger. Guns appeared from holsters throughout the room, all pointing directly at Emn. One Risalian ran to the comm and began tapping the screen furiously.

Emn stayed glued to the wall. Guns remained trained on her. No one spoke or gave orders. *They're so scared,* she thought, amused, as more cellulose flooded to her. *No one is doing anything. So I'll do something.*

Emn closed her eyes briefly and focused on healing her wounds—the swollen eye and the gashes on her face and arm all disappeared. Walls began to buckle. The ceiling bowed, and the lights went out for good.

"The first commands that she not be harmed!" a voice called out from the comm station. Emn looked towards the sound but found it hard to see. The starlight from the window was poor illumination.

"Does the first have a suggested course of action?" Aarn shot back. "The girl is *glowing.*"

Emn looked down at herself. There did seem to be a lot more light near her than anywhere else—which was funny, because she didn't know what was causing it.

The comm buzzed. "We're to contain her until backup arrives. A team is on its way."

Aarn turned back to Emn, hir voice soothing. "How about we all just stay calm? No need to do anything foolish."

"I'm not going to do anything foolish." Cellulose was swarming her now, the pieces she had not yet bound coating her very skin. Unnerved, Emn pushed at them, trying to make them back off, but it only pushed strands into one another. The cellulose coiled faster, forming bonds more quickly than Emn could detail. Energy coursed through Emn's body and sizzled from her hair and feet. She felt the capillaries under her skin begin to burst, the energy too much for them to carry. The room began to grow warm, and the vibration of the ship slowed and then stopped altogether. They were no longer moving.

"Stop it." Aarn pointed the gun at Emn's feet. "Or we will shoot you."

"No," Emn replied as calmly as she could. She stood up and began walking towards the door. The port was no longer of use to her. She'd sent her commands throughout the ship, and the cellulose was speeding to her from bow to stern—following her like little ducks, snapping as they neared her body.

Aarn took a deep breath and fired a warning shot that went straight towards Emn's heels. She watched the shot connect with her feet and felt a tingling as the cellulose from the laser bound to the loose strands that surrounded her, feeding into her energy pool.

Emn smiled. That was unexpected. Aarn's mouth hung agape, and xe dropped the gun, standing transfixed and motionless.

Emn wasn't sure who fired the next shot, but suddenly multiple blasts were singing through the air. Smoke began to fill the room from the discharge, and a burnt metal smell assaulted Emn's nostrils. She took a step back and watched with growing curiosity as the shots were absorbed upon impact, one right after the other.

Ping. A beam hit her hip. *Ping ping.* Two hit her shoulder. Another four crashed into her chest. Emn wobbled on her feet, the force of multiple blows throwing off her balance. Formed microfibrils now surrounded her so thickly that she was having a hard time seeing. Emn tried to continue towards the door, but each new shot shoved her slightly in another direction. Her mind hurt from the strain of holding it all together—the formed and free cellulose and the mass of energy circling her. The strands from the ship kept coming, and the laser shots were incessant. The energy swamped her system and threatened to overwhelm her. She wasn't quite sure what would happen if she lost control.

Pushing some of the extra energy into her legs, Emn tried to sprint to the door. Another gunshot caught her in the back and propelled her farther, slamming her small body against the doorjamb. Something sparked off the metal as Emn tried to right herself. She couldn't feel her legs.

Emn whimpered. She knew where she needed to go—her connection to the port had allowed her access to the ship's schematic. As the bolts continued to sizzle against her, it was becoming increasingly apparent that she wasn't going to make it. Frantic, Emn dropped to her knees and tried to establish a connection to Neek. She was far away, Emn knew, but with so much energy at her disposal, it certainly seemed possible. She didn't have anything to lose.

Neek! Emn screamed into her own head. She pushed the thought as far as she could, using the continued energy inputs from the guns to propel the message out—out of herself, out of the ship to...she didn't know where. She shot the message in every direction, amplifying it with as much energy as she could gather. *Neek, I don't know what to do!*

No response came. Emn hadn't expected one, not really, but she realized then that Neek wasn't anywhere. The lingering presence Emn had come to expect in the back of her mind was gone. She'd not even noticed it leaving.

Emn was vaguely aware of voices around her; some close—some far. She continued to smell burnt metal as the laser fire diminished and finally stopped. Had someone else come into the room? Her vision was so fuzzy that she couldn't tell. All she felt was the energy current. All she saw was a haze of cellulose, spinning into a thick shroud. Emn tried to gather the energy and strands together around her, but tendrils kept whipping off, bleeding into the air and disappearing.

A jolt to her physical body shook her out of her mind and brought her back to the present. Hands were trying to grab her and were drawing back with pained hisses. Nevertheless, the Risalians were persistent, clutching and dragging her back into the hallway in short bursts. Through her clouded vision, Emn realized in what direction they were headed: back to the cell. She panicked, the control she maintained over the wild energy surrounding her wavering. She had to get rid of the excess energy. It would rip her body apart, or possibly her mind, if she kept trying to maintain control. There was more cellulose on the ship than she had anticipated—more strands arriving each second.

Terrified at what losing control of the power would mean, Emn did the only thing she could think of. She focused, took a deep breath, and pushed as hard as she could, sending the energy and cellulose away from her small form. She sent it to the place where Neek's presence used to linger in her mind. The pilot could use the energy, surely. It would heal the stomach wound Emn had caused. Make everything right again. Maybe.

The current snapped and hissed from around her body and then shot out in waves. Emn watched with detached fascination as the white current sizzled along the curling metal of bulkheads, over the broken floor, and below the buckled ceiling, passing through the crumbling metal of the ship's confines.

Neek! she screamed into her head. *Neek! Neek, where are you?*

Eyelids heavy and ears ringing, she processed the smell of burning wood and, just underneath it, seared flesh. No matter how loudly she yelled, or how much energy she pushed into a seemingly endless abyss, she still couldn't find Neek. She was too tired to keep trying, the smoke around her too thick to breathe.

Emn gave in and let her consciousness slip away, the scent of burning skin following her into darkness.

CHAPTER 17: NEEK

"...confirmed. Repeat, our news team has confirmed that fifteen ships of unknown origin were spotted entering the Callis Wormhole. Their exit point is unknown. All species of the Charted Systems are urged to remain calm and report any incidents of unusual activity to the nearest Risalian peace force.

—Network broadcast within the Charted Systems, October 23rd, 2060 CE

The Ardulan stared at the dead woman in front of her. Medics moved around purposefully, inspecting charts, muttering to themselves, and occasionally lifting the black cloth to peer at the body underneath. While watching, she processed the antiseptic smell of the room and the dull yellow lighting that reflected off the polished wood surfaces. She felt the texture of the chair she sat on, cool and smooth. The impressions filtered into her mind and back out, barely registering.

There was a thought in the back of her mind, playing around the edges. She couldn't remember how the Neek woman had died, or how they had both ended up in the room. The woman seemed like she might be familiar—the image of her face just beyond her grasp. Instead, swirling fog filled her mind's eye and chased the feeling into the far recesses of her mind.

No instructions had been given, so the Ardulan sat patiently as she'd been taught. *Sit. Do nothing. Wait for instructions.* Words she understood in Common and Risalian. Now, for some unknown reason, her hands moved, fingertips sliding over the fabric of the dress. Even the smell of the room, which hurt her nose, was taken in and assessed. However fleeting, her senses were open, aware, and processing the sensory information as it became available.

A new medic entered then—a large one with pale skin and unruly brown hair barely contained under a surgeon's hat. A younger medic followed, covered from head to toe in scrubs without a single centimeter of skin showing. The bigger one handed a small, round chip to a doctor, who played a recording in a far corner outside the woman's field of view. He returned shortly, nodded at the big medic, gathered several instruments, and, motioning for his colleagues to follow, left the room.

"Whew!" a youthful voice murmured from underneath swaths of material after the last of the original medics left. The woman watched as white cloth was pulled away, revealing dark brown skin, brown eyes, and curly hair. The bigger man did the same, revealing more unruly brown curls and a wide smile.

"Hello," the large man said gently, making his way over the woman. "My name is Captain Yorden Kuebrich, of *Mercy's Pledge*. This is Nicholas St. John, my, uh, gunner."

The young man's posture straightened.

"We don't mean you any harm. We've gone to a great deal of trouble to break into this facility, and I'm afraid we're a little short on time. Maybe you could help us. We're looking for a friend—a tall woman with sort of blonde-red hair and green eyes. Copper skin. Strong temperament. We think she might be somewhere nearby." Yorden paused and looked quizzically at the woman. "Do you understand what I am saying?" He looked at her dress and then at her Talent markings through the opening in the side. His face clouded. "Ardulans everywhere now, apparently," the captain muttered.

The woman's eyes remained pointed straight ahead, unblinking. She nodded in assent and listened carefully.

"She looks like Emn," Nicholas breathed, cautiously taking a few steps closer to the woman. "Same dress and everything." The youth also looked at the opening in her dress and whistled. "Aggression Talent? Myth angle isn't working out so well, is it?"

"The *Pledge*'s sensors picked up engine residue consistent with Risalian transports when we flew here." The captain's eyes scoured the woman's face. "Chances are she's another construct. Neek should be able to help us sort it out when we find her."

"That'd explain the tattoos then, but not why Risalians are constructing Neek gods."

Yorden considered the woman again. "You understand Common?"

The woman nodded again.

"The woman I described, have you seen her?"

The woman shook her head. There were no faces in her mind, just the smells of the room, the brightness of the lights, and her perception of the weapons the two men had brought with them.

"Worth a shot." Yorden gestured to Nicholas. "You are admittedly better with cellulosic technology than I am. See if you can't log onto the computer system from the medical comm and find our Neek's whereabouts."

She watched the smaller man turn, head for the computer, and then sidestep to the table where the dead Neek lay. He hesitated but then peered under the sheet. When he turned around, his posture was rigid, his face ashen.

"Look at dead bodies later," the captain barked. "We have a job to do, remember?"

"I think you should look, Captain."

Scowling, Yorden took a quick step and ripped the sheet away. Underneath lay the Neek, her face a mass of tissue. One side remained intact, the expression frozen in surprise. The other half was scorched black, the dull light of the morgue glinting off the exposed yellow skull.

Nicholas jerked quickly away, and the Ardulan processed the sounds of stifled retching. Yorden's expression hardened as his face paled. He didn't speak. Instead, Yorden took one of the Neek's limp hands and remained silent, staring down at the body. After nearly a minute, he replaced the cloth over the Neek's face and scooped the body up into his arms.

"Come on, Nicholas," he called out dully as he moved towards the doorway. "Let's get out of here."

"These things don't happen in the Systems," Nicholas said softly to himself. "I thought you both had a plan. This wasn't supposed to happen."

Yorden paused and turned around, eyes blank. "Sometimes plans don't work," he said simply, his voice strained. "Right now we have to leave. With Neek...with our Neek dead, we have to find Emn. It's what she would want, what we discussed. Right now, our best course of action is to head back to the ship. We can regroup and figure out our plan from there."

Nicholas nodded and fell in step behind Yorden. The woman watched them pass through the doorway and realized she *wanted*. She wanted them to stay.

As the men moved just outside her vision, Nicholas turned back and addressed her again. "You didn't see her, did you? A little girl in a yellow dress, two triangle outlines under her eyes?"

She turned to look right at the smaller man. The girl in the yellow dress—that face she *did* remember. Even the fog in her mind couldn't obfuscate that image. She didn't know where the girl was, and she certainly couldn't communicate anything to the two men. Instead, she slowly shook her head.

"Thanks anyway," Nicholas said, smiling halfheartedly. He turned back and quickened his pace to catch up to Yorden, who was halfway down the hallway despite his struggle to balance the Neek's limp form in his arms.

The Ardulan woman watched as the two men carried the Neek out of the medical bay. She thought again about the girl. The feeling of *want* filled her. She wanted to see the girl, to help her. The two men—they also wanted to help the girl. Perhaps they would even find the girl.

The Ardulan noted that she could no longer see Yorden and Nicholas. She couldn't move without permission. The *want* persisted, even as the fog fought to block her perceptions and erase the girl's face from her mind. The woman realized that she could make a decision. She could decide to follow the men, to help them as she'd been trained. Perhaps they would be pleased. Perhaps they would let her see the girl when she was found.

The decision was quick. The woman struggled to hold onto the thin thread of her desire as she moved from the table to the doorway and continued to watch the men as they proceeded down the hallway. She took a step out of the door, intending to catch up, when something caught her eye. Tiny strands began to spark from the wood walls in time with Yorden's footfalls. At first they were sporadic and few, but they quickly increased in both frequency and magnitude. The woman watched, perplexed, as the sparking strands continued to generate and build, remaining lit and gathering with the others to form a thin tendril that wove against the bulkhead, following the two men.

Neek! she heard inside her head. It was a call from the girl in the yellow dress. A call for the dead woman. *Neek, I don't know what to do!*

The Ardulan stepped from the doorway and broke into a run, years of caution and training abandoned due to an impulse she couldn't explain. She didn't care about her orders, or that she was directly defying something she had been told to do. She cared about the girl. She cared about that strand and the voice behind it.

Her footfalls were loud on the floor as she ran. The men turned around at the sound, and Yorden stumbled, the Neek's body threatening to slip from his grasp.

"Quiet!" he hissed as the woman drew up towards them. "We didn't plan a loud rescue, just a well-timed, stealthy one. Stop drawing attention to our location."

Breathing hard from the exertion, the woman pointed at the arcing strand, still lazily weaving across the wall.

"What's she pointing at?" Nicholas asked in confusion.

"Damned if I know," Yorden responded impatiently. "Look, if you want to come, fine. I don't think the Neek government can get any more upset with us than they already are. But we have to *move*. Security will make a pass in another forty-five seconds, and we have to be back in the hangar bay before then."

The woman nodded but continued to stare at the strand, transfixed.

"Right then," Yorden grumbled as he turned back and broke into a light jog. "Let's get moving."

The woman matched their pace, and the strand followed along, always parallel with Yorden and growing steadily in size. The Ardulan's pulse raced. The girl's voice still rang in her head. *Neek! Neek, where are you?* The hair on the woman's arm rose. She blinked. Something exciting was coming. Something new. Something old. Something powerful.

Removing her gaze from the strand, the woman continued to trail the men as they rounded the final corner into the hangar bay. There, they encountered their first heaven guards, and Yorden halted them abruptly.

"Shit," the captain murmured under his breath. "They weren't supposed to be off lunch yet."

Nicholas placed his hand on the hilt of the containment rifle that the woman saw bulging in his pants pocket. "What do you want to do, Captain?" he asked in a hushed voice. "They haven't noticed us yet. They're too busy doing whatever over at that energy port."

Yorden didn't have a chance to answer. Alarm klaxons began blaring throughout the hangar. The guards spotted the three standing awkwardly in the entryway.

"The Terrans. They've got Emn with them!"

The guards broke into a run and pulled out their weapons, aiming straight at Yorden. The Ardulan watched the men, curious as to what they would do.

"To the ship!" Yorden bellowed. He sprinted to the far corner of the bay where a dilapidated ship was docked behind a skiff. Nicholas followed quickly behind.

The Ardulan stood her ground, concentrating on the weapons. Weapons were easy. Weapons were simple. The beings she'd chosen to be her new masters were in danger. There was weaponry present. She could help.

The woman sank deep inside her mind. She checked her small energy reserves and then refocused outwards. The crew shot at her new masters—one, two, three—four times in quick succession. The bullets flattened and fell short of their targets. She reached out and pulled at the disordered cellulose in the gun matrices, collapsing all the weapons into perfect balls.

Surprised, the guards pulled back, the metal falling with loud *pangs* onto the floor. Pleased at how easily the threat had been neutralized, she looked around for the girl's strand. The klaxon continued to blare loudly, the sound assaulting her ears as she searched.

When her eyes settled back on Yorden, she noticed that the energy was a strand no longer. In the moments she had let her mind focus on the weapons, the strand had spread into a wave that, with a loud burst of static, crashed over the Neek's body and stayed there. Pulsing, it slowly absorbed into the Neek's skin. The woman tried to follow the wave as it entered the body, but her mind became fuzzy. She was not of Science. Bodies were too hard to focus upon.

The klaxon silenced. The air stilled. She watched the guards split into two groups—the first running to the comm system and the second to the weapons storage locker. The woman heard Yorden utter a curse as strands hopped from Neek's limp body onto the captain, causing him to stumble. As his arm hair began to singe, Yorden dropped the Neek unceremoniously to the floor.

"Captain!" Nicholas called out.

The woman noticed that the black cloth had fallen from the Neek's legs when Yorden dropped her. Her bare legs glowed with a halo of white. They jerked back and forth and then stilled as the strand wrapped around her torso and head, causing each area to spasm.

"What is going on?" Nicholas begged.

"I don't know," Yorden replied, his eyes dark. "It was like getting a hand caught in an electric fence. Except instead of a hand, it was my whole body."

Nicholas looked around. "Any idea where it came from?"

"Damned if I know."

The Ardulan woman could see strands hopping in and out of Neek's skin, coursing along veins and massing near the giant hole in her face. Another Ardulan was healing her. That was strange, because she couldn't feel another around her. The little girl should have been too far away to carry out such a task.

"I can't carry her like that," Yorden said, his voice low. The captain glanced back at the Ardulan woman, and she returned the stare, awaiting an order.

"If they come back with knives, Captain, I don't think she can help us," Nicholas said urgently. "I read parts of the old Neek texts while we were at the house. Those marks on her side indicate she's an Aggression Talent, and knives, even though they're weapons, are supposed to be part of the Science Talent. Aggression Talents work on weapons with moving parts. I think. That or they actually have to be considered weapons and not tools."

"Then run, Nicholas," Yorden ordered, turning and pushing the youth towards the ship. "Run and fly the ship out of here. Take the Ardulan with you. No one else needs to die here today."

Nicholas stood his ground. "If you won't leave Neek's body, then I won't either."

"You're an idiot," the captain responded gruffly.

Unsure if Yorden had given her an order, the woman moved to stand next to him anyway.

"Orders, Captain?" Nicholas breathed.

"Don't die," Yorden snapped.

The hangar door opened and twenty heavily armored heaven guards entered the room, all brandishing long knives. Their leader, a short woman with close-cropped, cinnamon hair, carried a Dulan knife. The

Ardulan shuddered despite her conditioning as the hangar lights reflected off the dark material. The knife was something she knew, although she wished she didn't.

"Drop your weapons and step away from the Ardulan," the short Neek commanded.

Yorden merely snarled in response. Nicholas tensed and took a step forward, but he fell to the ground when one of Neek's prone legs jolted and kicked the back of his calf.

"You desecrate our dead," the leader snarled. "You try to abduct our Ardulan. You will now be killed for your intolerable actions."

"So we have no reason to lay down our weapons," Yorden quipped, his tone calm.

"Emn," the leader said gently, turning to the Ardulan. "Come away from them. You're not in danger anymore. They can't hurt you. Come back, and we will protect you from the off-worlders."

The Ardulan remained where she was. She'd made a choice, and it had stopped the funny feeling in her stomach. She would not move from the body and the strands that surrounded it. The strands belonged to the girl, and the girl was important. Focusing on the strands helped clear the fog, and the situation was plain. Her new masters were in terrible danger, as was she. They needed to escape.

When the Ardulan didn't respond, the leader motioned to her subordinates. "Those of you around Emn, sheath your blades. If the others resist, kill them. Don't lay your hands on the Ardulan."

A tighter circle formed around Yorden and his group. The Ardulan ignored them, the whipping current around the body suddenly increasing in intensity and recapturing her full attention. She made another decision. Slowly and deliberately, so as to not provoke the Neek, she stepped over to the body and knelt onto the floor.

"Don't give them your gun, kid," she heard Yorden instruct. "They'll kill us one way or another. Better to go out fighting."

Nicholas harrumphed in assent. More armored Neek surrounded them, but their focus seemed to be only on the men.

"Bind their hands," she heard the short Neek command.

The Ardulan looked up to see Yorden brandish his gun.

"Do you want to lose your eye the same way the exile did?" the leader asked curtly. The captain nodded sideways at Nicholas, who drew his gun as well.

"Fine. Do it your way," the leader muttered. She gestured to the other Neek.

"Time to shine," Yorden said grimly. When the first Neek broke the circle and advanced on Yorden and Nicholas, the captain fired. The Ardulan grimaced at the loud sound, but the Neek were not deterred. They ran at Yorden and Nicholas, knives tucked close to their bodies.

Nicholas fired, caging them in a Dulan Field. Another three went down, the *puppuppup* of Yorden's deadlier riot rifle echoing in the hangar bay. By the second round of shots, the rest of the contingent had climbed over or around the bodies of their colleagues and were engaging Nicholas and Yorden directly, knives slicing through the air in their attempts to connect with soft flesh.

The Ardulan woman wanted to help protect her masters but was unsure how. The Dulan fields and knives she could do nothing with, and only Yorden seemed to be using a gun. Instead, she reached under the blanket and touched the Neek's skin. Jolts of energy snapped onto her fingertips. Without understanding why, she took both hands and laid them on Neek's cold arm, ignoring the shooting pain that threatened to make her lose her grip.

The connection was instantaneous. Strands pulsed through the Ardulan's body, pushing away the fog and clearing her mind. She felt things rearranging, snapping into place. Sounds, smells, colors—everything deepened and intensified. She could feel the real Emn on the other end, afterimages of the child's panic and confusion a steady undercurrent to the energy.

There was something else there too...rather, there was some*one* else. Another consciousness swimming in the waves, trying to gain a foothold on...on her *body*. She watched in fascination as Emn's energy directed the strands inside Neek, repairing the tissue, connecting the blood vessels, and pulling and pushing with such force that the woman was overwhelmed with the sheer volume of tasks. Somehow, through all of that, the dead Neek's consciousness was tugged and guided and, finally, bound to the body by millions of shivering strands that raced in every direction.

It was too much. The woman drew her hands away and opened her eyes. As she did, her senses flooded. There were the sounds of the fight. Smells of body odor, metal, wood, and burning. She understood the sensory information—she contained it; she reveled in it. A smile crossed her lips for the first time.

The Ardulan remembered, then, why she was here, and the decisions she'd made. She looked down at the black sheet and saw Neek's legs grow still and the glow fade. This didn't seem right, so she tossed the blanket off Neek and ran her hands wildly over the body, hoping to find a lingering trace of energy.

The leader crashed to the ground next to the Ardulan, her arm bleeding. The Ardulan looked up, wary, but the guard's focus wasn't on her or her open wound. Instead, the Neek stared at the glowing body, her own form trembling.

Disinterested in the leader's discomfort, the Ardulan returned her attention to the Terrans' Neek. As the woman's gaze scanned the body, she finally brought herself to look at the head. Emn had finished her task. The Neek's face was whole. Her missing eye was back in its socket. The incidental burns from the impact area were gone as well. Her skin looked healthy. It even looked like she was breathing, and she watched the Neek's chest rise and fall in a slow rhythm.

The Ardulan turned back to the leader and watched the woman's face contort. Slowly, the leader's gaze turned to her, and she got to her knees in reverence.

"Praise," the guard murmured. "Praise to Ardulum. A miracle has occurred."

It took the Ardulan a moment to realize that the heaven guard was referring to her, thinking that *she* had somehow healed the broken body lying before her. It occurred to her then, for the first time, that the Neek did not treat her as the Risalians did. The Neek...the Neek revered her.

The thought made her head swim. When she tried to sort out just what that might mean, she again found herself distracted by the gunfire, slashing metal, and yelling in several languages. There were too many swinging arms to make out what was really going on, but it seemed like Nicholas and Yorden, or at least one of them, might still be still alive.

Could she help? She'd made the decision to do so once; making the same decision again didn't seem so difficult. With the fog gone, things seemed clear—crisper. Somehow everything in her world now seemed almost real.

Communication, however, was a problem. All the other beings had words and sounds. She had only movements. Perhaps the movements would be enough. With at least one Neek so intent upon her, it seemed plausible that a simple gesture might be understood.

She decided to try. The woman turned back to the leader and pointed to the fighting. Then she scowled and shook her head, miming disapproval.

"Everybody *stop!*" the leader yelled. The confused Neek halted midmovement, allowing Yorden to finish another volley of shots. Around Captain Yorden and Nicholas lay a pile of bodies—some frozen; some dead. Both humans were bleeding badly, Yorden down the side of his sliced shirt and back of his right thigh, and Nicholas from a knife embedded solidly just under the left side of his rib cage.

"Give up?" Yorden asked in a tired tone. Nicholas had squeezed his eyes shut and was holding his side. No one was paying either of the humans any attention. The heaven guards had dropped to their knees and were staring, first at the Ardulan, and then at the healed Neek.

"It's a miracle," the leader repeated. "She healed the exile. Now she's asked for the violence to stop." Her jaw hung agape. Several other Neek began praying and two Neek in the very back of the hanger started a hymn.

"To be healed by an Ardulan," someone whispered.

"To have the *exile* healed by an Ardulan," someone else responded. "She heals even those who scorn her."

"Captain," Nicholas whispered urgently. "Our Neek is…"

"Ugh," Neek groaned as she rolled over, her face a grimace of pain. The entire bay fell quiet. Nicholas's gun fell from his hands and clattered onto the floor.

"I feel like I was punched by a Nugel. Twice, in the eye." Neek rubbed her eyes and then opened them. The Ardulan smiled at Neek, whose expression slowly filled with a childish wonder.

"Neek!" Yorden yelled. "Holy *fuck*."

"Yeah," Neek managed. "Does someone want to tell me what is going on?"

The woman offered her hand and helped Neek into a sitting position. Neek rubbed her eyes again and then stretched her arms. "Funny," Neek said to the Ardulan. "I have a very distinct memory of the president firing a gun at my head."

"You were totally shot in the head, Neek!" Nicholas called out.

Neek swung around and took in the scene. The Ardulan assessed it as well. Kneeling Neek, frozen Neek, dead Neek, and the two humans bleeding in the middle of all of it.

"Guess I missed some fun," Neek commented dryly. Yorden managed a pained smile. "So if I was shot in the head, someone want to fill me in on why I'm on the cold floor of a hangar bay using both my eyes?"

"A miracle," the chief answered, her tone awed. "A miracle from Emn. Praise Ardulum!" The chanting rose up again from the kneeling Neek, their voices soft and melodious. The Ardulan woman stood awkwardly and looked to the humans, unsure what to do.

Neek eyed Yorden and Nicholas, before focusing on the Ardulan. "You?" she asked, her tone uncertain.

The woman shook her head. She tugged at her yellow dress and her braided hair.

"Emn?" Neek whispered incredulously. "But she...Aggression Talent... She's not even *here*."

The woman wasn't sure how to respond. The strands were gone, and so too was the girl's touch.

"Help me up?"

The Ardulan offered a hand, which Neek took. Leaning heavily on the Ardulan woman for support, she stood and addressed the guard. "My friends and I and Emn here—" Neek choked on the name. "—we need to go. We can't be here. I can't be here." She inclined her head towards the Ardulan. "It isn't safe for her here."

Yorden limped over and wrapped one of Neek's arms around his shoulders. "She chose us. You're on the wrong side."

The leader stood on shaking legs, and the other guards followed. She looked around, pausing on the dead bodies, the pools of blood, and the moaning wounded. "I don't understand," she whispered. She met the Ardulan's eyes then, her voice wavering. "We've always served. I don't understand why you have chosen the exile over the Heaven Guard, over our whole planet."

The Ardulan was confused. The Neek woman leaning on her seemed increasingly tense. The captain was turning a deathly pale, and Nicholas seemed to be battling unconsciousness. She didn't know how to explain about the little girl, about how she had to get to her. The Terrans needed a healer, but she didn't know how to ask for that, either.

"We need to get to our ship," Neek whispered into the Ardulan's ear. "We can find Emn with our ship."

That made sense. The girl was not on the planet. They'd need a ship to find her.

The Ardulan carefully transferred Neek's weight to Yorden. Taking several long, graceful steps, she crossed the distance to the leader. Bringing her hands together in a point, she moved them up over her head and then gestured at the Terrans and Neek.

"You want to leave?" the guard asked. "With them?"

She nodded.

The leader looked over her shoulder at the rest of the heaven guards. No one spoke, although the Ardulan could see wide eyes and shuffling feet.

"I...of course," the leader stammered. "Of course you can go. We just— We hoped you would stay."

Neek came forward then and took the Ardulan's hand. It was warm and made the Ardulan think of the little girl. She smiled.

"Oh, we'll be back. Promise." Neek grasped the sleeve of the leader's robe between two fingers, sliding across the green piping. After a moment, she tossed it aside and scoffed.

"Hard to believe how badly I wanted this. It's embarrassing." Neek looked the leader over and sniffed. "You want to protect Neek? Serve the Ardulans? Come with me. I think I might know how you can help."

Chapter 18: Markin Council Room, Risal

The Mmnnuggls have taken Oorin. Repeat—the Mmnnuggls have taken Oorin.

—Private Risalian network broadcast within the Charted Systems, November 1st, 2060 CE

Kelm felt like there was something off about the council room. It was darker, certainly, as the council seldom met in the evenings, but there was something else. Perhaps it was the dank, heavy air that seeped in through the window, or perhaps it was smell of decaying andal wafting from the plantation that bordered the capital. Regardless, the atmosphere was unnerving, especially considering their current circumstances.

"As it stands, we don't know what happened to the cutter or Ran," Xouy concluded. Xe gazed at hir colleagues and then sat, letting the weight of the words sink in.

"We know where the cutter is located, however, correct?" Sandid clarified, hir eyes staring unblinking at Xouy.

"We have its last known coordinates only," Xouy responded. "I pulled a skiff off sector 75 to investigate, and the pilot reports that the cutter is currently caught in orbit around the gas giant, Quinone, in the Minoran System. The Minoran government has sent several liners to monitor the cutter until our ship arrives, but advises that recovery should be done quickly before the cutter is stripped for parts by a salvage crew. The ship is completely unresponsive."

"The Minorans were never a species that liked to leave trash lying around," Sandid muttered.

"Then we're assuming no one is left alive?" Kelm asked.

"No transmission from the cutter in eight days. The positioning system beacon shows the ship not to have moved from the gas giant's orbit for the same amount of time. We'll know more once we get some people onboard, but yes," Xouy replied, hir eyes casting downward briefly, "we assume everyone is either dead or has, for some reason, left the ship. I've asked the Minorans not to board the cutter, for obvious reasons."

Silence hung in the moist air as the Markin digested the information. Kelm fidgeted under the table with the edge of hir tunic. The death of Ran was unwelcome, but the loss of the girl was devastating. At best, it might solve the issue of the mass Ardulan failures if indeed she was having some indirect telepathic influence, but the potential defensive loss to the systems... Kelm wasn't certain that could even be quantified.

"If we can't recover the girl..." Kelm started, unwilling to finish the sentence.

Sandid lowered hir face into hir hands and sighed. "Does it even matter anymore? The Mmnnuggls are well within the Charted Systems. More unknown ships arrive every day through breaches in our defense grid. Every day, I get reports of more lost Risalian ships, more outbreaks of violence within the Charted Systems. *Violence*." Sandid paused and raised hir head. "Violence from species that haven't so much as littered in the past fifty years."

"That might be edging into hyperbole, Sandid," Sald responded darkly.

Sandid continued unabated. "We've lost Oorin completely, and I have little doubt that the entire Callis System will fall within the week. The Callis Wormhole will be next, unless they've already claimed it."

"Ran should have sent ships to reinforce Oorin weeks ago," Raek cut in, hir tone accusing. "We tasked Cell-Tal with Oorin's security two months ago."

"I relieved Ran of that duty for the past several weeks," Kelm responded curtly. "Ran's focus has had to be entirely on the missing Ardulan."

"Fine then. *Kelm* should have sent ships."

"I didn't send ships because there weren't any to send," Kelm retorted, neck slits burning. "Would you prefer I took ships from the border and opened an even wider gap in our defenses? Perhaps I should have taken ships from inside the Systems—ships that are being used to protect the beings that look to us for their defense."

Raek opened hir mouth to respond, but Sald held up hir arms, palms outward. "Enough. I called this meeting because it is time that we the Markin make a hard decision. The Risalian people have long been the protectors of the Charted Systems, and it is our continuing duty to perform this role to the best of our ability. With the probable loss of the altered Ardulan, we cannot hold the borders any longer." Sald stared at Xouy. "With limited resources, which systems will we defend and which systems will be sacrificed?"

Sandid blanched. "Before we sacrifice anything, I'd suggest we attempt a parley with the Mmnnuggls. If there is any chance to negotiate, I say we take it."

Raek tilted hir head, seemingly biting back a retort. When xe did speak, hir tone was tensely civil. "I concur. Negotiating for peace may not be possible, but if we can meet with the Mmnnuggls, at the very least, perhaps we can finally get them to tell us *why* they're attacking. Perhaps we could even get some identification of their allies. This anti-Ardulan theory has merit, but I have a number of questions about how and why they have such information about the population of our ships."

"I agree that more information would be nice, but eventually," Kelm added, recovering hir temper, "we will have to make difficult decisions. Sald is correct. We cannot protect everyone within the Charted Systems—not anymore."

"If I may, friends." Sald tapped twice on the tabletop, and a holographic projection of the Charted Systems appeared, hovering just above the surface. "Risal is here—" Sald pointed. "—marked in blue. We are in a far corner of the Systems." Sald placed hir thumb and forefinger in the middle of the hologram and twisted hir fingers to the right, rotating the display. "The Mmnnuggl force is currently swarming here, in the Callis System. Oorin has fallen, and it is safe to conclude that the Mmnnuggls hold the Callis Wormhole, although as of yet they have not made a show of force to claim it."

Sald bent over the display and tapped the yellow line representing the wormhole twice in rapid succession. The wormhole vanished from the display. "As you can see, taking the Callis Wormhole was a strong tactical decision. The wormhole directly connects the Callis System—the Charted Systems' primary raw materials supplier—with the Minoran System—the Systems' financial center. Without the Callis line, the Alusian Wormhole will be the only method of connecting with Oorin."

"You're ignoring the Terran Wormhole on purpose, I assume?" Kelm said.

Sald nodded. "At this time, yes, since the Terran System, much like our own, lies at the edge of the Charted Systems. However, unlike Risal, Earth has neither resources nor strategic value."

"Are you suggesting that we withdraw from the Terran System?" Sandid asked.

"The Terran System would be one of my suggestions, yes," Sald said. "It is tactically unsound for us to spread our forces that far out to protect one small system with only one truly inhabited planet. I suggest we focus our energy here—" Sald tapped another line on the hologram and made a circling movement with hir finger. "—on the Minoran and Alusian Systems."

"If we assume that the Callis Wormhole is under the control of Mmnnuggl forces, does it not follow that the Minoran System might be also?" Raek interjected.

Sald nodded and tapped the edge of the table. Another holographic projection appeared directly above the Charted Systems display. "Today's financial report," Sald said, pointing at the scrolling text. "If the Mmnnuggls are in the Minoran System, their presence is minimal. It is vital that we get forces on Baltec as soon as possible. We cannot afford to lose both our mining and financial sectors. The Systems could not recover from such a loss."

Kelm leaned back in hir chair, considering. "So you propose concentrating forces in the Minoran and Alusian Systems and ignoring the Terran System. I'm assuming that means we would also be ignoring the Neek System, as it is another outlier."

"Reinforcing the Alusian Wormhole and its connection to the Callis System," Sald added. "We will, of course, continue to heavily patrol the Meral and Risalian Wormholes to ensure that our own means of travel are not interrupted. Should we lose control of Neek, however, we will be reliant upon our poor plantation andal. This could have disastrous consequences for Cell-Tal."

Kelm nodded, thoughtful. They could afford to lose Earth, but they could not lose Neek, not if they wanted to continue any type of technological progression. The irony of the thought made Kelm smile.

"We can worry about Cell-Tal after we get the Mmnnuggl situation under control, but I agree that Neek needs protecting, although we might not be able to manage it. At this point, saving the most sentient life should be our primary concern. I have another question, however." Kelm stood and touched the holographic Systems map, rotating the map one hundred eighty degrees. "Let's say for a moment that the Mmnnuggl insurgency is isolated within the Callis System and Callis Wormhole. I'd like to know how they got there in the first place." Xouy tapped the lines representing the Risalian, Meral, and Minoran Wormholes, turning the lines yellow. "Either the Mmnnuggls have access to routes of which we are unaware, or they traveled to Oorin through these three passages. That means that an *entire fleet* slipped through three separate wormholes without being detected."

"A disturbing thought," Sandid added darkly.

Sald nodded in agreement. "I'd say that a new wormhole is a more likely scenario than somehow sneaking a fleet through our space or possessing impossible technology."

Kelm rubbed hir neck slits. Of course the Mmnnuggls had better technology than the Risalians did. It seemed like every species outside the Systems had better tech than the Risalians. Clearly, they needed to work on establishing new trade routes once the current issues were resolved. Although if species outside the Systems used faster-than-light drives, that put Risal at a distinct disadvantage.

Raek repositioned hirself on the chair and cleared hir throat. "Back to the matter at hand. We sacrifice the Terran and Neek Systems and reinforce the Minoran, Alusian, and Risalian Systems." Raek ran a hand through hir long black hair, and Kelm watched a few pieces loosen from the main mass and float lightly with static. "Have any of you considered how long the Systems can survive without the mines of the Callis System? Do you propose a counterstrike to take back that system?"

Sald sat back down and folded hir hands. "One issue at a time, Raek. Are we going to focus our forces or not? We might lose Earth and Neek. Not indefinitely, but we need to be aware of the potential for heavy casualties."

Silence sat heavily in the meeting room. Kelm could hear footsteps just outside the door—footsteps of Risalians going about their daily routines, completely oblivious to the decisions being made meters away. The loss of andal would be devastating to Cell-Tal and Charted Systems technology, but the loss of life... Kelm had a hard time imagining it. All of those sentient beings with no idea what was coming, no way to defend themselves.

A scrape of wood on metal screeched through the silence as Raek pushed hir chair back and stood. Xe turned and looked squarely at Sald, hands clenched into fists. "I agree. I am willing to bear the responsibility and the associated consequences."

Sald nodded, and stood as well. "As am I."

Sandid joined them, glancing first at Kelm and then at Xouy. "I agree," xe added, weariness seeping through the confident tone xe was obviously trying to project. Without additional comment, Xouy scooted from hir chair and stood as well.

Kelm remained seated. Beings were going to die. *Sentient* beings. Children. Elderly. Their homes might be destroyed, their lands possibly ruined. Entire generations would feel the weight of this decision.

"Friend," Sandid said gently, breaking Kelm from hir thoughts, "we will not go down this path without unanimous approval."

Except what choice did they have, really? Try to protect everyone, and everyone could die. Sacrifice a few systems, save the majority. Risalians had done this for the Charted Systems for decades, had taken the task of defense upon themselves so that no other beings had to die. They couldn't keep that promise anymore, however—could no longer keep the innocence of the Charted Systems from the reality of the greater galaxy.

Kelm stood, each movement deliberate and measured. Xe studied each of the other markin, noting the purple-tinged neck slits, the pale blue knuckles surrounded by otherwise rich blue skin, the stress lines in the foreheads, and the bags under the eyes. It was obvious that none of them had come easily to their decision. It almost made Kelm feel better about what xe was about to do. Almost, but not quite.

"I agree," Kelm whispered, barely loud enough to be heard. "If diplomacy fails, sacrifice the Terran and Neek Systems and reinforce the Minoran and Alusian Systems. Secure the Alusian Wormhole. When the time comes—if the time comes...take back the Callis System by force."

* * *

With neck slits burning and mind awash in death, Kelm made the short journey from the council room to hir quarters. The lights were still on, despite the late hour, and Belm, Kelm's only offspring, bounded up from hir cushion and into Kelm's arms.

"Long meeting," Belm said, burying hir face in Kelm's tunic. The child wore no clothing of hir own. Status, and the appropriate tunic color, would be determined by a standard proficiency exam at maturation. Kelm knew better than to hope for blue—few Risalians even made a captain's yellow, and only zero point one percent of the population even qualified for Markin status. Most Risalians who tested high enough for Markin never got a glimpse of the post. Risalian law specified that only five could hold the position concurrently, and the post came with lifetime tenure. The rest of the would-be markin spent their days in training camps and executive service posts, waiting for the right combination of luck and death to be elevated to the highest rank in Risal.

Kelm knew that statistical probability favored the outcome of hir offspring wearing gray and serving on a transport ship. Except now those transport ships would become warships, and the gray tunics, the thirds, seconds, and firsts would be the ones to die. Belm was only a few years from maturation. If the war dragged on, if they couldn't resolve it soon... Kelm didn't want to think about Belm on one of those ships. Couldn't think about it.

Kelm glanced down at the dark head of hair burrowing into hir arm. Xe took the child's hand and gently stroked hir hair. "Yes, child, a very long meeting. Now it is time for both of us to sleep." Kelm produced a fake yawn, which had the intended effect of making the child yawn as well. "See? We're both tired. Let's retire and see what tomorrow brings, shall we?"

The child nodded, and Kelm scooped Belm up and carried hir to bed. "Dream of a bright future," Kelm said softly, turning out the light. Xe watched Belm curl into the thick, padded covering and smiled. The oncoming war might be out of hir hands, but Kelm knew xe had to find a way to protect Belm from being on one of those warships. Belm deserved a perfect future, and Kelm would use every resource at hir disposal to provide one.

CHAPTER 19: MERCY'S PLEDGE

This is an announcement for all members of the Charted Systems. Travel through the Callis Wormhole is, until further notice, restricted to sheriff purposes only. Interstellar travel will be rerouted through the Alusian Wormhole. In addition, the following materials will now be available in limited quantities due to supply chain disruptions: raw diamonds, titanium, refined methane, copper, and iron ore.

—General network broadcast within the Charted Systems, November 2nd, 2060 CE

"We should be able to see Quinone any moment now," Neek announced from her seat onboard *Mercy's Pledge*. Nicholas watched the tall woman battle fatigue while her fingers continued to fly across the computer screen—double-checking coordinates and maintaining constant communication with several Minoran contacts.

Nicholas stifled a yawn and squinted, hoping to spot the gas giant on the viewscreen. He knew none of the crew had slept much since escaping the Neek planet, to say nothing of having no time to do more than bandage their wounds. The heaven guards had escorted them past atmospheric security all the way to the Neek Wormhole entrance before intelligence personnel alerted the president—still alive, much to Neek's disappointment. Three additional Neek settees had then relentlessly pursued *Mercy's Pledge* through the Neek Wormhole and through the entire Alusian System. These ships were painted burgundy instead of crimson—a distinction Neek refused to elaborate upon, earning him a glare every time he brought it up.

The settees had tried to ground them near Missotona—the second inhabited planet in the Alusian System—but the captain hadn't let Nicholas fire on the unarmed ships. That bothered the Journey youth more than he wanted to admit. Nicholas understood not wanting to make matters worse, but at some point, self-preservation had to be taken into account. Systems law was pretty straightforward on self-defense, and he'd proven himself with the laser turret. Shooting ferries during a questionable encounter was one thing—trying to keep the *Pledge* crew alive after both the Neek and the Risalians had tried to kill them was entirely different. He was enough of an adult to make *that* distinction.

Mercifully, they had gotten a break at Craston, Neek managing to wedge *Mercy's Pledge* between two large Oorin drilling ships and flying tandem all the way to the Minoran Wormhole entrance. Neek had also managed to wheedle her uncle into giving her the comm number of Captain Elger Tang of the *Galactic Baltec Wind*, who happened to be privy to some rather delicate information about a derelict Risalian cutter currently in orbit around Quinone.

Nicholas wasn't sure, but it seemed like Neek had come back from the dead with a suspiciously high amount of luck on her side. Since there appeared to have been a unanimous, unspoken decision not to talk about Neek's death, Nicholas had chosen not to make any comments. He was tired of being verbally punched every time he spoke.

"There," Yorden said, pointing to a glowing speck in the upper right section of the screen. "Quinone is just ahead. Another hour and we should be in orbit."

"Captain Tang advises that we will need to proceed with caution," Neek said, and Nicholas noted the strain in her voice. "There are three Minoran liners securing the immediate area around the cutter. They are under orders from the Risalians to block any access to the ship until a Risalian salvage team arrives."

"We should be able to get an ID on the ship once we've got it on screen." Yorden glanced at Nicholas. "If it's the ship that has Emn, you'll be working the laser gun again."

"Hopefully it won't come to that," Neek murmured, her focus fixed on the computer monitor before her. "Captain Tang is already speaking with the other liner captains and explaining the situation."

Nicholas looked at the captain in confusion. "Do you really expect the Minorans to side with a ship full of criminals over the Risalians?" he asked. The idea seemed ludicrous.

Yorden raised an eyebrow at Neek. "An excellent question. Do we, Neek? Your miraculous return from death has given you a decidedly inflated streak of good fortune. I'd hate for it to run out now and land the *Pledge* on the bad side of yet another system."

"Captain Tang assures me that the Minoran government is sympathetic to our situation. She promises that she'll have responses from the liner captains in another few minutes." Neek sat up straight and wrenched her eyes from the console, scowling at Yorden. "Would you put the Ardulan on guns already?" She jerked her thumb over her shoulder, indicating Nicholas. "Nikki here has a much more successful track record with repairing frayed wires than shooting live ships, and the Ardulan is *trained* for combat with mechanized weapons."

The comment stung. He'd shot down more ships than Neek had.

Yorden looked warningly at Neek. "We've already had this discussion, Neek. I'm not having an uncommunicative, potentially abused and traumatized woman working our laser gun, no matter how good a shot she may be."

That was too good to pass up. "You let Neek use guns all the time," Nicholas pointed out.

Nicholas's comment earned him a glare from the captain and a snort from Neek. He grinned and shrugged his shoulders. She'd had it coming. "Just an observation, Captain."

"Apt though it may be," Yorden responded through clenched teeth, irritation in his tone, "my ship—my rules. The Ardulan stays in the cargo bay. Nicholas is on laser. You, Neek, get to figure out some way to get us on that cutter if it turns out it is the one that took Emn."

"It *is* the one that took Emn." Neek looked ready to argue, but then her screen lit up with a message.

"Captain Tang says the liner captains have agreed to let the *Pledge* dock on the far side of the cutter. That positioning will hide us from approaching ships." Neek paused her reading to push a stray strand of hair from her face before continuing. "The Risalian salvage crew is scheduled to arrive in just over an hour and a half. Captain Tang estimates at best a fifteen minute window between our arrival at the cutter and when we would need to depart in order to avoid visual contact."

"We only get fifteen minutes to access their database?" Nicholas asked incredulously. It'd take them that long to dock. "If they have any type of encryption, we're in trouble. Any chance you could, you know, sense her or something?"

He'd said the wrong thing. There was no biting retort, just silence from the pilot. Nicholas looked to Yorden, who stared back reproachfully. Unsure how best to apologize, he put his hand on Neek's shoulder. The muscles tensed.

"I didn't realize she was gone. I'm sorry."

It was enough. "Yeah, well, when your god falls in your lap, then is taken from you, you come talk to me." Her words were acerbic, but he heard the worry beneath them.

"Fifteen minutes to search an abandoned ship for information, when that information is in a language that none of us speak...it seems crazy. We can do it, just, well..." he trailed off.

Neek reached up and pushed Nicholas away, her fingers leaving small, wet spots on the top of his hand. "I died. I get to be a little crazy."

It was a fair point. Nicholas looked up at the viewscreen. Quinone had grown from a small dot to a fuzzy, yellow planet. Beside it hovered a long, gray rod and three small, gray specks—presumably the cutter and the Minoran liners.

"I think crazy is an accurate description of the situation," Yorden murmured in agreement. "One tramp versus a derelict Risalian cutter, an approaching Risalian cutter, and three potentially hostile Minoran liners." The captain turned to Nicholas. "Didn't you say your mother wanted you to be a lawyer?"

"Yeah," Nicholas responded wryly, thinking back to the argument he'd had with his mom before departing on Journey. She'd wanted him to take the law school entrance exam before leaving. He'd "forgotten" to attend the testing day, choosing to apply for placement on a transport ship instead. She'd found out. "That profession has more appeal with each passing moment."

* * *

Once the identity of the cutter was confirmed, Yorden ordered the immediate docking of *Mercy's Pledge*. Neek performed the maneuver flawlessly, the *Pledge* shaking only slightly at the connection.

"We don't have much time," Yorden said. "Grab a respirator from the wall panel on your way out. Who knows what happened to the atmosphere inside the cutter?"

A shiver ran down Nicholas's back as he snapped the elastic band that held the respirator around his head. The air coming from the gray mouth-and-nose cover smelled stale, and he wondered when the masks had last been recharged. The edges of the mouthpiece were sticky, which meant he knew for certain who had used it last.

"Watch your step!" Yorden called out, his voice muffled from the respirator as he stepped into the cutter. "We've got bodies."

Nicholas's eyes grew wide as he followed Neek into the cargo hold. There were six Risalians within his field of view, all wearing gray tunics and crumpled in horrible piles either on the floor or over storage bins, their faces frozen in silent shrieks. The floor and walls of the cutter were warped and jutted at strange angles, making it difficult to walk. It looked like one of those old Picasso paintings, and he really hated modern art. Smells filtered through the mask, only slightly diluted from the air scrubbers. There was the distinct smell of campfire and all of its components—seared meat, charred wood, and a lingering smokiness. In the woods, it would have been fine. On a ship, however...it made his stomach turn.

As the crew picked their way through the debris towards the door leading into the main section of the ship, Nicholas shuddered again and tried to will himself not to look at the bodies. *Such a horrible loss of life,* he thought to himself. The faces he was trying so hard not to look at continued to leer at him, eyes rolled back into their sockets and jaws wide. Nicholas caught himself imagining the screams and hastily tried to think of something else, the sounds his mind matched to the expressions too disturbing to consider.

"Bridge should be through this next corridor," Yorden called out as the cargo door opened and he stepped into the hallway. His foot broke through a particularly soft area of floor, and the captain fell, cursing loudly. "Thirteen minutes before we need to be back on the ship. Watch your step."

There were more Risalians in the hallway, some only partly visible from the buckled floor and remains of what appeared to be the ceiling above. All were clad in gray and all had the same horrifying expression on their faces. As the crew moved past briskly, the leg of Nicholas's flight suit caught on a clubbed hand jutting at a ninety-degree angle from one of the bodies. The sudden resistance pushed Nicholas into a panic. The floor groaned in response as he yelped and jumped, landing just behind Neek. The caught arm tore away from the shoulder, making a crisp *rrrrip* sound in the silent hallway, exposing cartilage and tendons. A large swatch of skin dangled from the forearm, the inside a much lighter blue than the outside.

"They're all so dark," Neek said, not commenting on Nicholas's shuddery breathing behind her. "Yorden, it's almost like they've been burned."

Yorden shivered too. "Or electrocuted," he responded tersely.

"Think something went wrong with the ship's electrical harness?" Nicholas asked. He'd had to repair the harness on the *Pledge* several times over the past few months. He'd received several nasty shocks, but nothing that would have led to this. "Maybe they got too close to the planet? What if they—"

Nicholas stopped talking as the crew turned a sharp corner. Yorden stumbled again but caught himself on the wall, which dented under his hand, and then looked down at the body beneath his feet.

"Is that..." Nicholas wasn't sure he could finish the sentence. The Risalian underneath Yorden was missing the back of hir skull and hir entire nose, but there was no mistaking the face.

"Captain Ran," Yorden muttered, his voice amplified in the silence. He took several wide steps to stay clear of the remains. "Looks like Cell-Tal's stock just took a hit."

"That's a laser wound, Captain," Nicholas said. "Do you think..." he trailed off and then tore his eyes from Ran, recognizing the door ahead. They could talk about the whys and wherefores later. Right now, they just didn't have time, and Nicholas had a reasonable idea of where they were. "The bridge door is just up there," he called out, pointing ahead. "At least, I think it's the bridge. That'd be an awful lot of bright markings for a bathroom, that is." He turned and gestured to Neek. "Hey, Neek, if we hurry we might be able to actually access their..."

Where was Neek? Exhaling loudly, Nicholas left the captain at the bridge door and backtracked down the last corridor. Just on the other side of the turn was Neek, frozen in place and staring down at some nondescript lump on the floor.

"Captain!" Nicholas called out to Yorden. The captain clomped back over and growled impatiently.

"Ten minutes, people—let's *move!*" Yorden began to head back up the hall, but Nicholas grabbed his arm and nodded his head at Neek. Yorden turned, his expression souring. "If it's a gun, Neek, just take it and keep moving. We don't have time to linger."

Neek continued to ignore both of them. The pilot shifted to the side and then knelt down beside what appeared to be a large, oblong plastic casing roughly the size of Nicholas's torso. Nicholas looked to the captain, who shrugged his shoulders. Unsure what else to do, Nicholas walked over and knelt down as well. Up close, he realized the surface was more like rough cotton, tan and grainy, with a faint shimmer.

"Why are we wasting time with dead Risalians?" Yorden asked. The question was direct, but his tone was softer than it should have been. Clearly Nicholas was missing something. Determined to figure out what, he brought his right hand up and ran his fingers lightly over the top.

"Gross," he said, a little too loudly, his voice echoing down the hall. "It's all sticky."

Yorden knelt down next to Neek, taking her hand in his. "Neek," he tried again, this time in little more than a whisper, "what is going on?"

Neek's eyes never left the cocoon. She ran two fingers down its length, her *stuk* absorbing into the casing upon contact. Nicholas saw a smile start at the corners of her mouth, but it never quite made it all the way across her face. Her body trembled, and she wrapped her arms around her chest, hugging herself.

"It's Emn," she said, her voice lilting.

"Huh?" Nicholas looked the casing up and down, trying to figure out what Neek was talking about.

Neek slid her hands under each end of the cocoon and lifted slowly until she was standing upright, the strange beige casing cradled gently in her arms.

"It's Emn," she repeated, her voice a wisp of sound. "She's in metamorphosis."

CHAPTER 20: MERCY'S PLEDGE

And when I saw what beauty lay
Beyond the clear night sky
I lifted up my voice in praise
Of that ephemeral lie

—Excerpt from *Atalant's Awakening*, published in the Charted Systems, 235 AA

"We're out of time!" Yorden called out as he yanked the respirator from his face and headed to the cockpit of the *Pledge*. "Neek, get the kid to the cargo hold with the other Ardulan and get back up here ASAP. Nicholas, to the laser. I'll disengage us from the cutter and get the engines started."

Neek paused long enough for Nicholas to remove her respirator before breaking into a sprint, her steps heavy with the weight of Emn's chrysalis. As she barreled expertly around the familiar curves of the *Pledge*'s hallways, she searched the back of her mind, hoping to feel a hint of the young presence that had so completely enveloped her when it pulled her out of the soundless void of what she now assumed had been some sort of Neek death-limbo. The death part, however, she was trying not to think about.

Her fingertips slid against the surface of the cocoon as she ran, the mixture of her *stuk* and the sticky, wet surface making it difficult to gain a firm hold. There was no mental trace of Emn anywhere, just a large, oblong shell that Neek was trying desperately not to drop.

When Neek finally reached the cargo hold, the Ardulan woman sprang to her feet and ran over to Neek, eyes wide.

"I need you to watch her for a while," Neek said, holding out the cocoon. "I've got some flying to do." The Ardulan nodded, taking the chrysalis into her arms. Neek turned and then hesitated. Reaching back, she ran three fingertips over the surface. *Be safe, little one*, she sent. She listened for a long moment, hoping to catch a glimmer of consciousness. Nothing came. A heaviness settled in her gut and, after allowing another few moments to pass, she nodded to the Ardulan and resumed her sprint back to the cockpit.

"System is up and ready for you," Yorden said as he vacated the pilot's chair. "Nicholas is in position. According to Captain Tang, we have maybe thirty seconds before the Risalian cutter arrives. It's enough to get us a head start. Do what you can." The captain brandished an old soldering iron and a handful of extra fuses. "I'll be on repair call."

Neek quickly took note of the system status report on the monitor and then switched the screen over to navigation. "Engaging engines," Neek called out crisply.

Mercy's Pledge began her slow acceleration from behind the cutter. "Captain Tang wishes us luck and hopes we found what we were after," Neek added, noting the scrolling message on the side of the screen. She turned to Yorden. "Anything you think we should share with her?"

Yorden considered for a moment, one hand rubbing his bandaged thigh. "Tell her everyone was dead, but that we did find the information we wanted."

Neek relayed the message. "*Pledge* has reached sufficient speed, Captain. Any idea *where* you'd like to go?"

"Callis Wormhole."

Neek merely raised an eyebrow.

"We don't have much of a choice," Yorden responded. "We left the Neek fleet searching for us in the Alusian System. Even if we went back there and managed to avoid the Neek, our next jumps would either be to Neek itself, through the Neek Wormhole, or through the Meral Wormhole to Risal."

"Hoping to return to Earth, Captain?" Neek asked as she entered directional coordinates into the computer. She wrapped both hands carefully around the ship's yoke and pulled to the right, causing the *Pledge* to arc seventeen degrees starboard as it continued to accelerate.

"Let's deal with the Callis System first." Yorden glanced at the computer screen. "Any sign of the new cutter?"

"No...wait, yes. The cutter just exited the Minoran Wormhole. They're coming up on our stern, so we won't be able to see them on the viewscreen."

"Time to the wormhole entrance?"

Neek tapped the upper left corner of the computer screen. "Four minutes, assuming no one starts shooting." She turned to Yorden. "If they *do* start shooting, we're on our own. Captain Tang says the Minoran government is only willing to stick their necks out so far for us. Obfuscated subterfuge is one thing; starting a violent incident that could lead to the dismantling of the Charted Systems is out of the question. Remember—she likes my uncle. She probably doesn't like me."

"I don't suppose there is any chance Emn might be able to help us out?" Yorden asked, raising an eyebrow.

Neek shook her head. "Unlikely. I don't know when she began metamorphosis, but she will be in the chrysalis for weeks, according to the books." The pilot narrowed her eyes. "If you *really* want a chance at getting out of this, the Ardulan gunner..."

Yorden growled, but his response was cut off when a proximity alarm began to beep on the console.

"The Risalian cutter is gaining fast, Captain. They'd have to be blind to not have spotted us."

"Let's hope the Minorans can keep them talking for a while," Yorden said, his hands clenching the back of his chair tightly.

"Yeah, well, they're not making any effort to communicate with us," Neek noted dryly. "I suppose we could take that as a good thing."

Nicholas dropped his head from the turret opening "Uh, Captain? If they fire on us, do you want me to return fire?"

Yorden nodded. "We beat a Risalian force once. Who's to say we can't again?"

Nicholas's voice wavered. "Does it always have to be us or them?"

"Yes. Neek, time to wormhole?"

"Another two minutes. The Risalians have docked with the dead cutter and have still made no move to contact us." Neek tapped the screen. "Captain Tang says that the Risalians have been in minimal contact with the Minorans as well. She says they seem distracted and very eager to board the derelict ship."

"An entire cutter is a lot to lose," the captain responded humorlessly. "They're in for a big shock when they open the hatch into the cargo hold. I'm hoping it will take them a while to process what happened on the cutter. We only need another minute or so."

"I don't think we're going to get it, Captain," Neek said, the tension rising in her voice. "The Risalians are undocking."

"Nicholas!" Yorden bellowed. "Get ready!"

"Their ship is pivoting. It looks like...yes, they're heading straight for us." Neek tapped a few additional buttons on the screen, her nervousness causing her fingertips to slip and smear *stuk* across most of the console.

"Time?" Yorden asked again.

"One minute, ten seconds. Our engines are at maximum, but they're gaining fast."

"Will they overtake us before we enter the wormhole?"

Neek's jaw clenched. "If not before, then most certainly while we're inside."

"At least they can't fire inside the wormhole," Yorden noted. "If we can get inside before they overtake us, we can buy some time."

A sudden blast rocked the ship. Neek gripped the console to brace herself as Yorden fell to his knees. She heard the telltale sounds of Nicholas crashing to the floor from his turret chair.

"We just ran out of time and luck," Neek said tersely as she yanked the yoke. The *Pledge* turned abruptly to port, the direction change sending data tablets and other loose objects skittering across the floor. "Best I can do is make a bunch of random movements and hope they don't manage to connect again."

"At least your government's armor upgrades appear to be working," Yorden muttered. He pulled himself up from the floor and brushed off the seat of his pants. "Nicholas! If you can get a shot, take it!"

"Okay, Captain!" the young man called back nervously. The turret creaked as Nicholas rotated it around, trying to get a decent angle on the cutter.

Another blast shook the *Pledge*. Expecting it, no one lost their footing. "Still no communication from the cutter," she called out. "We're about to enter the wormhole. Fifteen seconds."

The opening of the wormhole loomed before them on the viewscreen, spinning as Neek juked the *Mercy's Pledge* on a drunken route to the center.

A third shot racked the *Pledge*, but this time, the impact sent alarms blaring. Smoke filled the cockpit. Neek smacked her hand hard against the console as the computer screen flickered twice and then went dark. "Visual driving only from here on out."

"None of my shots are going anywhere near the cutter!" Nicholas called from above. "If they have an Ardulan onboard..."

"Count on it," Neek called back. "Entering the wormhole. Nicholas, kill the laser until we're out. You know the drill."

Mercy's Pledge entered the wormhole, the Risalian cutter now on top of them. Through the viewscreen, Neek could make out the clean, bottlenose curve to the cutter's bow. The lights from the ship illuminated their pitch-black surroundings.

"They'll shadow us until we exit," Yorden said. "Then we'll resume this delight. Nothing we can do in the interim except repairs."

Nicholas climbed down the ladder and stared at the mess of tablets and wires on the floor. Neek waved her hand trying to clear the thick smoke, her throat burning when she inhaled too deeply.

"How long will we be in the wormhole, Neek?" he asked.

Neek shrugged her shoulders. "No computer, remember? Last time we used the Callis Wormhole, it took about an hour. That's my best guess." She glanced at Yorden and then back at the viewscreen. "Noting my current mental state, Captain, I think I'll take some downtime. I'm going to check on Emn and our Ardulan gunner."

Yorden began to speak but then closed his mouth. Instead, he nodded and bent down to retrieve his soldering iron. "Nicholas and I will work on the computer and whatever else the Risalians managed to blow in that last shot. Be back here in forty-five minutes."

Neek nodded and glanced at Nicholas. He gave her an encouraging smile as she stepped out of the cockpit and into the connecting hallway.

The pilot spent several minutes wandering through the hallways and galley, letting her mind drift back to her home planet. She'd recognized most of the guards that had helped them escape. Many were classmates, a few of them her former teachers. How they'd looked at her—first as a reviled heretic, now as a feared confidant of an Ardulan. The images spun in her mind as Neek sorted them, considered them, dismissed them...

The only one who hadn't changed was her former roommate. Neek had noticed her push her way forward in the group until they were an armspan from one another. Her face was nearly the same—all juvenile hopefulness with a touch of something new. She had made Guard after all, which should have made the woman glow with pride, especially upon seeing Neek. They hadn't spoken, just stared. When they'd brushed past each other, just long enough to escort the crew onto the *Pledge,* a very different emotion had come through the connection. The *stuk* had relayed only grief, and a message she hadn't wanted to hear.

Your mother is dead.

It wasn't malicious. The message was buffered in sympathy, but it didn't matter. She'd been on-planet when her mother had passed, and she hadn't been able to get to her. Maybe they'd been dead at the same time. It didn't matter. Her mother's death, her own death, the nebulous possibility of a connection between Emn's electrifying whatever-it-was on the Risalian cutter and her miraculous recovery, and the Heaven Guard...it was just too much. Neek leaned back against the bulkhead just outside the cargo bay, willing the tears to come. Hoping for the relief that crying would bring.

Nothing came. Instead, her emotions fluttered in the emptiness left by Emn—the blank place in her mind that she had somehow come to rely on. The girl was locked in metamorphosis, their link severed now. Emn would emerge a different being from the child Neek had known. She would be calmer, more focused, if historical texts were to be believed. Her abilities would be heightened—adult versions of what she had toyed with as a first *don*. She would be an adult. She wouldn't need Neek. Neek would be alone, again—except this time, the "alone" seemed so much deeper.

She couldn't dwell on that, either, because the tightening in her chest was making her lightheaded. Instead, the pilot's thoughts moved to the Talent problem. Emn already possessed such incredible raw Talent. What limit would there be for this new Emn, the Emn she would have no connection with? Would she still require guidance, or would she choose to strike out on her own, perhaps avenging the wrongs done to her by the Risalians? Could Neek realistically still expect to be associated with a being so formidable? Andal help her, would Emn even remember her? Had Emn caused the destruction on the Risalian ship? Was she in control of her Talents? If not, could *anyone* control her Talents?

Her eyes were still dry, but her chest felt tight enough that she was gasping for air. Isolation in the hallway wasn't helping. Answers were just on the other side of the door. Answers that she likely couldn't get from Emn in her current state but might be able to get from the Ardulan woman. There were a lot of questions that hadn't been asked—that she hadn't wanted to ask—but she could no longer blatantly deny the facts in front of her.

Neek opened the door to the hold and stepped inside, eyes drawn again to the chrysalis and the adult Ardulan who watched over it. The answers were secreted away within the Ardulan woman, within the cocoon, and Neek was going to get them. It was time to solve the mystery of Ardulum once and for all.

CHAPTER 21: MERCY'S PLEDGE

All available ships to the planet Oorin. The war has begun.

—Encrypted communication from within the Charted Systems, November 2nd, 2060 CE

Neek ran a finger slowly over the chrysalis from one end to the other, feeling the lightly textured, now completely hard surface. She waited again, uncomfortably hopeful, for some sort of feeling—a presence of any form. But there was still no mental connection from Emn, no indication that any part of the child's mind was still intact. The emptiness hurt more, here, in the company of the chrysalis, than it had in the hallway. She should have been able to feel something, but her mind remained empty of a secondary presence.

"Guess you know a lot more about this than I do," she said, looking up at the Ardulan and attempting to smother her unease.

The woman smiled slightly, and Neek took a moment to survey the wrinkled, yellow dress and look of fatigue on the Ardulan's face. She briefly considered trying to make a connection to this woman as she had with Emn—a connection that might help quench the feeling of "not-loneliness"—but just as quickly tossed the idea aside. That didn't seem right, somehow, and the mere thought of it made her uneasy.

Instead, Neek brought her attention back to the chrysalis, its cottony surface tactilely pleasant under her moist fingertips. What was happening now, inside the fibrous cocoon? Was every synapse being recoded, every bone rebuilt? Would Emn's memories persist, or would she be like a clean textile when emerged—ready to be printed upon by anyone?

"She's okay in there, right? Everything is normal?"

The Ardulan took a long breath and sat back on her haunches, considering. Slowly, she placed her left palm onto the center of the chrysalis and closed her eyes. A minute passed—then two.

"Well?" Neek whispered impatiently. "Is she okay? I mean, she's still Emn, right?"

The Ardulan's eyes opened as slowly as they'd closed. She brought her hand back to her side and stared at Neek, her expression unreadable.

Neek slammed a hand on the floor in exasperation. "I don't understand! Can't you just nod yes or no?"

The Ardulan raised an eyebrow and nodded.

"Fine. At least you can answer *some* questions then." Neek pointed at the woman. "You and Emn, are you the same? Genetically speaking, anyway."

The woman tilted her head and considered. Finally, she shook her head up and down, then side to side.

"Yes and no? Great." Neek rested her head on her knees. "What about Ardulum itself? Did you come from a moving planet?"

The woman immediately shook her head.

"You came from Risal?"

A nod this time.

"There are more like you?"

Another nod.

"How many? No, wait, sorry. Stupid question you can't answer." Neek took a moment to form her next query. "The Risalians call you Ardulans. That name, it means a lot to my people. You saw the way the Neek treated you. Do you think..." she trailed off, not wanting to ask the question. Afraid of the answer. She rallied.

"Some type of genetic cousin of yours, at the very least, probably visited my planet. I guess my question is—" Neek bit her lip. "—do you think it was your people? That you, and maybe Emn and the others like you, are our gods?"

The woman continued to stare at Neek. She didn't blink, didn't turn her head. She made no indication she had even heard the question.

Neek smacked her hand on the floor. "Hey! Don't turn off now. You've got to know something. Ardulans are telepathic—Risalians aren't. Even as slaves you should have passed down some shared oral—erm, mental—history. Give me something. *Please.*"

The woman looked to the floor. She brought two fingers to her temple and then shook her head.

She knew she shouldn't be mad at the Ardulan. She had no right to be. It would probably get her damned or some other nonsense. But the unfairness of the situation, of sitting with not one but *two* Ardulans—neither of whom knew any more than she did—was beyond frustrating. The loneliness and events of the past several days overflowed and poisoned her words. "Just...just give me some space, okay?" Neek glanced around the bay and then pointed to the far corner.

The woman nodded and stood, retreating to the edge of the bay where she sat facing the wall, silent and still.

Guilt added to her mix of emotions. What Neek would ever dare speak to an Ardulan in such a way? What right did she have to speak to any sentient that way? She should apologize, she knew that, but she didn't have the energy. She would later, when all this was settled. Instead, she stared at the chrysalis again, a choking sensation rising up in her throat, causing her sounds to come out soft and garbled. She leaned in close to the area she assumed was the head and hoped fervently that this wasn't the moment in which Emn's ears were being rebuilt.

"So...hey." Neek stumbled over her words. "I don't know if you can hear me. Maybe you don't know who I am anymore, or even who you are. But, well, you're safe. You should know that." Neek sighed and tried to collect her thoughts. This had gone a lot smoother in her head than out in the open. "I was, uh, thinking about when you emerge. Maybe you'll need a guide to help you relearn things. Maybe you'll need a friend who kind of knows your history. Maybe you just want to find other Ardulans and want to mount an assault on Risal. Ardulum knows you're certainly capable of it."

Neek paused. Images swam through her head. Emn's destruction of the weapons systems on the Risalian cutter and the *Pledge*. The cutter of cooked Risalians. Their telepathic communication. The very fact that Emn had managed to make it to metamorphosis without her mother. Her mind wandered back to Neek and her childhood—to the games and stories, the nursery rhymes and worship services. Neek considered all the articles she'd read in *The Neek Journal of Science and Technology* over the years, the failing of the wild andal on her homeworld, and her people's technological and creative stagnation. She thought of her paternal uncle, the high priest of Neek, of her almost-placement in the Heaven Guard, and of the life that had been nearly hers.

The thoughts and dreams swirled through her mind, clashing and interweaving. Neek considered them and then sorted them: relevant, not relevant, plausible, implausible, coincidence, or possible divine irony. When she was done, she lifted her head, her eyes centimeters from the surface of Emn's cocoon.

"I just wanted to say...if you need some help when you come out, I would do it. Until you find your feet or whenever. Whatever you need. Whatever you are, whatever you are going to become—Ardulan or not—I want to be there to see it. I want to be there with you when it happens. I hope you'll let me. I don't know if I believe in Ardulum, but I do believe in you."

The Ardulan woman shifted, the sound breaking Neek away from her quiet declaration. She turned to see the woman staring at her, the same unreadable expression on her face. Neek stood abruptly, embarrassed, and motioned to the woman, her earlier unease threatening to again bubble to the surface.

"Stay with her. I'm going back to the cockpit. If—if she needs anything, come find me." Neek didn't wait for a response before turning sharply on her heel and walking briskly out of the cargo hold.

* * *

"You're back early," Yorden commented. His voice filtered up through a grated vent near Neek's head as she strode through the hallway. She glanced down just in time to avoid tripping over two large, hairy feet sticking out of an access panel.

"Computer up yet?" she asked, leaning in and aiming her voice at the vent.

"Nope. Last shot fried the entire system. We'll have to get a replacement."

Neek let out a loud puff of air. "Great. Flying blind. It'll add more color to our eulogies."

A loud clang came from the access panel, followed by a curse. "Damn upgrades!" Yorden yelled. "Fucking cellulose everywhere. Can't get *inside* anything anymore." There was a rustling sound, and then Yorden's torso and head slithered out from the opening at the bottom portion of the wall. "One of our engines is down, too. We're dead in space once we exit the wormhole. Again." He raised an eyebrow at Neek. "Why are you in such a festive mood?"

Neek's reply was cut off when Nicholas rounded the corner, covered head to toe in what appeared to be engine grease. The ship's lighting glinted off the lubricant, giving Nicholas a goopy glow.

"Something funny?" Nicholas asked sourly.

"Something up?" Neek asked, keeping her voice neutral.

Nicholas leaned a shoulder against the wall, exhaustion evident in his posture. Neek thought she saw a rust-colored stain on the youth's shirt and wondered if his knife wound had reopened.

"Yeah. I just took a look out the viewscreen. Looks like a few other ships joined us in the wormhole. I saw the tips of at least two. Couldn't tell what species they belonged to though."

Neek moved over to Nicholas and wrapped an arm around the youth's waist, letting him lean on her. "Come on, Nicholas," she said. "Let's go take a look."

The three walked to the cockpit in silence. Nicholas slumped heavily against her, and she could feel that he was breathing hard. "Worn out?" she whispered.

"Yeah," he responded. "And my ribs hurt."

Neek kicked a few of the fallen tablets from the corner of the cockpit, eased Nicholas to a sitting position, and gently prodded the wound. Nicholas grunted but didn't scream, although the way his eyes clenched shut told her a great deal. "Just sit here for a bit. Catch your breath. I don't think there's much any of us can do right now anyway."

"That's for damn sure," Yorden muttered when he caught sight of the extra ships. "I've only ever seen that type of ship architecture once before. We're being flanked by Nugels."

"Is that good or bad?" Nicholas asked.

Squinting, Neek made a full visual sweep of the screen. "Maybe three pods? Four? It's hard to tell since we're only able to look forward."

Yorden sat down heavily in his chair and gestured for Neek to do the same. "I don't know, Nicholas. I wasn't thrilled the last time we ended up in the middle of a Risalian-Nugel conflict, and the *Pledge* certainly isn't in better shape than she was back then."

"Yeah, you and I weren't nursing stab wounds, and Neek was still alive the first time," Nicholas added darkly.

Yorden smiled sympathetically. "We've got no computer and a shot engine. Realistically, we have no weapons and shielding that will last another four or five blasts at best. Our best course of action will have to be to exit the wormhole and hope the Risalians and Nugels are too busy killing each other to notice us drifting away."

Nicholas coughed and clutched his wound. "The Nugels probably won't fire on us, right? I mean, we saved their butts last time."

"We don't have any offensive capabilities, Nicholas. Therefore, we are left with assessing the situation as it develops and trying our best not to die."

Neek gave Yorden an intense stare and then leaned forward, jabbing a finger pointedly in the air towards the cargo bay. "*Or* you could use the Ardulan gunner to punch a hole through both lines and keep the Risalians off our tail until we can...until we can..." Neek searched for plausible scenarios and continued to flounder.

"Until we what?" Yorden asked, cutting her off. "Until we hopefully drift to Callis Spaceport? If that miracle were to occur, do you think anyone there would help us go against the Risalians? Or maybe we'll drift to the Terran Wormhole and bring the violence to my homeworld?" Yorden's voice was firm. "No, I think not. Whatever is happening—whatever is going to happen, it's happening here, now, when we exit the wormhole."

CHAPTER 22: RISALIAN CUTTER 32

No Ardulan construct is to be left alive.

—Intercepted communication from outside the Charted Systems to the Mmnnuggl Flagship *Llttrin*, November 6th, 2060 CE

They were all dead. Every Risalian on the cutter—including Captain Ran—electrocuted. Well, Ran was shot, too, but at this point that really didn't matter.

Markin Kelm couldn't get the smell out of hir nose, couldn't shake the crinkled, dark blue bodies from hir mind. What had remained of the cutter was entirely inorganic. The cellulose bindings, coatings, and interweaves within the biometals were all gone, leaving behind a fragile, metallic shell. It was a mercy that Xouy suggested Kelm investigate the matter personally. No captain should have been made to see this.

There wasn't a weapon in the Charted Systems that could accomplish this level of damage. As far as Kelm knew, there wasn't a weapon *anywhere* that could accomplish that. Xe had majored in Ardulan studies at the Markin Training Center on Risal, had completed a research study on Ardulan Talents, but this was beyond even a team of the creatures. Certainly the girl had shown some precocious Talent, but this was insane. The Genomics Sector had made a misstep in her creation. Funding never should have been given to Cell-Tal for the project. They had all made a grievous error.

Kelm swallowed hard, rubbing hir neck as xe did so. If the Ardulan girl on that cutter—the one body they hadn't found—was responsible, xe didn't know how recovery would even be possible. That kind of power couldn't be contained. *Shouldn't* be contained. The only option was destruction.

"We're exiting the wormhole now, Markin," the second said.

"Inform the Ardulan gunner to open fire the moment we've cleared the wormhole safety corridor. Take out the *Pledge* as quickly as possible. We'll worry about the Mmnnuggls afterwards."

"Yes, Markin," the second replied. Kelm watched hir walk purposefully to the weapons station and relay information to the second *don* Ardulan male sitting in the chair—an Ardulan who, up until now, had an excellent service record. Second *don*s were stable, Kelm reminded hirself. Powerful. They were in their physical prime without the caution that came to all life with age. If the gunner reacted before the girl did, if the shots broke through the *Pledge*'s armor quickly, it would be enough.

"We're clear of the corridor, Markin," a third called from the navigation station. "The Ardulan is opening fire."

Kelm watched the Ardulan male as his fingers flew over the touchscreen. Xe then turned back to see the corona of the first, second, and third laser flash illuminate the viewscreen, the light visible even though the weapons were being fired from the underside of the ship.

"Impact?" Kelm called out.

"Yes, Markin. All three shots were direct hits. The *Pledge* is leaking atmosphere."

"Finish the job—" Kelm's command cut off as the bridge flooded with light. The cutter hummed with its first impact.

"Multiple shots fired from the Mmnnuggl force," the third called out. Another blast rocked the ship, and Kelm had to grip the console before hir.

"Status of the *Pledge*?" Kelm spoke over the emergency klaxons.

"Last two shots went wide," the second responded. "The Ardulan is still sending off volleys, but he can't account for the *Pledge*'s sporadic juking."

Another Ardulan malfunction. The girl was onboard then—it was certain—and she was still alive. Kelm gripped the chair's armrests tightly, causing hir knuckles to crack. "How far away is the *Pledge* currently?"

More shots hit the cutter. The communications console erupted into flames.

Kelm tried to stay calm. Laser fire wasn't working. The *Pledge* could not be allowed to escape. Xe had to rectify the situation at any cost. Belm could not grow to adulthood in a galaxy of Ardulan influence. Belm had to be protected.

"The *Pledge* is less than thirty seconds away at top speed," a third said. "Possibly more if we lose an engine."

"Then take us to top speed before that happens," the markin said. "Aim this ship for the *Pledge*." A smiling child holding a stuffed *titha* danced across Kelm's vision, and the markin said a silent goodbye.

"Ram them?"

"Ram them."

"Yes, Markin."

"For the Charted Systems," a third whispered under hir breath.

"For the Charted Systems."

"For the Charted Systems," the markin echoed, joining hir crew's chant.

Then the tip of the cutter plowed through the *Pledge*'s starboard flank.

CHAPTER 23: MMNNUGGL FLAGSHIP

"Coming to you live from Baltec in the Minoran System, I'm Yiru Chang. As you can see behind me, panic has broken out on Baltec as residents crowd the spaceports in a frantic dash to make it off-world. The pandemonium comes after confirmation that at least fifty ships of unknown origin have been spotted in the Callis System, and that laser fire has been exchanged with at least one Risalian craft. It's good to know the Risalians are still looking out for the Charted Systems, even in the midst of this chaos."

—Broadcast from *The Galactic News*, November 10th, 2060 CE

Nicholas awoke with a raging headache and no idea where he was. A pale green light swung over his head. The air, smelling of antiseptic and wintergreen, was warm across his bare skin. He found himself momentarily enjoying the sensation of the breeze across his face and chest, down his torso to...

Nicholas sat up quickly—a little too quickly, his head spinning—and confirmed that he was naked. Not the kind of naked where someone had the decency to lay a towel over the more personal areas, but *naked* naked, and on an unfamiliar ship with no fabric in sight.

In the lime green room, there were three other beds, all empty. The wall closest to him lit up sporadically with small, red dots that stayed lit until another took its place. The bed had little in the way of anything resembling cloth and was far too firm for his liking.

"Good andal to you," a voice greeted in unaccented Common. Nicholas swung his legs over the side of the bed and stood—as much as he could manage with the low ceiling—to face the nondescript Mmnnuggl bobbing near the doorway.

The humanlike ears wiggled on either side of the sphere as it spoke again. "Ardulum spares you as well. Your friend recovered some time ago."

"Excuse me?" Nicholas stammered. "Where am I?"

The sphere bobbed once, both ears curling into tight ovals. "Short term memory loss is to be expected. Terran heads are soft. You're on the Mmnnuggl flagship *Llttrin*, in the medical bay. Our transports picked you out of the rubble of your ship after the collision with the *Risalians*." The Mmnnuggl said the last word with disgust.

"Yeah," Nicholas said slowly. Yorden had ordered them all into decompression suits before they exited the wormhole. Nicholas remembered Neek carrying him to the cargo hold and then returning to the cockpit to fly the ship. He remembered Yorden lifting a seal on the suit and sticking a long needle in his skin. He remembered the face of the sad-eyed Ardulan...

"You rescued us all?" Nicholas asked. "Neek, Yorden, Emn, the Ardulan woman—they're all okay?"

The Mmnnuggl hesitated, emanating a series of fast clicking noises. Its ears unfurled and curled back again even tighter. The sphere spun before floating towards the door. "Come, Terran Nicholas," it said. "I'll take you to see our captain. She can answer your questions more fully."

Nicholas took several hurried steps and then realized he still had no clothing. His cheeks flushed. "Think maybe I could get something to cover up with?" he called after the sphere.

The Mmnnuggl spun around again. "Are you cold?"

"No..." Nicholas stammered. "It's just, uh, Mister...?"

"My name is Gglltyll, and I am female."

"Sorry, Giltil." Nicholas stumbled over the name, his tongue thick in his mouth with the double consonants. "I'm not cold, but, uh, humans don't like to show their reproductive organs much."

Gglltyll bobbed twice. "Bipeds of the Systems also seem to require things in their hands frequently. The Neek is always picking things up. Very unusual. We don't have textiles onboard this ship and have taken yours to prevent microbial contamination, but your companion made a similar request. Some of our allies are bipedal and may have similar mores. If garments have been located within the fleet, the captain will know."

Nicholas glanced down and quickly resumed his pace behind Gglltyll. "I guess I should be grateful I'm *not* cold," he muttered.

* * *

By the time the pair reached the captain's office, Nicholas had such a severe crick in his lower back that he wasn't sure he'd be able to stand upright again. Once inside, he realized that it didn't matter anyway, since the ceiling was even lower in the captain's office than in the corridor.

"Nicholas St. John of the *Mercy's Pledge*. Eighteen rotations. Originating from Earth. An adult, by Terran standards, but a youth by Charted Systems dictate." The captain zoomed from head height to the floor and then back up, rotating as it did so. "I see that your body has finally healed. Your friend will be delighted to see you walking around."

Nicholas blushed. "About that... I don't suppose you might have some fabric around? Giltil said you were aware of the, uh, modesty needs of bipeds."

The captain floated closer to Nicholas and beeped several times in quick succession. "Yes. The Neek loudly informed us of her desire for clothing. We have many biped species in the Alliance with similar sizes to Terrans and Neek. We have a store of such clothing on one of our other pods. It will be brought onto the ship in the next few days."

Nicholas raised his eyebrows. Several *days*? He started to protest, but then thought better of it. "Thank you, Captain," he responded instead.

The sphere beeped again, ears rippling as the skin, or what Nicholas supposed was skin, of the Mmnnuggl shifted closer to a purple tint.

"Do you recognize me, Terran Nicholas St. John? We last spoke at a dinner reception on my ship at Callis Spaceport. I transferred a stasis chamber into your captain's possession. I am Captain Llgg." Llgg spun around three times counterclockwise and then zoomed in so close to Nicholas that the young man's nose touched the surface of the sphere.

Nicholas inched back uncomfortably and finally sat directly on the floor. That was a mistake. The floor was jagged, black metal and cut into his skin. "Of course, Captain. I remember the cargo in particular."

Captain Llgg backed away slightly from Nicholas and landed on the floor. Nicholas could only assume she was attempting to "sit" with him and make the experience less weird. It didn't help.

"Terran Nicholas St. John, I am going to speak with you now about Oorin. We were not honest with you. I apologize for that." The captain's voice sounded tired. "I have explained this to your friend as well. *Mercy's Pledge* offered a unique opportunity to stash awkward cargo. We needed a chance to regroup."

Nicholas tried to process that information. "So Emn wasn't a gift for saving your ship?"

"The modified Ardulan child?" Llgg rolled in a tight circle on the floor, edging closer to Nicholas. "The Alliance was unsure of the best course of action. Her time on the *Pledge* gave the Alliance leaders a chance to make a decision as to her fate."

Why does everyone else always get to decide Emn's fate? Nicholas wondered. Out loud, the young man cleared his throat before addressing the captain. "What was that decision?"

Captain Llgg rolled three degrees to her right, giving Nicholas the distinct impression that she was cocking her head at him.

"The Eld deliver the law. Assessment is required. Destruction is likely." Captain Llgg's tone softened. "Children of any species endear themselves to their caregivers. However, the Eld tolerate no imperfections. She is *not* of Ardulum. She is a curiosity for their amusement, and their amusement alone."

Nicholas flushed with anger but kept his mouth clamped shut.

"Risalians are tinkerers. Opportunists. They took the scraps of a great race and attempted to repair them. This was also not of Ardulum. Creatures such as the girl contain too much power. The Eld cannot allow this. It threatens Ardulum. It threatens the Eld."

"What are you talking about?" Nicholas asked. "Who are the Eld? Why do they get to decide what happens to Emn? She's powerful, sure, but you...they, can't just kill her for that!"

Llgg didn't respond, nor did she move. Nicholas tried to focus. How would Yorden handle the situation? Was tact required or some type of cultural deference? Morality was a social institution to some extent, but there had to be *some* intergalactic standards. Nicholas decided to take a chance.

"How does judging her on what she *might* do make you any better than the Risalians?" he asked quietly.

Llgg spun around once in agitation. "You do not understand," she said, voice terse. "The decision is not yours to make. You and Neek will be free to leave at your leisure—we will provide you with a small pod and safe passage through our fleet in thanks for your help with the Risalians and your unwitting role with the girl. Emn will remain with us. When reinforcements arrive, she will return to the Alliance."

"Wait, what about Yorden and the Ardulan woman? Why are reinforcements coming? Are we still in the Charted Systems? You can't just take Emn!" he blurted out, words tumbling over each other as his mind raced, any thoughts on cultural sensitivity forgotten.

The captain began to float back up and away from Nicholas. When she reached the interface, she touched the black panel lightly with her body. Three red lights appeared. The captain emitted a low whirring noise and was answered with a series of short clicks.

"A security team will escort you to your room. Neek and Emn are there, waiting for you. We are still in the Charted Systems. We are not far from where the *Pledge* exploded. Our recovery team was unable to locate Captain Yorden or the other altered Ardulan onboard. Reinforcements are arriving because the Alliance now has the power and the resources to stop the blasphemous Risalians and destroy their genetically manipulated monstrosities. There will be no more Emns, Terran Nicholas. No more child weapons and no more altering of the Gods' plans."

Nicholas was stunned into silence. Gods' plans? Were there *more* deities to contend with? If the Mmnnuggls were as superstitious as the Neek, no wonder Emn scared them. And what did she mean, Yorden hadn't been located? They were all together on the ship. How could he and Neek have been found, but no one else?

The security guards floated in, and Nicholas allowed himself to be led away, unable to form even the simplest response. Neek would know what to say. She'd know where Yorden was. It was probably all a plan, anyway. Throw the Mmnnuggls and Risalians and Neek and whoever else off so they could get Emn to safety. That had to be it.

The corridor arced perpetually, which made sense since the ship was a sphere, but having to hunch *and* constantly turn corners was not helping Nicholas's mood. When they stopped, Nicholas was relieved to see a doorframe that extended well beyond his head. "We've received word that the textile garments you requested are en route," one of the guards informed him. "We apologize for the inconvenience in the interim. Should you require anything else, please do not hesitate to ask."

Nicholas nodded his understanding. Another guard tapped its body against the door, which promptly slid aside, revealing a small room with some type of furry floor, a few pieces of what Nicholas assumed to be strangely shaped furniture, and a very large bay window.

"Neek!" Nicholas called out, forgetting momentarily that he was completely nude. "Are you in here?"

"Nicholas?" Neek called back. The young man took several tentative steps into the blissfully bipedal-designed room and spotted Neek sitting off in the back corner next to Emn's cocoon. Neek's face broke into a large grin when she saw him, and she sprang to her feet and ran over, enveloping Nicholas in a firm hug.

"It's really good to see you, Nicholas," Neek said breathlessly.

"Guess I missed a lot," Nicholas returned, becoming uncomfortably aware of the proximity of various body parts. "But it's good to see you, too." He felt Neek's hip jerk slightly, and the pilot backed away, a wry grin on her face.

"Sorry, kid. I got a little caught up in the moment. Didn't mean to make you uncomfortable. The nude thing may work for Nugels and Ardulans, but for the rest of us mere mortals, it's just awkward."

Nicholas blushed and turned away, pretending to find something interesting on the green-tinted wall while he waited for his body to settle down. He buried his toes in the thick ply of the carpet, trying not to think about what animal it could have come from. "Uh, Neek," he began tentatively, catching his big toe in a fur tangle, "Yorden isn't...I mean, he's not dead, right? And that Ardulan woman..."

Neek looked away. "Y—Yorden," she stammered. "Yorden gave you a sedative—it looked like you were going into shock. I went back to the cockpit to try to do a little creative steering. When the Risalians fired again...the blast stripped most of our armor and opened sections of the hull. Thank andal that Yorden thought of the decompression suits. We all got in them in time, even the Ardulan woman."

She paused, and Nicholas could hear the soft drops of *stuk* falling onto the floor. "I lost my grip on the main console and was pulled away from the *Pledge* before the cutter rammed us. I don't know what happened in the cargo bay, but I watched the Risalians aim right for the *Pledge* and skewer her through the midsection. She split apart a few seconds later. By the time the Nugels found me, they already had you and Emn onboard. They said they couldn't find anyone else and, with being locked in this room, I haven't been able to do much questioning."

"But it's a plan, right? You guys always have a plan. You knew the Neek would take Emn, that's why you went with her. You knew they'd try to separate you two, that's why Yorden and I stormed the capital building. This is just like those times, isn't it?" Nicholas was out of breath when he finished. He'd thought Neek would stop him halfway through—smile, pat him on the back. Realization dawned on him slowly, but Nicholas fought it. "Right, Neek?"

Neek's eyes finally met his, and the silence that stretched between them hurt worse than if she'd actually said something. Nicholas looked away then, too shaken to respond. Abstract death, death because you were defending yourself—it was horrible, but he could deal with it. This...

"He helped me out after I got exiled from my planet. Met him in a spaceport bar on Mars, talking big about his antique ship, how she was one of the first the Terrans ever put in space that could make it past Earth's moon. One of the first commercial spacecrafts." Neek sat back down next to the chrysalis and stared blankly out the window. "He was so proud of that fucking ship. So excited that I could drive it despite the insane upgrades he put in. Never cared about who I was, or that my whole planet hated me, or that he'd lose every Neek haul job by having me onboard."

Nicholas still couldn't bring himself to add anything. What stories did he have that could compare to Neek's decade of hauling freight with the captain? Maybe, when this was all over, they could sit and Neek could share some stories about Yorden—stories about close calls and contraband goods and a ship comprised more of tape than metal. They'd be safe stories, too, because Nicholas would know they'd pull through in the end. Yorden had always pulled through, until now.

"I don't really understand what he did, what you two did for a living, since it was smuggling—smuggling for the Risalians. But it was a good education, I think. I don't think I'd ever want to be like Yorden, but I'm glad to have met him. Glad I met the Ardulan woman too, however briefly." That sounded stupid and trite, but Nicholas didn't know what else to say. The reality of the situation hadn't hit him yet.

"Yeah," Neek agreed, her eyes wandering to the large window. The star field was stable, and Nicholas watched Neek's eyes flit from one star cluster to another, her mouth forming words that never sounded.

"What about Emn?" Nicholas managed to squeak out after the uncomfortable silence stretched too long. He walked slowly over to the chrysalis and squatted down, running his fingers over its surface experimentally. He would keep to safer topics, focus on the crew that had survived. "Feels warm and hard, not sticky like the first time I touched it."

Neek's response was lighter, as if she, too, was happy to move on to another topic. "When it starts flaking, that'll let us know that she's about done in there. At least that's what the old texts say." Neek took a heavy breath. "I know you just woke up, Nick, and things are pretty shit right now, but we have to escape—we have to get Emn away, but I don't know how to do that without endangering her. The cocoon is a pretty big target, especially if you're running down the halls with it."

Nicholas felt Neek's hand on his shoulder, her *stuk* wet on his bare skin. The familiarity was welcome. Not as comforting as Yorden's big paw of a hand, which always made the youth stoop a little from the weight, but comforting nonetheless. "We'll figure something out, Neek. No way we'll let the Nugels have her."

"We have to figure out how to not let the Nugels have *us* first." Neek shook her head and managed a tight smile. "I know this probably is not the Journey experience you were looking for, huh? Battles, death, war. It's a lot for anyone to handle."

"I adapted," Nicholas murmured. He could lighten the mood, too. "I mean, I can fire guns now. What do you think my mom'll have to say about *that*?"

Neek grimaced. "She'll never forgive us. You might have to consider a permanent life of petty space transport. The heretic lifestyle is also an option."

"I don't think transport cabin boy is a legitimate career path." The mental image of himself in brown cutoff pants with a mop in one hand, swabbing the cockpit of the *Pledge,* made Nicholas snort. Neek smiled back, but the sadness playing at the corners of her eyes sobered him. There wasn't any way to get around the weight of their current situation, apparently.

"Where do we go from here, Neek?" he asked softly. "The Nugels and their Alliance have declared war on the Risalians. Without the Risalians, the Charted Systems will fall apart. Emn's caught up in the middle of it all, and she can't even defend herself. We're naked, weaponless, and on a Nugel ship with no viable means of escape."

The corners of Neek's mouth twitched again. "That's not entirely true." She pointed to a pile of metal objects near a wooden bed that Nicholas hadn't noticed. "They gave us back all the loose parts from our suits. I was armed when we got in them. They must not consider us much of a threat, since they're going to let us go." She walked to the bed and picked up the knife with the curved blade. "We have a weapon."

"We have a vegetable peeler."

Neek grinned. "True. But don't you think the Nugels look pretty ripe?" Her smile broadened as she wove the blade through her thick braid, securing it with a loop of hair at the base. "C'mon, kid. Time for a plan worthy of Yorden and the *Mercy's Pledge.*"

CHAPTER 24: MARKIN COUNCIL ROOM, RISAL

We're holding position at Oorin, as instructed. Alliance vessels placed throughout the Charted Systems have spotted an estimated fifty Risalian ships moving from their posts at the border and heading towards our location. More Alliance reinforcements are arriving daily. We're set to outnumber the Risalians two to one. Ardulum smiles upon us.

—Encrypted communication sent from the *Llttrin*, November 12th, 2060 CE

Xouy was acutely aware of the empty chair to hir left. There hadn't been time to select a replacement for Kelm—there hadn't been time for anything really, except constant schematics, deployments, and fatality reports. The Markin were losing. The Systems were losing. If they couldn't drive the Mmnnuggls and their allies out soon, there would be nothing left in the Charted Systems worth protecting. Forget the loss of the Terran and Neek systems. Now the Risalian failure would be absolute.

Xouy watched the live-feed hologram flicker as another two Risalian ships materialized and joined formation with the rest of the fleet. The Risalian ships were holding position just outside of the Callis Wormhole, with the Mmnnuggl fleets on the far side of Oorin. For every Risalian cutter that arrived, it seemed like three times that many appeared of their adversaries. Xouy couldn't even begin to guess at the operational capacity of most of the unknown ships. Kelm had been their space technology expert, but Xouy doubted that even the late markin would have been able to separate warships from transports within the mottled Mmnnuggl fleets.

"Both sides continue to hold their positions," Sald said wearily, flipping text on the electronic sheet in front of hir. "Captains from several cutters report the continued influx of Mmnnuggl and unknown ships."

"Well, they're not coming through the Callis Wormhole," Raek said. "We haven't received any reports of a non-Risalian utilizing the wormhole since the *Mercy's Pledge* incident."

Raek's comment brought the conference room into silence once again. *We mishandled the whole situation from the beginning,* Xouy thought to hirself bitterly. *Maybe we've become too much like the other Charted Systems inhabitants—too quick to compromise; too slow to violence. We let our guard drop and the systems we swore to protect paid the price.*

The silence dragged on for several minutes, each markin buried in hir own thoughts.

"Risal will pay the price for our arrogance," Sald said finally. "We will pay the price. Thus far, the Mmnnuggl forces have shown no interest in any of the other systems, even those left undefended. They've chosen to take their stand against us alone."

"We're the only reasonable threat," Sandid cut in. "What resistance could Neek or Earth realistically offer?"

"At this point, I think we've realized that this isn't about conquering," Xouy cut in. Xe leaned over the table and switched the holographic display to a greater Charted Systems map. "More proof. Look here. The attacked intersects are highlighted in red. Now, look at the ships that were attacked at those locations." Xouy tapped an inset monitor, and images of Risalian cutters popped into the hologram. "If we look at the data starting just from the first incident with the *Pledge*—the first truly violent encounter with the Mmnnuggls—and ignore all previous encounters, the pattern we suspected emerges."

Xouy watched the other markin study the hologram, their heads nodding in defeated agreement. Xe leaned over and rotated the hologram, pointing at intersection 201. "Here, from two-oh-one to two-fifty, where we had the training ships for fresh second *dons*. Intersections twenty through twenty-five, where we attempted to reinforce the border with extra Ardulans. Somehow they *knew*." Xe sat back in hir chair and rubbed hir neck. "Kelm was right to be concerned. It's uncanny how they know which ships carry Ardulans."

"They targeted strategically." Sandid turned to Xouy. "It seems likely that the Mmnnuggls wanted to secure the upper hand before engaging us face-to-face. That would be a solid strategy for assuming control of the Systems."

Xouy shook hir head. "I thought so too, at first. But if taking control of the Charted Systems was the goal, why ignore Earth and Neek? If you argue that they went after the mining system to cut off our supply base, then why not also our financial center on Baltec? Why not take the Alusian System which has plenty of hostages, no defenses, and is situated directly in the middle of the Systems?" Xouy tapped the Oorin projection three times, and the planet lit up to a bright blue. "I think the motivation is less complex than conquering. I think that at first they simply wanted to destroy the Ardulans for some reason. Maybe the Mmnnuggls and this alliance of theirs met the original Ardulans and didn't like them. Who knows? The point is, I believe we had more than they initially thought. When hit-and-runs weren't proving effective, they decided to get our attention here, at Oorin."

"You're suggesting that we are playing into their hands by sending our strongest forces to Oorin." Sald growled, hir already purple-tinged neck slits turning an even deeper shade of violet.

"Yes. What we view as a last stand to defend the Charted Systems, they see as a well-planned chance to eradicate every Ardulan in our fleet. Eradication of us as a species may be an added bonus."

Sandid visibly considered the information, one of hir pointed teeth lightly puncturing hir lower lip as xe did so. "It fits with our intelligence reports. There have been no reported acts of violence against anyone on Oorin. No ships other than ours have been attacked throughout the Charted Systems. Xouy may be correct."

"What course of action does that leave us?" Sald's voice raised several octaves. "We're outnumbered at Oorin. We stay and fight—they win. If we pull our forces back, they will destroy those already stationed outside the Callis Wormhole, thus taking out over sixty percent of our Ardulans and over twelve thousand Risalians. After that, it would only be a matter of time before they picked off every last cutter."

Sandid scowled. "You make it sound like the Mmnnuggls have already won."

"Haven't they?" Sald pointed at the hologram. "If Xouy is right, we've already made our biggest misstep by sending the bulk of our fleet to Oorin. We will certainly lose those ships—we hadn't planned on the Mmnnuggl forces being so organized, or so very, very large."

Xouy made a sweeping movement with hir hand, causing the hologram to disintegrate. "Markin, if I may have your attention," Xouy said softly as xe brought up a template holo of the Charted Systems. Several quick taps of hir finger on the embedded computer screen created ship icons and numbers above each inhabited planet.

"Don't even suggest it," Sandid said, outraged. "I know what you're thinking, Xouy. We swore to protect the Charted Systems. The other species here, they don't understand war. They don't have weapons. Their ships barely have armor. If we bring them to Oorin, they will be slaughtered."

"Actually, I don't think so," Xouy responded calmly. "If we assume that the Mmnnuggl forces are acting upon some impulse to eradicate the Ardulans and have not done violence to any other sentients other than those responsible for the Ardulans..."

"The entire planet of Risal," Raek muttered under hir breath.

Xouy continued, ignoring Raek. "If we make that assumption, I think it is a logical step that the Mmnnuggls will *not* fire upon other species. At least, not without provocation. They took on Risalians because we alone defend the Charted Systems. We utilize the Ardulans. The other species, however—would they not be viewed as innocents in all of this?"

Xouy folded hir hands in hir lap and waited two long breaths, giving the other markin time to intuit where xe was going. "The Mmnnuggls encountered *Mercy's Pledge*, but no move was made against Captain Kuebrich or his crew. When our cutter rammed the *Pledge*, the Mmnnuggls searched for survivors."

"Of which we are *certain* there were none, correct?" Raek interjected.

Sald nodded in response. "We received reports from four separate empath Ardulans. There was no life in the debris."

"I conclude that the Mmnnuggls value life. Perhaps that is why they are destroying our Ardulans—our database notes numerous instances of species that disagree with genetic manipulation for religious or moral reasons."

"I really hope we're not dealing with religious fanatics," Sandid murmured under hir breath. "Anything we'd do would be like trying to reason with a Neek."

"Whether religious or moral," Xouy continued, "they're only after the Ardulans and then us by proxy. I suggest we disclose our current situation to the network of the Charted Systems. Offer beings a chance to stand with us and defend their homes. Be clear about the danger, but offer the various inhabitants a chance to fight for the peace they've enjoyed."

"What if the Mmnnuggls attack before any additional ships arrive?" Sald asked.

Xouy shrugged. "I thought you said we were going to die no matter what."

Raek scooted hir chair closer to the table and eyed the hologram closely. "You really think that a couple dozen transport ships will make the Mmnnuggls back down?"

"I don't know," Xouy replied, hoping the nervousness xe felt hadn't seeped into hir tone. "At the very least, it will make them reconsider. If six separate systems choose to take a stand against the Mmnnuggls, are prepared to sacrifice themselves to protect their way of life...it might give the Mmnnuggls something to think about."

Xouy watched Sald sit back in hir chair and rub hir neck slits with both hands. Xe let the passing lights of a ground transport distract hir momentarily from the decision before them, admiring the way the light reflected off the window glass and sent small, shimmering dots down the side of the nearby wall.

"If they just start firing," Sald started, hir voice wavering, "we'll have done worse than failed. We'll be responsible for the death of hundreds, if not thousands, of innocent lives."

"That's why we let them volunteer, Sald," Xouy responded gently. "I think you'd be surprised at the sacrifices beings are willing to make when they believe in a system—a system that protects them and their families, their cultures."

Sandid nodded slowly. "I agree. I think it's time to ask the Charted Systems to take responsibility for their well-being. We've lost approximately eight hundred thousand Risalians thus far in this war. I know the entire population of Risal would gladly give their lives in service of the Systems, and I think there might be some from other worlds that feel the same."

"I also agree," Raek said. "As long as it is only volunteers."

Sald sighed heavily. "All right. I'll send the notice to the Galactic News Network immediately." The large Risalian turned to stare at Xouy, hir eyes dark. "Then I'm getting on the next cutter leaving the system. If we're taking a stand together, as the Charted Systems, then I am going to be a part of it."

A smile broke out on Xouy's face. The tension in the room dissipated. Raek chuckled and slapped Sandid on the back. "We're all going, Sald," Raek said, smiling broadly. "We belong with our people, in life and in death."

CHAPTER 25: MMNNUGGL FLAGSHIP

I'd now like to read directly from a press release by the Risalian government:

Dear sentients of the Charted Systems,

The Markin Council of Risal would like to inform you that beings from outside the Charted Systems have broken through our defensive grid and have taken control of Oorin. These beings—primarily a species called the Mmnnuggls, as well as others—seek the complete destruction of components vital to upholding the framework of peace and prosperity we have built in the Charted Systems. We cannot defeat these forces alone. We invite you now to join us in our stand at Oorin. We Risalians understand that your ships do not have weapons— indeed, that you all abhor violence. The Mmnnuggls are unknown to you and do not have a history of attacking civilian ships; however, we cannot promise that this will last. We ask for your aid, but only if you are willing to give it. Together, we know that our combined presence will be enough to drive back the Mmnnuggl attack. Join us in protecting the Charted Systems, in protecting what is important to all of us—our home.

—Priority broadcast from The Galactic News, *November 12th, 2060 CE*

"I've never seen so many ships in one place," Nicholas breathed. He stood next to Neek in front of a floor-to-ceiling window in the sleeping area of their shared quarters. Neek surveyed him, pleased to see his skin take on a healthier hue despite all his recent wounds.

"Neek, do you know which species those ships belong to?" Nicholas asked softly.

Neek returned her attention to the window. The dim, green lighting sent wobbly patches of glare across the glass, but it was still easy to see the massing ships. She could just make out the edges of the Risalian fleet if she moved to the far right side of the window. Filling most of the view, however, were ships completely foreign to her. There seemed to be an infinite number of designs, from perfectly round spheres that reminded her of Mmnnuggls, to disc-shaped saucers. She saw an array of colors— mostly gray, but with blue, red, and purple undertones. Lasers and armor plating abounded in shapes and forms she'd never considered possible. The only thing the ships had in common, as far as she could tell, was that they all appeared to be made from the same cellulosic metal hybrid that the Charted Systems used for their spacecrafts.

"I don't have a clue, Nick," she responded finally. "There are Risalians, sure, and plenty of Mmnnuggl pods, but the others...they must be from outside the Systems." She pointed at a flattened disc— roughly the size of a Mmnnuggl pod-frigate—as it spun around a star-shaped vessel. "I *know* that's not a Systems design. That ship can't have ceilings more than one meter high. We don't have any species that could fit inside."

Neek reached back to scratch an itch lingering just between her shoulder blades, cursing the coarse, brown tunics she and Nicholas had been given hours earlier. It was an absorbent fabric, designed for a persistently moist species, and its wicking properties pulled at Neek's *stuk* and left her feeling dehydrated and irritable. "If we're going to do something, now is the time." She gestured towards the window. "No one is going to pay attention to a couple of bipeds in the middle of all this."

Nicholas pulled his attention from the window and turned to face the pilot. "Captain Lug said our ship would be ready in two hours. I think it's been almost three. We can get out of here any time we want, but what are we going to do about Emn?"

Neek closed her eyes and placed a hand on the window, steadying herself. Five days. For five days, she'd been trying to come up with a plan on how they might sneak the chrysalis off the ship. No matter what ideas sprang to mind, the sticking point was always the sheer size of the thing. There was no way to get it, undetected, onto a ship—especially when the chrysalis was poked and prodded hourly by a Mmnnuggl medical team hoping to sedate Emn at the moment of emergence.

"I don't see how we could leave with Emn," Neek said quietly. "She's too well guarded. We're too well monitored." She tapped the edges of the curved knife in her hair. "We don't even know if we're on a small pod or one of the big ones. We could maybe slice and dice our way out of a small one, but something cutter-sized...that's a lot of Nugels to impale."

"I'm not leaving without Emn," Nicholas said adamantly. "What about our plan?"

"Nicholas, we need to be reasonable about what we can accomplish. Getting Emn off this ship before she emerges is our number one priority, but we won't get anywhere if people are shooting at us." Neek ran a sticky hand over the irritating fabric, silently cursing the rough texture. Nicholas continued to stare at her, frowning.

She threw her hands up in exasperation. "We've been over this plan repeatedly. Yes, we have a chance—a *small* chance—if the ships outside start firing. There will be confusion and damage. Nugels will be stuck to those weird panel interface things. They don't really seem to understand the concept of hands, so if we can manage to convince them that bipeds need things *in* their hands at all times, we'd be marginally less suspicious if we tried to carry Emn's chrysalis out of here, but only marginally." She tapped the knife again, fidgeting. "If things *do* get rough, we will have to fight. We will have to *kill*. Do you understand that?"

"I'll kill if I have to."

Neek looked at Nicholas skeptically. "I thought morality wasn't negotiable."

"Shut up, Neek." Nicholas grinned. "If one of them disconnects and see us, and we can't talk our way out of it, we fight. I'm okay with that. She's just a kid, you know? She deserves a shot at life." He lifted his tunic off and laid it experimentally on the chrysalis. "Here, give me yours. Let's see how best to cover it. If we're going with the 'bipeds need walkies and things in their hands' ploy, we'd better at least cover this up."

Surprised, Neek took hers off and handed it to Nicholas. They'd talked about this course of action, sure, but she hadn't been serious about the bluff. Neek supposed it wasn't the absolute worst idea for getting off the pod. She helped tuck the tunic around the edges of the chrysalis and then glanced out the window. Her eyes caught a familiar ship design, and the untucked edge of the tunic fell from her hand onto the floor.

"Nick, isn't that a Terran shuttle? One of the new ones—not an antique like the *Pledge*."

Nicholas followed Neek's finger. "Yeah, I think it is! There are other Charted Systems vehicles now, too. Look! I see a Minoran Galaxtic liner, like, six different classes of Alusian ships, and there is a whole fleet of the Oorin mining ships. They're all flying into that big gap!"

Neek watched, amazed, as Charted Systems vessels began to exit the wormhole en masse. A Minoran galactic liner slid up alongside the Terran shuttle, two Oorin mining ships just behind. Moving to the far right of the window, she could make out even more vessels—a luxury cruiser from Craston, its bright lights flashing, and four short-range news skiffs. Nicholas whistled.

"There's a Risalian governmental transport ship over there too," Neek said, moving her finger and pointing emphatically. "The *Markin* are here. What is going on?"

A vibration began to build under their feet, causing Nicholas to momentarily look away from the window. "Neek..." he began uncertainly.

"They're powering their weapons," Neek said. "We're out of time. Looks like walkies it is." She hastily arranged the tunics over the top of the chrysalis and wrapped her arms around it, hefting one end into the air. It wasn't any heavier than when she'd picked it up from the cutter, but the weight distribution had changed dramatically. She could feel movement just underneath the surface.

"Come on, Nicholas," Neek said, nodding to the end nearest him. "Pick up your end and let's go. Now is our chance."

CHAPTER 26: CALLIS SYSTEM

Only the andal can guide you to your path. As the Ardulans move from first to second don, *from juvenile to adult, so too must the Neek journey within themselves. It is not enough to emulate. You must become.*

—Excerpt from *The Book of the Ascension,* first edition

Captain Llgg hovered against the black interface panel in her quarters, the connection sending packets of data directly into her brain. She curled the tips of her ears into perfect ovals and then released them, trying to send her frustration away. The Risalians had made a surprising move. She had not anticipated it. The Alliance rulers had not anticipated it, either. That the sentients of the Charted Systems would go to such lengths to protect the genetic mush perpetrated by the Risalians was obscene. They were idiots, the lot of them. Blasphemers, heretics, idolaters. They didn't walk in the light of Ardulum.

If the construct were her own offspring, she would have simply killed it. The Ardulans did not tolerate imperfection; therefore, the Mmnnuggl people did not tolerate it, either. Yet the Eld, rulers of the Alliance, waffled—made the Mmnnuggls wait. The longer they waited, the bigger the battle became. More lives would be lost to rectify the mistakes of previous generations. Llgg was not pleased.

An unexpected turn of events, her second-in-command messaged from his post.

An unfortunate turn of events, she responded. *Their numbers are not inconsequential. We have waited too long.*

Should we avoid the civilian ships or strike them down? another queried from Tactical. *Our maneuverability is superior. They are unarmed. They cannot offer resistance.*

Captain Llgg spun around quickly and then made contact again with the interface, accidentally clipping the lobe of her ear as she did so. *Their mere presence is resistance. They do not understand what it is they protect. There is no way to make them understand. We must rectify the transgressions of the past.*

We will fire only on Risalians if ordered, her second responded. *It is not of Ardulum to kill peaceful sentients.*

Weapons are charged, Tactical sent.

The Alliance ships report that their systems are also ready, came the response from Communications. *The Eld have given permission to proceed. The constructs are to be destroyed—all but the girl in our custody. They have given no guidance on targeting the unweaponized ships.*

Captain Llgg swayed back and forth against the interface. The Eld needed to protect themselves. They needed to protect Ardulum. If the ruling council would not make the decision, she had no problem doing so herself.

Attack, she sent. *Avoid the civilian ships to the best of your ability. However, you are authorized to take the steps necessary to neutralize any who get in the way. The Alliance has made its wishes clear—no Ardulan construct will leave this battle alive. Charted Systems lives are of no consequence to Ardulum, but the Alliance does not wish to begin a larger war.*

There was a momentary break in the feed as Llgg's statement was transmitted across the Alliance fleet.

Your message is received and understood, her second sent back finally. *The battle begins.*

* * *

Xouy, along with the rest of the markin, stood at attention on the bridge of their official government transport cutter, *Risal's Promise*. Their rigid posture as they raptly paid attention to the viewscreen did not go unnoticed by the ship's crew.

"Pull the *Promise* away from the front," Sald commanded. "We want to watch first to see how events develop."

A blast rocked the cutter and caused the markin to stumble into each other. Xouy grabbed Sandid's tunic for support. The neck seam ripped loudly.

Sandid shot Xouy an amused look when Xouy muttered an apology. "Relax, Xouy," Sandid said as xe squeezed Xouy's arm. "We're all new to this. Since I doubt we'll make it out alive, I don't think my tunic matters at all that much."

"No damage from the impact," a third called out to the Markin. "Our shields are holding. We'll be out of the battlefront in an estimated two minutes."

A spattering of small laser bursts impacted the viewscreen as a ship Xouy didn't recognize made a swooping pass. A small Risalian skiff vaporized just to the left of the screen, leaving the telltale gas signature floating across the space in front of the cutter.

Xouy continued to watch as the *Promise* navigated her way through the combat zone. The ship listed hard to port when a Mmnnuggl pod dropped a hydrogen bomb on their stern.

"Oof," Raek let out as xe picked hirself up off the floor. An alarm klaxon began blaring faintly in the distance. "We can't take too many more of those hits."

"Shields absorbed most of it," the third replied. "But the stern plating just chipped away. We're vulnerable in that area."

Xouy stepped from the line of markin over to the communications console. "Third, switch the viewer to show our stern."

The resulting image showed the protective shield plating scattered behind the cutter, several pieces still loosely attached and flapping back and forth against the hull.

"Would you look at how many there are," Sandid called out and gestured at the screen. Xouy looked past the stern and, amongst the impressive collection of streaming laser lights and explosions, saw an increasing number of civilian ships taking up defensive positions.

"They figured out that the Mmnnuggls won't fire on them," Xouy breathed. "They're shielding our ships!"

"Now, if only our ships could do some significant damage," Sald responded, hir tone sour. "Even with the civilian ships, we're outnumbered. Judging from the pieces of metal that keep floating past our screen, I'd say we're taking out one of their ships for every four of ours."

"Markin, we have a problem." A third looked up from hir console and pointed towards the front of the ship. "There's a Mmnnuggl pod directly ahead of us. It's preventing the *Promise* from moving any farther from the battle."

"Maybe someone should tell them that there aren't any Ardulans onboard," Raek suggested. "Just a bunch of government officials on an unarmed cutter."

"Markin, the pod is hailing us."

"Answer it," Xouy advised. "If they're talking, then they're not shooting."

The third tapped commands into the console. A series of loud clicks and whirrs sounded through the bridge, barely louder than the klaxon.

Sald raised an eyebrow and turned to Xouy. "How's your understanding of Mmnnuggl?"

"Terrible," Xouy responded. "I think the Capital Sector position would have a stronger foothold in xenolinguistics, Sald, than the Science Sector."

"Markin," a third called from the communications console. "May I offer a translation?"

Xouy stared expectantly. The third nodded and spoke loudly in an effort to be heard over the increasingly powerful klaxon. "The Mmnnuggl pod informs us that we will not be permitted to leave the engagement zone. We are warned that attempts at further movement will be met with force."

"Right." Sald clasped hir hands behind hir back. "Guess we watch from here. Third, stop the cutter." The third entered a swift command into the computer, and the stars in the viewscreen solidified. The battle unfolded in front of them—a mass of weaving ships and biometal flotsam. The Alliance ships spun through the mess of civilian ships and wreckage, trying to reach the Risalians.

Three hard blasts rocked the cutter in quick succession. "I thought we stopped!" Raek called, fanning smoke from hir face. Xouy and Raek gripped the edge of the wall for support as they both tried to regain balance, the ship now listing decidedly starboard.

"Crossfire," another third called out above the din as xe scrambled back into the chair. "One of our skiffs decided to use us for cover. The shots came from one of the Mmnnuggl ships that tracked the skiff."

"We'll be blown to pieces if we just sit here," Sandid yelled, choking on the smoke. "Our starboard stabilizer is shot. I say we *do* something, one way or another."

"Agreed," Xouy responded. Behind the Markin, the viewscreen lit up brightly as another Risalian cutter burst apart. "The captains know we're here, and they know not to give any special consideration to our ship. I don't think we'd be putting any lives in danger except our own if we engage a Mmnnuggl pod."

"We don't have any *weapons*, Xouy." Raek gestured around the bridge. "We've got communications, navigation, and a third who speaks Mmnnuggl. Unless you want to do a suicide ramming mission, this ship is useless."

Xouy nodded. "We can shield, just like those unarmed ships. We came out here to show solidarity with the Charted Systems inhabitants. I say we follow their lead."

Sald nodded in agreement. After a moment of hesitation, Raek and Sandid did the same.

Xouy smiled. "All right then. Third, take us back into battle. Pick one of our cutters and stay between it and an attacker."

The third altered course. The *Promise* made a tight turn, the force of the movement compounded by the loss of the starboard stabilizer. When the main battlefront was again visible on the viewscreen, Xouy paused, hir plan momentarily forgotten.

The Risalians were no longer outnumbered. Chartered Systems ships of every type and design littered the immediate space. More poured in through the Callis Wormhole by the second. The space was no longer filled with streaking lines of laser fire. Instead, Mmnnuggl forces flew by, fast and agile, trying to skim between the shielding ships to get a clear shot. With every group of ships that came through the wormhole, the task became more difficult. Systems ships began surrounding the Risalian cutters, creating massive biometal barriers.

"Which cutter would you like me to block, Markin?" the communications third asked. "None are without at least two shield ships."

None of the markin responded. All four stared dumbfounded out the viewscreen. Xouy couldn't believe what xe was seeing and shook hir head, almost expecting hir vision to clear and the real battlefront to materialize.

"I didn't expect this level of response," xe said slowly, the words dropping from hir mouth.

"It looks like every ship in the Systems is out there," Sandid added. "I estimate at least a thousand on the viewscreen alone."

"Your orders, Markin?" the third called again.

Xouy looked to Sald. "Yes, what are we going to do? Have we *won*?"

"I don't know," Sald responded. "For now, just hold position. If you're correct and the Mmnnuggl forces are only after the Ardulans, then we're about to see how badly they want them."

CHAPTER 27: MMNNUGGL FLAGSHIP

If light poured in through this tunnel
I would look up and know it was you
Like running water through a swinging gate
Sweeping through my conscious mind
Refreshing, refreshing my perceptions
Honing my rationale
Forcing an evolution of my senses
Until all I see is Truth

—Excerpt from *Atalant's Awakening*, published in the Charted Systems, 235 AA

"We look like two bipeds carrying a suspicious bundle of cloth the size of a chrysalis instead of two bipeds just carrying a chrysalis," Nicholas whispered as they eased their way down the corridor. The form in the chrysalis kept shifting, and the repeated need to rearrange the tunics slowed their progress.

"This was your idea, Nicholas. Little late to change your mind."

Nicholas scowled. "Hey! Being handsy bipeds is at least a semiplausible excuse for hauling something this size through a hallway."

Neck sniffed as they passed a transparent section of outer wall. The massing ships could be seen clearly, but the faint weave of the cellulose in the panel distorted their appearance. What was missing, however, was the streaking light of laser fire. Ships still moved, but the formation didn't make sense. Why were the civilian ships in the engagement zone? Why wasn't anyone firing?

Neek stopped their progression and set down her end of the chrysalis. Something was wrong, but she couldn't quite place what it was. "Nicholas," she said, gesturing to the window. "Come have a look at this."

Nicholas gently placed his end on the floor and moved to the clear panel. "We're moving. We've been moving. What's up?"

"It's different this time," Neek responded. "The ship types are different now, although if that's because there are more Systems civilian ships or because of where we are on the battlefront, I can't tell."

Nicholas turned from the window and shrugged his shoulders. The movement was tight, almost brittle, and Neek immediately regretted bringing this to the youth's attention. How much more Nicholas could take without breaking, she wasn't sure.

Neek wanted to mitigate her previous words, but was out of practice. Instead, she decided to plow through with the truth. She could get him a therapist later, if they lived. "If we are headed somewhere like the front lines, getting out of this mess without being shot at will be even harder, especially if the civilian ships are cluttering up the space." She bent back down and picked up her end of the chrysalis. "We don't have much time. Let's move."

Nicholas nodded silently and picked his end back up. They continued down the empty corridor, hunched over. The rough flooring tore at Neek's feet. Emn's chrysalis was heavy, and the stooping put even more strain on Neek's back. She shifted it slightly in her arms, trying to get a better hold.

"Docking area is to the left," Nicholas whispered as they reached a rounded T-junction that shimmered, floor to ceiling, with the black interface paneling. Neek nodded and turned. The two jogged as best they could to the next fork, where Nicholas again motioned that they should turn left.

The next bend brought them to a more populated area of the ship. The corridor had a long black interface on the right side where twelve spheres were currently attached and lightly bobbing. That left precious little space for them to pass without brushing the wall on the opposite side, which was lit up with little red dots. Neek slowed to a walk and eyed the Mmnnuggls carefully.

"What do you want to do?" Nicholas whispered under his breath.

"Just keep walking and try to keep away from the wall and the Mmnnuggls," she responded. "Maybe they don't see like we do. If they're linked up to the ship, it's possible they're not even paying attention. If anyone says anything, we're just on our way to the ship. Decided to hold our clothes instead of wearing them. Since they don't use textiles, anything we do with garments will be strange. Let's bank on being too foreign to bother with."

Halfway through the corridor, Neek had to shift Emn's weight again. As she slid her left arm towards the middle of the chrysalis, one of the tunics unwrapped and fell onto the floor. Green light reflected off the silver casing right onto one of the Mmnnuggls. Before Nicholas could rewrap the chrysalis, the sphere rotated towards them and pulled away from the interface. Its top ear cuff curled, folding the ear effectively in half.

Neek didn't waste any time. She set her half of the chrysalis down, tugged the knife from her hair, and plunged the curved metal tip into the mouth opening. The Mmnnuggl screeched and tried to pull back, but caught on the tip of the blade. Neek brought her arm down quickly, keeping a tight hold on the handle. The momentum drove the Mmnnuggl down into the floor, where it split in two, leaking a purple, viscous fluid onto the jagged floor.

None of the remaining spheres took any notice.

Neek wiped her blade on her tunic and then picked up her end of the chrysalis, knife still clutched firmly in her hand.

"Effective," Nicholas whispered. "Also gross. I thought you wanted to talk your way out of this, not kill beach balls?"

"If you have any complaints, you can deal with the next one." Neek's left hand slid to the top of the chrysalis, and she had to catch it with her hip to keep from dropping it. "Damn it, I can't keep a solid grip."

"That would be because you are covered in Nugel goo."

Neek glared. "No," she shot back, "it's because the surface is changing again. Don't you feel how smooth it is?"

Nicholas pointed to a small pile of white flakes near where the tunic had fallen. "There's also those. We're running out of time."

Neek cursed, the thumping in her chest an unwelcome addition to her thinned *stuk*. Time. They were always short on time. The two resumed their jog, and Neek tried desperately to remember her assigned reading on Ardulan metamorphosis. What was the time frame after the scaling? An hour? A day? She fervently hoped it was longer than ten minutes.

"We're almost there," Nicholas huffed when they reached the next junction. "Should be behind those doors up ahead."

They approached the round hatch slowly. When they were within an arm span, the door rolled to one side, allowing them access to a docking bay with a mercifully high ceiling. Neek entered first, backing in and trying to minimize the squelching sound her wet feet made on the floor. The small transport pod Llgg had mentioned stood in the center of the small hangar, the boarding ramp lowered. No other ships were in the bay, but pieces of biometal were strewn about the floor, in various stages of decay. A long window stretched across the back of the bay, giving an excellent view of the ships outside. Two Mmnnuggls hovered on an interface just beside the ship and paid neither her nor Nicholas any attention.

It looked too convenient, but Neek wasn't going to question it. She stood back up to her full height and nodded towards the ship. "Let's try walking again," she whispered. "Nice and slow. Nothing suspicious. Avoid the debris. Board the ship, hide the chrysalis, pull the ramp, engage the engines. Then we can blast the hangar door open and get out of here."

Nicholas reached around the chrysalis and grabbed Neek's right arm, halting her movement. "Neek," he breathed, "take a look out the window. We're right in between both sides now."

Neek studied the layout. There were more and more Charted Systems crafts as they rotated. A breath later, all she could see were Systems ships, the last Mmnnuggl pod falling off the edge of the screen. If only Systems ships were in view, that meant the Mmnnuggl ships were behind them. That meant... Realization hit. They were leading the attack. Every Risalian would be aiming for this pod. This would be their primary target.

"Run!" Neek pushed the tunics from the chrysalis to Nicholas, transferred the chrysalis to her arms, and nudged Nicholas forward. She followed Nicholas's sprint as fast as she could, kicking the debris out of her path. She felt the surface of the chrysalis sloughing in thin sheets as she ran. They couldn't afford to be cautious anymore.

As she took the first steps up the boarding ramp, the *Llttrin* shuddered. The movement was enough to send Neek off-balance. The pilot wobbled on the ramp and lost her footing, sending both herself and the chrysalis crashing to the floor. None of the Mmnnuggls turned to investigate, instead remaining locked to their interfaces.

The *Llttrin* shuddered again. Nicholas reached Neek and offered her a hand up, which she took. Another shudder and Emn's chrysalis rolled back behind the boarding ramp. Hands inadvertently free, Neek tossed her tunic back over her head, securing the knife in a side fold, and glanced out the window. Laser fire had resumed, but it was no longer discriminate. Charted Systems civilian ships began exploding at an alarming rate, bursting into rainbow hues before Neek's eyes.

"We missed our window," she whispered.

"Jesus, they're firing on *civilians!*" Nicholas put his hands on either side of his head. "That's just not...our ships don't have any weapons! The Systems civilian ships don't have any chance of surviving. Neek, we have to *do* something."

Neek shook her head. What could they do other than protect their own lives? At least the Mmnnuggls were too busy coordinating attacks to pay any attention to them. She reached over to wrap an arm around Nicholas, hesitated, and then brought her arm back in. She watched three Terran shuttles disintegrate as a pod cut through them with laser fire. A Minoran galactic liner split in two, each half taking out six nearby Risalian skiffs in its wake. An Oorin mining frigate took three shots from a pod and began to list, inertia pushing it from the engagement zone. A formation of small, unidentified ships followed, peppering it with laser fire until it broke apart.

For a moment, she imagined herself out there, in a settee, weaving in and out of the fray, exploding Mmnnuggl ships. It was a ridiculous notion, because settees didn't have weapons, but at least she could fly one. Even if they got onto the gifted Mmnnuggl pod in front of them, what guarantee was there that she could fly it? For that matter, what guarantee was there that it had weapons either?

"Nicholas," Neek began. She understood all too well the desire to act. "We'll never make it through that much fire, especially in a ship I've never flown before."

"I'd rather be blown up than drugged and hauled to another system," Nicholas hissed. "I'm sure Emn would feel the same way. Let's take our chances. You're supposed to be the reckless one, remember?"

"You don't understand the first thing about what is going on out there, do you?" Neek glared at the youth, *stuk* streaming from her fingers. "I'm not taking Emn on a suicide run. We will die if we leave this ship now, and Emn is in no place to cellulose us back into existence."

She gestured around the bay. "This space is defensible. There might be another break in fire we can take advantage of. We need to be patient. For the time being, we are trapped."

Without waiting for a response, Neek turned back to the window. Nicholas moved to her side and stared as well. Laser fire filled the darkness of space, illuminating the void in the brilliant flashes. Four Alusian luxury liners broke apart when a small Mmnnuggl pod rolled across their surfaces, depositing bombs in its wake. With their minimal shielding, they disintegrated immediately. A formation of Terran shuttles scattered as two large Mmnnuggl pods corralled them on either end. Two additional ships that Neek didn't recognize caught the shuttles as they fled, destroying each in turn.

"This is a nightmare," Neek whispered.

"It's a slaughter," Nicholas said simply, his voice flat.

"It is the only way to end the threat," another voice said behind them.

Nicholas and Neek swung around to find the two Mmnnuggls from the interface only a couple of meters away, hovering halfway between the floor and ceiling.

"You are not authorized to remove the altered Ardulan from this ship," the second one said.

"Security has been contacted," the first added.

Neek brandished the knife. "You want a threat?" The ship shuddered again.

The first Mmnnuggl tipped itself slightly to its left, both ears folding in half. "*You* are not a threat. The construct threatens unaltered species. There is a threat of interbreeding. There is a threat of mutation. You risk angering the Gods by challenging their edict."

Neek stepped forward and swung the knife wide, trying to back the Mmnnuggls off. "How are you *not* angering your Gods right now?" she demanded. "Those ships are unarmed. You are killing civilians whose only desire is to protect their homes and families."

The second Mmnnuggl floated closer to Neek and stopped just out of arm's reach. "You are Neek," it said, the tone relaying confusion. "You approve of the use of Ardulans as weapons? Of their captivity and alteration?"

"Of course not," she spat angrily. "But these people you're killing, they don't share my culture. All they know is that the Risalians have kept us safe."

"Even if some did know *how* the Risalians managed the peace," Nicholas said, "how could they be forced to choose between a people they've never met over peace and prosperity for their children? Kind of a cruel thing to ask of a sentient."

"The decision is not yours to make, Terran Nicholas," Captain Llgg said as she entered the hangar and floated over to the other Mmnnuggls. "The Alliance has chosen to end the suffering of the altered Ardulans. The Risalians will have to maintain their peace another way. We Mmnnuggls will protect the galaxy from those that threaten it."

"You're not protecting the galaxy by slaughtering thousands of beings!" Neek yelled. Her mouth felt parched. Dehydration wasn't surprising, given her excessive *stuk* production and the stupid wicking tunic. "Are you completely insane? What can you possibly hope to gain from all this?"

The captain remained silent, bobbing up and down gently in the quiet bay.

Neek looked back over her shoulder and stifled a scream as ship after ship exploded, the empty space between the two forces now heavily littered with wreckage. She watched the Risalian cutters attempt to maneuver into shield positions for the Charted Systems ships while the smaller Risalian skiffs peppered the Alliance fleet with ineffectual laser blasts. Even when the unarmed ships ceased blocking and attempted to flee, they were shot down, the Alliance exterminating everything in its path. Ship wreckage clogged the viewscreen, most of it from familiar crafts.

Rage welled in Neek as she surveyed the flotsam: Terran, Minoran, Oorin, Alusian, and Risalian. Bits of ships she didn't recognize. Mmnnuggl. But no Neek.

"Chen's ships are out there," she whispered to Nicholas. "The Minorans, Captain Tang, everyone we know. Everyone who cares enough to protect the Systems."

Nicholas gripped her hand. "You don't know for sure that the Neek aren't out there, too."

She shook her head. "The elite pilots of the Heaven Guard can't be bothered to leave our world, it would seem." Neek paused and looked at the floor. "I wonder if my uncle is addressing the planet about it, right now. I wonder if the president..."

"Neek," Nicholas said, his voice pleading. "This *isn't your fault.*"

The pilot ignored his comment. The president, her uncle, the fucking Heaven Guard, *fucking Ardulum*. Thousands, maybe millions of sentients were dying because of a goddamned planet that *didn't even exist*.

The *Llttrin* jerked to port as a bright streak of yellow shot across the viewscreen. Neek watched the hydrogen bomb impact the Risalian government ship, which slid in front of a cutter just in time to take the hit. The Markin's ship exploded in a wide ring, debris scattering so forcefully that several pieces smacked into the reinforced glass of the hangar window. The small impacts reverberated throughout the empty, metal corridors and rooms of the *Llttrin* and assaulted Neek's ears with thudding, low echoes.

Neek stood rigid and silent as she and Nicholas continued to watch what was left of the battle. Neek began to follow the bright line of another hydrogen bomb when something caught her eye.

In the corner of the hangar, where the dim, green lighting failed to adequately illuminate the space, stood a tall figure. It was bipedal, of that she was sure, but the gloom masked all but a vague outline.

She was unwilling to risk calling attention to the form, but Neek guessed at its identity. *Run*, she thought, trying to aim the command into the small section of her mind where she had hoped Emn might someday return. *Stuk* congealed on Neek's fingers, but she knew that, without reinitiating physical contact, it would be impossible for the girl to hear her.

"Neek?" Nicholas asked as he wiggled his now sticky hand in hers. "What's wrong?"

"They're dying," came a clear, strong voice from the dim corner of the hangar. The Mmnnuggls bobbed in agitation, and Captain Llgg let off a series of high-pitched whistles.

Neek watched the tall, humanoid female step out from the shadows. She had Emn's face, but the features were extended, the cheeks hollow instead of puffed with youth. Her hair had darkened, seeming nearly black in the poor lighting.

Neek couldn't move. She couldn't speak. The facial markings were still present, but now every vein on her body appeared black under the too-pale skin, arcing and angling into complex geometric patterns.

Pale and dark and etched like stone. The line repeated over and over in Neek's head. She couldn't form a new thought, emotions circling the recurring words. Her Emn was gone, replaced by...by what?

A quick series of *tick clack tick*'s came from Captain Llgg. The other Mmnnuggls scattered. One joined the captain in hovering a meter away from Emn while the other connected with the interface.

"Remain where you are," the captain ordered Emn. "Under orders of the Eld, you are to be transported back to our headquarters for evaluation."

Emn turned towards Neek and smiled. They were almost the same height now, Emn just a bit taller. Neek wanted to speak. She wanted to run to Emn and pull the girl—rather, the woman—onto the ship with Nicholas and get *away*. Did Emn even know who they were? Would she consider Neek and Nicholas as friends or foes? What was she even capable of?

"Emn," Nicholas called out. The word echoed through Neek's ears, but no emotion chased them into her mind. "You have to run. They're going to sedate you and take you with them whether you want to or not."

Neek needed to act. She needed to do something, get Emn and Nicholas to safety, but her feet wouldn't move. She couldn't take her eyes from the woman in front of her. Decades of ethos assaulted her, battering the already tortured walls of her mind, overwhelming her senses. Rational thought was a luxury, and she was emotionally poor. All Neek could think was that she had been wrong. *Wrongwrongwrongwrong.* And she was about to pay for her arrogance with their lives.

"She won't be mistreated," Gglltyll said, floating into the room. Four other Mmnnuggls followed. All of them were covered in a shiny liquid that dripped onto the floor as they continued forward. Neek identified the smell as a powerful sedative commonly used on *litha* before slaughter.

The Mmnnuggl medics surrounded Emn and, still, Neek couldn't move. She watched the smallest rush Emn, goo splattering onto the floor as it accelerated. Emn sidestepped at the last moment, a move that appeared so calculated, even the Mmnnuggl paused before reversing for a second pass.

"Didn't you take the Heaven Guard vows?" Nicholas whispered into her ear as a second Mmnnuggl attempted to back Emn into a wall. "Vows to discover or protect or something like that?" The goopy Mmnnuggl began bouncing near Emn's legs, the thick liquid spattering in a wide arc that Emn was still managing to avoid. "She's right in front of you, Neek. Your Ardulan. Your answers. Don't overthink it."

Nicholas's words finally hit home, breaking through the jumbled, chaotic entanglement that was her memories. None of it mattered—not the ships, the robes, the religion...hell, not even the science. It was stupid to remain hung up on the past when her future was right in front of her—if they managed to stay alive.

Neek threw her knife at the other Mmnnuggl. It spun three times before contacting, the side of the blade embedding deeply into the sphere and sending it crashing to the floor.

The effect was satisfying. Action was good. Action she could deal with. Neek recovered her knife and, setting her sights on Gglltyll, pulled her tunic from her body and stretched it taut between her arms. The three remaining medics headed towards Emn while Gglltyll sped towards Nicholas. Neek intercepted Gglltyll at an angle and tossed the tunic over the top of the sphere.

Gglltyll emitted a series of high-pitched whistles and slowed her speed. As the sphere began to rotate to dislodge the fabric, Neek threw herself underneath, gathered the edges of the tunic together, and yanked down. Caught by surprise, Gglltyll slammed into the floor.

Neek looked up to see Emn surrounded, staring intently at the Mmnnuggls. The three medics spun in a tight circle around the Ardulan before attacking all at once. The mysterious liquid flowed off their round bodies as they made contact with Emn's skin, absorbing immediately.

"Get away from her!" Nicholas yelled as he tried to swat ineffectually at the spheres. They zipped gracefully out of his way and headed towards Neek.

Gglltyll struggled against the fabric binding and tried to regain her height. Neek punched the sphere three times in rapid succession, hefted the tunic-wrapped Mmnnuggl from the floor, and threw her over her shoulder. As the medic spheres dashed towards her, she spun the tunic in a wide arc. She struck the leading sphere with Gglltyll's chirping body, releasing the tunic at the highest point in the arc. Gglltyll and the medic flew into the nearby wall and slid to the floor with a satisfying crunch.

Nicholas was on the two remaining medics before Neek had a chance to collect herself. He shoved the first off its path to Neek and wrapped his arms around the other one, wrestling it to the ground and pinning it with his body. The first medic recovered its course and slammed into Neek's stomach. She lost her wind as she landed on her back, the sphere spinning in tight circles on her pelvis and shrieking.

"Neek!" Nicholas yelled. Gasping for breath, the pilot grabbed at the Mmnnuggl's ears, pulling them in opposite directions as hard as she could manage. The shrieking turned into chittering, and the mouth slit opened widely. She heard scuffling sounds from Nicholas's direction but nothing from Emn, which concerned her even more. Frustrated with the delay, Neek brought her left knee up into the back of the Mmnnuggl, holding tightly to the ears as she did so. The Mmnnuggl surged forward as Neek braced her arms against the tension, keeping the sphere in place. She heard a quick ripping sound, and a thick, purple liquid began to drip from the Mmnnuggl's ears. The mouth slit opened wide, nearly separating the Mmnnuggl in half, and Neek found herself staring into a fleshy, purple mouth.

"I don't know how to subdue it!" Nicholas yelled. "I keep punching, but nothing is happening!"

A thick, wet proboscis began to extend from the slit. "Go for the ears," Neek shouted back as she tried to pull the Mmnnuggl to the side. "Get *off* me," she hissed. This time, when she brought her knee up, she released the ears. The Mmnnuggl, expecting to again be held, overcompensated and was sent spinning over Neek's head. Momentarily free, she sprang to her feet and dealt several quick kicks to the left ear of Nicholas's Mmnnuggl. The sphere emitted a high-pitched whine and, on the fourth kick, lay still.

Nicholas stood, and both he and Neek looked around. The medic she had flung away stayed back, and Captain Llgg and her guard remained off to the side, watching. They had a few moments of reprieve. Neek turned and slowly approached the young woman.

She was still standing, but weaving, her eyes fighting to stay open. Nicholas reached out, put her arm around his shoulder, and tried to move them both towards the ship.

"Come on, Emn. We have to get out of here," he said, dragging her slumping form. Neek wrapped the other arm around her shoulder and tried to help them both to the ship. Their mental connection flickered as their skin touched, but the sedative kept the link nebulous.

Captain Llgg moved directly into their path, preventing them from continuing.

"If you stay this course of action, we will be forced to sedate you as well," she informed them, her tone even and crisp. "Your actions against the medics were unwarranted."

Emn's body drooped farther, and Nicholas lost his grip. The sudden change in weight distribution caused Neek to lose her hold as well. Emn fell to her knees on the metal floor, the impact forcing a harsh exhale from her lungs.

Terrified at what it would mean if they couldn't get on their ship, Neek dropped down and tried to figure out how best to move Emn. Nicholas feigned leaning down to assist Emn but came up quickly, bringing his fist in contact with the Captain Llgg's right ear.

The captain sputtered to the floor and rolled, a loud stream of high-pitched whistles echoing through the chamber. The guard advanced and surrounded Nicholas, taking turns in attempting to attack while he jumped and dodged.

They couldn't do this alone. Neek turned back to Emn. *Stuk* running freely from her fingertips, she brought a hand to Emn's shoulder, determined to make their connection work. Then she hesitated. Emn's breathing was shallow, but there was another sound coming from her. Neek listened as a *crackle hiss* began to build in intensity, Emn's body starting to form a white corona. The sound and light built until Neek had to cover her eyes or risk being blinded. She heard Emn forcefully exhale, and the crackling quieted to a dull hum.

"Neek?" a lower version of Emn's voice asked, at least, lower than what Neek had heard in her head. Nicholas spun around to face them. Neek could only stare. Emn was speaking. *Emn was speaking and she was an adult and the markings...*

Emn tentatively rested a hand on the arm across Neek's face, the touch sending a gentle vibration through the pilot. Neek lowered her arm. The strange liquid that the Mmnnuggl medic had transferred to Emn lay in a puddle on the floor. When Neek looked back up, the eyes that met hers were clear and focused.

"It's all right, Neek," Emn told her, smiling. "I haven't forgotten. I will protect the Systems' ships. It's just taking me a bit to get used to this body, these abilities." She removed her hand and stood.

Speechless, Neek watched as the light around Emn began to grow again. The walls and interface panels near them seemed to come alive and glisten, and Neek got the distinct impression that the floor was getting softer. Metal particulate began to flake, first near Emn and then in a growing concentric ring as her luminescence grew brighter by the second. The black veins on her body gleamed in the dim, green light and her straight, dark hair lifted slightly with the energy she was generating.

"Let's deal with the Mmnnuggls first," Emn said quietly to Neek. Confused, Neek let Emn push her gently away and watched as the young woman headed towards the remaining spheres. Nicholas had finally tripped and lay prone on the floor. Llgg accelerated towards his head. Emn reached out her hand and caught the captain just before impact. A loud *pop* filled the air, followed by a long series of sizzles and clicks. Llgg drooped and fell to the floor, just missing Nicholas's body. Smoke curled up from the open mouth slit, and the room filled with the smell of burning metal. The Mmnnuggl at the interface detached and went to Llgg's aid.

The remaining medic and Llgg's guards rushed Emn. She arced her arm wide and caught each in turn, a loud *smack* emanating upon contact. Each dropped heavily to the ground, rolled a full rotation, and then lay still.

Another high-pitched whistle sounded through the bay. Neek looked over her shoulder to see Gglltyll shake off the tunic and bob drunkenly to the interface, her body trailing thick lines of purple. Emn followed but, instead of touching the sphere, she placed her hand on the black panel. The lighting in the hangar surged momentarily. Gglltyll began to vibrate up and down as yellow-white energy arcs hopped from the interface into her round body. The vibrations intensified, and this time, Neek was certain the floor was getting softer—although whether it was from metal and plastic detritus, loss of cellulose, or both, she couldn't be certain. She was *certain* there had been a ceiling above them only moments ago. Technically, there still was, but now it was to the deck above.

Emn pulled her hand away. The lights dimmed, and the sphere dropped to the floor, unmoving.

"The battle," Neek managed to get out as her heart and mind raced. "Can you stop it?"

"I can stop the ships," Emn replied, "but not the beings. The Alliance ships are linked through a single network, which I can access through this panel. I can begin a chain reaction that will transmit to the other ships. They will be unable to counter."

Emn closed her eyes and placed her hand back on the interface. Nicholas crawled over to where Neek continued to kneel, and the two stared fixedly at Emn. The hissing sound of an electrical current rose as the lights in the hangar again flared and then went out completely. It took Neek a moment to realize that the only reason she could still see was that Emn hadn't stopped glowing.

Neek counted her heartbeats in an effort to calm her racing pulse. *One.* Emn was alive. *Two.* Emn was talking. *Three.* She wasn't a child anymore. On four, Emn's head jerked up and her face pointed to the now-absent ceiling. Tendrils of what looked like electricity began to whip and snake off her body, the wall next to her folding into a dangerous convex curve.

"What is she doing?" Nicholas whispered to Neek. "If she takes much more from this ship, it won't stay together!"

"You're assuming she is limited to this ship," Neek whispered back.

"That's terrifying."

Neek didn't respond. Stillness took hold of the hangar, and Neek realized that the humming had stopped. Emn's glow was fading from her right side and feeding into her left, traveling up her legs, through her torso, and coursing out of her left hand and onto the interface. The energy collected there, a snapping and hissing ball of radiant yellow-white. Emn allowed the energy to build until she had a writhing orb twice the size of her head. She then took a deep breath and moved it into the interface.

The hangar went dark. Light streaked back in almost immediately from the window at the opposite corner of the bay. Neek and Nicholas spun around to see every Alliance vessel stop dead and begin to glow. The light around each ship increased to an overpowering brightness, and then, at exactly the same time, every Alliance ship went completely dark.

"Fastest computer virus ever," Nicholas breathed.

Neek watched as the battle became decidedly one-sided. Risalian ships saw the opening and drew together, massing their firepower on one listing Alliance ship after another. The Risalian cutters targeted the ships with denser hull plating, their powerful lasers more than capable of slicing through the hull when the other side wasn't attempting to counter.

Alliance ships exploded. The number of combatants on each side leveled.

"This isn't much better!" Nicholas called back to Emn. "Can you do something about the Risalian ships?"

"No," she responded, and Neek realized her voice sounded strained and tired. "I...it doesn't work like that. I can't access Risalian systems through a Mmnnuggl interface." Emn opened her eyes and turned to look at Neek, her hand remaining on the interface. "I'm sorry, Neek," she said softly. "Even if I could access one of the Risalian ships, the structural integrity of this ship is too low to keep removing cellulose. We're adrift, just like the rest of the Alliance fleet. I only left enough power in each ship for environmental maintenance." A smile crept across the woman's face. "See? Not a god. I'm just..."

Nicholas cut her off. "You're a target. We all are, sitting here in a dead Alliance ship." He grabbed Neek's arm and began pulling her to the small pod. "The Risalians have no way of knowing we're on here, and they probably wouldn't care anyway. We have to go, *now*, before someone..."

All three were thrown from their feet when a blast rocked the *Llttrin*. Neek silently cursed the loss of power to the stabilizers, as anything that wasn't bolted to the floor, including them, suddenly smashed against the starboard wall and then hurtled to port. The floor started to crumble around them, and anything that wasn't affixed to a wall crashed into the deck below.

The *Llttrin* made four complete rotations before coming to a stop. Neek landed facedown on three dead Mmnnuggls and gasped as the wind was knocked from her again.

"The shielding on this ship is thicker than most," Emn said as she pulled herself from under an assortment of unrecognizable metal instruments and several Mmnnuggls. Bits of extruded plastic, porous from the cellulose removal, clung to her hair. "That blast was probably from a cutter. The *Llttrin* can take several more before it breaks apart."

"Let's not leave it a chance." Nicholas had held onto the pod during the blast and was still clinging to the boarding ramp. "I'll get Neek," Nicholas said to Emn. "Can you get this ship started?"

"Yes."

As Nicholas navigated the floor debris to Neek, Emn ran up the boarding ramp into the small ship. The distinctive sound of engines whirring to life began to resound through the hangar. Neek gratefully accepted Nicholas's assistance, and the two managed to get up the ramp just before another shot hit the *Llttrin*. Three more shots followed in quick succession. The small ship skidded across the hangar floor before righting itself as Emn closed the ramp and began the ignition sequence.

The floor finally gave way, and Neek held her breath as they entered free fall. Emn engaged the ship's thrusters just before impact.

"Please tell me we have weapons!" Neek yelled as she gripped the wall paneling in a desperate bid to stay upright.

"Yes. I'm going to make an exit." Emn turned the ship to face the external wall and fired two quick shots. The panel blew out just as a final volley of laser fire hit the *Llttrin*. The larger pod broke apart, pieces intermingling with the already thick debris cloud. Emn, both hands firmly placed on the flat black panel in front of her, sent the smaller ship charging into the battle's engagement zone and away from the wreckage.

Neek recovered her breath and paused long enough to grab another coarse, brown tunic from a pile near the cockpit, shrug into it, and tuck her knife snugly in the folds. She refrained from speaking. She wasn't certain what might come out of her mouth.

"I'm glad the Mmnnuggls thought to give us a change of clothes in this thing," Nicholas remarked. "I wonder how they thought we'd fly it?" The young man draped another tunic over Emn's shoulder. "Here. One for you, too."

Neek moved to stand behind Emn. The pod's viewscreen was huge and wrapped around the walls of the cockpit. It gave an excellent view of the battle, which was now weighted heavily in the Risalians' favor.

Neek considered Emn for a moment as the Ardulan expertly dodged between Risalian ships taking shot after shot at prone Alliance vessels. The little pod had the same dull, green lighting as the pod frigate, but, without the electric halo, Emn looked more like the second *don* she was instead of the imposing being she had appeared as on the *Llttrin*. She was more like Nicholas, really, than the omnipotent god Neek had so irrationally feared. A woman, just like her. Nothing more.

Neek took a relaxing breath and moved her focus to the battle outside. "Can you hail any of the Risalian ships?" she asked.

Emn turned her head and smiled. "You're talking. That's good. Yes, I can hail a Risalian ship. I can hail all the ships if you want—Risalian and others."

Nicholas turned to look at Neek and raised his eyebrows. "What are you thinking?"

"I'm thinking we should give a little battle update. See if we can't talk some sense into our blue protectors."

Emn snorted at the word "protector" but turned back to the interface and closed her eyes. "The connection is established. Let me know when you want to begin broadcast."

"Ready?" Neek asked Nicholas.

"Your show," he responded, holding his hands up. "I'm just a Journey youth, remember? Just here for the ride."

"Hell of a ride." Neek responded wryly. The pilot put her hand on Emn's upper arm. "Ready..." The words died in her throat.

Upon contact, the *stuk* once again ran from her fingers and onto Emn's bare skin, forming a bridge. Emn flooded back into her senses, but this wasn't Emn the child. This presence was adult—competent and confident. It had complex language and goals, and a blinding sense of purpose. It felt...it felt Ardulan. An image of a planet flashed across her mind—an orange planet streaking blue light. She couldn't tell if it was from imagination or memory, but the vision was too bright and made her want to look away.

Neek blinked and wavered on her feet. The sensory input from Emn blocked her sight, and her breathing became stilted. The *stuk* thickened. A roaring sound filled her ears, and Neek brought her hands up to cover them, though the gesture proved ineffectual. Removing her fingers from Emn's arm dissolved the connection, and the presence receded, leaving a wisp of consciousness in the back of Neek's mind—a consciousness that was both familiar and utterly disconcerting in its aplomb.

Neek saw the smile on Emn's face when she finally managed to open her eyes. "Hell of a ride," Emn repeated gently. "Ready to talk to everyone, Neek?"

"Yeah," Neek responded heavily, again pushing her emotions away for a more convenient time. "Turn it on." There was silence from Emn for a moment, and then she nodded.

"Greetings, members of the Charted Systems. Myself—a Neek—and a Terran Journey youth have commandeered a Nugel pod—the only pod you see still in operation." She paused and took a breath. "The Nugels are from outside the Charted Systems, as are the ships with them. They've come here to destroy the so-called Ardulans—a race of beings that the Neek people consider pivotal in our culture's development. Sort of. It's a long story."

Again, Neek paused. This time, she sent a questioning look to Nicholas, who gave her a supportive smile. She continued, her voice noticeably less confident. "The Nugels are now gelded—dead in space save for minor life support. They cannot fight back. You slaughter them now as they slaughtered you less than half an hour ago."

Static erupted through the feed, and all three of the pod's occupants winced. A voice cut through, their tone stern. "This is Captain Lorn of Risalian Cutter 17. I'm ordering all Risalian forces to continue pursuit. If we eliminate the threat now—if we make a strong showing—the Mmnnuggls will not reenter the Charted Systems. We can end this threat here, today."

"Can you get communications back, Emn?" Neek whispered urgently.

"I'm trying," Emn said. Her forehead wrinkled in concentration. "Captain Lorn has three communication Ardulans on hir ship. They know how to do this better than I do."

"Can't you talk to them?" Nicholas asked. "I thought you were all telepaths."

Emn frowned. "I've never talked to anyone that way except my mom and Neek, and the healer on the cutter." She pursed her lips and considered. "I think I can do it. I just have to find them."

Neek sent reassurance through their new mental connection and cautiously placed a hand back on Emn's shoulder, noting with surprise as she did so that her fingertips were dry, the *stuk* uncharacteristically absent. *I believe in you.*

Emn looked at her. *You don't believe in anything, Neek,* she sent back. *Not really, anyway.*

That stung. Neek pulled her hand away.

"Neek?" Nicholas asked. "You all right?"

"Yes," she responded, a little too quickly. But her voice hadn't wavered. That was good.

Neek leveled her gaze at the viewscreen, watching the civilian ships cluster together and hold position well away from the front. It looked like about twenty Risalian ships were still attacking the Alliance fleet. The rest had stopped, as if unsure what their next course of action should be.

With their connection still present, Neek watched with fascination as Emn let her consciousness sink into the interface, into the computer's main core. Cautiously, so she did not start a chain reaction, Emn pulled a handful of loose crystalline cellulose from the metal matrix of the console and bound it together, releasing a short burst of energy. Just like before, it coursed through her, charging her skin and causing sparks to flare where her hands touched the interface. She drew on the energy and reached out towards the cutter, searching for someone who could hear her.

Emn's consciousness brushed past thousands of minds on her way through the battle. Most were closed off and foreign, but on the Risalian cutters and in the skiffs, there were minds that were open and empty. When Emn hit Cutter 17, it was the same. She found six Ardulan minds onboard, all *empty*. Neek felt Emn's hesitation before Emn drew another surge of energy from the ship and mentally yelled as loudly as she could to every mind she could contact.

Stop it! Stop fighting! Stop helping the Risalians!

The words echoed back into their minds, almost as if they had hit the inside of the empty skulls and ricocheted. Emn pulled out another ball of energy, preparing to try again, when Neek put a hand on her shoulder and squeezed.

Emn, wait.

Emn brought herself out of the computer far enough to visually take in what was happening. In an almost complete duplication of the Alliance force, the Risalian ships had stopped dead. Skiffs in midpass cut their engines and allowed the momentum to continue carrying them across the battlefield. Pilots made no move to steer and three of the skiffs collided with a frigate pod. The resulting explosion took out all four ships. Debris haloed from the engagement zone and spun slowly outwards, disappearing into space. Afterwards, all was still.

Nicholas let out a long breath. "Whatever you did worked. Nice job."

Neek nodded and turned to Emn, who was sagging into the interface. Unsure of what exactly had transpired, Neek cautiously reached out. "Can you open the communication again? We should finish the conversation with the Risalians."

Their minds were still spooled tightly together. Neek watched as Emn again searched for the empty minds, ready to send another string of commands. Where before there had been hundreds of minds, now there seemed only half that. Confused, Emn reached out again and found even fewer. With growing frustration, she picked a Risalian cutter at random and tried to make a solid connection to just one Ardulan, the lead gunner. Emn slipped into the gunner's mind, and the woman acknowledged Emn briefly with a flicker of thought before whatever small consciousness she had disappeared. Emn did not think to pull away, so both she and Neek watched through the Ardulan's eyes as her vision blurred and the ground sped towards her—before everything went dark.

Realization hit. A moment later, Emn's eyelids flew open and her mouth dropped. She slumped to her knees, breaking her connection to the interface.

"They're dying!" Emn yelled. She balled her hands into fists and punched both into the floor. "I told them to stop letting the Risalians use them, and they're killing themselves! Just stopping their hearts and...and..."

Neek knelt beside Emn and wrapped one arm around the Ardulan's shaking form, unsure whether she was comforting herself or Emn. A blistering emptiness passed through their connection before Emn skillfully tempered her presence.

Nicholas was next to them a moment later. "Can you tell them to stop?" he asked, his voice panicked. "God, it's like we stop one bloodbath and another begins!"

"Can't," Emn whispered. She rested her head against Neek's shoulder and closed her eyes. "They're all dead. All of them. The war is over. I'm the only one left alive."

CHAPTER 28: MMNNUGGL POD

The Markin are dead. The Ardulans are dead. The Mmnnuggl fleet retreated. The war is over. There were no victors.

—Transmission from Captain Enoch to the Markin Training Center, November 18th, 2060 CE

Neek sat alone in the captain's berth of the Mmnnuggl pod and counted back in her mind. It was five days since the battle at Oorin ended. Five days since the Alliance withdrew from the Charted Systems. Three days since Risal installed a new set of Markin. One day since the Risalians released a priority network announcement that they were discontinuing the Ardulan program and required civilian volunteers to help run sheriff operations.

Neek let out a long breath and flopped onto a thick, round pillow, staring at the ceiling. She knew Emn was in the cockpit with the interface and assumed Nicholas was there, too. She should have been there with them, but there was an added awkwardness now to the whole situation. She was a pilot, a good one, but she couldn't fly the ship—it required a mental link that she was incapable of sustaining. That left her feeling useless, and she was unsure how to, or if she should, discuss the issue with Nicholas and Emn. They were each under their own unique stressors, and Neek didn't want to add to them.

Not that she was in a great place mentally, either. The Systems were in disarray and communication lines were chaotic. It had been impossible to get a call through to her homeworld to check on her family. Yorden, the only person she'd been able to call a friend for the past decade, was dead. Her home, her real home on the *Pledge,* was gone. And now...now the only people left that she could remotely call friends were a Journey youth and...and Emn.

It was even harder, now, to be around her. Neek tried not to care anymore about the god thing, the *Ardulan* thing, but it was a different Emn that piloted the stolen pod. This Emn was confident. Undaunted. She was no longer haunted by memories of her mother or of the Risalians. She interacted with Nicholas with ease, smiled and laughed at jokes, and discussed the financial ramifications of the war with an analytical mind.

Emn also wanted something from Neek. The pilot could see it in the way Emn looked at her with patient eyes and subtle nods—except Neek couldn't begin to imagine what Emn could need from *her*. The emotions in the Ardulan's mind were complex now—mature—and Neek was having a hard time making sense of them, or making sense of anything, really, including her place in the postwar Systems or the Mmnnuggl pod itself.

Neek's mind wandered as she stared at the ceiling, pale green lighting doing nothing for her mood. Emn's markings and abilities were unlike anything ever documented on Neek. Emn was, in a way, so much more than any Ardulan Neek had ever read about. She was also was still here, still on the ship. She hadn't left after the battle or made any comments about parting company. She wanted to be with them, it seemed—with Nicholas *and* Neek. How Neek would manage an extended voyage with an Ardulan and a Journey youth remained to be seen, if indeed they did all decide to stay together.

A smile played at the corners of Neek's mouth. An Ardulan for a crew member. It was a crazy idea. Whether a potential construct of modified cells, the product of directed breeding, the descendant of an ancient species, or whatever Emn was, it meant Ardulum—the planet—had a possibility of existing. *That* was an entertaining thought.

There was a soft tap at Neek's door. She sat up and crossed her legs on the pillow, irritated at the interruption. "I don't really feel like company," she called out. "Just tell me when we get to Craston so we can refuel."

The door opened, and Emn stood in the doorway, barefoot. Two days ago, they'd stopped briefly on Baltec to purchase items for the ship, including clothing, with money borrowed from one of Yorden's contacts. It had been hard to find anything that fit. The selections were limited due to the wormhole and supply line disruptions, and the beings that flitted through the markets had been wary and unsure of their future.

Emn stepped into the small room, wearing a gray, strapped dress that stopped just above her knees. Neek was glad they'd found something to fit her, especially something that fit well. The gray drew attention away from her translucent skin and onto the fine, black veins, giving the Ardulan the look of a tattooed Terran.

"We're exiting the Minoran Wormhole. I put the ship on auto. A chime will sound when we enter Craston's orbit." Emn took a tentative step closer. "I'd really like to talk to you, if you don't mind."

The intensity of Emn's gaze sent shivers down Neek's spine. Did Ardulans make eye contact? She couldn't remember if any of the texts spoke about it. Was she supposed to make contact back? What was the protocol for addressing a second *don*? It was the most asinine debate she had ever had with herself.

"I guess," Neek responded in a noncommittal tone, realizing that Emn was far less likely to be aware of protocol than she was. Neek's chances of offending the young woman were small.

She gestured to a pillow sitting against the near wall. Emn smiled slightly, but sat next to Neek on her pillow instead. Neek promptly scooted as far away as she could get. It was one thing to not know protocol. It was another to sit right next to a maybe-god you maybe believed in.

"I make you uncomfortable," Emn commented. She stared at Neek, eyes unblinking. Neek thought her tone sounded a little hurt.

"That's not really new," the pilot responded. She ran a hand through her loose hair, moving the reddish-blonde strands away from her face. Emn watched the movement and then copied it, her own hand gliding smoothly through the straight, dark hair that reached just past her shoulders.

The two were silent for several minutes. Emn stared at Neek, who tried to find anything in the small room to look at besides the other woman.

It was Emn who broke the silence. "I'm sorry," she said.

Neek shrugged. "It's all right. I'll get over it."

Emn looked away and toyed with the hem on her dress. "I wanted to tell you that I appreciate everything you did for me. You, Yorden, Nicholas—I would have died without you." Emn paused and looked back to Neek for a response. Neek shrugged again.

"I wanted to tell you, too," Emn continued, her voice softer, "that while I was in metamorphosis...I could hear things. I couldn't see, but I could hear through the casing. I heard what you said about wanting to be with me, to see what I'd become."

"I said I believed in you, too," Neek retorted, more harshly than she intended. "But I seem to recall you telling me that I don't really believe in anything."

"I didn't mean it like that, Neek. I meant...you don't believe in your home religion. I don't mind that. But I can feel you, even when we're not connected by touch. Your presence to me is just as strong as any Ardulan's. Why not believe in our connection or your friendship with Nicholas?" Emn covered Neek's hand with her own. "No one is asking you to reconcile a lifetime of religious indoctrination with the events of the past week."

Neek snorted and pulled her hand away. "You're a kid, just like Nicholas. The things I am dealing with...they're more complex than you think."

"Because your family couldn't protect you? Because your world wanted to control you? You think I don't understand that?"

Neek stood abruptly and walked the three steps to the other side of the room. She placed her hands on the wall and let her head hang. "I've let this debate rest. It's done. I don't care if you are an Ardulan, or a Terran, or strange, mutated Nugel. What you are *not* is a fairy tale. You can't be a fairy tale. You're too real to be a god." She was sure her voice wavered. "I need you to not be a god."

Emn considered. "I wasn't like all those Ardulans that died at Oorin. They were empty—their minds were blank. Even my mother didn't have a mind like yours or mine. I'm different from all of them. Maybe I'm more like a real Ardulan than you think, but that still doesn't make me a divinity." She smiled. "I'm just Emn."

Emn got up and walked over to Neek. She placed her right hand next to Neek's left on the wall, their fingers centimeters from each other. "Ardulan or not, I want to find out who I am. I want to find other beings like me. I don't want to be alone." She wrapped her hand around Neek's and brought both their hands away from the wall. "There's nothing here for you, Neek," Emn said softly as the connection between the two tightened and Emn's presence flooded Neek's mind. "The Charted Systems will take years to put themselves back together. Transport jobs will be limited, legal or otherwise." Emn smiled and took Neek's other hand in hers. Neek felt her face color. They were too close. Why were they so close?

"My journey lies beyond the Charted Systems. I want you to come with me. Nicholas too, if he wants. I'm going to find Ardulum, and I want you there with me when I do. Maybe if we find the planet, you can finish your journey. If they're just like us, then they're not gods. I'm not a god. Everything can be okay."

Neek swallowed, her throat dry. Emn took a step closer and closed her eyes, moving her consciousness into the link the two shared.

Please, Atalant. I need you, and I think you need me.

Neek broke at the use of her child-name. Tears spilled down her face, and she began to tremble. This wasn't a settee, and this wasn't a family reunion—it was something so much more than any of that. The pilot tugged her hands away from Emn's and wrapped her arms around the younger woman, pulling her into an embrace. She held Emn tightly for several long moments, letting the smell of andal from Emn's hair permeate her senses. She had no intention of leaving either Emn or Nicholas, although she'd not managed to verbalize that to either of them. The last time she'd been on her own in the Charted Systems, she'd ended up clinging to life in the back alley of a spaceport, wallowing in her own self-destructive tendencies.

Emn shifted slightly in Neek's arms, turning her face and looking Neek directly in the eyes. "Neek?" she asked softly, her breath warm against Neek's skin. "Are you all right?"

Neek stared back and kept her face motionless. Emotions swirled just underneath the surface, threatening to break free right at that moment, where Emn would witness them all. Instead of letting that happen, Neek opened her mouth and spoke with as little wavering as she could manage.

"All right," she whispered into Emn's ear, pulling the younger woman back and lingering in the strength of Emn's embrace. "To Ardulum, then, or however far we can get in this rotund excuse for a spaceship. I don't care. The Charted Systems, the Alliance, Ardulum—it doesn't matter. Wherever your path leads, we'll be together."

ABOUT THE AUTHOR

J.S. Fields is a scientist who has perhaps spent too much time around organic solvents. She enjoys roller derby, woodturning, making chain mail by hand, and cultivating fungi in the backs of minivans. Nonbinary, but prefers female pronouns. Always up for a Twitter chat.

Email: chlorociboria@gmail.com
Website: http://www.chlorociboria.com
Twitter: @galactoglucoman

Coming Soon from J.S. Fields

Ardulum: Second Don
Book Two in the Ardulum Series

Chapter 1: Eld Palace, Ardulum

This is a Galactic News Network special report. Aid agency reports coming in outline a new species found on Risalian ships in the aftermath of the Crippling War. Our Risalian sources confirm the species as "Ardulan," a nonsentient beast of burden. The bipeds resemble Terrans and Neek in appearance but have unique subdermal bruising. All specimens thus far recovered have been deceased; however, the newly-appointed Markin request that should a live one be found, it should be turned over to the Council immediately.

—Excerpt from wideband news broadcast in the Charted Systems, December 2nd, 2060 CE

It was his Talent day. *His* day to be here, in the old palace. His day to meet the Eld and complete his metamorphosis.

Arik pushed a sheet of black hair from his face—streaked with red from a summer tending andal trees—and began a slow, deliberate procession towards the Talent room. He passed under a high andal archway built in the traditional encased knot style, reliefs carved into each aborted branch. Reaching out as he passed, Arik ran a finger over one of the raised knots, noting the texture created by chisels and pyrography. He gingerly picked his way over andal floorboards, worn to unevenness from generations of youth making this same journey. The lustrous, black heartwood reflected the sunlight falling from the glass ceiling, but Arik didn't turn his eyes from the glare.

Four more steps and a turn brought Arik around the final corner. He faced the door to the Talent room and paused. His heart rate increased, so Arik rested his back against the andal wall paneling, digging his nails into the soft, white sapwood. It was comforting to be so close to Ardulum's native tree, reassuring to embed himself in it, if only slightly. His pulse calmed. His breathing slowed. Arik took two more calming breaths and pushed off the wall. He nudged the door ahead with his foot, and it slid silently open, revealing the room inside.

As with the hall and receiving room, natural light filtered in from the glass ceiling. Here, however, it was muted. Outside, the canopy of several large andal trees swayed in the breeze, casting patchwork shadows on the floor. Arik walked forward, trying to keep to the darker, shadowed areas, and approached the rulers of Ardulum.

In the center of the room, the three eld sat on ornate, wooden thrones, each watching him with reserved amusement. Arik supposed humor was a good sign. Perhaps the Eld had a soft spot for young second *don*s on their Talent day. Perhaps being the only one present meant the Eld were not tired from numerous ceremonies, and Arik would get their full attention.

Arik stopped when he was within an arm's length of the Eld and then let his gaze flicker around the hall. Towering sculptures of past elds, carved in great detail in black andal heartwood, loomed over the thrones and stared ominously at Arik—their freshly polished faces glistened in the baronial light.

A deep male voice broke the silence. "You come before us, Arik of the second *don*, fresh from metamorphosis. What do you bring?" The male eld, who looked to be the oldest of the group, stared unblinkingly at Arik as he stroked the worn wood grain of his throne seat. His two Talents were carved into the throne base, easy for Arik to see: Hearth and Mind. It wasn't a bad pairing to have. The Eld were the only ones on Ardulum to have more than one Talent, of course, but Arik liked the balance created when the Talents encompassing protection and construction intertwined with the Talents surrounding critical thinking and mathematics. The male eld was likely an excellent architect, which, if the palace suffered any ill effects after the next move, would be a key skill to have.

Arik's stomach growled loudly, and the youth sheepishly placed a hand over it, hoping that somehow the Eld hadn't heard.

"Arik?" the male eld prompted again, his tone gentler than before. "What do you bring to offer to us, your Eld?"

Arik closed his eyes tightly for just a moment and brought his mind back to the present. Andal help him, he could smell the wood cooking, the sweet odor wafting from the kitchens on the lower floor. Arik's stomach growled again, and his mouth started to water.

Focus! he scolded himself as he fumbled momentarily through his tunic pockets. *This is the biggest day of your life. Stop thinking about lunch!* Finally, his fingers came across his offering—the form of a small child whittled from andal from his parents' plantation. The carving was crude and made only from sapwood—Arik had never had great fine motor skills, but the figure had understandable appendages and a reasonably detailed face. Arik hoped it was enough.

"I bring you this gift," Arik said slowly, his voice wavering and squeaking to a higher pitch on the last word. "May it show my devotion to my spiritual journey, so I can leave my childhood and discover my Talent. Please accept this offering and guide me onto my new path." With shaking hands, Arik knelt and held the carving up over his head. The coarse weave of the andal mat dug into his knees, and Arik had to stop himself from reaching down to scratch.

A cool hand touched Arik's wrist briefly before removing the carving. "We accept your offering, Arik of the second *don*." The female eld reached down and put a small finger under Arik's chin, lifting his face up. "Rise and receive your Talent."

Arik got to his feet, suddenly aware of how close he was to these mystical individuals. He'd never been this close to the Eld before and likely never would again, so he took a moment to study their faces. They were old, older than the oldest third *don* Arik had ever seen—and yet, their fingers were elegant, their bodies strong and well-muscled. The male eld looked to be from one of the southern provinces. His hair still had dark streaks shooting through a mass of silver, and his skin was closer to olive in its translucency. The female, blessed with Talents of Mind and Aggression, was tall, her sharp chin well above the other elds' heads. Her hair was uniformly cinnamon save for her temples. She, too, looked to be from the south. However, the gatoi, of Science and Hearth, was much paler, zir skin containing next to no melanin. Zie was from the farthest northern province, then, where sunlight rarely penetrated the thick andal forests. The birth rate was skewed in favor of gatois in that region, although Arik wasn't certain whether that was a natural phenomenon or whether it came from parental selection.

The male eld cleared his throat, and Arik again snapped back to the present. The Eld were still staring at him, unmoving. Was his offering not enough? Was there another component he had forgotten? His mother and talther, his gatoi parent, had helped him carve it, staying up late each night since Arik's emergence and guiding the young man's wavering chisel with steady hands. A week wasn't much time to construct an offering. Did others bring more elaborate gifts? Should he have done something in line with what he hoped his Talent might be? Dizziness threatened to topple him, the smells from the kitchen permeated, and he had to work to control his breathing. His mind wandered. The increasingly saturated smell of cooked andal spun through his head. Was he *in* the kitchens? It certainly seemed that way now. How had he ignored the intensity of the smell before? It was almost like standing in the rotisserie himself, the scent of sweet spice invading his nostrils.

The female eld smiled slightly at the male, who gave a knowing wink. Arik teetered in a near panic, vision straying between reality and his wandering delusions.

"Peace, young one," the gatoi eld said as zie stepped forward. In zir hands, zie carried a small wooden bowl filled with pale mucus. Zie dipped two fingers into the bowl, coating them, and then held zir hand out towards Arik. "Step forward to begin your journey."

Arik's empty stomach rolled. He knew the mucus was synthetic, but what it represented brought the taste of bile to the back of his throat. Determined to not embarrass himself further, Arik took a confident step towards the gatoi eld and closed his eyes. For the past year, he'd been instructed in the ritual that was about to take place. He would not mess things up now—not on his Talent Day, no matter how strange and ostentatious the performers or how heavily the air hung with the smell of food.

"I am Eld," the gatoi eld said steadily as zie outlined Arik's face with the mucus. "I am the vessels that transport power."

"I am Eld," said the female, taking the bowl from the gatoi. She swirled her smallest finger in the mixture and then coated Arik's nose. "I am the fibers of strength." She handed the bowl to the male, who had stepped forward as well.

"I am Eld," the male said, pinching Arik's chin between two mucus-coated fingers. "I am the rays that store our knowledge."

Arik counted silently to fifteen in his head as he'd been instructed. The tingling at the mucosal contact points radiated from his face down to his neck, absorbed into his skin, and congealed into a tight, painful lump just above his heart.

"I am Arik of the second *don*," he said when he finished the count. Gently, slowly, Arik moved his consciousness into himself to where the lump lay just under his skin, pulsing in rhythm with his heartbeat. He watched it for a moment, external stimuli forgotten. He was both slightly revolted and slightly in awe of this *thing*, this synthetic chemical compound that would, in just a few seconds, stimulate his adrenal gland and cause the production of a massive number of hormones—hormones that would determine how he would spend the rest of his life.

Arik let his mind touch the lump. The mass dissolved, its components seeping into his bloodstream and heading directly for their target. Arik's body became warm—and then hot. He broke out in a sweat, the salty liquid beading on his yellow skin and reflecting in the bright overhead lighting. He shut his eyes and was forced to his hands and knees when the chemicals hit his adrenal gland and the hormones began to affect his other cells.

Cells changed. Cells morphed. His blood circulated in the normal direction, paused for a fraction of a second, and then reversed. His metabolism increased, and his internal body temperature shot up even more. Veins bulged in his wrists and began to burst, blood seeping under the skin and forming bright-violet bruises. Arik felt like he couldn't breathe anymore. The heat was too intense. He began to pant and fell onto his right side, body curling into a fetal position.

As abruptly as it began, the heat began to recede. Arik could feel his cells calming, the veins in his wrists closing. Sweat stung his eyes, seeping past his eyelids, and Arik brought his left hand up to wipe them clean. When his vision cleared and he brought his hand away, Arik saw his new markings for the first time—three linked, black circles on the inside of his wrist surrounded by a bruised haze of extra subdermal blood. His smile grew slowly as he moved into a sitting position and looked up at the Eld.

"I am Arik of the second *don*," he said clearly, his voice resonating, crisp and strong, through the chamber. No wavering. He could be proud of that. "I am of Science."

"And there your Talent shall lie," the female responded. "Stand, Arik, and leave this palace. Return to your home and begin your apprenticeship."

Arik's face broke into a broad grin. He clasped his hands behind his back and stood, his previous discomforts forgotten. Arik took a moment to straighten his tunic before bowing to each eld. "I thank you, Eld, for showing me my way."

The Eld smiled back but remained silent. Remembering that he was to leave promptly, Arik turned and took several confident steps towards the door, being careful to stay within the confines of the woven mat. Pride filled his chest—pride at his Talent, pride at the way he'd conducted himself, and pride that he could go home and apprentice to a Talent that would not take him away from his family or his andal saplings. With the Talent of Science, he could stay and work his ancestors' andal plantations—could tend the young trees he'd grown up with. His entire family was of Science. They would be proud of him.

Several steps into his departure, the smell of the cooked andal began to waft towards him again. What should have been a pleasant, understated smell was pungent and slightly curdled. He tried to ignore it, quickening his pace. The soft *slack slack slack* of Arik's bare feet hitting the polished andal floor was suddenly joined by the deep sounds of a heartbeat.

Slack du-dumn, slack du-dumn, slack...

Arik spun around, confused, and looked for the source of the noise. It took another three seconds of *du-dumn du-dumn* before Arik realized that it was *his* heart he was hearing, the beats becoming more rapid in his agitation.

Arik swallowed, his throat dry. His muscles twitched under his tunic, the fibers itching his skin. He glanced at the Eld, a peculiar expression on their wrinkled faces.

"I...I don't feel well," Arik said, mostly to himself. He cringed when his own voice sounded too loud in his ears. His heart was trying to escape out of his chest, and no amount of controlled breathing seemed to help. The smell of the andal wound through his head and then down his throat, causing Arik to gag. Thoughts of simultaneous choking and hyperventilating filled his mind. Unsure of what else to do, he moved his consciousness back inside himself, trying to find the cause of his distress.

What he saw shocked him. This wasn't the body he knew—did not resemble anything of his. Here, capillaries burst just under his skin and leaked perpetual blood out of his circulatory system. Hormones raced everywhere, transmitting across his chest and up into his brain. Something was happening near his throat, too. Loose blood pushed ligaments around, unwrapping and changing their positions, and pooled just under his larynx. Cartilage scavenged from around his thyrohyoid ligament sidled closer, surrounding the blood.

Arik opened his mouth in an effort to call over the Eld but was shocked when all that came out was a gurgle. He tried again, forcing more air out through what had once been his larynx. Again, only gibberish.

He grew hot, a red flush surfacing not just on his cheeks but across his entire body. Arik watched in stunned horror as the purple veins that had always been just slightly visible under his skin—the veins that had already started to fade after his time with the Eld—darkened to black.

Once more, Arik looked to the Eld, desperate for guidance. They'd moved closer. The gatoi reached a bony hand out to Arik, zir expression unreadable.

Help? Arik sent frantically on a telepathic thread. It was unacceptable to speak to Eld in such a manner, but he was in trouble. They had to know!

None of the eld responded to Arik's mental query. The hand remained out and open, all the eld staring at Arik expectantly. Not knowing what else to do, Arik reached out. His whole right arm was covered now in arcing black veins that grouped into geometric patterns just under his skin.

I'm dying, Arik thought to himself. *The smell of the andal is actually going to kill me.* He let his fingers touch the tips of the gatoi eld's hand, and his mind cleared. The contact sparked through Arik, and he snapped his head up, eyes wide. The gatoi eld stared back, unblinking, as pieces of emotion began to filter into Arik's mind. Discomfort, unease, disappointment. That didn't seem right. He hadn't done anything wrong—something had just misfired, that was all. He was still Arik, still of Science. A healer could fix his larynx, he was sure of it. He wasn't quite sure *why* all of this was happening, but surely the Eld knew. Surely others had had this same problem.

The intensity of the connection became uncomfortable, but when Arik tried to pull his hand away, he could not. The gatoi eld had a tight grip on Arik's wrist. The male eld moved behind Arik in two fluid steps and placed his hands on his shoulders, pushing down to keep Arik in place. The female grabbed his other hand around the wrist, her longer fingernails digging into his skin.

Time seemed to be slowing. Arik felt his heart rate depress, the blood in his veins decrease in flow rate. His mind became muddled again. Something was wrong, and he needed to speak to the Eld about it. Why couldn't he speak? Why wouldn't the words come out?

Dark spots began to swim before Arik's vision. His heart didn't seem to be beating anymore, and Arik thought that was wrong somehow. The blackness increased. Arik slumped. The male eld backed away quickly, and Arik's body hit the wood floor with a thump, his head bouncing once after the initial impact. Words leaked across the darkness: *defective, unsuitable, terminate.*

Terminate?

Arik opened his mouth to make a sound to indicate his distress, when his brain, starved of oxygen, finally shut down.